LINDSAY McKENNA

D0032115

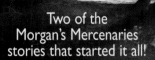

Two of the
Morgan's Mercenaries
stories that started it all!

MORGAN'S
LEGACY

Other Morgan's Mercenaries titles available from bestselling author

LINDSAY MCKENNA

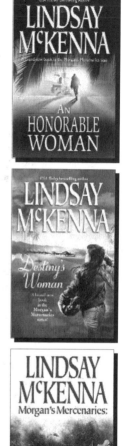

ISBN 0-373-21871-0

9 780373 218714

50650

EAN

PSLM0204IFC

Dear Reader,

I don't know about you, but I'm absolutely thrilled *pink* to see a reissue of this four-book series! I can remember that when I wrote it, I felt like I was in an emotional storm. I get completely involved with my characters' lives just like you do!

Even though Morgan Trayhern and his family are fictional creations of mine, I must tell you that they are alive and well in my head and in my heart. Over the years, I've received hundreds of letters and e-mails from you telling me the same thing. I feel the world loves the Trayhern family, if your sentiments are any indication!

Originally, I'd penned *Morgan's Mercenaries: Love and Danger.* I'd envisioned four books. I had written enough about Morgan, Laura, their son Jason and daughter Cathy in the years earlier that I wanted to invest some quality time with them. As you well know, no family ever escapes "life" and all its drama, intensity, hardships and triumphs. Up to that time, nothing of much import had happened to Morgan or his family. I knew I wanted to write, one day, about his children (*Firstborn*, Jason's story, is coming out in June 2004!), and in order to write about them, readers had to know a lot more intimate details about the original family I'd presented.

Because Morgan lives in a dangerous world, it spills over into his personal life—and it affects everyone around him. In these first two books, you will read about how Laura Trayhern is rescued, and then, their son Jason. The results of these wounds will create further tension, problems and hurdles for each character to overcome in the later years. I hope you enjoy *Morgan's Wife*, Laura's story, and *Morgan's Son*, about Jason, his firstborn son. As always, I love to hear from you.

Warmly,

Lindsay McKenna

And watch for these upcoming releases from

LINDSAY McKENNA

MORGAN'S HONOR
coming from Harlequin in April 2004

FIRSTBORN
coming from Harlequin in June 2004

DAUGHTER OF DESTINY
coming from Silhouette Bombshell in July 2004

LINDSAY McKENNA

MORGAN'S
LEGACY

Silhouette Books

Published by Silhouette Books
America's Publisher of Contemporary Romance

SILHOUETTE BOOKS

MORGAN'S LEGACY

Copyright © 2004 by Harlequin Books S.A.

ISBN 0-373-21871-0

The publisher acknowledges the copyright holders
of the individual works as follows:

MORGAN'S WIFE
Copyright © 1995 by Lindsay McKenna

MORGAN'S SON
Copyright © 1995 by Lindsay McKenna

Visit Silhouette at www.eHarlequin.com

Printed in U.S.A.

CONTENTS ·

MORGAN'S WIFE   9

MORGAN'S SON   307

To my readers,
who love Morgan and his family as much as I do.

MORGAN'S WIFE

Prologue

"Are you about ready?" Morgan Trayhern poked his head into the bedroom and looked inquiringly at his wife.

Laura turned, the string of pearls Morgan had just given her as a seventh-wedding-anniversary present poised in her hands. She smiled softly, holding the luminescent necklace toward him.

"Will you? It's only fitting." As he stepped into the room, Laura's heart swelled with a fierce tide of love. How had seven years fled by? She watched his usually stoic features relax slightly as she laid the strand in his badly scarred hands. How much Morgan had suffered, Laura thought as she turned her back to him. He had come so far since they'd met on that fateful, rainy day at the Washington, D.C., airport.

She closed her eyes as Morgan leaned lightly against her back. He was wearing a suit in honor of the occasion—celebrating over dinner at a posh Alexandria restaurant. As he slipped the pearls around her neck, a tiny shiver of expectation accompanied his fingers' gentle path.

"Mmm…"

Morgan smiled slightly as he carefully worked the small gold clasp. Laura wore a camellia-scented perfume. Like her, the fragrance was heady, making his senses spin.

"Seven years," he murmured close to her ear as he slid his hands along the expanse of her shoulders. "Can you believe it? I can't." He never would. Laura was his bright, shining dream against the dark, nightmarish world that probably would never completely stop haunting him. Post-traumatic-stress disorder didn't necessarily go away with time—at least his hadn't. Laura had stood by him—and suffered with him—through the gut-wrenching flashbacks. Before Laura, Morgan never could have fathomed a person of such strength and courage that she'd *want* to remain at his side during those tortured times.

Responding to his gentle pressure, Laura leaned against him, feeling his warm breath on the side of her neck as he pressed a kiss against her temple. Her nostalgic glow gave way to more urgent feelings and she eased away just enough to turn in his arms and face him. Placing her hands on his broad shoulders, she smiled up into his serious gray eyes.

"I can."

With a sigh, he brushed a few wayward strands of hair back from Laura's cheek. She wore a simple ivory silk suit that showed off the pearls to perfection. Her blond hair fell in soft waves to her shoulders, arousing in him the urge to tunnel his fingers through its thick, silky mass. His mouth curved ruefully.

"I don't know. It hasn't exactly been heaven living with me, has it? More like a living hell at times."

The scar on Morgan's face from that long-ago hill in Vietnam presented a constant reminder to Laura of the deep, invisible scars he still carried in his heart and soul. She touched his other, recently shaved cheek. "No marriage is perfect, and neither are we. But these have been the best seven years of my life, darling. If I died right now, I'd be happy with exactly what I have here—with you." She glanced fondly toward the partially open door to the dimly lit hall. "We have two wonderful children, a boy who worships you and a baby girl who adores you just as I do." Her eyes filled with tears. "No, these years haven't been hell for me, they've been heaven."

Morgan felt the tension that inevitably gathered in his neck and shoulders with rising emotions. He cupped his wife's delicate face and looked deeply into her luminous blue eyes. "I still don't know how you can stand being around me sometimes, Laura. I guess I'll never understand it. But it doesn't matter. I love you with my life," he breathed against her mouth. He kissed her fully then, parting her lips, tasting the love she effortlessly gave to him. The emotional nourishment she provided was part of the miracle he realized his life to be. Laura was a beacon of strong, steady light for him and for their children. He hoped, as he kissed her, that he was imparting just how deep his love for her ran in him.

As he felt her lips meet and match his fervor, Morgan heard a distinct *click*. The marine part of him went on instant alert, though he was loath to break their molten embrace. A chill moved up his spine: another warning. One he couldn't ignore.

Breaking away from Laura, he gripped her shoulders, already turning toward the door leading to the beige-carpeted hall. "Stay here," he said in a low voice.

Laura gasped. Three men, dressed completely in black

to the dark ski masks covering their heads, appeared soundlessly at the bedroom door. She didn't even have time to raise her hands to her mouth to scream as they drew their weapons. Morgan reacted instantly, thrusting himself in front of her. Too late!

The *pop* of the guns wasn't the sound of bullets. Laura felt a sting in her left shoulder, and everything became slow motion, like single frames of film passing before her. Two of the men fired at Morgan, and Laura saw two small darts strike him in his neck and chest.

She was disoriented by the intruders' eerie silence as a burning sensation spread rapidly through her, radiating from the area where the first dart had struck her. Looking down, she saw very little blood. Her vision blurred, and her knees suddenly turned to jelly. Morgan gave a strangulated cry, turning toward her, his eyes wide with warning and fear. At the sight of that fear she tasted abject terror.

How many times had Morgan worried about attack from any of the countless enemies he'd made running Perseus over the past seven years? Laura's breath was becoming chaotic, and she struggled for air. She staggered and fell to her knees, automatically reaching for the edge of the bed.

Morgan dropped suddenly and heavily, like a bull that had been shot in the head. He lay unmoving nearby, on his back, one arm extended toward her. Laura stared, feeling her mouth go dry. She looked up. All three intruders warily entered the room, their weapons still raised. A hundred questions swirled in her head as she fought the effects of the drug racing through her system.

She sagged to the floor, oddly conscious of the brush of the lavender carpet's nap against her hands, even as her terror mounted. Had they killed Morgan? Was she dying? Oh, God, no, the children! *The children!* The thought made Laura whimper, and with everything that remained of her rapidly dissolving strength, she tried to rise. But her weakened muscles would not cooperate, and darkness shadowed her blurred vision.

With a moan, she fell back toward the carpet and knew nothing more.

Chapter One

Jake Randolph looked grimly at the small contingent of Perseus mercenaries gathered around the oval oak table in what Morgan called the ''War Room.'' Here, plans were laid for covert missions around the world. Jake clenched his jaw. ''Morgan, Laura and their son, Jason, have been kidnapped,'' he said, his voice harsh in the room's tense silence.

Wolf Harding had just appeared in the doorway. ''Who's behind it?'' he growled.

Jake sighed wearily. ''We don't have details yet—but we'll get to that in a minute.'' He'd been without sleep for forty hours. He'd just returned from a mission when the kidnapping occurred. Sean Killian and his wife, Susannah, arriving to baby-sit for Morgan and Laura, had discovered the Trayherns missing—except for their baby daughter, Katherine Alyssa.

''Son of a bitch,'' Wolf snarled as he stalked into the

room. He'd just gotten off a flight from Montana. When he noticed that Morgan's faithful assistant, Marie Parker, was part of the group, he quickly apologized for his lapse of manners, then crossed to the coffee dispenser and poured himself a cup.

Jake looked at his watch. "Killian discovered them missing at 1900 yesterday evening." He picked up a plastic bag. "They were shot with tranquilizer darts." He looked toward Killian, who stood in the shadows, his back against the wall, his face unreadable, as always. "Tell them what you found."

Killian looked at his friends. He and Wolf and Jake had been on a number of mercenary missions over the years, and the two men were like brothers to him. "Their front door was standing partly open. I thought that was odd— especially in November—so I told Susannah to stay in the car until I could check it out. Inside, I saw nothing until I reached the master bedroom. There were a few drops of blood on the carpet, and that drug dart was under the bed." Killian scowled. "I checked the kids' rooms, and the boy, Jason, was gone. Katherine was still in her bed, asleep."

"Were there signs of a struggle?" Wolf demanded, taking a seat to Jake's left. Papers were scattered across the large, highly polished table. He noted the worry visible on Marie's usually calm features. He took a sip of the scalding coffee and grimaced.

"Very few," Killian answered abruptly, folding his arms across his chest. "Once I made sure the place was secure, I brought Susannah in and called here. Jake had just come in off a mission, and I told him what I'd found." Killian pointed to one of the many pieces of paper on the table. "Marie received this message on the Perseus fax at 2100, two hours after the kidnapping."

Wolf reached for the paper. He frowned as he read it aloud: "Don't try to find Morgan Trayhern and his family. They are scattered around the world. If you want to see any of them alive again, Perseus will stop its attacks against the Peruvian Cartel."

"Yeah, Wolf, our friends down south," Jake muttered. He eyed the Cherokee man, whose dark features had paled considerably. "I know the three of us have fond memories of Ramirez and his cocaine syndicate. Wolf had been captured, tortured and nearly killed under the drug lord's hand, and Killian had fared only slightly better.

"Son of a bitch..." Wolf darted another apologetic look at Marie. "I'm sorry," he rasped, suddenly getting to his feet, the paper clenched in his large fist.

"It's all right, Wolf," Marie whispered, dabbing her eyes. "What should we do, Jake? I don't know how to run Perseus without Morgan's input. I have no idea how to start a search for him, or if we should. Please, can you take over? At least for now?"

Jake looked at the other two men. Wolf had been out of the mercenary business for nearly a year, working a sapphire mine in Montana with his wife, Sarah. Killian, who now took only low-risk U.S. assignments, was out of the loop, too. Though Perseus employed nearly a hundred mercenaries, those teams were locked into missions that couldn't be aborted at a moment's notice. Grimly, Jake realized he was the only available player who was up-to-date on everything.

"Unless anyone has a problem with it, I'll run Perseus—until we can get Morgan back," he offered.

Killian eased away from the wall and sat down at the opposite end of the table, facing them. "We're going to need a lot of government interface on this. Have you contacted the CIA? The FBI? And what about the DEA? They know more about the Peruvian Cartel than we do.''

"All of that's been initiated," Jake said. He took a long swig of coffee. His mouth tasted bitter, and his eyes smarted from lack of sleep. He'd already called Shah, his fiancée, in Oregon, to let her know what had happened. He should have been home by now. Instead, she was on a flight east to be with him. He wouldn't be going home now until Morgan and his family had been located and rescued.

"I've got Pentagon Intel specialists watching for messages of any kind. Part of the problem is satellite time. If we don't get it, we can't intercept potential messages between countries on satcom. It's pretty clear Ramirez is behind this, but that doesn't mean Morgan and his family are in Peru.''

Killian looked at his watch. It was 1900 on Tuesday, November 22. Thanksgiving was two days away. "We need to do some long-range planning," he murmured, looking up at the weary group. "I think we should keep the local police out of this. We've already got every arm of the government involved at a high level. The Alexandria police won't add anything except potential media coverage that we certainly don't need. I say we keep this as undercover as possible. That way the cartel won't be able to anticipate our moves.''

Jake rubbed his face. "Are we in agreement that we should try to locate and rescue Morgan and his family?''

Wolf nodded. "We don't have a choice. Killian and I know better than anyone what Ramirez is capable of. That bastard will torture Morgan to death an inch at a time. He's a murdering monster.''

"And what about Laura?" Marie asked tearfully. "What will he do to her?" She gazed around at the set faces of the men, seeing the grim lines of their mouths. None of them would meet her eyes. "Oh, dear…"

"Look," Wolf said impatiently, standing again, "we can't afford to let our imaginations get the best of us. We need cold, clear-headed tactics." He nailed Killian with a searching look. "Will your wife take care of Katherine? She's Laura's cousin, right?"

"Yes. I'm sending Susannah home to Kentucky—to her parent's farm. She and Katherine will be safer there."

"Have Morgan's parents been contacted?"

"No," Jake said heavily. "I was waiting until we could get a group of us together to figure out our plan of attack. But they need to be called and informed now."

"I can do that," Marie volunteered, making a note on her pad.

"Fine. Wolf, your specialty is communications. I want you to be our liaison with the Pentagon. Killian, I need a lieutenant to talk things over with, someone to help me make final decisions."

"I'll hang around," Killian said dryly.

Jake smiled a little and rubbed his stubbled face. He needed a hot shower, a shave and some sleep. The first two he could get, but sleep would have to wait.

"First we'll try to intercept communications traffic and get a lead on where they've taken the family members," Wolf said, thinking out loud.

"From the message, it sounds like Ramirez has separated them," Jake said. "They could be anywhere in the world. Anywhere."

"It's like searching for three needles in a haystack," Wolf agreed unhappily, pacing the length of the room.

"I know." Jake moved his shoulders to release some of the tension that had accumulated there.

Killian looked at Jake. ''Who's going after Ramirez and his goons?''

''I don't know yet,'' Jake admitted heavily. ''We're shorthanded. I'm going to go through the mission roster with Marie to try to cut loose some people to help us.'' He knew neither Wolf nor Killian would go. Wolf had quit the mercenary business almost a year ago, and he and Sarah were going to marry at Christmas. Killian was happily married and not about to risk everything—especially with Susannah four months pregnant. Jake didn't blame his friends for not volunteering for this kind of mission. If he took it, he knew Shah would raise all kinds of hell. Of late, they had grown inseparable, and Jake didn't want to risk their happiness on this level of danger.

Besides, the three of them had worked together for a long time, knew one another and how they thought. In a crisis like this, they'd be more useful in a behind-the-scenes overseeing role. ''Somehow we'll find the teams,'' he muttered.

''Do you want me to contact Alyssa and Noah?'' Marie asked.

''We'd better,'' Jake said ruefully. ''If we don't, there will be hell to pay.'' Lieutenant Commander Alyssa Cantrell was Morgan's younger sister, a navy pilot. Jake had no idea where she and her husband, Clay, were stationed. He did know that Commander Noah Trayhern, Morgan's brother, was in the Coast Guard and, with his wife, Kit, lived in Miami, Florida. Noah and Morgan's parents, who lived nearby in Clearwater, would be easiest to reach. ''Try to contact them through nonmilitary channels if you can, Marie.''

She rose, nodding, but gave him a questioning look.

''Ramirez has enough money to buy state-of-the-art telecommunications equipment that rivals anything the military has," Jake explained. "If we send these messages via the military, he might pick up on them and get an idea of our movements. I don't want him to know a damn thing if we can help it."

"I see," Marie acknowledged. She tried to smile, but failed. "I'll have dinner brought into the War Room for all of you."

Jake nodded. "Thanks, Marie." After she left, he turned to his comrades. "This is a hell of a bind."

Wolf stopped pacing, his hands on his hips. "Ramirez will kill them. It's only a matter of time."

"Yes," Killian agreed quietly. "He likes long, slow deaths. You know that, Wolf."

Harding nodded, his mouth a tight line. "I'm more worried about Laura. She's the one really at risk."

"Ramirez won't be easy on her," Killian agreed. "When I was first captured in Peru, I was taken to a different cell block from you, Wolf. Ramirez and his goons raped women prisoners as part of their torture to get them to talk. No, you're right—Laura has problems."

"And what the hell will they do with the boy?" Jake asked, his voice frustrated. "I mean, the kid's innocent."

Killian gave him a flat look. "In our business, no one's innocent."

"Why didn't they take Katherine?" Wolf wondered aloud.

"Probably because women are considered worthless—second-class citizens—in South America," Jake muttered. "She wasn't worth taking. You know how South American men think the world of their sons. Boys carry on the family name and honor. I'm sure that's why they took Jason."

"Do you think he's at risk?" Wolf asked.

"I don't know," Jake hedged. "Knowing Ramirez and

his twisted mind, he'll probably stash the boy away somewhere and raise him in the cocaine empire. That's the way Ramirez is, you know. He'd think that was the ultimate revenge on Morgan—turn his son into a cocaine trafficker—or worse, a coke addict.''

Wolf cursed and began pacing again. ''There's no question we've got to get to them. The sooner, the better.''

''First,'' Killian said, ''we need a lucky break. Someone has to pick up communications between Ramirez and his worldwide cartel. We've got to get a clue to where they are.''

''Our second problem is finding a team that can undertake the rescue once we do locate them,'' Jake reminded his friends.

''What do we have so far?'' Jake demanded of his team. He was clean shaven, dressed in fresh clothes, and had even managed to snatch a little sleep. It was 2000 the next evening, and the three mercenaries were back in the War Room. Marie sat at the opposite end of the table from them, taking notes. A messy stack of papers still covered the shiny oval surface. On the wall, a map of the world had been pulled down for reference. Disposable cups littered the room, silent testimony to too many cups of coffee, and the burning stomachs and frayed nerves that went with them.

''The Pentagon is working double time on telecommunications,'' Killian reported. The Joint Chiefs of Staff have approved satellite telecommunication time for us. They've put a team of Intelligence people from the CIA on it, along with other military specialists. We're getting more help than I anticipated.''

''Good,'' Jake grunted. ''Wolf?''

''I'm getting help from the FBI and DEA. They're

checking all flights from the East Coast to see if we can figure out how Morgan and his family were taken, and in what direction they went.''

''Do you think there's a chance they're still in the U.S.?'' Jake asked.

''No. The FBI thinks they're off U.S. soil.''

Before Jake could speak, the door flew open. He reared back in surprise, automatically on guard. A Marine Corps officer, a lieutenant colonel, stood in the doorway, one hand on the knob, the other on the doorjamb. His face looked stormy; his eyes were narrowed in anger.

''Just what the hell has happened to Laura Trayhern?'' he snapped, moving into the room and shutting the door behind him. ''And what the hell are you doing about it?''

Jake stood. He'd been in the Marine Corps himself for many years before leaving to work for Perseus. The officer in front of him was in his middle thirties, lean as a cougar. Jake noted the gold parachute emblem above his dark green, wool shirt pocket and the full set of colorful ribbons denoting his time in service. The officer stood rigidly, his hands curled into fists at his sides, his eyes accusing as they swept the room, then settled on Jake.

''Who are you?'' Jake demanded in a deep tone.

''I'm Colonel Jim Woodward, Intel, over at the Pentagon.'' He gave a disdainful look around the room again. ''Where's Laura? What's happened to her?''

Jake held up his hand. ''Calm down, Colonel Woodward. Are you part of the liaison the CIA put on telecommunications?''

''Yes,'' he said tightly, ''I am. I've been pulled to oversee the operation. When I found out Laura was involved, I had to know a hell of a lot more than I was being told. That's why I'm here. I'm an old friend of hers, from before she married Morgan. Now will someone fill me in?''

Jake nodded. "Have a seat, Colonel."

Jim listened without interrupting. By the time Jake Randolph finished briefing him on the kidnapping, he couldn't seem to settle his rapid pulse or ignore the fact that his hands were sweating. Laura was in danger. His heart contracted at the thought. It was nearly impossible to keep his face carefully arranged. When Jake asked if they'd been able to intercept any likely communications yet, Jim stood.

Taking a piece of paper out of his breast pocket, he handed it to him. "I know where they've got Laura. We just picked up a sat-tel link off a small Caribbean island known as Nevis. It's a tiny spot in the Windward Islands, off the coast of South America. The message is cryptic, but we got a lead on the transmission."

Jake frowned as he studied the paper. "How do you figure this, Colonel?"

"I don't know who transmitted—yet. I've got the CIA working on that angle right now." Jim jabbed a finger toward the paper. "But it was transmitted from Nevis to someone in Dresden, Germany. It reads, 'The Tiger is caged.'"

"Why would that be Laura Trayhern?" Wolf demanded.

Jim held on to his disintegrating anger. "Before Morgan came into Laura's life, we had a relationship. I used to call her Tiger." He felt heat creeping into his cheeks. "It was a nickname I gave her because she was the only civilian woman writer working at the Pentagon archives." He felt foolish divulging the intimacy, but he had no choice.

"I don't know…" Killian began. "Isn't that a bit of a stretch?"

Woodward glared at the narrow-faced man sitting to

Randolph's right. "Not when the CIA has already confirmed that Nevis is home to a world-class drug dealer by the name of Guillermo Garcia."

"Garcia," Harding growled. "Damn, he and Ramirez have been in cahoots for twenty years."

Jim smiled grimly. "I'm right and I know it. 'Tiger' is Laura."

"How would Garcia know that?" Jake demanded.

"He's probably drugged her and gotten a lot of personal info out of her," Killian interjected.

Just the thought of Laura being drugged, having her life bled out of her, made Jim sick to his stomach. "It's just a matter of time until I get more info pinpointing Garcia as her captor. I've already gotten permission to move one of our spy satellites to that part of the Caribbean. Right now—" he glanced at his watch "—a U-2 spy plane is in the air, on its way to take photo reconnaissance over the island. I guarantee you, with those photos, we can pick up a gnat's rear end at fifty yards. If my photo people see anything to suggest Laura being there, we'll have our proof."

Relieved, Jake nodded. "I'm damn glad you're heading up the Pentagon effort, Colonel Woodward. You obviously know what you're doing, and you've provided more information than any other source so far."

"Well," Jim rasped, "my association with Laura goes back a lot of years. She's a special woman...." He avoided Jake's probing gaze, cleared his throat, then looked back at him. "What plans do you have for infiltrating that compound on Nevis, Mr. Randolph?"

Jake smiled for the first time, just a little. "We might be short on the information files, Colonel, but one thing Perseus does do well is mercenary work of any kind. This type of mission is right down our alley."

"I doubt it," Jim challenged. He focused on the men one by one. "I thought this situation through on the way here. The dossier on Garcia I've got coming over to you from the CIA is substantial. They've got a blueprint of his estate, which is behind an iron fence ten feet high. He's got guards and Doberman pinschers posted around his ten-acre kingdom. Nobody comes and goes from Nevis without him or his people knowing about it.

"If you sent one of your men to the island, they'd find out instantly. They'd tail him, and chances are, they'd take him out at first opportunity. You don't know what's involved here." He went over to the map and tapped the Caribbean area. "You need a HAHO," Jim said, using the military acronym for a high-altitude, high-opening parachute drop, "onto that island in the dead of night. And you'll need a specialist with maximum military parachute experience. Do you know how small Nevis is? It's not much of a target. But if you tried to parachute from a lower altitude, Garcia would spot you, and you'd be dead before you landed.

"Then *if* you get your man on the ground, he'll need jungle experience. Nevis is heavily wooded and, because it's so small Garcia's people will certainly spot you, if the locals don't. That is, unless you utilize maximum stealth technology."

"Hold it, Colonel," Jake said heavily. "We have those kind of people on our payroll. Morgan rarely hires anyone who's not ex-military. We've got ex-Delta Force and former Marine Recons. The problem is, we're stretched too thin. We don't have a team we can pull to take this assignment."

"You what?" Woodward's mouth fell open and he snapped it shut. "You don't have anyone assigned to fulfill this mission? It's a priority."

"Don't you think we're upset about it, too?" Jake retorted, his voice irritated. "Unfortunately, Colonel, this world of ours is full of trouble spots. Many of our teams are on dangerous missions. We can't just extricate them without jeopardizing their lives, or other people's lives, in the process. It doesn't make sense to lose two to six lives to save one." Jake tapped a bunch of computer printouts. "I've gone through our mission list twice. The teams with experience are in situations where they can't be pulled. The ones that can be pulled don't have the background you're talking about. I'm not about to put an inexperienced team into the type of situation you're painting for us. We don't throw our people's lives away like the military does."

Woodward smarted under the remark. He felt heat rising from his throat into his face. Whenever he got angry, his face turned red, and he knew it. "This is an unconscionable position. You've got three lives—one of them the man who owns this damn company—at stake, and you don't have anyone to run a rescue mission?"

"Back down," Wolf snarled, crossing his arms over his chest and returning Jim's glare. "We're doing what we can with the resources we have."

"I won't back down." Jim held his gaze for a long moment. "All right, then I'll volunteer for the mission."

Jake's brows knitted, and he studied Jim for a long moment before speaking. "This is personal, isn't it? Between you and Laura?"

"That's none of your business, Randolph. What is your business is that you've got someone to take this mission. I can get orders cut to allow me to do this. I'm a Recon. I'm HAHO qualified. I've been in more jungles than I care to think about. I've been in Panama, Grenada and other South American venues on deep undercover assignments.'' He stopped, his voice low and shaking with tightly held emotion.

Jake glanced around the table, assessing his team for some inkling of their thoughts. Killian stirred and placed his arms on the table, clasping his hands in front of him. He glanced up at Woodward.

''Laura is married to Morgan. They love each other,'' he said quietly.

Jim recoiled inwardly. ''Don't insult me with facts I already know.''

Killian held his stare. ''Mercs who have an emotional involvement with the person they're trying to rescue don't live long.''

''That may be your problem, Killian, but it's not mine.''

With a shrug, Killian looked across the table at Wolf.

Wolf said, ''You'll need a partner. We never go in alone. It's two or nothing. Do you have someone in mind who has the same qualifications?''

Jim hesitated. ''Two?''

''Yes,'' Jake rasped, ''two people on every mission. That's Morgan's law, and it's a good one. If one partner is injured, the other can always bring him out.'' He lowered his voice. ''We have no time for heroics, Colonel. We work as a tightly knit unit and watch each other's backs. I know Recons. I used to be one. You don't go gallivanting off by yourselves, either. You have five men to a team and you know the value of working together.''

''I don't disagree with you, but I can't honestly think of anyone who would volunteer for such a dangerous assignment. The one man who might be willing, a sergeant, is laid up in the hospital with a broken ankle right now.''

Jake shook his head. ''Colonel, this mission doesn't go down without two team members.''

Wolf slowly unwound from his chair. He rubbed his temple and looked first at Woodward, then at Randolph. "I know someone who can do it. Her name is Pepper Sinclair. Her brother's a Navy Top Gun and a test pilot. She's a team leader for the National Forest Service's smoke jumpers. In fact, Pepper is in the Hotshots, the elite, highly trained group that goes into dangerous forest hot spots or wildfires. She's got over two thousand parachute drops and is ex-army." Wolf smiled a little. "Matter of fact, I've known her for nearly a year now, and her background is impressive. She was the only woman ever to complete Army Ranger training—but they wouldn't let her graduate because she was a woman."

Jake twisted to look in Wolf's direction. "What'd she do then?"

"She quit the army. She was an officer, and she resigned her commission in protest over their decision. Pepper went into the smoke jumpers because it was the most dangerous career she could find where nobody cared about her gender. She's got six years of military service behind her, and she was in Panama and Grenada, too, so she knows jungles. I think she's around thirty years old, and she's got a good head on her shoulders. Pepper doesn't go off half-cocked on anything." Wolf studied Woodward. "And in this case, that might be important, because, Colonel, I think you're in this way over your head emotionally. You're carrying a torch for Laura, whether she's married or not, and that's going to get you into trouble on this mission."

Jim opened his mouth to protest, but Harding went on.

"I know the question you're all wanting to ask. Would Pepper volunteer for something like this? I don't know, but I can sure call and ask. She's good friends with Sarah and me, and I think she'd be interested."

"She'll get good pay for it," Jake said hopefully, liking the suggestion.

Wolf's smile broadened a bit. "Pepper isn't turned on by money. She's a competitive person and she likes challenges."

"This is hardly a game!" Jim protested vehemently.

"Pepper doesn't play games, Colonel. What I'm saying is that she's as solid and trustworthy as they come. Hell, she leads a Hotshot team. You probably don't know a thing about smoke jumpers, but I can fill you in. You're a Recon, the best warrior the Marine Corps produces. Well, in the smoke-jumping world, Hotshots are the equivalent. We had a forest fire north of Phillipsburg, where we live, and I got to see Pepper and her crew up front. That fire was bearing down on our small mountain town, with seventy-mile-an-hour winds pushing the blaze.

"Of all the teams that could have been put on the line between that fire and our town, Pepper and her staff were chosen. She served as commander over ten Hotshot teams. I worked with her on tactics and strategies for the fire and I saw her parachute in with a team that I thought for sure would be burned alive. She went in there with her walkie-talkie—and with her people, who would go to hell and back for her—and she did the impossible. She got the fire to move, and Phillipsburg is still standing, thanks to her guts, intelligence and experience."

Jim sat down. "I'll be damned if I'm going in with a woman," he said harshly. "They aren't qualified for this kind of a drop."

"She's ex-army, ex-Ranger. Ranger training is similar to Recon," Wolf droned. "And you know that."

Jake nodded. "It's an excellent idea, Wolf. Can you call Pepper now and fill her in?"

"You bet." Wolf excused himself to make the call.

Woodward stood up. "You can't be serious about this, Randolph."

"I'm dead serious. You don't know Wolf, nor do you know his background and experience. If he says Pepper Sinclair can do it, I believe him." Jake held the officer's shocked stare. "I do know one thing for sure, however. If you take this mission, you're doing it the Perseus way, not the Marine Corps, John Wayne style. I've got three people I love very much on the line right now, and I'm not going to blow it by putting anything but two first-rate people on this mission. Do you understand that, Colonel? Because if you don't, or if you give me grief about it, I'll make a call to the JCS and tell them we don't want you. Do I make myself clear?"

Angrily, Jim moved around the table. "Don't threaten me, Randolph. I'm damn well capable of pulling off this mission *alone.*"

"It's not a threat, Colonel. It's a promise."

Was Randolph bluffing? Jim wasn't sure. As a matter of fact, he didn't like the loose way Perseus worked at all. This decision by committee wasn't in the least like the military. He rubbed his jaw as he assessed Randolph, who sat like a mountain in the chair at the other end of the table.

"Even you can see the folly of Harding's idea," Jim insisted.

"Really? What's that?"

"A *woman,*" Jim said in exasperation.

Jake grinned tiredly. "Colonel, one thing Morgan Trayhern has made very clear to everyone at Perseus is that in his opinion, women are just as good, and usually better, than any man at this work."

"That's ridiculous!"

"Not in our book." Jake tapped the table deliberately

with his index finger. "And as long as Morgan is alive, we're running his company his way. You got that?"

Biting back the anger that warred with his fear for Laura, he sat down. "This woman could be killed."

"It's an equal-opportunity business, Colonel, just as women in the military can be killed as easily as men. Bullets don't consider gender."

Stymied, Woodward sat very still, evaluating his options. He knew no one was better qualified than he was to rescue Laura. But to have a woman—a civilian, of all things—along on such a dangerous mission was beyond his imagination. He wasn't usually so temperamental— but this was personal, just as they had accused him of earlier. Jim knew his emotional involvement could be a detriment to the mission. Somehow, he had to separate his feelings from the job to be done, and concentrate on surviving.

"I want your promise on one thing, Randolph," he insisted.

"What?"

"If this Pepper Sinclair is stupid enough to volunteer for this mission, I want the opportunity to put her through her paces. If she can't or refuses to do a HAHO, or in some way is not militarily qualified, I have veto power."

"With an attitude like yours, she's sure to fail whatever task you set her," Jake said tightly.

"Dammit, I have a right to protect myself in this mission. I don't care how glowing Harding's report is, if she can't stand the heat, she doesn't come with me."

Jake glared at him. "I propose an alternative plan, Colonel. If Pepper volunteers, you can set up the tests you need to feel comfortable, then you can both report back to me. I'll make the final decision."

In that moment, Jim disliked Randolph intensely. "I can set up the tests?"

"Any and all you want, understanding that we don't have much time. Once the CIA gets a fix and confirmation that Laura is on Nevis, we want to initiate the mission immediately."

Satisfied, Jim leaned back in the chair. "Fine. I'll bet you a hundred dollars right now that Ms. Sinclair is going to fail miserably at the tests I've got in mind."

Randolph smiled uneasily. "You're on, Colonel. A hundred bucks."

Jim crossed his arms, wondering about the outcome of Harding's phone call to Sinclair. He prayed she'd turn him down. What woman in her right mind would volunteer for a high-kill-ratio assignment like this? He didn't look too hard at his own answer to the same question.

Chapter Two

Tension thrummed through Jim Woodward as he stood waiting for Pepper Sinclair to walk through the partially opened door. It was 0700 on Wednesday, November 23, and she was due in from a red-eye flight from Butte, Montana, at any moment. Harding had gone to the airport to pick her up and would brief her on the way in, so she'd be up to speed by the time she reached the Perseus office.

Jim didn't want a woman with him on this mission; it was that simple. She could have taken first in Hawaii's grueling physical-endurance contest, the Iron Woman, and it wouldn't have mattered to him.

His sensitive hearing caught the sound of voices in the reception area, where Marie had her neatly organized office. Warm, husky laughter—distinctly feminine—drifted to where he stood. Jim tried to stay immune to that rolling, mellow sound, but it was impossible. It wasn't Marie's laughter, so it had to be Pepper Sinclair's. His mouth turned down. Why did she have to have such a provocative laugh?

He stood tensely, hearing Wolf's deep voice and Pepper's well-modulated one intermingle as they chatted amiably. He didn't know Harding well, but knew he wasn't the type of man to be chatty, so it must be Pepper's presence drawing him out.

Whatever Jim was prepared to see, it wasn't the physical reality of Pepper Sinclair as she followed Harding into the room. She was tall—probably close to six feet—medium-boned, with dark walnut-colored hair softly brushing her proudly held shoulders. More surprising, she was wearing a long red-and-yellow calico skirt that touched the tops of her comfortable, brown leather shoes. Her white blouse, with touches of lace around the throat, was partly hidden by a pale golden deerskin vest adorned with conchs. Long beaded earrings nearly touched her shoulders, giving her a somewhat Native American look, except for her pale, almost-translucent skin with a sprinkling of freckles across her nose.

Pepper's face was oval. Her nose had a slight bump and fine nostrils. Jim looked downward to lips curved in an impish smile, then his gaze moved back up—and into eyes as blue and clear as a Montana sky. His heart gave a hard thump, underscoring the impact of those eyes—the pupils edged in breathtaking turquoise, the frame of thick, dark lashes. Her dark brows were arched and full, offering a second frame for the magnificent eyes. Her cheeks were flushed, their rosy pink enhancing her classic bone structure.

But more than her striking and unexpectedly feminine looks, it was Pepper's direct, fearless gaze that caught Jim completely off guard. The look combined maturity with a woman's confidence—yet glinted with a girlish aspect that somehow strengthened its impact. Jim was chagrined to feel his palms growing damp. Meanwhile, his errant heart refused to slow its pounding beat.

Jim tried to suppress his reaction to Pepper. It didn't help that he'd expected a sturdy, mannish sort of woman with a tough, no-nonsense attitude—a hardened outer shell for this female smoke jumper who damn near walked on water, according to Harding. Jim's gaze ranged from her long, narrow hands to the graceful way she walked toward him, to those mesmerizing blue eyes....

"Colonel Woodward? I'm Pepper Sinclair. Glad to meet you."

Her grip as she took his hand told Jim instantly that she wasn't as weak as she looked. Her firm, confident handshake, warm and dry, conveyed strength and capability. If it had been a man's handshake, he'd have been impressed. In a woman, he didn't know how to react.

"Ms. Sinclair," he said, hating the clipped abruptness in his tone as he stared challengingly at her.

"I'll leave you two to get acquainted," Wolf said dryly. He pointed to the counter on the left. "Pepper, if you want coffee, help yourself."

"You saved my life again, Wolf." Pepper laughed and waved to her friend as he stepped out of the room, closing the door quietly behind him. She shifted the strap of her deerskin purse off her shoulder and laid the bag on the oak table, then moved toward the coffee machine. The tension in the room was palpable, and she knew full well it was emanating from the marine standing rigidly next to the table, watching her every move like a predator ready to strike.

"I don't know about you, but four hours on the red-eye makes me thirsty as a horse." She glanced back over her shoulder at the officer, who was scowling heavily.

"Coffee, Colonel?" she asked pleasantly. "Or would you prefer to take out your weapon of choice right now, shoot me and put yourself out of your misery?"

Shocked, Jim opened his mouth, then closed it. Her eyes were serious, but her voice dripped with honey and her mouth curved in a rueful smile. "I see Harding has been talking behind my back," he said finally.

"On the contrary," Pepper said smoothly, finding a clean white mug and pouring the fresh coffee into it, "Wolf was merely honest with me about potential problems and dangers. He did inform me that you were against using a woman on this mission."

Jim moved to the table, hating himself more as he snapped, "Ms. Sinclair, when it comes to life-and-death matters, all the cards get laid on the table. Nothing and no one is spared. And you're right—I don't want a woman on this mission."

Pepper turned. "I couldn't agree more with the truth of your first statement, Colonel. We're both in the business of life and death, aren't we?" She took a sip of coffee. Too bad Woodward was such a sourpuss, she thought. Because the man was undeniably a handsome devil, in a rugged kind of way. His green eyes were glittering like shards of ice in her direction right now, though, and his square face was set—like concrete. His black hair was militarily short and neat, and she liked his darkly tanned looks. Lines in a face told her much, and Woodward had his share. Creases at the corners of his eyes spoke of a great deal of time spent outdoors. The lines bracketing his mouth said something different, though. Lines of pain, possibly. But from what? Or who? His size, posture and attitude reminded her of their local college football captain. Fleetingly, Pepper wondered if Jim had played football in college. She smiled to herself and decided not to ask. Pulling back a chair, she smoothed her skirt and sat. Woodward stiffly took a seat opposite her, his hand folded in front of him, his knuckles white.

"We aren't in the same business, Ms. Sinclair. Not by a mile," he said tightly.

Pepper held his angry, defiant gaze. "Let's talk about your anger at the idea of a woman going on this mission with you, shall we?" she asked, her voice calm and steady. "I believe in gut-level honesty, so maybe that would be a good place to start in this messy little situation we seem to find ourselves in."

Jim reeled internally at her unexpected bluntness. Her quiet voice belied the strength of her demand. He grasped at a notepad with several items neatly printed on it and slid it around in front of him on the table, using the moment to collect his scattered thoughts. "I'm not angry at you," he said coldly. "I'm angry at the concept of Perseus installing a two-person team on this mission, when I feel I'd be more successful alone."

Pepper's smile was equally chilly. "Spoken like a politically correct officer in line to make general someday. Congratulations, Colonel Woodward. It's a great reply, but it's hardly complete and honest, don't you think?"

Under any other circumstances, Jim had to admit, he would have liked Pepper immediately. She wasn't conventionally beautiful. Her chin was stubborn and pronounced, and her aristocratic nose didn't match her full mouth, the corners of which always seemed to curve slightly upward. Her features were like puzzle pieces that shouldn't fit together, but somehow did, to create a whole more magical than the sum of its parts. A rebellious lock of hair fell across her broad brow, and she brushed it away, as if she'd made that effortless gesture unconsciously all her life. He bought more time by opening his briefcase and placing a couple of books on the table.

"Are you always this acerbic, or are you doing it as a special favor to me?" he asked finally, seeing the laughter flash in her eyes, though she didn't allow it to transfer to her mouth.

"I consider my answers honest," Pepper responded. "Maybe you're looking for political correctness or diplomacy. I'm neither of those, Colonel. I learned about both things early on as an army officer, but I'm a civilian now. I no longer have to play those word games with you or anyone else." She smiled slightly. "Thank goodness."

Jim found it difficult not to smile in response to the warmth shining from her eyes. In fact, he could feel her warmth—as real as if a beam of sunlight had suddenly struck him. Who was this woman? "It's not my nature to be base," he offered.

"Since when is honesty considered baseness, Colonel?"

His fingers tightened around the ballpoint pen in his hand. "If we're done sparring, can we get down to the business at hand?" he said through gritted teeth.

"Fine, let's do it." Pepper tried to feel anger toward Woodward, but it just wouldn't surface. He was obviously uncomfortable, backed into a corner of sorts and unhappy about her appearance on a mission he wanted to perform solo. She set the cup to one side and pulled out her own small notepad and a pen from her purse. "What's on your agenda, Colonel?"

"You. I told Jake Randolph I intend to put you through your paces. If you don't measure up to my high standards, you aren't going."

"I believe you agreed that Mr. Randolph will make the final decision," Pepper said smoothly, holding his glare.

"Besides, what gives you the right to question my credentials while assuming yours are beyond question?"

"I'm a Recon Marine. My credentials *are* beyond question."

Pepper leaned back, slowly tapping the table with her index finger. "I'm a country girl, Colonel, and I've lived most of my life in Montana. Maybe we're kinda simple folk out that way, but you know what? We let people prove themselves through their acts. Your walk is your talk. I could understand your concern if I didn't have a military background. I could also understand it if I'd never jumped out of a plane with a parachute. But what I see going down here is a wounded male ego overreacting to the fact that I'm a woman. If I were a man, I think you'd drop this pretense. Back where I come from, that doesn't go down well. I'm a team leader for twenty smoke jumpers. I'm responsible for a lot of lives, and I've never lost one. I'm not about to start now with yours or my own. I found out a long time ago that ego and pride are expendable."

Her voice dropped slightly. "Colonel, I appreciate your concern about my qualifications, but it's not necessary. I probably have more time logged in parachute jumps than you do."

"All at low altitude."

"I took Ranger training. I've participated in HAHOs."

Frustrated, Jim said, "I'm not going to fire any more shots across your bow. We need to get down to business. I've outlined the next three days." He pushed the neatly printed paper toward her. "I'm going to test your map- and compass-reading ability. I've arranged for a HAHO and have preplanned the jump zone with the military boys at Andrews Air Force Base. It's set up and ready to go for tomorrow at 0700. The jump onto Nevis will be at night. But as much as I'd like to schedule day and night practice HAHOs, we just don't have the time. A day jump will have to do.'' Jim watched the soft fullness of Pepper's lips tighten a little as she carefully read his outline. Her fingers were slim with largish knuckles, her nails closely trimmed. There was no wasted motion about her, he had to admit, and in spite of himself, he savored her unique mix of serenity and efficiency.

"I feel like I'm back in Ranger training," Pepper said mildly, sliding his notes gently back across the table. If Woodward weren't so intent on making her dislike him, she thought, she might like to explore him personally, as a human being and a man. But the set of his square jaw warned her off. He was trying to intimidate her into quitting. Well, it wouldn't work. As the only female ever to go through Ranger training, she'd had plenty of experience with intimidation attempts by men far more dangerous to her than Woodward—but he didn't know that. "I'm assuming you'll be with me on these exercises? That you'll participate in the HAHO, too?"

"Of course."

Pepper grinned. "To watch me fail?"

"I expect you to."

"Colonel, you've just pushed a favorite button of mine—I love a good challenge. My whole life has been about dancing on the edge of a sword."

Jim almost smiled. Again that unsettling turquoise warmth from her eyes enveloped him, and he felt his heart beating harder in his chest. There was something arresting about Pepper that he couldn't quite put his finger on. At least, not yet.

"Tell me a little about yourself, Colonel. Personal stuff."

Her directness scuttled him. He eyed her. "Why is that important to the mission?"

"If I'm going to succeed at all your tests, I need to know more about my partner than his military title. I want to know something about the man." Her eyes narrowed briefly. "What makes you run, Jim Woodward?"

Jim pushed his chair away from the table and stood up. "You have a damn needling habit of being nosy, Ms. Sinclair."

"And you have a damn needling habit of questioning my credentials when what we really should be doing is planning how to save Laura Trayhern."

The set of her jaw, with her chin jutting out, challenged him, as did her incensed gaze. So she was angry, after all—but for the right reasons, Jim realized. "Believe me," he said, trying to hide his emotion in a gruff tone of voice, "no one wants to save Laura more than I do."

"I understand from Wolf that Laura is a personal friend of yours." Pepper watched his cheeks flame red and saw sudden shyness in that imperious gaze he was trying to control her with. Maybe Woodward wasn't such a jerk, after all. For a moment, she'd glimpsed a real man behind that egotistical marine facade he was employing to try to scare her into quitting.

"Laura and I go back a long way," Jim muttered offensively, as he turned and walked to the window. In the distance he could see the Capitol and the Washington Monument outlined against the dawning colors of the horizon. "We met when I had my first tour at the Pentagon. Laura was—still is—a military-defense author. It's rare for a woman to find success in the field, and she's considered authoritative on a broad range of military subjects." His voice dropped. "She's an incredible woman…all that intelligence, that ability to comprehend…''

Pepper watched Jim Woodward's face soften tremendously—as if he'd forgotten she was in the room. The incredible tension around him dissolved as he spoke of Laura. "And she married Morgan Trayhern?" Pepper asked quietly.

He shrugged. "Morgan Trayhern crashed into our lives, and she ended up with him."

The sudden flatness of his tone belied his pain, his confusion over that issue, Pepper realized. No longer was he the tough marine officer; for a moment he was a human being struggling with unresolved emotions regarding a woman he loved.

"Are you presently in a relationship?"

Jim shook his head. "No, not a serious one."

"Any family?"

"Just my parents, until recently. They died in an auto accident a year ago." Jim turned. He felt oddly sad and didn't try to cover it up. Pepper's gaze was assessing, the warmth still there, continually surrounding him like sunlight. The genuine care and sincerity radiating from her was very real. Vaguely, he acknowledged that good leaders had that kind of charisma. Despite her almost-brutal honesty, Jim admired those qualities. He could understand now why men would work under her command without having male-female issues. Yes, she was personable and easy to talk to—too easy.

"I'm sorry to hear it," she murmured. No one deserved to have their parents ripped from them like that. Trying to establish a less-traumatic line of conversation, she asked, "Are you an only child?"

"Yes. And I was spoiled rotten."

"I have an older brother, Cam. He's married to a wonderful woman named Molly. They have three children now, and I like playing Auntie Pepper to all of them.'' She smiled fondly as she thought of her brother's family.

Jim tried to resist her husky voice, but it was like a soothing balm to the sadness he still held in his heart over the unexpected loss of his parents. It uplifted him, and he noticed the luminous quality that came to her eyes when she spoke about her brother. ''He's the naval aviator?'' he asked, remembering Harding's comments about a Top Gun brother.

''Yes. Molly used to be in the navy, too. They met at test-pilot school a number of years ago. She's such a homebody, a real hausfrau who enjoys being a mother and parent. Cam lost his first family in a freak airplane accident, so I'm really happy to see them together. I'm glad she decided to resign her commission and become a civilian.''

''Surprising words from a gung ho career woman—or are you?''

''What do you think?'' Pepper would play his game against himself. She wasn't about to become cannon fodder for him or any military man stuck in the ''women should be barefoot and pregnant'' mind-set.

Jim rubbed his jaw and held her gaze. ''I don't know what to think about you—yet,'' he admitted. ''I know what I thought you were, but my original assessment isn't turning out to be as accurate as I expected.''

''I'm sure you expected me to come striding in here wearing men's clothes and acting like 'one of the boys.''' Pepper countered. ''Well, I would have at one time, Colonel—back in my army days. I became that way to protect myself from the men who wanted to tear me down and make me quit.'' With a slight shrug, she added, ''When I joined the Smokeys, I lost that facade: I discovered that the men and women who jumped into fires didn't care what gender I was so long as I could do the job. I was allowed to be myself, to flourish and grow into the woman you see now.'' Her smile was frank. ''I think it's nice to be a woman and do a first-rate job, whether it's perceived as masculine or not. Don't you?''

''Touché.''

''An honest answer. How refreshing, Colonel. Be careful, it could become a habit.''

Instead of being stung by her rejoinder, Jim laughed. And it felt damn good to laugh, as if an incredible weight he'd been carrying on his shoulders had slipped free for just a moment. That load had been there in some form ever since Laura had married Morgan, he realized. Getting up, he went over and poured himself a cup of coffee. Silence flowed back into the room, but the atmosphere was less tense than it had been.

''Since we're exploring each other,'' he said, coming back to the table, ''tell me a little about yourself. Do you have a significant other?'' He wondered what kind of man would be drawn to her.

Pepper slid her fingers quickly through some strands of hair. ''No…not anymore.''

Jim heard the pain underlying her soft answer. He also saw, for the first time, a look other than happiness in her eyes. Pepper had a real vulnerability to her, even if she held down a decidedly male career with success. In his experience, the military molded women into a male image in order to help them survive. The military was unforgiving if someone—man or woman—showed vulnerability of any kind, so he was fascinated by Pepper's ability to maintain that quality.

Pepper struggled with a sudden deluge of emotions that brought back her raw, unhealed past. She saw at least a shred of real concern mingled with the curiosity in Jim's eyes. Afraid to release that genie of past suffering from its well-stoppered bottle, she straightened her spine. "Since we've both laid our cards on the table, why don't we get down to the real business?" she said, her voice suddenly brisk. "What's on the agenda today? I'm sure you've got something up your sleeve."

Jim pulled himself from his reverie, realizing he was staring at her. Embarrassed by his own breach of officer-like etiquette, he murmured, "We're going over to my office at the Pentagon. My attaché called to say they've got reconnaissance photos of Nevis Island taken by a U-2 flyby."

With a shake of her head, Pepper got to her feet and slipped the purse strap onto her shoulder. "Amazing how all that old military lingo I thought I'd forgotten comes right back."

"Once in the military, always in the military," Jim said as he opened the door.

Pepper's smile was still laced with pain. "There are some parts of it I wish I could forget," she muttered, slipping by him and out the door. In the front office, she saw Wolf and Jake, their heads bowed together over some military information, talking in low tones. She went over to Wolf and touched his arm. The civilian clothes both men wore couldn't hide their military bearing.

"Wolf, I'm going with Colonel Woodward over to the Pentagon."

"Fine…we'll see you when you get back." Wolf gave her a brief, assessing look. So did Jake, who she'd met earlier.

Pepper smiled a little, reading his mind. "Everything went fine," she lied. Wolf had a habit of sticking up for friends rather boldly and sometimes to his regret. Not wanting Wolf to dislike Jim any more than he already did, she felt the white lie would help reduce office tension to below the boiling point. As she turned, she saw the oddest look in Woodward's gaze—an almost wistful expression combined with such heat that it threw her off guard.

Woodward didn't like her because she was a woman in a military man's slot. Okay, so why was that look so tough to decipher? Sighing at the knowledge that Woodward was something of an enigma to her, Pepper grabbed her Pendleton coat off the hook and followed him out of the Perseus office.

The late-November chill was matched by a gray sky that threatened the first snow of the year, and Pepper was glad to get into the heated Pentagon building. As she walked at Jim's side, she smiled to herself, once again surrounded by uniformed members of all four military branches walking the halls of this military icon. The tile floor was polished to perfection, and hundreds of pieces of artwork, depicting and honoring war from the ground, water and air, decorated the walls of the octagon-shaped building's outer ring.

Jim was aware of the stares Pepper was receiving from more than one gawking officer. He tried to ignore her natural grace—the way she moved was more like water flowing than like the steady, deliberate steps he took. Maybe it was that effortless ease, he decided sourly, that made nine out of ten officers do a double take. Disgruntled, he had to admit that any man worth his salt would certainly look at Pepper. An old saying came to his mind: "She was easy on the eyes." It was a decided compliment.

His office was tucked away, compared to many of the others. When they'd made their way in, Jim shut the door after Pepper. His natural inclination was to be a gentleman, to take her coat and hang it up for her. But a contrary part of him said, let her take care of herself. As he stood, debating which to do, Pepper crossed to the small closet, matter-of-factly hung up her coat and purse and turned toward him.

"What now?"

"This way," he muttered unhappily, preceding her into the interior office—his private space. His secretary had yet to come in, and with Thanksgiving tomorrow, many people in the Pentagon would be working only half a day, anyway.

Pepper stepped into Jim's small enclave and looked around at the officious degree certificates and awards hanging on the walls. She was impressed. Woodward was more than a Recon. He had a degree in engineering from Ohio State University and had graduated with honors. Curious, she moved to a wall hung with several framed color photos. Most were of him with graduating officers, but one exception drew her attention.

The photo showed a younger Jim Woodward, his arm around a much smaller, delicate-looking blond woman. Both were smiling, obviously happy, with champagne glasses lifted in a toast to the camera.

"Who's this?" Pepper asked, turning to him. Jim was behind his desk, riffling through a pile of papers that had been stacked there for his attention.

He looked up briefly. "Oh…that's Laura Bennett—I mean, Trayhern. Morgan's wife."

Pepper returned her attention to the picture. "How old is this photo?"

"Eight years." Frowning, Jim stopped reading the message in his hand and looked up. Pepper's profile was clean, even pretty. Her dark hair fell softly around her face, completely natural and untamed. He liked that about her—her utter naturalness, with no apology for the way she looked or dressed.

"What was the occasion?"

Jim set the paper aside. "It was taken down in the Pentagon archives. Laura had just sold a manuscript to a publisher. It was her first hardback book. I bought some champagne, and she and I and the people she worked closely with down there—who'd helped her bring the book to life—celebrated late one afternoon."

Smiling, Pepper nodded. "You both look very happy."

"We were...." Shaking his head, he muttered, "Come on, we're going to the photo lab. Those pictures of Garcia's fortress are available. Ready?"

"Sure." Pepper followed him out of the office. They walked, it seemed, forever, taking an elevator two floors down and into a more dimly lighted area. The photo laboratory had a small sign on its door. Jim ushered her in. The place smelled of chemicals. Without preamble, he led her into a smaller niche where several black-and-white photos lay on a hardwood table covered by thick glass. A naval-intelligence officer waited for them. She was dressed in a dark blue wool uniform with a white blouse and a black tie at the throat. Her black hair was neatly coiffed, barely touching the collar of her jacket.

Jim introduced Berenice Romero, a woman in her early thirties, to Pepper and immediately asked, "What have you got for us, Berenice?"

"Garcia's mansion, Colonel." Berenice smiled a hello at Pepper as she responded, then used a pencil to outline the shape of the main house and grounds on one of the photos. "This is his fortress. Garcia's got a ten-foot-high wrought-iron fence surrounding the main compound.

Guards are posted every quarter mile, and Doberman pinschers walk the fence line, too. Take a look at this.''

Leaning over the photo, Jim squinted through the film magnifier she handed to him. ''Oh, yeah…big, black Dobermans. You can even see their teeth, can't you?'' He smiled a little and handed the magnifier to Pepper, who also took a look. When she straightened, he said, ''Still want to go, knowing those dogs are more than willing to rip us apart and call us breakfast?''

''Dogs like me.''

''Those dogs don't like anybody.''

Berenice chuckled. ''Colonel, by accident, our flyby caught something else interesting.'' She brought out another picture and laid it on the table. ''It's a jeep. I think you'll be interested to see who's in it.''

Jim took the magnifier and leaned over the photo. He choked back a gasp. ''Laura Trayhern…''

''Yes, sir.'' Berenice beamed triumphantly at Pepper. ''We had no way to know for sure if Garcia had her, but for once we got lucky. I'm sure they didn't expect a flyby or they wouldn't have transported her during daylight in an open jeep like that.''

Pepper nodded, noting the strained expression on Woodward's face as he handed her the magnifier. He had paled considerably, obviously shaken by the photo. She leaned over to study the minutely detailed photo, focusing on the jeep. Laura, her blond hair streaming behind her, sat in the passenger seat next to a driver dressed in battle fatigues. A handgun of some sort was pressed against the back of her neck by a soldier sitting directly behind her, and his hand gripped her shoulder.

''How awful for her,'' Pepper whispered as she returned the magnifier to Berenice. She glanced at Jim, who immediately turned and walked a few steps away. Sensing his anguish, Pepper said nothing more, but when he returned to the table, his eyes were suspiciously bright.

"We've got a mission report on Garcia for you, too," Berenice said, noting Woodward's reaction. "Come with me, sir."

Pepper remained at a distance as they moved to a small, comfortable office, where four steel gray chairs were arranged before a desk. Berenice moved behind the desk and sat down. She handed them each a sheaf of papers and gestured for them to sit.

"Guillermo Garcia is the top drug lord in the Windward Islands," she began. "This is a color photo of him. You can see he's short and overweight. His most distinguishing feature is his face, pockmarked with deep scars. He's fifty years old—an autocratic tyrant as murderous as his boss, Enrique Ramirez, of Lima, Peru.

"Garcia has been a pain in the neck to us since the early eighties. The FBI infiltrated his organization in Florida and Texas and managed to collar most of the U.S. bosses, but Colombia refused to extradite Garcia. However, it scared him enough that he moved his profitable operation from our country to the Caribbean. Now he's had ten years on Nevis to set up another empire, which has proven equally profitable."

"Berenice, do we have an operative there?" Jim fervently hoped so.

"No, sir, we don't."

"Damn," he muttered, then glanced apologetically at both women.

Nodding slightly, the lieutenant continued the briefing. "Garcia calls his fortress Plantation Paloma." Berenice looked at Pepper. "*Paloma* is spanish for *dove*."

"Rather an irony, isn't it?" Pepper drawled.

"To say the least," she agreed. "Garcia is as cold-blooded a killer as Ramirez. All the bosses who work for Ramirez pattern themselves after him. When you make your jump, if Garcia discovers either of you, he'll kill you without question. Although we don't have an operative on Nevis right now, the CIA is working to come up with one. At one time we had an informant.'' She frowned. ''She was a local Nevis woman, a laundress for Plantation Paloma. She was in Garcia's employ for five years, and we were able to gather a great deal of useful background information about his fortress from her. Unfortunately, Garcia somehow found out she was working for us.''

''What did they do to her?'' Pepper asked quietly.

Jim looked up. ''You don't want to know.''

''Don't protect me, Colonel. Just because I'm a woman doesn't mean I can't handle the gory details.'' Pepper looked at Berenice, who obviously agreed with her.

Stung, Jim nodded. ''All right, give her the information, Lieutenant.''

''Yes, sir. Garcia is known to use truth drugs on anyone he suspects isn't loyal to him. They shot the operative full of a truth drug, and she spilled everything. After that, Garcia threw her to his men, and she was gang-raped.'' Berenice sighed. ''We know because we found her body on the beach at the opposite end of Nevis from the fortress. One of the locals found her stripped of her clothes, and the CIA autopsied her body.'' The distaste in Berenice's voice was obvious. ''Garcia is a torturer—an expert. He picked up his methods from Ramirez, who's nothing short of a sadist.'' She handed Pepper a photo from the file.

Pepper's stomach rolled as she stared at the photo of the woman's body lying on a morgue slab.

''That's who we're going up against,'' Jim said in a steely tone. He met Pepper's narrowed gaze. ''And that's why I don't want you along." He jabbed a finger at the offending photo. "Now do you see why I'm against you coming on this mission?"

Bile coated Pepper's mouth as she laid the photo down and pushed it slowly in Berenice's direction. The lieutenant picked it up and slid it to the bottom of the file. Swallowing against a dry throat, Pepper rasped, "Don't you think he'd do the same thing to you, Colonel? What makes you think a murdering bastard like that cares if you're a man or a woman?"

Jim scowled and leaned back. Pepper was right, but he had hoped the photo and briefing session would discourage her. "There's an old military saying—'Take no prisoners.' Garcia doesn't. And you're right—he'll do the same to a man as he will a woman."

Rubbing her brow, Pepper whispered, "My heart aches for Laura Trayhern. I mean, what has Garcia done to her already? My God…"

Jim's heart lurched in his chest at her whispered words. He saw tears in her eyes and felt unexpectedly touched by the depth of her reaction to Laura's plight. He didn't think anyone else had fully appreciated the terrible trouble Laura was in. As Pepper wiped tears from her eyes, his heart swelled with an unknown emotion. He dug in his back pocket for his handkerchief and handed it to her. "Here…"

Pepper nodded, taking it from him. "Thank you." She dabbed at her eyes, not caring whether her companions approved of her nonmilitary emotional response. As an officer like Lieutenant Romero, she wouldn't have dared allow the tears to show. But as a civilian, Pepper wasn't about to apologize for wearing her emotions close to the surface. Not anymore.

As she dried her face, Pepper glanced at Woodward,

expecting to see his face set with disapproval—just one more mark against her in his hard, military book of life. Instead, she saw a surprising softening in his glacial green eyes—and some unknown emotion touched her fleetingly.

Maybe, she thought as she refolded the handkerchief and handed it back to him, he lived vicariously through other people's emotions, unable to be in touch with his own or show them. Berenice Romero sat quietly, and Pepper saw dampness in her eyes, too.

"What an ugly little monster Garcia is," Pepper said, her voice tight with feelings. "All this does—" she pointed to the folder where the highly offensive photo now rested "—is make me that much more determined to get in there and rescue her."

Jim said nothing, but secretly he was thrilled by the determination in Pepper's tone. Her eyes, too, glinted with a new light. Gone was the warmth, replaced with a surprisingly steely anger. "You'll need more than desire fueled by anger on this mission," was all he said, as he pushed the handkerchief back into his pocket. "Please continue the briefing, Lieutenant."

"Yes, sir." Berenice cleared her throat and placed three more black-and-white photos before them. "Garcia's Dobermans not only patrol Plantation Paloma, they're trained to kill. They're also trained not to take any meat or other food that could be tainted with a drug to render them unconscious."

"Has the CIA come up with anything? A dart gun or something?"

"Pheromones, Colonel."

"Oh?"

Pepper leaned forward as Berenice showed them a photo of a small capsule containing a clear liquid.

"The CIA labs have developed a unique way to control

the dogs—the hormones of a female Doberman in heat.''
She smiled a little. "All you have to do is create a di-
versionary trail with the hormones along the fence line,
in the opposite direction of your entry point. The dogs
will follow the scent. Garcia made a mistake in having
only male guard dogs. They'll choose the female scent
over their guard duties. Great idea, isn't it?''

Pepper grinned at the lieutenant. "I know this is a sexist
comment, but isn't that just like a male?''

Both women laughed. Jim didn't think it was very
funny but, reminding himself that women in the military
took more than their share of sexist prejudice and harass-
ing remarks, he gracefully allowed them their joke.

"Do we have a diagram of Garcia's plantation?" he
asked.

The lieutenant became somber. "Yes, sir, we do." She
handed each of them a detailed diagram. "Our operative,
because she was a laundrywoman, was in every room of
the plantation. Garcia's home is a two-story wooden structure, painted white. The upper floors include many guest
rooms and his personal suite. The lower floors are mainly
offices, with a telecommunications room, satellite feeds
and anything else he needs to stay in touch with his people
around the world. He also displays a multimillion-dollar
collection of old-master paintings about the house.''

"Has the CIA projected where they might be holding
Laura?''

"She's probably being kept in one of the second-floor
rooms in the right wing, where there are bars over the
windows and a guard is posted.''

Jim's stomach knotted. Unconsciously, his hand closed
into a fist. The possibility that Laura had already been
drugged to gain whatever information she had was a for-
gone conclusion. The Perseus team had assured him that

Morgan never discussed business with her—to help prevent her from becoming a terrorist target. But…his mind railed against even thinking what other atrocities might have been done to her. Closing his eyes momentarily, he struggled with his anger—and his grief—over Laura's situation. She didn't deserve any of this. If only she hadn't married Morgan…

With a sigh, he opened his eyes. Both women were watching him in the building silence. "What else, Berenice?" he asked in a strained tone.

"I've arranged an 0700 HAHO over the woodlands of Virginia for you. The C-130 will drop you from twenty thousand feet. Another team with a HumVee will monitor you from the drop zone." She pulled out photos of the landing area, which was covered with thick stands of oak, ash and beech trees. "We've tried to duplicate as closely as possible the landing zone chosen for you on Nevis. It's heavily wooded, so the potential for injury is high."

Pepper studied the photo carefully. "Looks just like the forests we chute into, Colonel, except that these aren't pine trees." She looked at him. "Are you used to landing in this kind of stuff?"

"No, I'm not," he admitted darkly.

"Welcome to a lot of getting hung up in trees, then." Pepper leaned back, feeling good about being able to contribute something from her area of expertise. "We have special chutes made so that we can pretty much zero in on which set of trees to land between. Of course, even if we're able to do that, we still get batted around by tree limbs. There isn't a time when we aren't bruised. At the worst, those limbs can act like spears, and gash an arm or leg."

Pepper tapped the photo on the table. "And even if you're lucky and experienced, and the wind is your friend that day, you still can get hung up fifty feet off the ground. Then you have to cut yourself loose and do a free-drop to the terrain below, which may or may not be rocky. Or if you manage to make the mark and go between the trees, you may not have the luxury of flexing your knees and bending and rolling when you hit the ground, the way parachutists are taught. Which leaves you open for at least a sprained ankle, and potentially a broken leg.''

"Do you ever make a landing without some kind of injury?''

"Never,'' Pepper said matter-of-factly. "I work long hours with my team on precision landings, Colonel. We pick the most thickly wooded, steepest slopes, ones with boulders under the trees, to practice on, because, you have to understand, we may land within a mile of a roaring forest fire. The winds around a fire are very different, far more dangerous and unreliable, than those of a straight-forward parachute drop like this HAHO. For this one, at least, we'll have weather information in advance. We'll know what the wind directions are and won't have to worry about vortex winds swirling at five thousand feet to throw us off course or into some trees.''

As Jim listened to her husky urgent voice, a sense of admiration threaded through him. Pepper obviously knew her craft. And he didn't have much experience with heavy-tree landings. If anything, he could be the albatross on this trip.

"Colonel, I strongly suggest we wear support gear around our knees, elbows and ankles.'' Pepper held up her hands and gestured to her elbow. "We usually wear tight, hard elastic wraps around joints that are likely to be injured. I wear them especially tightly around my ankles. If I can't walk once I'm on the ground, I'm useless to my team.''

Jim snorted. "We don't do that in the military, Ms. Sinclair. If you want to wear them, go ahead."

Pepper stared at him. "I can't believe you'd dismiss this safety feature so easily, Colonel. What if you hurt yourself on this HAHO exercise tomorrow morning? What good will you be to the mission then?"

Jim glared at her. "Give it a rest. I'm not going to impose my jumping habits on you, Ms. Sinclair, so don't shove your ideas down my throat."

"Good teamwork comes from working together, Colonel," Pepper said hotly. "Teamwork means sharing our experiences, deriving the best ideas from all parties concerned, then instituting them for everyone. Safety is my first and only consideration."

"Hitting the target accurately is mine. And you had better hope you hit it, too, or you aren't going on this mission." Jim rose, feeling the tension in himself, seeing the anger in Pepper's huge blue eyes as she slowly stood in turn. Tearing his gaze away, he looked down at the lieutenant.

"Thanks for the briefing, Berenice. You've done a good job, as usual."

"Thank you, sir."

Pepper moved to the door and opened it before Woodward could get there. She was stunned by his refusal to work together. Worried, she walked down the hall, making her way back to his office. She was too angry to walk back with him. His secretary was in his office this time— a woman with short blond hair and pretty blue eyes, dressed in a pale pink business suit. Nodding to her, Pepper went straight to the closet and got her coat. It crossed her mind that Woodward's secretary resembled Laura Trayhern somewhat—she had the same hair and eye color and was petite in build. As Pepper turned, shrugging into her coat, Woodward entered, his jaw set, his eyes grim.

"I'll get you a manual on HAHOs, then take you to another area to be fitted with gear," he said abruptly.

"Fine." Pepper's nostrils quivered with anger. What a bullheaded person he was turning out to be! Did she even want to try this mission with him? If he'd been one of her staff, she'd have kicked him out for lacking the team spirit that kept them successful and safe on the toughest jumps. She decided she would call Wolf later from her hotel room and talk more with him about the situation.

Vaguely, she heard Woodward talking to his secretary. His voice was no longer hard or clipped, but personable— even warm. She turned, realizing what a difference there was in his attitude toward her and toward his secretary. So he could be human, after all. He just didn't like her, didn't want her around and didn't believe she could contribute anything of value to the mission.

To hell with him. She stepped out into the hall to cool down. Arranging the deerskin purse on her right shoulder, she waited for Jim to reappear. When he did, she didn't want to admire him in his dark green wool uniform, the cap, with its shining, black patent leather bill, settled on his head. He was a stalwart warrior type, the epitome of the Marine Corps' finest, and he knew it. Pepper's anger dissolved as she appreciated him from a purely physical standpoint. The man was ruggedly handsome, there was no doubt, in a dangerous kind of way. Despite his stubbornness, Pepper found herself drawn to him—and then berated herself for allowing her feminine side to overlook the facts: the man was a danger to her—and to the mission.

Chapter Three

The chill in the C-130 as it leveled off at twenty-one thousand feet at 0630 the next morning sent a shiver through Pepper. It was below freezing. She stood, legs apart, balancing herself as the Air Force bird bobbed around in the choppy air, hitting continual pockets of turbulence. A yellow ribbon of color lay along the horizon in the clear, cloudless dawn. The high-pitched whine of the four turboprop engines and the cavernous expanse of the empty C-130 reverberated through her as they strained in the thin atmosphere en route to the drop zone. In fifteen minutes, the rear of the C-130 would yawn open, and she and Woodward would leap from the edge of the ramp into the sky, four miles above the earth.

She hadn't gotten much sleep last night. Instead she'd pored over the manual on the military parasail used in HAHOs, a specially made parachute that was wedged shaped, like an arrowhead. Although it was similar to the ones she used in smoke jumping, it had small differences, and that's what she had absorbed until three o'clock this morning, when she'd finally fallen asleep on the couch in her hotel room.

Glancing up, Pepper saw Jim standing about six feet from where she had anchored her booted feet on the metal grating. He was busy making last-minute checks on his gear, too. His attitude hadn't changed since yesterday, and in fact, she'd seen him give her a look of disdain when she'd pulled protective elastic coverings over her elbows, knees and ankles. Pepper didn't care. She had too much to lose by allowing him to push her into jumping without her safety gear. She hadn't done a high-altitude jump into a deciduous forest before, and she didn't want to take a chance that the limbs might not give way as easily as pines did—providing the potential for even more risk. Falling at fifty miles an hour and hitting a tree limb as thick as her arm would be enough to break bones.

Unlike her usual jumping gear, she'd been fitted with a walkie-talkie on her belt, the earphone snug on her head and the lip piece settled against her mouth so they could literally talk to each other during free-fall, if they wanted to. A tight cap imprisoned her hair, with a heavy, military-style helmet over it, strapped beneath her chin. She wore a number of bulky items, but she was used to carrying an ax and a shovel, as well as maps, compass, water, first-aid kit and other items, when she jumped into a fire situation. Woodward also had outfitted her with a specially made—to his specifications—Beretta pistol in a thigh holster. She carried eleven clips of ammunition for it, and an HK submachine gun with six hundred rounds and thirty magazines rested in her backpack. The equipment she carried today included everything they would jump with two days from now over Nevis. Today was Thanksgiving. A hell of a way to celebrate it, she thought.

Automatically, her fingers went to her chest, where the nylon straps bit into her green-and-tan-and-black uniform—''tiger'' utilities, designed to blend in to the jungle environment. The knife—her own—she'd brought with her for emergency situations, such as to cut away shroud lines should her first parachute fail and the second one have to be deployed. The main chute was on her back, the reserve in front, and she'd personally packed them late yesterday evening.

Woodward had packed his own this morning on the floor of the hangar at Andrews Air Force Base, where they'd taken off from. Pepper had watched him off and on, becoming convinced that he did know what he was doing. After all, he'd informed her icily, he had made five hundred jumps. He was no novice. Still, with two thousand under her belt, she considered him less experienced and would keep an eye on him during the jump—just in case. Pepper smiled to herself, her hands ranging knowingly across her bulky gear. If Woodward knew what she was thinking, his male ego would surely smart under her decision. But out in the field, she was responsible for her people, and she always felt like a mother hen of sorts.

Jim watched Pepper covertly within the deep shadows of the C-130. The vibration of the deck beneath him moved through his booted feet and up his legs. He'd made hundreds of jumps from this type of plane, but he worried about Pepper and the fact that it had been five years since her last HAHO. He wrestled with telling her his concerns. His cool, professional attitude toward her wasn't really the way he wanted to treat her. Despite his anger yesterday, her eyes continued to hold that warmth toward him. Mentally, Jim kicked himself. Dammit, he liked Pepper.

He wanted to call her by her first name, but something wouldn't let him. She probably realized it, since she always called him by his official title or last name. Seesawing from his chaotic emotions over Laura, Jim moved slowly toward Pepper.

Thanks to their headsets, he wouldn't have to yell above the din that always permeated the interiors of these cargo planes. Reaching out, he placed his hand on her upper arm.

"Are you checked out?"

Pepper nodded, wildly aware of his unanticipated touch. His grip on her arm was hard without hurting, and she could tell he was monitoring the amount of strength he used. Her skin tightened beneath his fingertips. "Everything's okay."

Jim felt the firm strength of her body. She was solid, and he was sure she was in top shape due to her job. Still, he longed to soften his hold on her arm and run his hand in an exploratory motion upward, across her shoulder. Why? He'd seen a shadow come to her eyes the moment he'd touched her. Did she consider his touch an invasion of her privacy? Forcing himself to drop his hand to his side, he said in a cold voice, "The jump master said ten minutes 'til they open the cargo-bay door for us. Remember, you jump first and I'll be ten seconds behind you."

Pepper nodded, knowing he wanted to go second to watch her performance in the jump. "Fine," she said, striving to keep the irritation out of her voice.

"Once we hit the LZ," he said, using the common designation for landing zone, "you'll take the compass and map and get us out to the pick-up point where the HumVee team is waiting. It's a ten-mile hike."

Pepper smiled grimly to herself. She knew Jim was not only testing her jumping ability, but checking out just what kind of shape she was in. She would have at least fifty pounds of weight on her back after the jump, and she was sure he didn't think she could go ten miles with it. Little did he realize she carried as much, sometimes more, into a smoke jump. Her team worked in shifts for almost twelve hours at a time, doing the grueling physical work of cutting fire breaks through stubborn brush. If only he knew that she was questioning *his* physical condition. Eight hours a day in a posh Pentagon office made for soft officers, not hard ones. She'd find out just what kind of shape Woodward was in—one way or another.

Exactly ten minutes later, a red light began to blink. Pepper moved to the starboard side, a bit ahead of Jim. Holding on to the cable above their heads she watched the maw of the C-130 slowly groan open. Whirring and grinding sounds clashed with the noise of the plane. Icy wind blasts began to buffet her body, pummeling her sporadically. As the ramp dropped, she saw the beauty of the night sky above them, a few stars still twinkling. Below them, dawn brushed across a thick carpet of barren, gray trees, which had already lost their leaves in fall's arrival. The hills of Virginia were rounded, but many were steep, and they'd been specially chosen because they resembled Nevis's volcanic terrain.

The jump master, a twenty-year veteran, stood opposite them. The wind whipped into the cargo entrance, striking Pepper heavily. She spread her legs a bit to take the invisible fists of air punching through the aircraft. The wind was biting, far below freezing. Although she wore black nylon gloves, she took them off at the last moment before she expected the light to flash green, indicating "jump." Jamming the gloves into a thigh pocket, she took a deep breath and felt her heart start a pounding but steady beat.

Pepper never tired of the adrenaline rush that accom-

panied such a jump. With it, all her senses became excruciatingly alive. She sensed movement behind her, knowing Jim also was getting ready for the jump. Fear struck
at her, too. She hadn't made a jump this high in a long
time. Talking to herself, telling herself it was the same as
any other, she managed to dissolve some of the initial
anxiety.

The light flashed green. The jump master gave her the
hand signal.

It was like taking a long, summer walk down the slop-
ing, greasy ramp of the C-130. Then Pepper took the leap,
plummeting downward, keeping her hands, arms and legs
tucked tightly against her body. The slipstream slammed
into her as she tumbled clear of the aircraft. She gasped.
It was icy cold. Her goggles protected her eyes from the
tearing wind and enabled her to look around. She peered
up to see the C-130 moving away from her, then glanced
down at the luminous dials on her watch, counting ten
seconds. Woodward had jumped, though she couldn't see
him in his dark camouflage gear against the still-darkened
sky.

Spreading out her arms and legs, she stopped her rock-
like plummet. The wind beneath her became a cushion
against her flattened body. Stabilizing, she checked the
altimeter on her wrist, then glanced upward. At fifteen
thousand feet, they were to meet and pull their chutes
simultaneously.

Finally Pepper saw Woodward. He was coming rapidly
toward her out of the darkness, his body like an arrow
except for the hump on his back where he carried his
weapons and gear. Bringing one hand in, she got ready to
pull her rip cord. Woodward threw his arms and legs out,
braking his plummet. When he was no more than twenty
feet away, she saw him jerk his cord. To her horror, before

she could pull her own, she saw his released chute begin to stream.

No! Pepper stopped herself from opening her chute and watched in dismay as Jim tried to open his by jerking on the shroud lines repeatedly. It wouldn't flare and catch the wind, and Pepper knew a parachute that streamed had little chance of opening. She saw him frantically take out his knife and cut away the shroud lines before he got tangled in them as he continued making slow, awkward spirals downward. Like Pepper's, his emergency chute was attached to his chest harness, and he quickly jerked it open. As she watched, the parasail started to open nicely, then developed a fold and crumpled. The horror on Woodward's face spurred Pepper into action.

Without thinking, she dove toward him. She'd have to be careful to avoid getting tangled in his reserve chute, and she made a sign for him to cut it away. She saw him shake his head as he frantically tore at the lines, trying to force the chute to open at least some of its cells, so it would catch the air and balloon out.

Fifteen thousand.

Pepper wanted to scream at him, but she didn't. She'd forgotten she had a mike and could speak to him.

Twelve thousand.

"Jim! Cut the chute away! I'll come in, and you grab my harness. I'll open my chute and we'll go down together."

She heard his heavy breathing, watched helplessly as he made large, corkscrews, fighting the chute all the time. Stubbornly, he jerked the lines again and again, trying to force the cells to open.

Ten thousand.

Pepper became alarmed. "Cut the chute!" she screamed.

He refused.

Eight thousand.

Breathing hard, Pepper again dove toward him. Dodging his chute, she made a grab for his shoulder harness. There! She slid her fingers strongly around the nylon straps. The thick material bit deeply into her hands and the two of them began to tumble slowly, like a huge, eight-legged spider in the sky.

"Cut the chute!" Pepper pleaded hoarsely, tightening her grip on his harness. She felt more than saw Jim hacking at the shrouds. He didn't think she could rescue him, much less hold on to him, but she'd proven him wrong.

Six thousand. It was now or never.

"Grab my harness front!" she screamed, and she jerked at her rip cord. She felt his hands grab on to the crisscross of nylon over her chest. Her eyes trailed upward with the opening chute, which streamed, then flared perfectly. Pepper had little time to prepare for the opening. Woodward weighed more than two hundred pounds with all his gear, and he had gripped her harness with both hands, the front of his body pressed tightly against hers.

The jerk was tremendous. Pepper groaned, but kept her hands locked around Woodward's upper arms, knowing he could easily lose his grip on her harness as the chute yanked them upward. Her muscles screamed. She shut her eyes and pulled hard. Fire seemed to roar through her body as every muscle went rigid against the reverberation of their combined weight.

Jim grunted as the pull of gravity fought the jerking, upward motion of the opening chute. It felt as if an invisible giant had gripped his legs and was pulling him downward with all its might, almost forcing him to let go of Pepper's harness. His gloved hands were sweaty and his fingers began to slip. He felt Pepper's tight grip around his upper arms, but his fingers were slipping even more. No! He gasped again, struggling. The terror of falling to his death tore through him. His grasp continued to weaken despite his panicky knowledge of what could happen.

In that instant, his entire life began to flash before his widened eyes. He saw everything—things he hadn't remembered since he was a young boy. He saw the death of his mother and father. He saw himself on the deadly parachute drop into Panama City. Accompanying the inexorable vision of his life, he felt every emotion with heart-stopping clarity. The replay was pulverizing, and he gasped again, realizing he was going to die.

Somehow, Pepper must have sensed his situation. Jim was amazed when she pulled him upward, with a strength few men would have possessed. Adrenaline flashed through his body, and he squeezed his eyes shut, pressing his face against her belly region, her gear mashed against him, jabbing into his flesh. His fingers stopped slipping. He crushed his helmet and goggles against her, gasping for breath. Due to her one, upward motion, he was able to affix his fingers more tightly to her harness and prevent a fall to his death.

Breathing hard through her mouth, Pepper gave a quick, cursory glance around them. Thank God the chute was open and working perfectly. But where were they? She couldn't look at her compass or altimeter, since both were strapped to her wrists. She felt Jim clinging to her, their bodies fused together, their tangled legs dangling as they fell rapidly through the denser air nearer the ground. The parasail, without any pulling of shroud lines, drifted at the whim of the wind. The sky was getting lighter, though the sun wasn't up yet. Pepper could clearly see the woods below them, coming up fast. Too fast.

They were at three thousand feet, she estimated, and

their rate of fall, because the chute was too small for their combined weight and gear, was a lot more rapid than it should be.

"Jim!" she gasped. "We're about three thousand. We're coming in too fast!"

He grimaced and felt a terrorizing weakness numb his arms. Did he have the strength to hold on until they landed? He didn't know.

"There's nothing we can do!" he rasped, trying to glance out of the corner of his eye. He dared not move. Dared not try to readjust his position. If Pepper's grip weren't so secure, he wasn't sure he could continue to hold himself in place, with the sixty pounds of weight on his back tugging him away from her and her lifesaving harness.

Gasping for breath, Pepper said in a hurried voice, "Okay, okay. We're about twenty-five hundred feet. We're heading into what appears to be a slight opening in the trees. Try and stay loose. Try not to tense up too much. We're gonna hit the limbs. Be flexible, but hang on."

It was frustrating not being able to see where they were going. Jim tried to steady his breathing. He felt Pepper flex her knees, a signal that they were close to the canopy. He could still die. They both could. The thought of Pepper being killed almost shattered him. What a brave, strong woman she was, he realized mere seconds before they smashed into the treetops at over eighty miles an hour.

The crunching and snapping began, and Jim felt the initial branches giving way beneath them. As they fell, the chute slowed their forward motion. Heavier, less-forgiving branches swatted at him, bruising the backs of his legs. He grunted as another smacked him hard across the shoulders. The pain was instantaneous and he almost let go. At once Pepper's hands tightened.

The sounds intensified as the crackling, popping branches stubbornly gave way. They were falling. Falling through space.

Jim hit the ground first, and Pepper's entire weight came down across his lower legs. Crying out in pain, he jerked his hands free of her harness and tried to cushion the force of his contact with the ground by rolling end over end, dirt and rocks flying up around him.

Pepper rolled headfirst across him and down a brush-covered gulch. She kept herself tucked as much as possible, her arms across her face to protect it, her legs drawn up. It was impossible to tuck as she wanted to, carrying so much weight. Finally, she hit a large bush and came to a sudden stop, landing flat on her back, the breath knocked out of her, her arms and legs sprawling outward.

Opening her eyes, Pepper took in the dawning sky above her and the many broken limbs where they had fallen through the thick, nearly impenetrable canopy. Panting for breath, she automatically went through a swift, physical check of herself. *Jim!* Her heart thudded powerfully in her chest. Was he alive? Dead? Suddenly, concern for him overwhelmed every other sense, avalanching through her with unexpected force and leaving her stunned as nothing had in the past six years.

Slowly, she forced herself to roll over and dizzily rise up on her hands and knees. Searching desperately she called out his name, her voice a terrified croak.

"Jim! Where are you? Answer me!" Pepper fumbled frantically with the harness straps, working quickly to free herself from the cumbersome pack.

"Dammit, answer me!" Her voice broke with emotion. What was going on? She never behaved like this in the

field. Jerking the helmet off her head, she dropped it on
the ground, her hair spilling around her face and shoulders
as the cap came with it. Off came the goggles. Peering
through the gray early-morning light, Pepper thought she
saw a lump far below her on the brushy hill. "No..." she
said in a half whisper. Breathing raggedly, she stumbled,
fell, then made it to her feet. As she picked her way down
the sharp incline, she saw the dark lump define itself into
Woodward, lying in a ravine filled with dried leaves,
rocks and small bushes. He was sprawled on his back, his
left leg tucked up under his body, his arms thrown outward. His head was tipped back, mouth open.

Was he dead? Badly injured? Her mind spun with questions and ways to get help here as fast as possible. They
had a radio. She could call for a rescue helicopter. Powerful emotions captured her, and tears flooded into her
eyes. Arriving at his side and falling to her knees, she
sought and found the jugular vein in his neck with shaking
hands. A sob racked her body and she felt out of control,
pulverized by these violent feelings toward him. It was
crazy! She was crazy.

"Jim?" Her voice wobbled. Tears blurred her vision as
she frantically searched his wan features, even as her fingers located a strong pulse. Thank God. Pepper saw his
lashes flutter as she called his name again. Getting up, she
moved to his left side, where his leg was folded beneath
him.

"Don't move, Jim. Don't move," she crooned, placing
her hands on his hip and knee. "You might have a broken
leg. Just wake up easy. Easy..."

Pepper's husky voice entered Jim's burgeoning consciousness. He was aware first of her voice, then of those
strong, sure hands on his left thigh. Groaning, he opened
his eyes. Pepper was kneeling over him, her face drawn

in tension, her tearful gaze fixed on him. Shaken by the change in her features, the panic in her eyes, he reached up for her.

"We made it," he mumbled. "We're alive...." A miracle in itself when he'd been so certain he was going to die. Struggling toward consciousness, he slid his hands over her shoulders. Life and death. How close they'd come to dying. Tears were rolling down Pepper's pale cheeks, and Jim dug his fingers into her shoulders as a fierce joy suddenly swept through him. Never had he needed someone as he needed her at this moment. His careening emotions had steamrollered his normal, controlled responses. A wild feeling thrummed through him and he pulled her down, crushing her to him as his arms slid across her back.

"You're alive, you're alive...." he rasped, burying his face in her thick, silky hair. Jim groaned as he felt her surrender to his need to embrace her. He felt her sob once more, her cheek pressed against his. The dampness of the tears, the softness of her skin dizzied him, convinced him of the fact that they weren't dead. For one powerful heartbeat out of reality, Pepper clung to him, held him as tightly as he was holding her. She was warm. Alive. Moving his face away from her cheek, he released her and tunneled his fingers through her hair. As she eased away, her face bare inches from his, he drowned in the splendor of her anguished, sky blue eyes. And Jim saw desire there. Desire, heat and need. The realization tore at his disintegrating control and pummeled senses. He saw Pepper's lips part. The ache to kiss her was almost his undoing. As his fingers tightened against her face, he saw her eyes flare wide with shock.

Pepper gasped and placed her hand on his heaving chest, wildly aware of his strong, cool hands framing her face. What was wrong with her? She shouldn't be embracing him! What insane fear had made her lose her perspective? Her professionalism? She saw the burning hunger in his eyes for her alone. Shaken badly, she pulled out of his grasp, knowing that if she didn't, she was going to lean forward those final scant inches and bury her lips against his very male mouth.

Trembling violently, she sat back, perplexed. She tried to recover from her faux pas by examining his injury, but her face was burning with mortification. What was happening to her?

As he lay there, reorienting himself, Jim realized that if Pepper hadn't saved his sorry neck, he'd be dead. What had made him reach out and embrace her like that? Chaotic feelings sheared through him. And what the hell had prevented him from cutting those second shroud lines to release the reserve chute? Ashamed, he admitted the answer he already knew: he hadn't trusted Pepper to rescue him, because she was a woman.

"Your leg," she whispered tautly, giving him a quick glance. His cheeks were flushed, his look one of utter discomfort. Swallowing hard, she murmured, "How does it feel?"

"It hurts," he grunted, avoiding her darkened eyes, seeing the shame in them. "Look out, I'll try to move it."

Surprised, Pepper staggered to her feet. "Can you?"

"I think so...." He grasped at any straw to lessen the tension, as if some invisible, throbbing sensation lingered palpably between them. Even if his leg was broken, it could refocus their attention on something other than their torrid, intimate embrace of moments ago. Jim sat up with difficulty, the pack he was wearing still weighing him down. Then, easing his body slightly to the right, he brought his left leg out and straightened it.

"You're lucky," Pepper said, a wobble of relief in her voice. She touched her damp cheek and wiped at the last of the tears. Inadvertently, she looked up at him. His gaze burned with an emotion that scorched her, and she looked away, shaken even further. "Brother, are you ever lucky. I thought you'd busted your femur in a compound fracture or something." She knelt at his side again. Whether she wanted to or not, she had to touch him. Resting her hands gently on his leg, she examined the length of it. Feelings she thought had died years ago swept through her as she explored his muscled limb. She felt a throbbing sensation seem to leap from him to the palm of her hand. Confused, she struggled to force the raw, newly awakened feelings aside.

Jim grimaced, fighting a hot awareness of her closeness—of her care. Her touch was galvanizing, and his skin tightened when she grazed him. Frantic to get himself back under control, he rasped, "I'm too hardheaded to break a leg. I should have had my head examined, though."

Surprised, Pepper looked up into his darkened eyes. "What do you mean?"

"You saved my neck despite my stupidity. Thanks." He held out his hand to her.

Stunned, Pepper slowly raised her own hand. Should she touch him again? Last time they'd ended in a torrid embrace. Shyly, she slid her fingers into his. There was nothing weak about his grip, and she gloried in its secure warmth. "You're welcome, Colonel Woodward," she said in a strained tone.

Jim didn't want to release her hand. He was entranced by the length and grace of her fingers, almost at odds with Pepper's obvious tough strength—both physically and mentally. If she hadn't had the presence of mind, as well as the experience and skill, to rescue his sorry butt from that situation, he wouldn't be here shaking her hand in a symbolic gesture of peace.

"Call me Jim," he said gruffly, reluctantly releasing her. The surprise that flared in her eyes astounded him. It was at that moment that he realized just how much of a bastard he'd been to her. Shame wound through him, and he forced himself to check out his left ankle instead of staring into Pepper's beautiful, vulnerable eyes.

Pepper watched him pull away the bloused material around his jump boot. *Call me Jim.* The husky inference in his voice had gone through her like hot sunlight on a cold winter's day. And the look in his eyes had stunned her—as if she were seeing his tough military facade melt before her eyes. The change was arresting, filled with promise. His mouth had lost its usual hard line, and his eyes had lost that icy glitter that warned her to back off. Most of all, Pepper was drawn to the tenor of his voice— strong yet decidedly gentle.

Shaken, she sat back, resting her hands tensely on her thighs as she tried to digest his change toward her. Finally, she forced herself to look around. "I have no idea where we are…Jim," she admitted hesitantly.

He glanced up as he freed his ankle from the trouser material. "Let's worry about that later. Can you help me unlace this boot? I think I've sprained my ankle."

"Sure…" He was asking for her help. Pepper didn't quite know how to take this sudden attempt at teamwork. Was he feeling grateful because she'd saved his life? Would it last? Did it have anything to do with the sudden intimacy he'd established? Her hands trembled as she tried to untie the double knot on the boot.

"I'm still shaky." She laughed with sudden shyness.

"I'm shaking inside," he admitted, watching her slim

fingers work out the tightly bound knots. Her hair fell in soft waves, and he had the maddening urge to reach out and thrust his fingers through that mass again. As he remembered its softness, his hand lifted slightly, as if by its own accord. Jim jerked it back. It was an idiotic urge. An insane one, he realized, chastising himself. Pepper's mouth was slightly open, revealing her full lower lip. The color was high in her cheeks, and he could see she was shaken by the ordeal they'd survived. Or was it by his unjustified embrace—his need to feel her strong, feminine body against him and prove he really was alive?

"I could have died," he croaked, the realization starting to fully sink in.

Pepper glanced up at him. Jim's eyes were dark with the harsh reality of his words. "I know...." Her voice broke, and she avoided his sudden, sharpened gaze.

Jim's heart began an erratic pounding in his chest. Suddenly, he felt a trembling that seemed to start deep inside him and spread outward. He had a wild urge to blather almost hysterically. Fighting the feeling, he rasped, "I saw my whole life flash before my eyes." He shook his head as Pepper began unlacing the now-unknotted jump boot. "I've heard of guys seeing it, like a movie in full living color, when they thought they were going to die. But it's never happened to me...."

Swallowing against a dry throat, Pepper nodded, her heart still pounding wildly in her breast. Where Jim had gripped her shoulder, her skin still tingled in memory. "We were lucky. Hold on, I'm going to try to get this off you." She rose and positioned herself at his feet, then carefully eased the boot off his left foot. Pulling off his heavy cotton sock, she grimaced. "You're right," she said, glancing up at him, "you've got a dilly of a sprain." The skin around his ankle was already turning bluish purple and swelling. Prodding the region gently with her fingers, she felt a lot of heat coming from it.

Jim was fervently aware of Pepper's long, thin fingers moving over his swollen ankle. Miraculously, wherever she touched him, the pain momentarily ceased. "You look like you've done this kind of thing before," he observed.

Pepper gave him a slight, one-cornered smile as she finally managed to get some control over her rampant emotions. "Too many times." Placing his foot on the ground beside her, she slowly stood. "On myself and other members of my team. Sprains are pretty common in our business."

Jim held her narrowed gaze. He was seeing the professional side of Pepper now, and he admired her coolness and common sense. "If I'd worn that ankle brace as you suggested, I might not have a sprain right now," he groused.

Pepper realized what it took Jim to admit his mistake and was grateful he'd abandoned his combative attitude. "It's a learning curve," she offered hoarsely, not wanting him to feel any worse than he did already. She wasn't one to rub salt in anyone's wounds. Good leaders didn't berate their people. Instead, she would try to support his decision to wear it next time. "I'm going back up the hill for my pack. I've got a first-aid kit with me. Just lie still" was all she said.

Jim lay back on the rough ground, feeling pretty damn humbled by Pepper and her forgiving attitude. She had every right to nail him with the fact that he'd not only refused to wear the joint and ankle braces but had openly challenged her idea. Angrily, he rubbed his face. What was the matter with him? He didn't normally act like such a jerk. Never with anyone under his command in a military situation. And why had he reached out and grabbed her? Held her in a hot, powerful embrace that had driven him to the edge of his control? He'd come so close to molding her parted, tear-stained lips against his mouth. So close. What the hell was happening to him? Looking up, he scowled at the horizon. The sun was rising, the sky turning a pale, translucent pink and yellow.

Pepper, he decided, was her own woman—and he wasn't used to dealing with a woman with such a high confidence level. He had some thinking to do about women, he conceded. He was just beginning to grasp the full weight of their potential. Pepper was a role model, a stunning example of what could be. Perhaps that was what made her different in his eyes, and explained his unexpected attraction to her. He had no direct experience with a woman like her—at once feminine and vulnerable, yet shored up by an incredible confidence that radiated from deep within her, translating into every action she took or decision she made.

Jim knew men like that. Hell, he was like that himself. A sour smile pulled at his mouth as he made the realization. If Pepper had been a man, he would never have questioned her experience. And he would have instantly reached out for help as he plummeted from the sky. With a shake of his head, he decided that once they got out of this mess and back to Perseus, he needed to sit down and have a long talk with her. First he would apologize for being such a jerk, as well as for his intimate behavior toward her, which was completely out of line—as sexist in its own way as his initial lack of trust had been.

Touching his ankle, which had quickly swollen to the size of a ripe cantaloupe, he wondered how he would be able to make the jump two days from now. He'd screwed himself up by rejecting Pepper's advice. Damn. He had a lot of ground to cover with her on their return to civilization.

"We're in luck," Pepper said as she approached Jim. She held out two small kits. "I not only brought my first-aid kit, but I packed my homeopathic kit, too." She saw him look up, felt his green gaze lock onto hers. For a moment she was speechless. The undiluted warmth in his eyes caught her off guard again. Slowly kneeling at his left side, Pepper fumbled with the first-aid kit, even as she fought the clamoring desire still burning within her. Heat stabbed at her cheeks, and she knew she was blushing.

"I'm in luck you were along," Jim stated. He saw Pepper's face flame red. The blush made her even more becoming, if that was possible. Her fingers worked the lock on the kit, as an ache built inside Jim's chest, and he fought another totally inappropriate urge to reach out and kiss her. The slightly curled length of her hair, now in disarray from the dampness of the cold November morning, enhanced her natural beauty.

Pepper made an effort to smile while avoiding his gaze. His eyes were like magnets, drawing hers, she decided as she opened the second kit. "We shared a close call. Stupid reactions always happen afterward," she stammered.

Jim nodded. "Yeah—stupid things…" Like grabbing her and wanting to kiss her until they breathed the same air. Stupid things like that. "I'm just glad we're alive," he told her unevenly. "Maybe that's why I grabbed you.… I don't know.…"

Pepper felt the heat in her face intensify at his muttered apology. She refused to look up at him as she dug into her kit. "That's all it was," she agreed breathlessly, "a close shave with death. Nothing more…" Wasn't it? Pepper was unsure. Her even, stable world seemed to be fragmenting before her very eyes. Hadn't she made decisions in the past to commit herself to her job, to her friends and her family—*not* to a personal relationship? Yes, absolutely. And in the six years since that decision, she'd made it stick. Ever since John's death. Until now. Pepper felt wary and shaken in a way she hadn't experienced before.

Jim frowned. Though his unexplained actions toward her were far from all right, she was kindly trying to provide a way out for him—despite her own discomfort. Now was not the time to examine his actions.

He watched as she drew out a small green tube and squeezed the clear, thick contents onto her fingers. "What's that?" he asked, making an effort to get their conversation onto something safe and impersonal.

"Arnica. It's a homeopathic remedy that I use for any kind of muscle sprains or strains." Pepper took in a ragged breath, relieved to be talking about anything other than their embrace. She gently slathered the ointment across his swollen skin and amended her earlier concerns: Jim was in tremendous shape—for an office type. "You must jog or something," she murmured, concentrating on covering the entire sprained area, "because if you didn't work out, you'd have broken something in that fall."

Jim glanced up at the thick trees on the hill above them. "Yeah…it was a hell of a fall, wasn't it?"

Her laughter was strained as she set the ointment tube aside and expertly wrapped his foot and ankle in an Ace bandage. "A hell of a fall," she agreed.

"How are you?" Jim realized he'd been remiss in asking after her condition. Had she sustained any injuries?

Panicked over his sudden interest, Pepper stammered, "A lot of bruises, but otherwise I'm okay." She looked up and brushed her hair aside. The concern on Jim's face tugged at her, and she felt her breath jam in her throat. Her heart pounded briefly, underscoring the look of care radiating from him. Again heat prickled her cheeks, and she quickly looked away, her fingers trembling as she continued to wrap his ankle.

"You're blushing," he muttered, unwilling to acknowledge his blame in her response.

"I haven't done that in years," Pepper said, frowning. Six years, to be exact.

"It's becoming," he admitted gruffly. Shocked at the intimacy that seemed to continue to insinuate itself at the least opportunity, Jim snapped his mouth shut.

"It's an embarrassing disease."

He cast desperately around for some impersonal comment, but words he didn't intend to say tumbled out of his mouth. *"You're a woman who wears her heart on her sleeve."* When Pepper raised her chin and looked at him, he realized she was so self-sufficient that few people probably ever considered she might need a little care or a tender touch herself. He could give her that, he realized suddenly. To cover up his error, he said, "Recons take care of their own. You're no less important than I am." He noticed a number of bloody scratches on the backs of her hands. Without thinking, he reached down and captured her right hand. Gently, he laid his palm over it. "You're hurt, too."

Stunned by his gesture, Pepper jerked away. "Oh…it's nothing. Scratches are nothing…." Her heart was pounding. She felt curiously exhilarated and at the same time wary. "I guess I'm not used to my team making a big deal over something like this," she muttered. "During a fire there isn't time to pay attention to minor injuries. We're always getting bruised, scratched and cut. It's no big deal."

With a shake of his head, Jim said, "I guess I really

didn't realize the kind of danger you and your team jump into.''

''Most people don't. Why should they? As far as I'm concerned, there are a lot of unsung heroines and heroes doing my kind of work. We're rarely given media coverage, but our work is intense and very dangerous.'' Pepper closed the first-aid kit. ''Of course, people in the military aren't acknowledged much, either.''

Jim nodded in agreement as Pepper took a small, amber vial from the other kit and opened it. ''Here, take these,'' she said.

Jim stared at the small, white pellets she placed in his open hand. ''What are these?''

''They're sugar pellets that have been medicated with a high dose of Arnica. Just put them in your mouth and let them melt away.'' She smiled a little and closed the lid on the vial. ''You'll see a miracle happen with that ankle of yours—the swelling should go down within the hour. Otherwise it will never be in good enough shape for a jump one day from now.''

Jim wasn't about to argue with Pepper. He put the pellets in his mouth. They tasted like sugar, not medicine. Pepper rose, carried the kits back up the hill, then returned to Jim's side. In the meantime, he shrugged out of his pack.

She handed him the radio. ''I think we need to call for backup. You're in no shape to walk ten miles.''

''Roger that,'' he agreed sheepishly. He took the radio from her and made the call. He no longer questioned Pepper's abilities. She'd saved his life. She'd dealt with his injury with grace and without recriminations. Soon the helicopter would be hovering over the hill above them and they would be winched up on a cable, one at a time, since there was no appropriate landing area. But first Jim silently promised himself one thing. Tonight, at his condo, he and Pepper would have a long, serious talk. It was time.

Chapter Four

Pepper was unprepared for the flurry of activity that met them back at Perseus. The helicopter pilot had called in, alerting the team of their near disaster. As she entered the office, she was met by a number of people, some of whom she didn't know. Wolf and Killian guided Jim to another room, where Dr. Ann Parsons, the ex-Air Force flight surgeon who worked for Perseus, was waiting.

"Pepper," Wolf said as he came back out, "I want you to meet Morgan's brother, Commander Noah Trayhern, and his wife, Kit."

"Glad to meet you," Pepper said, extending her hand to a tall, spare officer with gray eyes. Noah Trayhern was dressed in his winter Coast Guard uniform, the dark blue wool a contrast to his tanned features and penetrating gaze. She liked his firm grip.

"Same here," Noah said with a tight smile.

Pepper extended her hand to the woman at his side. Kit

Trayhern, tall as well, smiled warmly at her, offering an equally firm handshake. Her long, dark brown hair, alive with red highlights, was tied back with a red ribbon that matched the tasteful red suit she wore with a lacy white blouse.

Marie approached Pepper. "You look worn out. Are you all right, dear?"

"I'm okay." She looked down at her camouflage uniform and gave a slightly embarrassed laugh. "Dirty, bruised, but no worse for wear." She was acutely aware of Noah's assessing look, sure he was measuring her against what had happened and determining whether she had what it took to successfully complete the coming mission.

"Let me get you some coffee," Kit Trayhern offered. "You look like you could use a cup. Actually, from what we've heard, maybe you'd rather have a stiff drink."

Smiling sheepishly, Pepper nodded. "No thanks. If I drank alcohol, I'd probably ask for whiskey, straight up. Thanks, Mrs. Trayhern."

"Call me Kit. Come on, let's go into the War Room. Marie made a fresh pot when she heard you were coming in."

Pepper wondered how Jim was doing and wanted to find out, then thought better of it. She followed Kit into the Conference Room and gratefully sank onto a chair Noah pulled out for her. He closed the door, and he and Kit joined her at the table, coffee cups in hand.

"Can you tell us exactly what happened out there this morning?" Noah asked.

Without preamble, Pepper told them the story, leaving out only the fact that Jim had refused her help in the air and that he hadn't worn the safety bandages. She had no desire to embarrass him. On the flight in, she had sat next to him and had felt him withdrawing deep into himself. She'd wondered what he was thinking about, but then, the fact that they'd nearly died was enough to turn anyone inward for a while.

Kit sighed and smiled softly at Pepper. "We feel lucky to have you on this mission, Pepper. You've got the right stuff."

"Bruised but right," Pepper answered tiredly. She glanced at Noah. Did he feel the same way? The officer was somber, worry showing in his gray eyes.

"Have you heard the latest?" he asked.

"No. What?" Pepper sipped the hot coffee with relish.

"Wolf said still no communiqués have been intercepted to suggest where Jason or Morgan might be held. No more transmissions from Garcia, either. It's as if they know...."

"Darling," Kit whispered fervently, reaching across the table and touching his arm, "everyone's doing all they can."

"I know that," he said, scowling. He set the white mug on the highly polished table, sliding his long fingers around it. "I worry that if you go in to rescue Laura, they'll kill Jason and Morgan. We just don't know what they might do."

"Look," Kit said, removing her hand, her voice growing more adamant, "I know Garcia and Ramirez from my days as a detective in Miami. Laura isn't safe there. She's at serious risk. If we know where she is then Perseus needs to mount a mission as swiftly as possible to get her out."

Pepper saw Noah's face become rife with unspoken emotions, including obvious anguish. "I don't have a police background," she offered, "but from my days as an army officer, I know you don't avoid one objective because others might suffer. I'm sure Ramirez is expecting

Perseus to back off. So we may have some element of surprise on our side.''

Exhaling loudly, Noah stood, his dark brows drawn together. ''We're dealing with the lives of my brother, his son and his wife.'' He looked down at Pepper. ''Dammit, I wish I could go instead.... I wish—''

''Noah, please...'' Kit said softly.

Pepper watched Morgan's younger brother struggle with barely contained emotions. She noted the glimmer of tears in his eyes, then he abruptly turned and walked deliberately to the other end of the room, his back to them.

''How much do you know about the Trayhern family?'' Kit asked her.

''Only what Wolf told me on the way in from the airport the other day. I know Morgan has gone through hell regarding the Vietnam War and that he was used by the CIA against his will.''

Kit nodded. ''Then you realize how much trauma everyone's suffered.'' She rubbed her brow. ''It's awful. I mean, this family has finally gotten back together. We have three beautiful children. Morgan's parents live in Clearwater, Florida, and we visit them all the time. Alyssa, Morgan's sister, is the youngest. She's married to Commander Clay Cantrell, and they're both pilots in the navy. They don't have any children, but they come and visit as often as they can, Pepper. We're very close-knit. Morgan's parents are in shock over the kidnapping. They're flying up this afternoon to Perseus, to meet you and Colonel Woodward, but it's a frightening situation for all of us. I'm an ex-cop, and I've had dealings with far too many drug dealers. They're the scum of the earth, as far as I'm concerned.''

''Do you think Ramirez will try to attack you? Or Morgan's parents?''

Kit shrugged and looked at her husband, who stood silently, his profile silhouetted against the map on the wall. He was clearly suffering. ''It's the right question to ask. That's why we've flown in with our entire family. Right now, Susannah Killian is playing baby-sitter not only to Morgan's Katherine, but to our children as well, at a hotel in Fairfax. Talking to Jake, I get the feeling they're worried about another hit from Ramirez. Anyone in the family could be vulnerable to attack. I think Jake wants all the Trayherns to go into hiding.''

''It wouldn't be a bad idea right now,'' Pepper agreed slowly. ''Especially if we hit Garcia and manage to take Laura away from him. I don't know how quickly or *if* he'll retaliate—or against whom.''

''You can bet it will be our family,'' Noah growled, turning and walking slowly back toward them.

''Then you agree with Jake?'' Kit asked.

''I do.'' The tall man picked up his coffee mug and took a swallow of the hot liquid. ''I don't put anything beyond the realm of those murdering bastards.''

Pepper could feel a number of new aches developing in her body. She needed to get out of this uncomfortable uniform, put arnica oil on her own minor injuries and take a long, hot bath. But she tabled her own discomfort for now because, by understanding some of the Trayhern family, she might be able to understand more about Laura and her potential actions or reactions—which could be important if they were able to get to her.

A knock on the door interrupted their conversation. Wolf poked his head in and looked at Pepper. ''Colonel Woodward is asking for you. Got a minute?''

''Sure.'' Pepper excused herself and followed Wolf down the hall. Jake and Killian had just left the room where they'd taken Woodward earlier. The looks of relief

on their faces told Pepper the good news. Trying to settle
her suddenly pounding heart, she entered the room. Jim
sat on a gurney, his left pant leg rolled up to just below
his knee. The doctor, a woman in her early thirties, was
just closing her black physician's bag.

"Pepper, I wanted you to meet Dr. Parsons," Jim said.
He felt a tremendous rush of feelings as Pepper entered
the room. Despite her disheveled state, she managed to
look beautiful, he thought. "I told her you gave me those
funny-looking sugar pills, and that they made the swelling
go away on my sprain."

Pepper shook Dr. Parson's hand. "It's a homeopathic
remedy, Doctor."

"Oh," Ann murmured thoughtfully. "That's a complementary form of medicine that's catching on here in the
U.S., isn't it?"

"Sure is." Pepper noticed Jim's gaze on her and felt a
little uneasy. "I've got a doctor friend in Anaconda, Montana, who teaches classes on homeopathy. I'd gone to her
about three years ago with some pretty severe muscle
strains from a bad jump. She used homeopathy on me,
and I was back at work two days later. It made a believer
out of me, so I took classes from her over the years, and
I always carry a small kit of remedies with me no matter
where I go."

Ann raised he eyebrows. "Sounds interesting. Maybe
you could give me her name and phone number." She
pointed to Jim's untaped ankle. "By rights it should look
fat and purple by now, but there's no swelling. He told
me how badly he'd injured it, and I just couldn't believe
it."

With a laugh, Pepper said, "It was the size of a healthy
cantaloupe out there at the LZ, Dr. Parsons. I gave him a
high dose, and I knew it would take down the swelling."

"Good thing," Ann said, "otherwise Colonel Woodward would be grounded and someone else would be taking this mission." She smiled warmly. "Good job, Ms. Sinclair."

When the flight surgeon had left, Pepper turned to Jim. She examined his ankle closely. "Looks pretty good. Are you as impressed as Dr. Parsons is?"

"More impressed," he said quietly. He saw the strain in Pepper's face. "You look the way I feel," he commented.

"I'm getting a bit achy from my bruises and the letdown that always comes after a jump like that," Pepper said, standing awkwardly in front of him. Despite what they'd been through, Jim appeared relatively unfazed. His short, dark hair was plastered against his head, with several strands falling across his wrinkled brow. Some smudges of dirt trailed along his jaw, but otherwise he looked as good as new. The front of his uniform was open, revealing the strong column of his neck and some of the well-sprung dark hair on his chest. He was pulverizingly masculine, Pepper realized belatedly. She'd been so busy shielding herself from his attention that she hadn't noticed the details of him as a man—until now.

"I need to go back to my hotel room and clean up," she croaked.

"You should," he agreed, then added, "Later, will you come over to my condo?"

"What?" Startled, Pepper halted on her way to the open door. She had a great deal of studying to do today—manuals to read and details to memorize.

Jim opened his hands. "Tonight? About 1900, will you come over?" he repeated.

Her heart started a traitorous beating in her breast. "Well...I—"

He saw her hesitation. Saw the fear in her glorious blue eyes. "Please?" He said it softly, with just a slight, pleading edge. Pepper's face visibly relaxed and most of the wariness left her eyes.

"Sure..."

"It's personal," he admitted softly, then looked around the room. "I need to say some things to you in private, Pepper."

Swallowing convulsively, she nodded. "I'll be there...."

Pepper's mouth was dry. It took a lot to make her nervous these days, but the possibility of intimacy—of the kind of unexpected feelings Jim had somehow managed to arouse in her in such a short time—had her running scared in a way that far surpassed the risk of jumping out of a plane into a raging fire. She knocked on the solid oak door of Jim's condominium. It was in a posh part of Georgetown—a redbrick building covered with dark green ivy that gave it an old, austere look. The building suited him, she thought. He was old-fashioned in many ways, clinging to certain traditions just as they ivy clung to the brick. The door opened, and Pepper's heart bounded once to underscore her surprise.

Jim wore civilian clothes, a pair of comfortable, navy blue chinos, a collegiate white shirt open at the collar and simple brown loafers. He looked approachable. Far too approachable, her heart warned. And when his mouth curved in a sincere welcome, Pepper became tongue-tied, which wasn't like her at all.

"Come on in," he invited, standing to one side and gesturing for her to enter. He wondered if he'd ever quit being surprised by her. She wore a long, dark green corduroy skirt and a soft mohair sweater of pale pink and green. Her hair, which had been matted and snarled after their ordeal this morning, glowed under the hall light, with golden strands sparkling among the dark brown ones. She wore no makeup, but she didn't need any. The flush of her cheeks emphasized the guarded look in her glorious blue eyes. Instead of shoes, she wore black suede boots and carried a purse to match. As she stepped inside, Jim inhaled the fragrance of her perfume; it reminded him of jasmine blooming in spring.

"Are you sure you're a smoke jumper?" he teased as he quietly shut the door.

Pepper smiled uneasily. "Are you sure you're a Recon Marine?" she countered.

"Touché." As he reached to help her off with her coat, his fingertips brushed her shoulders, and it was as if a shock ran through him. Jim felt a powerful desire overwhelm him. Never had he wanted to kiss a woman more than in this fleeting moment. It cost him every ounce of control to keep from doing exactly that. He hung Pepper's coat in the closet and motioned for her to follow him. "I guess neither of us look like our jobs, do we?"

"I make a point of not looking like my job. Otherwise I'd be a mess all the time," Pepper said in a strained voice, her skin tingling where he'd barely grazed her shoulders. She quickly looked around. The condominium was spacious and tastefully decorated. The ceilings were high, in keeping with the traditional style of older East Coast buildings, with ornate plaster patterns detailing the expanse. The hall was painted beige, the walls holding a number of original oil paintings, most of them landscapes. As she entered the living room, Pepper smiled to herself. A gray-and-white cat sat on the burgundy-striped sofa. The room was large, with a television in one corner, a stereo unit in another. A mahogany coffee table stood in front of the couch, with fresh fruit overflowing from a cut-glass bowl. The chairs, in shades of burgundy and navy, were complimented by a beige carpet.

"Did you decorate this?" she asked, impressed as she scanned the walls, where more pictures hung.

"I couldn't have in a million years," Jim admitted, stuffing his hands in the pockets of his chinos. If he didn't put them somewhere, he was going to touch her. He felt good as he saw the radiance in Pepper's face as she examined the room. She didn't miss much. With a chuckle, he added, "My only contribution to the interior designer's touches was this alley cat. Frank, meet Pepper. Pepper, this is Frank."

Pepper smiled and crossed the room, to gently stroke the large cat's scarred head. Both Frank's ears were partially gone. "Looks like he's been in more than a few fights."

Jim took his hands out of his pockets again, trying to contain his nervousness. "I found him on my porch one morning last winter," he said, coming around to the end of the couch, where Frank lay purring contentedly. "The garbage truck had hit him, and he crawled up on my stoop and waited for me to come home."

Pepper straightened and looked directly into Jim's eyes. "He must have known there was something special about you. That you'd take care of him. Cats have good instincts."

Ruefully, Jim held her warm, searching gaze. He didn't deserve Pepper's forgiveness for what had almost happened today, yet he knew he already had it. Could he have been as generous, if he'd been in her shoes? He doubted it. "It was a little rough at first, because he had a broken front leg, and he wasn't too happy about being incarcerated here, unable to go outside."

Pepper's mouth softened. She melted beneath his dark, hooded look. Again she saw a smoldering fire banked in his eyes—a fire that had something to do with her. Struggling to maintain an air of neutrality, she forced her voice to remain even as she said, "Well, it looks as if Frank has since made the adjustment from scrappy alley cat to fat cat."

"Yeah, he has. Come into the kitchen. I'm putting the final touches on our dinner." Jim forced himself to move, to break the almost-tangible connection that seemed to establish itself between them anytime they were together.

Pepper followed him at a distance, relieved to have his focus shift away from her. "Did you buy Chinese? Or stop at a local fast-food joint?" she teased. Jim walked with only a hint of a limp, she noticed. Silently, she gave thanks for her knowledge of homeopathy. Despite her confidence in her own abilities, Pepper knew she couldn't pull off such a mission without Jim's help and knowledge.

As they walked from the carpeted living room into any airy, light green kitchen with green-and-white polka-dotted curtains framing the window over the sink, Pepper smiled to herself. Jim might be like any other bachelor, but he didn't live like some of them did.

"A number of men on my team are single," she said, stopping a few feet from him, her hip against the kitchen counter, "and their apartments are in sorry shape compared to yours. I feel like I've stepped into *Better Homes and Gardens.*"

Jim pulled a bottle of chardonnay out of a bucket in the sink, where it had been chilling. "I hate to burst your bubble about me. Not that I haven't already, but this place was decorated this way before I bought it—from a general and his wife."

"Ohh..." Pepper met his sheepish smile and watched him pour the white wine into two crystal goblets.

Jim handed a glass to Pepper, his fingers barely meeting hers. For an instant, he saw surprise register in her eyes. She felt it, too, he thought. But just as quickly, he saw her hide her response. In that moment, her full vulnerability became excruciatingly apparent. Without thinking, he removed the glass from her hand and placed it on the counter.

"Come here," he rasped, stepping toward her and settling his hands on her shoulders.

Pepper's lips parted in surprise as she felt Jim's hands holding her. Shock turned to heat as she gazed wonderingly up into dark eyes that held her helplessly captive. *He was going to kiss her.* The thought was there, along with a rush of desire that made her move into his arms and lift her chin to meet his descending mouth. She had no time to analyze what was taking place, or why. She could only obey her heart, which cried out for closer contact with Jim, and personal consequences be damned.

As she felt herself enveloped in his powerful arms, her body coming to rest lightly against his as he drew her even more tightly against his hard, angular contours, a sigh of surrender broke from her. Pepper felt as if she were in a waking dream—a beautiful one filled with a raging desire that refused to be ignored. Her lashes swept downward, and she slid her arms around his neck, waiting. The instant his mouth captured hers in a demanding kiss, she responded with equal intensity. The heat of his mouth moving across hers, taking her, stamping her with his very male scent and taste, shattered every barrier she'd ever erected. His warm, uneven breath fell across her cheek as she opened her mouth even more to his deepening exploration. The slight prickle of his recently shaved face brushed hers. His hand moved upward, cupping her cheek, angling her mouth to an even more advantageous position, and she drowned in the splendor of his quest.

Lost in the molten power of his mouth, of his hard, straining body pressed to hers, Pepper felt a moan of pleasure coming from deep within her. A lightning heat swept through her, overriding her logical mind and connecting wildly with her heart—with a raw desire that was being born out of the fire of his searching, hungry kiss. Then, somewhere inside her, an alarm went off, a warning so primal that Pepper pulled away from the mouth that pleasured hers. That one movement broke the dream. Her eyes flew open. She felt Jim ease his grip on her, his eyes opening and focusing narrowly on her, like a predator gauging its quarry. Panic spread through Pepper.

"No…" she pleaded brokenly, placing her hands flat against his chest. "Oh, no…" The still-throbbing need within her belied the shattering knowledge that Jim should never have kissed her. She shouldn't have kissed him. As Pepper stumbled out of his embrace and gripped the back of a chair for support, she stared up at his stormy face, met the burning gaze that clearly said he wanted to claim her again. Her lips were still wet from his kiss. Her body ached to complete what she knew they both wanted. Shocked at how thoroughly her emotional barriers had been lowered, she touched her brow, confused. How could she have let this happen? She was as much at fault as Jim was. All he'd done was brush her fingers when he'd handed her the glass of wine. A small, grazing touch!

Shakily, Pepper stared at him in the building silence. His chest was heaving, his breathing ragged. His hands were drawn into fists at his sides. He looked as if he were fighting some inner demon to stop himself from moving the few feet to where she stood. The hunger in his eyes was unmistakable. And how badly she found herself wanting to walk right back into his arms!

"Pepper," Jim rasped, opening his hands, "I'm sorry...." And he was. Shaken by what had just occurred, he backed away. His heart was pounding in his chest. He felt the tightness of his body screaming for relief, screaming to complete what they'd started. The look in Pepper's eyes mingled fear, accusation and sultry desire. She'd liked the kiss as much as he had; he knew that. But her grip on the back of that chair spoke of the depth of her devastation. Jim's mouth tingled in the aftermath of their fiery sharing. He could taste her on his lips. He longed to taste her everywhere—and give her even more pleasure. As he studied her in the tense silence, he knew with every particle of his being that he had given her pleasure. The knowledge made his heart sing, lifting him in a sort of heady euphoria he'd never realized existed.

"I think," he began in a strained voice, "that almost dying this morning is still with me." He wanted to take full responsibility for the kiss, even though she'd come willingly into his arms. "I'm sorry, Pepper. Really sorry..."

Trembling inwardly, she nodded and pressed her hand against her breasts, fighting for control of her frayed emotions. "I— yes, I think it was that...." she answered shakily. After all, there had to be some reason she'd done something so foolish!

"If you'll excuse me? I'll be back in a minute." Jim turned without waiting for her permission. If he didn't leave now, he feared he would walk right back over to her and take her. The vision of carrying her to his bedroom and making hot, hard love with her clamored in him. His leaving would break that damnable tension that seemed to stalk their interactions. And he'd take the opportunity to splash cold water on his face and get a grip on his unruly emotions.

When Jim had left the room, Pepper grabbed her glass from the counter and lowered herself to a chair. Her knees were shaking so badly she wanted to sit before she fell. In three gulps, she downed the wine. The alcohol took the edge off her frazzled emotions, soothing some of the shock out of her system, and Pepper was grateful to have time to pull herself together.

By the time Jim reappeared, nearly ten minutes later, he seemed back in control. No longer did she see undeniable hunger in his eyes. Instead, his mouth was an unhappy slash as he slowly walked to the sink and picked up his glass. Without a word, he drank the contents, then poured them both a second glass.

"I think," he began gruffly, "I owe you an apology for a lot of things regarding my behavior—"

"No," Pepper whispered. "It's all so crazy, Jim. I've had close calls before. I know what they do to me—to other people." She was blathering to cover her real feelings—her genuine need for him. It was totally inappropriate. Insane. "Stuff like this happens. Let's just chalk it up to the day, can we, and forget it?"

Working his mouth, Jim stared down at the wine in his glass. "Yeah—okay, you're right, of course." *Forget?* How the hell could he forget her warm, flowing response to his kiss? But she was right. Somehow, he had to put it behind him. Savagely, he reminded himself that Laura was the important one right now. At the thought of her, he felt his body shutting down, becoming less sensitized to Pepper's presence. Relief raced briefly through him.

Pepper took another gulp of wine. "It's already forgotten," she said, but her voice came out unexpectedly husky. *Liar.* Unwilling to analyze why she'd blindly walked into his arms in the face of everything she believed—no, *knew* to be true, she lifted her glass. "Let's toast to something. Anything."

Jim nodded. "Good idea." He frowned and thought for a moment, then touched the rim of his glass lightly against hers. "To a lady with more brains and courage than I gave her credit for." He lifted his glass, his gaze steady on her widening eyes. Taking a sip, he waited for her to drink. "Well?"

Pepper shrugged and tried to calm her alarm over his continued intimacy. "Bygones are bygones, Jim. It could just as easily have been me in trouble this morning." Her face serious, she lifted her glass to him, then took a small sip of the light, oak-flavored wine. The sincerity in his eyes and voice shook her, and she didn't want him to see the depth of her reactions to him. Casting around for some safer topic, she noticed a wonderful scent emanating from the oven. "Whatever you're cooking, it smells good," she said, forcing a cheerful smile. Right now, eating was the *last* thing on her mind.

Jim remained serious as he sat down opposite her. Something was driving him to remain intimate with Pepper. He ignored her attempt to lighten the mood. "I think you hold a lot of secrets," he said quietly, meeting her startled look. Setting his glass aside, he added, "I've had all day to think about you—us—and I've come to the conclusion that I know very little about you, Pepper." One corner of his mouth curved upward. "I do know that you're smart, gutsy and humble. You could have told Perseus about my attitude, the problems we had before and during the HAHO, but you didn't." He drilled her with a look. She colored fiercely. "Why? You had every right to."

Gazing down at her wineglass, Pepper murmured, "Look, I had that stuff pulled on me all the time in the army, Jim. It got worse when I demanded to take Ranger training. Every man there, almost without exception, was just waiting to gig me on something, to report me, to show my weaknesses to the world. I know what it's like to be singled out, to be the underdog." She gazed into his dark, somber eyes and saw another, hard-to-define emotion that set her heart to beating harder in her breast. "It would have been different if you hadn't realized your mistakes. But you did. Why pour salt in your wounds? I knew you were hurting." The larger, more encompassing truth was that she had been hurting for him, too.

"Maybe that's the difference between a woman being in charge and a man."

Relieved that the talk was turning more toward professional generalities, Pepper sighed inwardly. "There are many differences between the genders," she agreed slowly, tracing the rim of her glass with her fingertip. "I can tell you I don't treat my team of twenty the way I was treated in the army."

"Good leaders are rare, and you're one of them." Jim rubbed his jaw and said, "You made me feel ashamed of myself out there today, Pepper. It wasn't your fault. It was mine. I'd been a first-class jerk to you from the moment we met." He sighed, then smiled tentatively. "I wanted you to come over tonight so I could tell you that. To say I'm sorry and mean it. I didn't want to say it at Perseus, where we might get interrupted." He couldn't explain away their kiss, though, and he didn't even try.

Pepper felt the heat in her cheeks again, but this time she didn't care. The dark green warmth in Jim's eyes was sincere, blanketing her with a wonderful range of emotions that made her feel so incredibly alive. How long had it been since she'd felt that wonderful rush through her heart, which made her take a long, unsteady breath? Too long. "I knew you were sorry, Jim. Thanks for having me over, but it wasn't necessary."

He slowly got up and moved toward the kitchen cabinets. "I disagree. When I got home this afternoon after the debriefing, I kept asking myself who *is* Pepper Sinclair? Where'd she get her nickname? Does she have another name? What about her personal life?" He brought down two china plates edged with gold and placed them on the table.

When he turned and met her steady gaze, Jim saw real anguish, combined with fear. Why?

Pepper sat very still beneath Jim's heated inspection. She was seeing another surprising facet to this unusual man. His voice had gone low and husky, and her heart responded powerfully to his gentle inquisition. "I don't know that any of that matters," she said defensively.

"It matters to me," he said. Pulling out a drawer, he chose some flatware and brought it over to the table. "Rangers and Recons have a lot in common. They work as teams, and I know you understand the importance of that. You can't be on a team for any amount of time without getting to know your buddies, warts and all. There's a kind of unspoken marriage that happens—a personal closeness that binds the team together." He straightened and looked into her uncertain gaze. "You know what I'm talking about." And she did. He knew she understood very clearly what he was saying and what he was asking from her. But would Pepper drop that invisible wall between her professional life and let him in? Jim believed that sort of melding would be absolutely necessary if they were to survive the coming mission. But was she willing?

The silence in the kitchen seemed deafening to Pepper.

She watched as Jim drew a Yankee pot roast, replete with potatoes and carrots, from the oven. He said nothing further as he proceeded to make a thick, brown gravy. Part of her wanted to bow to his request. It wasn't an extraordinary one, under the circumstances. At 0300 they would make a high-risk jump over the island in complete darkness—a jump that amounted to "out of the frying pan, into the fire," given what awaited them on the ground. Jim was right: they had to establish that bond now, no matter how painful it was to her.

Although dinner was delicious, Pepper ate little. She began to appreciate Jim's social abilities as an officer when he kept up a steady stream of polite small talk during the meal. Inside, she felt wary, knowing that after dinner the polite talk would turn serious—and personal. Her decision never to become personally involved with a man again was under assault. Pepper reminded herself what was really important in her life: her family, her friends and her team. The only thing she knew of that could stop her from accomplishing her goals was a romantic relationship. For that very reason, she had to fight her alarming attraction to Jim in order to maintain her promise to herself.

"Let's go in the living room and have dessert," Jim suggested. Pepper had barely eaten anything on her plate. He'd felt the unmistakable tension in the kitchen after he let it be known he wanted to get to know her, the woman, not the smoke jumper. Oddly, the shoe was on the other foot, he thought, frowning as he cut two slices of freshly made cherry pie. Placing them on dessert plates, he took them into the living room.

His pet had already made himself comfortable on Pepper's lap when he came in, and he chuckled.

"Frank's got an unerring instinct about people who

love cats.'' Jim handed Pepper the pie, fork and paper napkin. Sitting down on the couch less than a foot from her and the contented alley cat, he noted Pepper's wary expression. Could he blame her? ''It's a good thing you left the army,'' he said slowly.

''Oh?''

''You don't hide your emotions very well.'' He gestured to her eyes. ''You broadcast everything in them.''

With a groan of desperation, Pepper continued to stroke the cat, setting her pie aside on a nearby lamp table. She wondered if the animal had sensed her trepidation and come over to assuage it. Cats and dogs were psychic in that sense, and Pepper was grateful for Frank's comforting presence and the excuse to do something with her hands. Jim was too close, and she felt trapped. Clearing her throat, she said, ''I did find it a minus in my work in the army, but it's been a plus in my job as a team leader with the smoke jumpers. Maybe because I've got five other women on my team, and we're used to looking into one another's eyes and reading how we're feeling or what we're saying, on almost a telepathic level. Over time, the men have learned to communicate the same way.'' With a shrug, she added, ''My team functions as one body, one brain. They've been with me two years or more…and we more or less grew up together out there in those forest fires. They're like my extended family.'' Smiling a little, she noted, ''They *are* my other family.''

''I see….'' Jim noticed the softening in her eyes when she spoke about her team. Without thinking, he reached out and touched her hand—and saw the fear come back into her eyes. ''We've got less than nine hours to develop that level of communication, Pepper. The mission we're going on could easily kill us. I want us to survive, and I know the mechanics of that kind of survival.'' He moved his hand back to his lap. "We need to talk about ourselves. Us."

Pepper's mouth went dry. Her skin tingled pleasantly where Jim had so briefly touched her hand. Despite her fears, a part of her wanted his continued touch. It had been so long. So long… "It's hard for me to just sit down and talk about myself."

Wryly, Jim said, "I can tell. How about if I go first?"

Pepper met his gaze and felt a kind of warmth she'd never encountered before. What magic was going on here? Was the inner Jim Woodward really so different from his Marine Corps image? "A-all right."

He set his dessert plate on the coffee table and placed his hands on his thighs. "I was born in Maryland—very near Annapolis, as a matter of fact. My father owned his own software company, and my mother enjoyed staying at home. I wanted to become an engineer like my dad, so I went to Ohio State, where they were known for excellence in that area. When I graduated, my dad convinced me to put in six years as an officer. He said his six-year hitch in the corps had served him well for the rest of his life.

"I agreed, and went into the Marine Corps, following his footsteps." With a grin, Jim said, "It turned out to be a career. I like my work. I prefer field assignments to sitting behind some officious desk at the Pentagon, but this is what I have to do right now to punch the ticket to get to general someday. Well, that's pretty much my background." He opened his hands and gave Pepper an encouraging smile. "How about yours?"

Her hands stilled on the gray-and-white tomcat in her lap. "Well…I was born in Montana. Actually, Cam came first—my brother. Our dad was a silver miner near Anaconda."

"And your mother?" Jim was curious about Pepper's role model. He couldn't imagine her mother as a woman satisfied with being a housewife and parent only.

Pepper grinned. "She was a real hell-raiser, born way before her time. Mom is a CPA—that's how she met my dad. She worked for the silver company that gave Dad his paycheck. He found a mistake on his check one time and went into the front office to find out who'd made the error. Mom told me later the sparks flew."

"I'll bet they did." Jim chuckled. He watched the way Pepper's eyes and face became animated as she spoke of her family. How easy it was for her to plug into her emotions. He envied her that ability.

"My mother is also a horsewoman, and she rides to this day. She was twenty-nine years old when she met my father, so she already had a pretty independent life established."

"You're a real Montana gal, aren't you?" Jim observed.

"I'm a Westerner not only by birth, but by heart, too," Pepper answered. She petted the cat fondly. "My mom was born in Anaconda, so I guess it's in my genes. My dad is a real outdoorsman, and he taught us to fish and hunt at an early age. I couldn't enjoy killing those beautiful animals, so I quit hunting and fishing and stuck to horseback riding. Cam loved hunting, though, so he always went with Dad. I will say this—my father and brother hunted and used the food. They never killed for sheer sport."

Jim realised how important that was to Pepper, and he found himself mesmerized by the graceful way she used her hands to punctuate her statements. Finally, he was becoming privy to the woman inside the confident smoke jumper. "What made you go into the army?"

"Dad asked me the same thing," Pepper said wryly. "Mom thought it was a great idea. She said the military would teach me discipline and organization. She was right—it did. But it taught me a lot more. When the army wouldn't let me attend Ranger graduation after I was the top student in my training group, I resigned my commission. I went back to Montana to find my roots and see if I couldn't give back to the land that had bred me, in some way."

"Why?" Jim asked quietly.

Startled, Pepper glanced up at him. In the shadows of the large room, his high cheekbones and square jaw seemed emphasized. She felt herself automatically acquiescing to his reassuring steadiness. "I guess…well, I've never really thought about it, but I love the wide-open, blue sky, the miles and miles you can go without seeing another person. It's serene, but at the same time teeming with wildness and beauty."

"Sort of like you?"

Shaken badly by his insight, Pepper frowned. "I don't know about that."

"I think I do," Jim said, settling back more comfortably against the couch cushions. "It sounds like your mother and father really supported your being all you could be, not caring that you were a girl."

She nodded. "My parents have always been way ahead of their time, that's true. Cam and I were raised in a pretty even-handed way in that sense. Not that I wanted to play football in high school or anything."

"But you didn't go out for cheerleader, either."

She laughed. "No, I didn't. I was with the band. I played saxophone for four years. And, since I had my own horse, Mom and I would compete in shows on weekends." Her hand stilled on the cat's back, and she said,

"I had a happy childhood. I'm very close to my parents, and to Cam and his family."

Jim sensed the tension still stalking Pepper. "So how'd you get the name Pepper?" he teased, his mouth curving into a smile.

Flushing, she laughed. "Oh, that…well, I guess I was a pretty active baby. Mom told my father about five days after I was born that I was like a hot pepper bouncing around in the crib. I wouldn't lie still. I was always moving my legs or arms or rolling back and forth. So Pepper stuck."

"What's your given name?"

"Mary Susan." Pepper wrinkled her nose. "I can't imagine anyone calling me that, though. It sounds so foreign!"

Laughing, Jim shrugged. "It's not a bad name."

"I know," Pepper grumbled good-naturedly. "My mother named me Mary, after her mother, and my father named me after his mother, Susan. Go figure." Her laughter was husky. "However, I did know there was hell to pay whenever my mother or father used my given name instead of my nickname. That meant I was in *big* trouble."

Jim chuckled. Then he sobered a little and said in a quiet tone, "Cam's married, and it sounds as if you really dote on your family. How come you haven't married?"

It felt as if a spike had been driven through her heart. Pepper sat very still, wrestling with her unleashed emotions. Her hands rested on Frank, and she stared down at the animal. Finally, her tone strained, she said softly, "I was going to get married…but that was a long time ago. Or sometimes it seems like a long time ago. Then again, sometimes it seems like yesterday.…"

Jim said nothing, holding his breath. He saw the anguish in Pepper's eyes and heard it clearly in her voice. Something tragic had occurred, there was no doubt. "Go on," he coaxed gently, "what happened?"

With a one-shouldered shrug, she whispered, "I met Captain John Freedman when I was in the army, six years ago. A lifetime ago..." Pepper raised her chin and stared blindly across the room, not really seeing it, lost in her past. "He was an incredible man. He didn't care if I was wearing a uniform. You know how a lot of men are— they see a woman in uniform and automatically write her off. Well, John didn't. I was wary of him, because I'd been hurt before by other officers, in a few attempts at relationships that ended badly. He was so patient. That was one of the many things I liked about him.

"John was a Ranger and head parachute instructor at the school. He taught me about parachuting, and pretty soon I was skydiving with him and his friends. I came to love jumping." She compressed her lips. "I came to love John." Pepper felt tears coming to her eyes and she self-consciously wiped them away. "He gloried in me, in who I was. I didn't have to play any games with him. I didn't have to fit into his idea of what a woman should be. He accepted me just as I was, without apology.

"We had known each other a good year, and we'd decided to get married. I wanted to marry a man who didn't hold a prejudice about women's roles. I knew..." Pepper swallowed against a lump forming in her throat. "I knew the kids we'd have would be raised in the same kind of environment Cam and I had been raised in. I was excited about life—about spending it with John and watching our kids unfold like unique flowers, watching them blossom...."

Pepper closed her eyes, pain making her voice hoarse. "Two days before the wedding, we went skiing with the army skydiving club. It was a celebration John's friends had arranged for us. He was a wonderful skier. He was good at anything he did, to tell you the truth. I'd skied all my life, being from Montana, and it was just one more thing we had in common." Pepper felt the lump in her throat hardening. Helplessly, she opened her eyes, her voice cracking. "He died on the slope that day in a freak accident. A broken neck. We—we were skiing together, and his left ski hit something under the snow. Later, we found out it was a rock. He fell and rolled. I went on, thinking he'd get right up again. When I looked back and saw him lying in the snow, I thought he was playing a joke on all of us, because he did that kind of thing." She stopped, struggling with her grief for a moment. "It was all so crazy. Crazy. I went back and saw his best friend, Steve, turn white with shock when he leaned down to see how he was. As I came up, Steve told me John was dead. I couldn't believe it. I stood there, frozen."

Pepper dragged her gaze to the ceiling and fought back tears. "I don't remember very much after that...." Anguish wrapped her in its persistent embrace. Pepper didn't tell Jim that since John's death, she'd made a decision never to fall in love again. She'd decided it simply wasn't worth the risk. She knew she couldn't survive a second such loss. The decision had been easy—born out of the fires of her grief. And she'd lived by her promise for six years, successfully sidestepping any romantic attachment—until now. Unable to explain why Jim touched her in that forbidden region of her heart, she felt confused and scared.

Jim groaned. Without thinking, he moved to her side and placed his arm around her tense shoulders. Her pain was mirrored in every aspect of her face and lovely, tear-filled eyes. He couldn't stand to see her suffer this way and wanted somehow, to soothe her. This time, his embrace wasn't one of passion, but one born of a need to help her. He saw the desolation in her eyes as she looked at him. "I'm sorry, Pepper. Really sorry."

She sat with her hands pressed to her face, bent over but not crying. He felt the grief in her taut muscles, in the way she held back the tears. Again following his instincts, he lightly caressed her thick, silky hair. He wanted to do more. Much more. Fighting to keep his touch light and comforting, he rasped, "At least you got to know what love is about. You had some time with him."

Pepper felt Jim's hand on her hair, appreciated the tenderness of his touch. She hadn't believed he was capable of such a thing. Blinking, she took in his serious, shadowed features through eyes filled with tears. Jim continued to surprise her with his humanity, his range of emotions and his willingness to share them with her. When he removed his arm from around her shoulders, she felt bereft. Alone. For a moment, she had experienced that wonderful sense of togetherness that only a man and a woman could forge between themselves. She and John had had that once.

She studied Jim in the silence, memorizing each nuance of his features, from his dark tormented eyes to his compressed lips and the softening lines in his face. She wanted to say, *Who are you? Why is there such a chasm between your officer image and this Jim Woodward? Which is the real man?* Whatever the truth, Pepper knew she didn't dare open up to him the way her wayward body and emotions were pleading for her to do. She couldn't afford the gift he was offering her. The price was too high, as she knew from bitter experience.

It took her long moments to pull back from her own grief and realize what Jim had just admitted to her. She

saw the agony in his green eyes and found it unbelievable
he'd never loved a woman.

"I don't understand," she said brokenly. "You must
have loved before."

"Not like you have," he admitted, staring down at his
clasped hands, resting between his thighs. "I envy what
you had with John."

"You can't be serious. Surely there's been a woman in
your life."

"Oh, there have been women, but not at the level of
what you had with your fiancé." Jim saw such sadness in
her expression at his words that it tore at him. In that
moment, he realized Pepper had never truly gotten over
John. He found himself unexpectedly wishing he could
evoke that much emotion in her—and knowing it could
never be.

It didn't make sense. Pepper sat silently for a long time.
"You come across different than you really are," she said
finally.

Jim angled a look in her direction. "What do you
mean?"

"When I first met you, Jim, you were hard and cold. I
didn't like you much." She lowered her lashes, her voice
tight with hurt. "I know you didn't like me, either."

"And I was wrong," Jim rasped. "I'm sorry for hurting
you, Pepper."

"I'm not asking for an apology. I know you've changed
your mind." She grimaced. "It's just that I see such a
difference in you now from when I met you. You're like
two different people." She had to bite back the words:
And I like the man I'm with now. But was he the real Jim?
There wasn't time to analyze it, so she went on. "I know
a lot of people wear a facade, a social mask. I have a
friend like you. He's a pretty vulnerable man, but he pro-

tects his vulnerability by putting up this tough exterior. When Joe first joined our team, I had real problems with him, until a crisis occurred. Then he dropped those barriers, and I could reach inside and touch the real person. After that, we became good friends, and he never put up that barrier again toward any of us."

"Maybe I'm the same way," Jim murmured. "I don't know. I don't spend a lot of time analyzing myself." He shrugged. "Maybe I should."

"The military doesn't encourage that kind of thing," Pepper said with disgust. "They mold you into little mannequins trained to march, act and react the same way. I do understand how that can affect you, Jim. It's tough for me to believe you haven't ever fallen in love, though."

"Maybe I have and didn't realize it."

Pepper frowned, considering. She gave him an assessing look. "What about Laura Trayhern? When I was in your office, I noticed the picture of her was the only really personal one you had on the wall."

"Laura?" Jim straightened. "She's always been special to me."

"Yes, but did you date her before she married Morgan?"

"Oh, a few times." He stood up and jammed his hands in the pockets of his pants, frowning.

"You said she's special to you. In what way?"

With a shrug, Jim walked around the coffee table. "I don't know…I never thought much about it, to tell you the truth." He turned and gave her a slight smile. "Laura is…well, you know…"

"No, I don't know. Put it in words for me, Jim."

"She's just special." He frowned, thinking. "You want an example? Well, when she'd come into my office at the archives, I would feel better, happier. Not that Laura singled me out, or anything like that, for a long time. She was like this bright ray of sunshine down in that dark hole. Everyone in the archives responded to her.

"I admired Laura because she had beauty and brains— and she also had moxie. She was a go-getter, and she had the endurance to see whatever research project she was working through to the end. My office was at the entrance to the archives, and I enjoyed hearing her laugh whenever one of the staff told a joke. She was like a breath of fresh air in my life, that's all I can tell you."

"And how long did you know her?"

"Two years. Before Morgan turned up, I'd been taking Laura out some. They weren't official dates, but she'd happen to be leaving the archives at lunchtime when I was going, and I'd invite her along. Things like that." He shook his head, lost in memories. "She is just an incredible person, that's all." He omitted the fact that they'd kissed once—a kiss he recalled as vividly as if it had happened yesterday.

Pepper studied his expression, her heart squeezing with realization. Jim was in love with Laura. Didn't he know that?

Chapter Five

"Perhaps," Pepper ventured cautiously, "you care for her more than you realized."

Jim gawked at her. *"What?"* The word came out strangled, filled with shock.

"Maybe that's why this mission is so hard on you. I mean, it's understandable," she went on in a quiet voice.

"Wait a minute." He held up his hand. "You're wrong." But was she? Jim wasn't so sure anymore. He wanted to dismiss her words but an unexpected catch in his heart told him to look more closely at her observation.

"I don't think so," Pepper said, noting the confusion in his eyes. She did believe that Jim had never been consciously in touch with the fact that he loved Laura. She had met men like that before—so divorced from their feelings that they hadn't a clue about what was really happening deep within them. If Morgan hadn't come along so suddenly, Jim's love for Laura might well have surfaced in time. Not everyone closely tuned in to what their heart wanted—men and women included—and Pepper accepted that.

Sitting down on the couch again, Jim quickly reviewed his past with Laura. "She's been married for seven years and I see her only infrequently at the Pentagon. She still comes by occasionally to use the archives, and we're still friends, but—" he looked up at Pepper "—that's all."

Pepper didn't believe him for a moment. His tone of voice changed every time he spoke Laura's name or shared something about the extraordinary woman. Why was *she* feeling suddenly bereft, then? Pepper didn't know. "At first I didn't realize I loved John, either. It just sort of grew out of our friendship over a long period of time," she offered lamely. "Since he died, I've had a lot of time to think about our relationship." She opened her long, thin hands. "I was overly focused on my career—I wasn't looking for love or a relationship. I did plan to have a family, but much later, when I'd achieved my goals in the army."

Jim propped his elbows on his knees, with his chin resting in his clasped hands. "About the time I met Laura, I was in high gear careerwise, too. It was my first assignment to the Pentagon, and I knew I was being watched closely by the upper echelon. I was basically blind, deaf and dumb to anything outside what was necessary to keep my career on the fast track." He gave Pepper a curious look, noting how the room's shadows softened her face, making her even more beautiful. She had great depth, he was realizing, and from the grief still visible in her gaze, he began to understand what it had cost her to come clean with him about the love of her life.

"I've certainly never been in love to the depth you were with John."

"It's been hell," Pepper admitted. "The experience taught me a special sort of euphoria. But with him no longer around, I've been lonely in a way I never knew could happen."

With a soft snort, Jim rose and put his hands in his pockets. "My parents had the kind of love I want."

"Oh?" Pepper wondered if Jim was at all aware of his magnetism, of the way his natural strength and confidence coupled with this surprising tender side acted as a beacon to her. Surely other women had been privileged to know this side of him. If she believed what he was saying—that he had never, truly fallen in love—then she had to recognize the importance of this moment with him. If he didn't show this side of himself to others, why was he revealing it to her? Shaken by the possibilities, Pepper sat very still. It was automatic for her to embrace what was in her heart as well as what her mind told her; to separate them was folly. On the other hand, she had to be careful not to act on those feelings—if it might signal the risk of a potentially romantic relationship.

She knew it was often easier for men to separate their emotions from rational thought—and not even acknowledge the danger. From the moment she'd met Jim Woodward, he'd called to her heart—against her head's warnings—which could be why his aloofness and negativity toward her had cut so deeply, hurting her much more than it should have. She studied his thoughtful face and wondered again why he was revealing this very private side of himself to her. Could his love for Laura have forced him into the position? In her heart, Pepper had to believe he still loved the woman. It explained why he had barged into the Perseus offices and demanded to take the mission. And it also might explain his violent stand against Pepper coming along on the mission. Love made people do crazy

things, she knew from experience. It wasn't out of the
range of possibility that Jim subconsciously saw himself
as the white knight coming to rescue the damsel he loved.
And he didn't want any help in doing it, perhaps to prove
to Laura once and for all that he was a man worth loving,
a man willing to risk his life for her.

Jim continued thinking about his parents' marriage. "It
was silly things, I guess," he said finally with a short
laugh. Giving Pepper an embarrassed look, he pulled his
hand out of his pocket and opened it. "Things like sharing
a cup of coffee at the dinner table after we kids left to
play. Sometimes my dad would take my mother's hand
and stroll down the street in the evening, just before
dark." His voice lowered with feeling. "I always knew
they loved each other. My dad didn't show affection easily, but in those small ways, he showed he loved my
mother very much."

"I think most men, even of this latest generation, are
still struggling with showing their feelings."

"It seems to come so much more naturally to women,"
Jim agreed.

"It's natural because we were never taught, as boys are,
that it's wrong to show our emotions. You men are the
ones who get it in the neck, so to speak. You're taught
it's not masculine to cry, to reach out, to touch and express. What a sad thing society has done to you. And
everyone suffers for it."

With a grimace, he nodded. "I won't argue with you."

"Maybe that's why you were so slow to let Laura into
your life," Pepper suggested gently.

"Maybe," Jim agreed, with a slight shake of his head.
He held Pepper's velvet blue gaze. Did she realize how
beautiful she was? He almost voiced his feeling, but
thought better of it. Her dark hair was free and soft around

her face, lighted with golden strands. He recalled touching that silken mass and found himself wanting to touch it—and her—again. Her mouth showed such vulnerability, its soft fullness always pulled into an expression that underscored how she was feeling. Jim liked discovering that about her. She might be a woman of extraordinary talents, but under it all, she was gloriously feminine and had never abandoned her heart or her feelings.

"You know," he murmured, "you're a lot like Laura, in some ways."

Pepper's chest squeezed in pain. She didn't want to be compared to her, because she knew she could never live up to the image Jim held of the other woman. "I don't think Laura and I share much in common."

His mouth curved ruefully. "More than you realize."

A warmth cascaded through Pepper as she stared up at him in surprise. Laura was ultrafeminine and delicate. In comparison, she was plain and gangly, far from the ethereal beauty Laura was. Her heart wanted to embrace Jim's statement, but her mind and the decision she'd made after John's death stopped her. She glanced down at her hands, at her practical, blunt-cut nails. She never wore fingernail polish or earrings. Nor did her job allow for dresses, perfume or many of the smaller appointments that, in her mind, made a woman feminine.

Jim saw her frown. "You both possess an inner strength. You're passionate about what you believe in. Laura was passionate about helping Morgan after she was injured and he rescued her. She saw *through* him, somehow, to the man beneath the armor." He shook his head. "I certainly didn't. When I met him for the first time, all I wanted to do was pick a fight with him." His voice grew gentler. "You both live, breathe and move through your emotional instincts." His mouthed twisted in a sad

smile. "I find that commendable. Courageous." He
touched his own chest. "If I tried that, I'd be laughed out
of the corps."

"Laura put you in touch with your heart, maybe for
the first time," Pepper pointed out, even though it was
painful to admit that truth. She saw Jim's mouth curve
more deeply in response.

"Yes, I guess she did. Laura always has had a way of
making the men in her life take responsibility for how
they felt—even when we didn't know what we were feeling in the first place." He eased onto an overstuffed chair
opposite Pepper. Her long skirt added to her naturally
graceful appearance, and he liked the way she slowly
stroked Frank's gray-and-white fur. What would it be like
to be stroked by those long, narrow hands—hands that
had saved his life with their inherent strength just this
morning?

Jim's mind gyrated forward to the mission. *Pepper
could be killed.* The thought was pulverizing to him, and
he stared at her hard, noting the shadows that lovingly
emphasized her features. Her lashes, he realized, were
thick and long, while her eyebrows reminded him of
gently arched bird wings. The combination gave such startling definition to her soulful eyes that Jim felt as if he
could get lost in them forever. Something was always going on in Pepper's eyes, in a way he'd never experienced
with another woman. Her eyes broadcast her emotions so
clearly that it aroused a powerful response in him.

For a split second out of time, he knew that Laura could
die, too. The overwhelming emotions that came with that
flash of awareness rocked through him, a vivid reminder
of his own equally fragile hold on life. This mission could
kill all of them. Easily. He struggled internally to reject

that knowledge, but his military mind and training coldly confirmed the possibility.

His focus returned to Pepper, who appeared lost in thought. She might never find love again, he realized sadly. Her heart was still in John Freedman's hands, even though he was dead. After this mission, provided they survived, Jim would never hear Pepper's husky laughter again or see that wonderful bevy of emotions mirrored in her eyes. She was rare, he realized—a rare woman who had the courage to make of her life exactly what she wanted. If life told her no, she went in another compatible direction, reweaving the fabric of her goals and continuing to move toward her heart's desire.

Looking back at himself, Jim gave an internal, derisive laugh. He'd merely had to punch the military system's ticket to get what he wanted. He'd never been told no, as Pepper had. All he'd had to do was play the game the way he was told, and the next rank would follow. Oddly, his successes didn't fill him with the kind of satisfaction he was sure Pepper experienced over her many battles, wins and losses. She might have had doors slammed in her face, but she'd never let it defeat her.

If there was anyone he'd choose for a mission this dangerous, he had to admit, it would be Pepper. She wasn't a killer, but that wasn't what was needed here. Her brains, flexibility and unique ability to turn a setback into a success would come in very handy. Jim knew he provided certain strengths to the mission, but Pepper's input and observations would be easily as valuable as his own.

But despite his discovered faith in her, he couldn't stop worrying about the chance of Pepper dying. His heart lurched violently in his chest at the thought. Much as he would like to deny it, the possibility was real. A maelstrom of feelings rose sharply in him, encircling his heart.

Pepper was murmuring soothingly to the cat, her head bent over him, her mouth curved in a soft smile. For a moment, Jim enjoyed watching her, then, unexpectedly, Laura's face shimmered before him. Where had that come from?

Rubbing his chest, he rose suddenly. He excused himself abruptly and went into the kitchen, wrestling with a gamut of unexpected emotions. Placing his hands on the sink, he looked out the window over the sparkling neighborhood lights of Georgetown. The porcelain sink was cool against his damp palms. His heart wouldn't settle down. Maybe Pepper was right, after all, about his feelings for Laura. Did they go beyond mere loyalty and friendship? At the same time, his response to Pepper was new, something he'd never encountered—even with Laura. But maybe that was why he hadn't fallen in love during all these years—because his heart was still in Laura's hands. He frowned. The only way he could think to find out once and for all how he felt about Laura was to see her again. He knew it was wrong to love another man's wife—and he was very aware of how deeply Laura loved Morgan. He'd seen for himself the reality of what existed between the couple. So where did that leave him and this confusion of emotions squeezing at his heart?

Grimly, Jim studied his hands, still resting on the sink. Pepper's insight had blown the lid off something he'd been carrying around for years but had never realized until now. He'd never really considered his feelings for Laura. At first, he'd been too busy chasing his career up out of the depths of the archives. Then, when he'd realized Laura was drawn to Morgan, he'd slammed the lid down on whatever emotions he'd had.

With a shake of his head, he sighed. Morgan might already be dead. Laura could be a widow. Would he want to step in and try to start afresh with her? There were no easy answers. Yet his response to Pepper was wildly spontaneous and breathtaking, and Jim had never felt more uncertain in his life. What was real? What were mere idealistic dreams that would never be fulfilled?

The discovery of his chaotic feelings was painful, yet strangely euphoric. Somehow, subconsciously, he thought, he'd been looking all his life for a woman who possessed Pepper's unique combination of qualities. She was completely comfortable with who and what she was—and was not. No, she wasn't a magazine-model beauty. And maybe she wasn't beautiful in the same way Laura was, but that didn't matter. He pictured his mother. She'd been a strong, quiet woman with a deep passion for life—much like Pepper. Above all, Jim realized, he wanted people in his life who had commitment—as he did. Pepper's commitment to herself was mind-boggling in the sense of how much she'd accomplished in face of sometimes severe opposition. Fleetingly, he recalled that his mother, who'd had artistic leanings, had been refused schooling at a college where she'd wanted to take art courses, because her high school grades had been too low.

Closing his eyes, Jim went back to that time. He'd been ten years old, far too young to understand his mother's tears as she'd told his father that the college had turned her down. Jim recalled crying that evening in his bedroom, alone and unseen. He'd cried for his mother—for her dream being shattered by an unfeeling institution that looked at grades rather than the quality of her talent. From that day forward, he remembered, his mother had changed in subtle ways. She had never again tried to draw. She had put her box of paints away in the attic, never to retrieve them.

Releasing a ragged sigh, Jim opened his eyes and stared

blindly out at the city lights. He felt anger at the insen-
sitivity of the college's treatment of his mother. Pepper,
too, had her passion for life, but she'd somehow managed
to sidestep that awful trap of failure. He smiled at the
thought. Pepper came from a younger generation of
women, who had been told it was all right to fight back,
to fight for their dreams.

A sizzling sort of electricity moved through him. It was
a feeling he'd never experienced with Laura, and he knew
it had to do with Pepper. He liked her more than a little,
despite the small amount of time they'd shared. Their
bonding had occurred through a life-and-death situation,
Jim realized, and that kind of connection was soul deep,
transcending time and space. He'd learned that in Desert
Storm, Panama and Grenada, where he'd felt that same
bonding with the marines he commanded.

Pepper, despite his poor treatment of her up to that
point, had saved his miserable life out there in the sky.
She'd reached beyond the hurt he'd delivered, wrapped
her strong hands around his arms and held him. She
hadn't let his pettiness stand in the way of risking her life
to save his. Yet even as he savored his feelings for Pepper,
Jim's heart cried out for Laura, for what might have been
and could be in an uncertain future.

"Damn..." he rasped, straightening. He glanced toward the living room. Turbulent emotions soared through
him as he digested what Pepper quickly was coming to
mean to him. And at 0300 tomorrow morning, she could
die. She could miss the island and, with sixty pounds of
gear on her back, drown in the ocean. She could hit a tree
and be fatally gored. A bullet could find her, or one of
those dogs could tear her apart. Worst of all, she could
fall into Garcia's hands as his prisoner. And Jim knew
what the drug lord did to women. Sickened, he turned,

his stomach rolling with nausea. It was heinous enough that Garcia had Laura; it was unthinkable that Pepper could fall prey to the sick bastard, too.

"Jim?"

Pepper's voice was soft. Questioning.

He turned abruptly on his heel. "I haven't been a very good host," he said, more gruffly than he intended because she'd surprised him.

Reeling from the sudden hardness in Jim's tone, Pepper stepped back from the kitchen entrance. The old Jim Woodward—the hard, unfeeling marine she'd first met—was back. Part of her was relieved. With Jim in this mode, it was easy to respond to him on a strictly professional basis. Anything beyond that was too dangerous for her to contemplate, anyway, she reminded herself. Gathering her thoughts, she said, "I'm tired. I'm going to try to get some sleep before we meet over at Andrews at 0130."

Cursing himself, Jim started toward Pepper. He saw the quizzical look in her eyes—and the pain. He'd hurt her again. Scrambling for a way to apologize, but not knowing how to go about it, he followed her to the door. He retrieved her coat from the closet and helped her on with it.

"Thanks for dinner," Pepper said woodenly, suddenly drained by all the events of this very long day. She was an emotional wreck. As she slung her purse over her shoulder, she saw anguish in Jim's eyes and had no idea what was going on inside of him. Had it been something she'd said? But what? She had no idea.

"I'll see you later," Jim rasped, opening the door for her. It was the last thing he wanted to do—let Pepper out of his sight. He was consumed by gnawing hunger to ask her a hundred different questions about herself, about her growing-up years and her family.

Stung by Jim's inexplicable withdrawal, Pepper stepped out onto the sidewalk leading to the curb, where her rental car was parked. The November air was icy cold—but nothing like the chill that enveloped her insides. As she pulled on her gloves and walked quickly to the car, her chest began to ache. Dammit, she liked Jim! At least her silly heart did, she chided herself, as she slid onto the cold vinyl seat and shut the door. The street was well lighted and lined with trees, their bare branches lifting skyward into the darkness. Wind stirred the dried leaves along the curb and sidewalk.

Pepper started the car and drove slowly down the street. Why had Jim left her alone in the living room so long? She grimaced. Even if it had been something she'd said or done, he hadn't needed to disappear like that. He was a mature adult. He at least could have stayed and made small talk. The Marine Corps drilled officers on small talk for social occasions, Pepper knew, but Jim hadn't been willing to do even that much. Frowning, she made a turn that would take her to her nearby hotel.

Why had he turned so gruff? He'd been accessible, then ten minutes later, he'd been closed off. Perhaps, she ruminated, he had got in touch with the fact that he still loved Laura Trayhern. Bothered, Pepper wondered how or if that knowledge would affect his performance on the mission. It had to affect him. Whether he wanted to believe it or not, he was human, and dammit, he had feelings.

Angered, Pepper drove to the hotel and went directly to her room. After a long, hot shower, she slipped into her cozy flannel nightgown, which fell to her ankles. Going to bed was the easy part. Going to sleep was another story. Her mind swung from the manuals to the HAHO, to Jim and John. Every time her heart touched on Jim, she became a mass of vibrant feelings. Frustrated, Pepper got up and started to read another manual to distract herself from the thought of Jim Woodward, but even that didn't work. Finally, she started pacing her hotel room.

Jim still loved Laura; Pepper was sure of it. Desperately, despite her roiling response to the idea, she wanted it to be true. She couldn't dare risk true love again, so it was just as well that Jim was otherwise involved. As the clock ticked toward one a.m., she tiredly rubbed her smarting eyes. She should have tried to sleep, not think. Her mind was spinning with data to remember—radio codes, satcom codes, what to do if they got separated. What to do if she was captured. That last thought scared the hell out of her. Pepper didn't want to die. At the last moment, she wrote a letter to her parents—just in case. Then she wrote a letter to Jim, too. She tucked both of them away in her purse, which she would be leaving behind at Perseus, along with the rest of her luggage. If she died, her personal effects would be gone through and the letters delivered.

The seriousness of the mission impinged upon her more than ever as she slowly pulled off her nightgown and began to dress in striped utilities that the Marine Corps had provided. She could die tonight—in a variety of ways. Even so, Pepper found herself repulsed at having to carry weapons. She didn't want to kill anyone. It simply wasn't in her. And she might have to. She pulled on thick, dark green socks as she explored her feelings. Even as a child, she hadn't wanted to shoot deer or catch trout with sharp hooks. Some of her passion for smoke jumping came from her role in stopping the destructive fires that inevitably killed the wildlife in their paths.

Pepper knew she'd be hard-pressed to squeeze a trigger to kill someone. She didn't doubt Jim would do it—probably because his survival instincts were more sharply honed. But despite her hitch in the army and getting through Ranger school, she was less than sure about her ability to take a life—even in her own defense. Pepper shook her head. Why was she taking this mission? Wolf had told her about Laura and Morgan. She liked Wolf and knew he was a man of honor. If he wanted her help, she didn't question it. Wolf was like part of her extended family, and if he needed her, she'd be there.

Pepper decided that her morals and values were terribly confused. On one hand, she'd dive into life-threatening danger at the blink of an eye, yet she was loath to pull a trigger to kill another person—even one intent on killing her. Go figure. Well, it was too late to change her mind, although these weren't really second thoughts. Her heart centered on Jim, and Pepper knew unequivocally that she was a balance to him and the skills he brought to the mission. He wasn't a killer, either, but he would kill in self-defense—although she believed that if he had to, he'd regret it.

As she pulled her thick, shoulder-length hair up and back into a ponytail, Pepper looked at herself in the bathroom mirror. What a contrast, she thought. Her big, blue eyes didn't seem suited to the military uniform she wore. She looked vulnerable, not tough and soldierly. Maybe that was what Jim was concerned about.

Sighing, she realized that she had no answers to the various dilemmas she faced. A part of her liked Jim and was glad to be there for him on this mission. Another part was willing to do what was necessary to rescue Laura Trayhern. And part of her didn't want to go at all—because of Jim, who stirred the coals of life brightly within her. Somehow the danger he presented to her very soul seemed to outweigh the many external threats.

* * *

By the time Pepper arrived at Andrews Air Force Base, she was a mass of nerves. Wolf drove her there, his face set and hard. He said little on the way, and as Pepper stepped out of the vehicle and toward a small office inside a hangar, the tension was electric. There, squinting in the bright lights, an Air Force team met her and began helping her into her parachuting gear. Pepper felt as if she were in a surreal movie. Where was Jim? Four people worked with her, saying little, the strain obvious in all of their faces. In half an hour, she and Jim would board the C-130 that would take them across the Gulf of Mexico to the Caribbean for the drop.

Wolf remained nearby, and Pepper felt reassured by his presence. The pack she would carry on her back was loaded with ammunition and weapons. Pepper made sure that her knife was situated, as always, on the front of her harness, with easy access, though she hoped this time she wouldn't be cutting away shroud lines.

The door opened. Jim, already in his tiger utilities, appeared in the doorway. His face was grim, his eyes hard. Pepper swallowed convulsively, suddenly wondering if she really ought to go on this mission. She could die. Jim could die. The thoughts shook her, and as she held Jim's glittering gaze, Pepper *felt* his raw, boiling emotions. Though he hadn't said or done anything, she experienced his feelings as if they were her own. What was going on? Had she suddenly become psychic?

Pepper acknowledged that during critical fire situations, her intuitive abilities were nearly clairvoyant, probably because of the adrenaline, which automatically heightened everyone's senses. She watched Jim skirt her to talk in low tones to Wolf, who stood, arms crossed, listening intently.

Jim was ignoring her—again. She felt hurt as well as

relief wind through her as she turned toward the two men. Her talk with Jim earlier tonight—their unexpected intimacy—had been wrong, she realized, as she followed the jump master out to a waiting vehicle that would take them to the C-130 warming up on the runway.

"Pepper?" Wolf reached out, his hand wrapping around her arm to halt her forward progress.

They stood on the tarmac, the light from the hangar casting eerie shadows across the huge base. Pepper looked up into Wolf's face and saw the worry in his eyes. "I'll be fine, Wolf. Stop worrying." She gripped his hand.

"Just be careful," he growled. "Sarah won't forgive me if you don't come back."

She nodded somberly. "I know." Sarah was her best friend, and Pepper knew how much Wolf loved her. "I'll be back."

He reluctantly released her hand. "I'll be praying."

Pepper smiled weakly and waved goodbye to him and to the uniformed men and women standing around him. She found herself walking next to Jim, who seemed to appear out of the darkness. His profile was sharp. His eyes revealed nothing. Most of all, she saw the forbidding set of his mouth—a single line. Swallowing against a dry throat, Pepper climbed into the vehicle. The doors slammed and they lurched forward, gears grinding.

Darkness closed in around them, except for the dull glow of the dashboard lights. Pepper sat in the back seat, alone. She felt horribly deserted. If only Jim hadn't retreated so far inside himself. She knew that certain members of her team reacted like that before a jump. Still, she wished for some friendly sign from him, some humanity.

The C-130's engines were whining, the four turboprops spinning and invisible in the night. Jim and Pepper boarded through the rear ramp, and she hauled her gear on board, taking a seat next to the jump master, a grizzled-looking sergeant in his mid-forties. The load master, a woman sergeant, gave the signal, and the ramp began to come up, the sound of clashing metal echoing through the cargo plane's cavernous hull. Soon the inside of the aircraft was dark, the gloom broken only by a few small lights.

Jim had sat opposite Pepper, on the other side of the aircraft. He wouldn't look at her, she noticed. Instead, he fiddled with his pack, going through last-minute checks on various items. His movements were sure, brisk and economical. He knew what he was doing. He'd done this many times before—and she hadn't.

Squelching the urge to go over her own pack again, Pepper sat quietly. The C-130's engine whined at a much-higher pitch, and the aircraft began trundling awkwardly down the runway toward the takeoff point. The vibrations went through her, launching the faint smell of hot oil and metal. The human element was lacking in this mission, she realized. The weapons were cold steel. The plane was metal. Even the air crew with the C-130 seemed stoic and robotlike. At the moment only Pepper and her rising internal panic seemed frighteningly soft and human.

Her palms were wet, and she rubbed them against the fabric on her thighs. Her heart wouldn't settle down. Every time she thought of the coming HAHO, and all the possible problems, she broke out in a sweat. This time, if Jim's chute didn't open, she wouldn't see it. The darkness would mask the view of a partner plummeting to certain death. So many harrowing possibilities ran through Pepper's head. What she wanted, what she needed, was Jim's closeness. She tried to reassure herself that her need to be close to Jim and feel his touch was a normal desire she always had before a risky jump—a way to know she was

connected to the rest of her team. Still, her stomach tightened, and an odd tingling at the base of her spine as she
looked at his strong, reclining figure, scared her more than
she wanted to admit. Maybe she should be thankful Jim
had shut himself off from her, she thought suddenly, dash-
ing fiercely at unexpected tears that threatened to spill
from her eyes. She was alone in this mission, as she ultimately was in life. She had her family and friends and
that was enough—more than enough. She sat up a little
straighter in her seat.

As the C-130 rumbled through the air toward Nevis,
Pepper thought about her past. While the hours passed,
she was able to review her entire life to date—the good
experiences and the bad. All of them had been instructive
in some way, and she was grateful to realize that. As she
continued to sit on the vibrating seat, tired but wide
awake, her hands in her lap, she was glad she'd left her
parents that letter.

And Jim… She stole a glance through the gloom. He
was lying down, his back to her, curled up on some nylon
seats across the aisle. Pepper admired the possibility that
he might be able to sleep so close to a jump. She couldn't.
She thought again of their dinner together and realized
just how much she'd come to like him. That brief moment
where he'd been human, warm, even tender with her, had
shown her the real man beneath his harsh military facade.
Her heart cried out at the injustice of it all. But he was
in love with Laura. That's why he'd separated from her,
kept his distance. His mind and heart were focused on
Laura's rescue—not on what might be frightening Pepper,
what her needs might be.

Pepper understood those things without bitterness.
Surely she was old enough, wise enough, to allow people
to be themselves. Although she might not agree with Jim's

behavior, especially under the circumstances, she wasn't going to try to change it—or him. But didn't he realize she was scared, too? That she might need a brief touch on the shoulder, a slight smile or sign from him? Wolf had given her that before they'd left. But then, Wolf was different from Jim. He'd been through the fires of hell with Sarah, Pepper knew, and she had brought him out of his own closed world.

Feeling sad as never before, Pepper decided she would lie down, too. She stretched out on a row of uncomfortable nylon seats, her arm beneath her cheek, and closed her eyes. Exhaustion swept over her. Too much had happened too quickly. As much as her mind counseled against it, her heart ached with the pain of Jim's reproach. Her feelings toward him were good and true and strong—yet he pushed those genuine emotions away. *Because he loved Laura.*

Pepper shifted, trying to shut out the overwhelming noise of a C-130 in flight, and to ignore the bone-jarring vibrations. She could die, and Jim would never know what lay in her heart. Tears matted her lashes, and she struggled to hold them back. Even as she fought her rampant emotions, she fell into a deep, exhausted sleep.

Chapter Six

A hand gripped Jim's shoulder. Instantly, he was awake. The jump master leaned over and said, "It's time to get ready, sir."

Shaking off the much-needed sleep, Jim nodded and moved into a sitting position on the nylon seats. Removing the black covering from his watch, he saw that it was 0200. They'd be over the target in an hour.

Automatically, his gaze ranged through the gloom. The jump master must have sensed his worry, because he leaned down again. "She's been sleeping almost as long as you have, sir. Shall I wake her?"

"No, I'll do it."

"Yes, sir."

Jim took the can that contained the colors they would use to darken their faces before the jump. His heart twisted in his chest as he drew closer to where Pepper slept. Her long body was tucked along four of the nylon seats, her hand beneath her cheek. She looked angelic, her lips softly parted, her hair in mild disarray around her serene face. He felt guilty at the thought after his concerted effort to remain apart from her during the flight.

As he knelt down, one hand gripping the nylon for support as the aircraft bumped along, he had a wild, nearly uncontainable urge to reach out and touch her hair. The only thing that stopped him was the fact that the jump master was probably watching him. Instead, Jim settled his hand firmly on her shoulder and squeezed just enough to waken her.

Pepper felt a strong, warm hand on her shoulder. Her eyes flew open. She blinked, thinking she was dreaming. Jim was kneeling over her, a concerned, unguarded look on his face. His eyes were shadowed, but they burned with a fire she felt go through her as surely as morning sunlight after a cold Montana night. No longer was he hard and unapproachable. No, this man was the one she was helplessly drawn to, against her better judgment.

She savored the feel of his hand on her shoulder and the strength and care it conveyed. When Pepper realized she hadn't moved, but had only stared up into his eyes like a child for that long, undiluted moment, she made an effort to sit up. Her hair fell in tangles about her face, and she used her fingers to tame it into some semblance of order. Jim's nearness was agony. He had removed his hand, but not himself. Why not?

Confused, she looked at him.

"It's time to get ready," he said. He handed her the can containing black, green and tan coloring agents. "Cover your face, neck, hands and lower arms," he explained, then forced himself to get up before he did something crazy like kiss her senseless.

As he rose to his feet, Jim knew he should return to his

side of the aircraft, but he couldn't do it. Instead, he settled a chair away from Pepper and used her open tin to start camouflaging his own face. Covertly, he watched as she slowly applied the greasepaint to her lovely features. When they jumped, they would be completely invisible to anyone on the ground.

As he sat, absorbing the din and heavy vibration of the aircraft, Jim was surprised at how much Pepper meant to him. It was all so crazy, he decided in frustration. He continued applying the greasepaint to the exposed skin of his hands and forearms, wishing himself anywhere but here. Without question, he wanted to rescue Laura, but his heart longed for anything but the danger he knew they would be parachuting into. He'd had no time to talk to Pepper, to share his chaotic feelings, which were as surprising to him as he was sure they would be to her. Just as their kiss had been....

With a slight shake of his head, he finished smearing on the agent, feeling completely at loose ends. One part of him, the warrior, was focused on the mission to rescue Laura. But the man in him was torn between Laura and Pepper. Pepper was like a delicious, mysterious flower that had yet to open in his presence—a rare, beautiful orchid hidden deep in the jungles of the Amazon, waiting to be discovered, to be touched, to be loved.

Loved? Jim got to his feet, unable to stand being so near her. He was going to end up doing something foolish and embarrassing if he didn't move. Such a large part of him wanted to get to know her—all of her, on all levels. As he made his way back across the belly of the aircraft to the seats against the other wall, Jim realized he had to rise above his personal dilemma and focus on the mission. He needed to rescue Laura and find out just what she really meant to him.

No woman in his life had stunned him as Pepper had. Not that she'd meant to. No, he'd seen with painful clarity just how much she'd loved Captain John Freedman. He couldn't talk openly to people. He didn't possess those magical qualities that held Pepper in thrall.

Sitting down, his mouth grim, he began putting on his gear, plus the elastic joint protectors Pepper had brought along for them, with the help of the load master. Angrily, Jim forced his focus to the business at hand, but every once in a while he stole a look across the aircraft to where Pepper was being helped with her own gear. He saw the strain on her face and the fear in her eyes. That was a healthy sign. Beneath his own emotional state, he felt that same fear and trepidation. But his mind and heart were centered on Laura and Pepper.

Life was so screwed up, he decided disgustedly as he shrugged on the sixty-pound pack containing his two parachutes and everything else he'd need for the mission. Pepper had walked into his life, sent him reeling emotionally, but her heart was still trapped in the past—just as his apparently was. He had no time to savor her and discover her. Instead, they had a mission staring them in the face, and either, or both of them could die at any point. Never had Jim felt the surge of anger he felt now. How unfair life was. How damned unfair to all of them.

Compressing his lips, he thanked the load master and adjusted his headset.

"Pepper?" he said, trying it out.

Instantly, her head jerked up. "Yes?"

"You hear me okay?" Jim was barely whispering into the mike placed against his lips. Her husky voice sent a wave of need through him, one so excruciating that he had to take a deep breath to steady himself.

"Y-yes. Fine."

Jim heard the fear in her voice. Without thinking, he crossed the cargo plane to her side. The jump master had finished helping her on with her pack and had gone to his position near the ramp.

Reaching out, Jim slipped his hand around Pepper's upper arm, his eyes meeting her shadowed gaze. "Are you okay?"

She drew in a ragged breath. "Scared to death, if you want the truth. I mean, I'm nervous about the jump, but I'm more scared of what waits for us on the ground."

He gave her a tight smile. "It's healthy to be scared. It will keep you alive."

Pepper gazed up at Jim's dark features, at his eyes, glittering with some unknown emotion. "You look like we're going for a stroll in the park," she observed, trying for levity. His hand hadn't left her arm, and she desperately wanted to move closer to him. Did Jim realize the strength and confidence he exuded? How it helped her steady her own frayed emotions?

"I'm scared to death, too," he rasped, meeting and holding her gaze. Pepper had tucked her glorious hair beneath a helmet, black knit cap and positioned the headset over it. Her once-tan skin was streaked black, green and brown.

"I'm glad to hear it. My knees are feeling weak. I'm shaking."

"It's okay," he soothed, losing the hardness he wanted to keep between them. If Pepper realized how much he ached to have her, to discover her as the wonderful, unique woman she was, Jim knew she would retreat permanently from him. He squeezed her arm and found himself wanting to slip his around her shoulder to reassure her.

With a nervous laugh, she said, "I haven't been this

scared in a long time. Maybe on my first jump into a fire with my team, but not since.'' She felt bereft when Jim removed his hand. To her surprise, though, he didn't move away, instead remained only inches from her, as if to shield her with his tall, stalwart body.

"Fifteen minutes," the jump master informed them.

"Roger." Jim checked the altimeter on his right wrist and the watch on his left. "Is all your equipment in working order?"

"Yes." Swallowing hard and suddenly very thirsty, Pepper bit back the rest of what she wanted to say. She felt like babbling nervously to bleed off the fear that crouched in her chest and knotted her stomach. She could die in the jump. She could miss the island and drown. She could be gored by a tree limb.... Sitting down awkwardly with her pack, she fumbled with her bootlaces, tying them into double knots. Jim stayed close, and stymied, she wondered why. Was he worried she wouldn't or couldn't fulfill the mission now that she'd admitted her fear?

Her three-hour nap had left her feeling groggy. If only they'd had another day or two to rest up before the mission. Pepper felt strung out emotionally, uncertain about how Jim saw her, or even if he trusted her at all with this mission. The urge to turn, slip her hands around his broad, capable shoulders and press herself against him was very real. Too real. She told herself she was human, seeking comfort from an understandably scary situation. It was normal to find solace with another person. But why Jim? His heart was held captive by Laura Trayhern, whether she knew it or not. His love was bound up in the past.

"Five minutes," the load master said, hitting the switch that caused the giant ramp to open. Grinding sounds filled the cargo bay.

Pepper tried to still her pounding heart, without success.

She got up and walked across the deck, with Jim at her side. Her mind whirled with a litany of what needed to be done and in what order. Everything hinged on her parasail opening without a hitch, and she worried about Jim's jump. This time if something went wrong they wouldn't be able to help each other. Although they would be in radio contact via their walkie-talkies, silence was a must. In fact, until they were established on the island and sure they hadn't been spotted, hand signals would be their only means of communication, for fear of someone overhearing them or discovering their position.

Jim gripped Pepper's arm, when the ramp opened fully and a gusting wind began to tear through the cargo bay. At twenty thousand feet, the air was freezing cold. He felt the aircraft begin to bank, bringing them east of their target, Nevis.

"One minute," the jump master warned.

Jim's fingers dug into Pepper's arm. "Listen," he rasped, his face very close to hers. "I want you to be careful. No heroics, okay?"

Startled, Pepper felt his warm breath on her face as she was pulled against him. She opened her mouth to reply, caught up in the fierce, burning light in his dark green eyes.

"Dammit, Pepper, this isn't how I wanted it. I wanted time…time with you. We don't have it. You're special. I just wanted you to know that…."

Stunned, she stared up at his grim features. One of her hands was resting against the pack on his chest, and she swayed slightly off-balance as the plane tilted. She felt his hand tighten on her arm to steady her. Somewhere in her mind she realized that Jim could have held her at arm's length and helped her regain her balance, but he hadn't. He wanted her close, as close as they could get under the circumstances. The helmet on his head, the tight chin strap, the greasepaint and the darkness combined to give his face a dangerous look. She felt his eyes burning into her, touching her heart, her soul. Not believing what she'd just heard, she said brokenly, "There are so many ghosts from the past, Jim...."

"Thirty seconds," boomed the jump master.

Cursing softly, Jim released Pepper and moved ahead of her. It was too late to talk. He saw the jump master's grim face and watched the blinking red light that would turn green any moment now. The C-130 suddenly straightened out into level flight after the deep, tight turn. Wind whipped against him. Fortunately, his goggles protected his eyes. His mind revolved forward to the mission at hand. God willing, they'd find Laura and get her out alive.

So much could go wrong. So much.

The light flashed green.

The jump master gave the signal.

Jim moved down the ramp and leapt off its lip. Almost instantly he was hit by the power of the slipstream. He groaned and righted himself in the icy night air. Twisting to look upward, he heard the plane but couldn't see if Pepper had jumped yet. But he didn't have time to worry. Watching his altimeter, he pulled the cord when he reached ten thousand feet. The parasail opened flawlessly, jerking him upward as his gear sagged down, tugging mercilessly at his body.

Where was Pepper? All he could see under the quarter moon was the glinting of light on the smooth water of the Caribbean below. A few stars twinkled. He didn't have time to look around. Checking his compass, he pulled at the lines, directing his parasail in a slightly more westerly direction. The winds weren't cooperating; in their briefing earlier, the weather forecaster had warned them of this. Where the hell was Pepper? Again Jim twisted his head, but was unable to locate her.

He was panting hard, his breath coming in rasps. If he could just steady his breathing, he might be able to hear her. Wrestling with his chute in the uncooperative winds, he saw Nevis coming up. The dormant volcano sat on the western end of the island, near Plantation Paloma. In fact, Garcia had built his fortress at the bottom of its velvety green slopes. Again Jim checked his compass and made another adjustment. If he wasn't careful, he'd overshoot the whole damned island.

At five thousand feet, he was drifting silently toward the northern coast. He could see the white beaches now, and the black glint of the water. The iciness had changed to warmth, and he felt a trickle of sweat down his rib cage. It was hurricane season, so the humidity was high. He would feel his parasail slowing in the heavy wet air as he came closer and closer to the island. Making some last-minute adjustments on the lines, he aimed for their agreed-on LZ—a small clearing about half a mile inland that had been photographed by the U-2 flyby.

Where was Pepper? Jim couldn't look for her now. He could only pray she was somewhere nearby, probably five thousand feet above him, coming down safely. The wind was fickle. He bobbled. Yanking the lines, he steered the parasail farther inland. Two thousand feet. The trees formed a thick, continuous canopy. Automatically, he bent his knees and forced his lower body to relax. If he hit the LZ, he would have a clearing about the size of a football field in which to land.

Another gust of warm wind coming in off the ocean hit him and spun him around. Damn! Gritting his teeth, Jim saw the canopy flashing beneath his boots. One more yank. There! The meadow opened up beneath him. Instantly, he prepared to land. On the very best of days, he was able to land on his feet. But the sixty pounds of gear was pulling him off-balance. Rather than risk a broken ankle, he pulled the parasail around at the last possible moment to face the wind. There was lift, about fifty feet above the ground, then, gently, he was eased downward.

It was a nearly perfect textbook landing. His feet hit the wet grass and he bent his knees, absorbing the shock. The parasail fell to the earth, and he quickly jerked it toward him. Breathing hard, Jim looked around for Pepper. Anxiously, he searched the sky. All too aware of the wind gusting off the ocean, he narrowed his eyes against the dark sky.

The sudden breaking of tree limbs made him freeze. To the left! Jim jerked around, dropping his chute and kneeling. The crash continued, a crescendo of snapping branches. Pepper had landed in the trees! Quickly releasing his harness, he dragged everything under the jungly growth at the edge of the meadow. He pulled off his helmet and substituted a utility cap in the same camouflage colors as his uniform. The submachine gun was in his hands as he raced quietly along the edge of the meadow toward Pepper, a hundred questions racing through his mind as he hurried toward the sounds.

Voice communication was impossible; he couldn't risk it. Looking up, he finally spotted her. She was hanging about forty feet above the ground, dangling at the end of her lines from a huge rubber tree. He could hear her ragged breathing. Without a sound, he set his weapon aside and began to climb the tree's gnarled expanse. As he drew closer he could see that Pepper was tangled in her lines, so she couldn't just cut herself free and drop. Damn.

Pepper tried to steady her breathing and avoid making

any more noise than she already had. When she saw Jim climbing the tree toward her, she nearly cried out. Biting her lower lip, she waited silently. He was like a dark panther scaling the smooth-barked tree almost effortlessly. Pepper knew she was in trouble. The shroud lines had somehow become wrapped around her neck and arms. If she tried to cut loose, she might garrote herself. Worse, the branches above her, supporting her for the moment, were not stout. She was hanging tenuously at best.

She knew enough not to move. But had Jim ever cut someone out of a tree before? she wondered. In smoke jumping it was a common procedure, but she wasn't sure if he'd had the experience. She saw him study the situation. Their eyes met and he grinned a little. A flood of feelings tunneled through her. She tried to smile back but didn't succeed. Knowing she shouldn't break radio silence, Pepper merely waited, watching as he moved gingerly out on a limb above her. Good, he knew he had to cut the lines tangled around her neck and arms first.

Relief sped through her as the lines were shorn and fell past her. Just as she reached for her own knife to cut the remaining lines and fall, Pepper heard a loud crack. She jerked her gaze upward as the limb Jim had crawled out on broke beneath his weight. With a gasp, she watched in horror as it tore from the trunk behind him. He had no time to prepare for the fall. A cry escaped Pepper as he fell past her, and hit the ground, hard.

Rapidly, she unhooked her heavy pack and let it drop first. Then she grasped her knife and began cutting her lines, one by one. Hanging precariously, she bent her knees, preparing for the coming fall. Jim had crawled off to one side. She could make him out in the dim moonlight, his back against the trunk of the tree. Dropping, she hit the ground, her bent knees taking the shock. She rolled, absorbing more of the shock, and dried leaves and dirt flew up around her.

Gasping for breath, Pepper scrambled to her feet and hurried back to Jim, falling to her knees at his side. She saw the grimace of pain in his face and followed his gaze to his lower right arm, which he held tightly against him. Even in the darkness, she could see blood oozing through his uniform.

"I cut it," Jim rasped, throwing his head back, the pain flaring up his arm and into his shoulder. To hell with communications blackout. He had to talk to Pepper.

Gently, she eased his hand away from the wound. Jim's sleeve had been ripped open. Pulling it aside, she gasped. "It's deep."

"Tell me about it," he groaned softly. Looking around, he said, "Do what you have to do. We have to get out of here."

Pepper felt guilty. If she hadn't landed in the canopy instead of the LZ, Jim wouldn't be injured. Compressing her lips, she shoved herself to her feet and went to retrieve her pack. Her fingers were already bloody, a sign that his wound was bleeding heavily. Locating her first-aid kits, she took them back to him.

"Take this," she said in a wobbly voice, putting several white homeopathic pills directly into his mouth. "It's arnica—good for sprains as well as hemorrhage." Setting the kit aside, she drew out more items.

"I cut it on that damn branch I was on," he muttered angrily.

"I know…I'm sorry, Jim."

He held her guilt-ridden gaze. "You couldn't help it. The wind was all over the place." He stopped, a wave of pain flooding him. Finally, he gasped, "I'm just glad you're okay."

"I'm fine...fine...." Pepper quickly dumped the contents of the bottle directly into his wound. It was too dark to see much of anything. All she could do was disinfect the gash, then wrap it in a dressing and an Ace bandage. "I can't do much until it's lighter."

"I know. Just wrap it tight. We've got to move."

Nodding, she worked quickly. Though her fingers trembled, she was fast. In no time Jim was pulling down his torn sleeve. She helped him stand. He wavered for a moment, caught himself and straightened.

Anxiously, he searched her drawn face. "No injuries?"

"No..."

He reached out, unthinking, and brushed her cheek. "I was worried...."

The brief caress sent her heart skittering wildly. Shaken by his unexpected tenderness, Pepper pulled away. "Let me put my pack on and we can go."

"I'll bury the chutes and other gear." Jim tested his right arm. To his dismay, it hurt even to pick them up. The injury held far greater ramifications than he wanted to admit. Without his right arm, he was damn near useless.

By the time Pepper had situated her heavy pack, Jim had dug a shallow hole and laid the equipment in them. She noticed he wasn't using his right arm, instead pulling leaves and debris across them with his left hand. Helping him finish the job, she knelt next to him.

"The arm is bad, isn't it?"

"Yes." Grimly, he caught and held her gaze. "Listen, I'll take point. Whatever happens, we can't engage anyone in a firefight. Do you understand? I can't even count on using my fingers to pull the trigger." He looked with disgust at his right arm. "Maybe it's just as well," he muttered. "We'll do what Recons do—be quiet and not engage the enemy.'' He drilled her with a hard look. ''Do you think you can do that?''

''I don't want to kill anyone, Jim. I never did. It's fine with me.''

With an abrupt nod, he forced himself to his feet. Luckily, he hadn't lost too much blood before Pepper wrapped up his wound. He knew enough about anatomy to realize that his luck could have been worse—an artery could have been torn open and he could have bled to death. And he knew what the jungle environment with its high humidity and decaying bacteria would do to a wound like this. Once the sun came up, he'd have Pepper sew up the wound and give him a shot of antibiotics from the supply of medications they carried in their first-aid pack. Infection in the jungle was the surest killer of all, and those antibiotics could be the only thing ensuring he finish this mission. And he was going to finish it.

Pepper allowed Jim to take the lead. They walked quietly but quickly toward the unseen volcano. The surrounding trees were mostly coconut palms. According to the LZ information, they'd landed in a coconut plantation. The soil was tilled, dry and easy to navigate beneath the arms of the flowing palm trees, which rattled in the gusting winds. Pepper's heart settled down and her senses took over. Although she carried a submachine gun, she didn't want any part of using it. In the distance, a dog barked once. They froze and waited. No more barking. Jim moved on, more shadow than human being.

Pepper's throat felt like sandpaper by the end of the first hour's hike. Jim had kept up a fast, steady pace, and where they could, they trotted. Her shoulders ached from lugging the gear, and she was glad when Jim gave the hand signal to stop and rest. They were out of the plantation now and into the jungle itself, which was more tangled and harder to navigate. Twisted roots kept tripping her up, and she'd fallen too many times to count. Her shins were bruised and sore.

Pepper eased to her knees and unsnapped the pack. It fell behind her, and she wanted to groan with the pure pleasure of getting rid of the thing, but didn't dare. Worried about Jim, she turned and devoted her attention to him as he came and sat down next to her. The dawn light finally allowed her to get a good look at his injury for the first time.

"Well?" he demanded, watching her face closely for reaction. He knew it was bad.

"It's deep," she said in a choked voice. She laid his hand on her thigh and opened the first-aid kit. "The bleeding's stopped. That's good."

"I got lucky on that, at least," Jim agreed. Pepper's face was glistening with sweat, and a few dark brown curls had escaped from beneath her knit cap. Though her long fingers barely grazed the skin around his wound, he felt their warmth, with a tingling sensation that momentarily eased some of the throbbing pain. He concentrated on her lips—that full, lower lip—remembering what it was like to kiss her. Remembering her passion and generosity…. The loss of blood was making him light-headed. For a moment Jim allowed himself the indulgence of really looking at Pepper. She was beautiful….

"Did anyone ever tell you that you have a beautiful mouth?" he asked almost dreamily.

Stunned, she gazed at him. His face was sweaty, his mouth grim from the pain she knew he was feeling. "What? Oh…no, they haven't." She felt heat sweep across her cheeks, and she avoided his burning, intense stare. Taking out some surgically clean gauze that had been soaked in disinfectant, she steeled herself to begin scrubbing out the wound. In the light, she could see it was free of splinters or debris, but it had to be as clean as possible before she taped him up.

Jim leaned back against a tree trunk, honing in on Pepper's face. Anger sizzled through him. Well, what was wrong with the perfect Captain John Freedman that he'd never noticed Pepper's lovely mouth?

She began to scrub. "I'm sorry...."

His mouth tightened and he stiffened against the pain. "Somehow, I think I have this coming. I was such a bastard to you earlier," he groaned.

Pepper shook her head and bit down hard on her lip. She knew how much pain Jim was in as she continued to cleanse the wound. "It's the mission." And his love for Laura Trayhern.

Fire leapt up his arm, and Jim felt sweat pop out across his face and under his arms in reaction. He shut his eyes tightly, fighting off a dizzying faintness. "I was thinking about you," he gasped. His lips lifted away from his gritted teeth. He fought swirling dizziness—and more pain. Finally, it was over.

Pepper watched Jim worriedly. He lay in a prone position now, sweating heavily and breathing raggedly. His eyes were tightly shut. She couldn't blame him. Pulling the antibiotic syringe out of the pack, she gave him the shot in his upper right arm, above the injury. Much of what she did in fire-fighting situations was coming back to her, and she was grateful for her paramedic training.

Glancing around, she saw hundreds of trees, mostly rubber trees and palms of all sorts, silhouetted against the coming dawn. Odors of decay mingled with the salty smell of the ocean and some unidentifiable, exotic floral fragrances. Focusing on Jim's wound, Pepper located the surgical strips that would pull the edges of the wound together. At least he wouldn't have to be stitched up.

"This is going to hurt," she warned in a low voice. She used one hand to pull the wound together, and instantly he became rigid, his entire body convulsing. Hating to hurt him, she quickly taped the adhesive across the wound, closing it. In a matter of a minute, she'd completed her task. Breathing shakily, she began to rewrap the wound in clean gauze to protect it.

Jim wiped sweat from his eyes. He felt awkward using his left hand, but he'd better get used to it—it was the only one in working order. Concentrating on Pepper, he absorbed her clean profile as she worked over him. Her touch was exquisitely gentle, and in his hazy, shorted-out state he wondered if she made love with that same kind of touch. It was a crazy thought in an even crazier situation, he told himself harshly.

"I wish," he rasped unsteadily, throwing his arm across his eyes as she worked, "that we were anyplace but here right now."

Pepper smiled grimly and glanced at his face. His mouth was a line of pain. "That makes two of us." She completed the bandaging and stretched an Ace elastic around the gauze to further protect it.

"I keep seeing us talking over a candlelit dinner. I know some good restaurants in D.C. You'd like them, too. Quiet places. Intimate. Where good conversation can go on and on...."

Pepper felt mild shock over his rambling. Was Jim out of his head? Impossible. But his words were disjointed, ragged sounding, filled with fervency. Was he teasing her? Her heart said no, her head said yes. She remained kneeling beside him, more uncertain of herself than she'd ever been in her life.

Chapter Seven

"We've lost the time advantage," Jim said when she sat back, the bandaging of his arm completed.

"What should we do?"

Jim looked up through the canopy of palm fronds and heavy rubber-tree leaves. Daylight was already upon them. In another half hour the sun would be up. He didn't want Pepper to feel bad that her getting snagged in a tree had wrecked their initial timing. Being injured was something he hadn't counted on, either.

He slowly sat up, his back against the tree for support, and rested his right arm across his belly. Pepper remained kneeling and alert, slowly perusing the area with her sharpened gaze. There was little to be wary of now. But as they neared Garcia's fortress, her watchfulness would pay off.

"I worked out two plans with Jake," he said quietly. "The first involved striking before dawn, but that oppor-

tunity's gone. The second is to hit them tomorrow at 0300.
Noah Trayhern is sitting off the coast of Nevis, on a Coast
Guard cruiser with a helicopter platform. If we get to
Laura and can spring her, we're to meet at the beach south
of Garcia's fortress. I showed it to you on the map.''

Pepper nodded. ''If I hadn't blown it by getting hung
up in the tree, we might be there now.''

Jim sat up, reached out with his left hand and gripped
her arm. ''Things happen, Pepper. Let it go.''

She shrugged. ''At least our chutes opened this time.''

He breathed deeply. ''Yes, there's plenty to be grateful
for.''

''Do you really think you can continue the mission with
that arm, Jim?''

It was a fair question. He held her worried gaze. ''We
don't have a choice. You can't do this alone, and I'm not
going to call in air support for further medical help. No,
we'll do it. We're just going to have to be particularly
careful—and quiet.'' He scowled. ''But if we get in a
firefight, I'm going to be next to useless.''

Feeling bad for him, Pepper said, ''I don't want to kill
anyone. I have real issues over that, Jim.''

''Fine time to tell me.''

She saw his mouth quirk. ''Seven years ago, when I
was young and wild and going through Ranger school, I
thought I was capable of killing. At least I convinced myself I could do it.'' Pepper shook her head. ''I'm older
now, and looking back, I'm glad they didn't graduate me.
I liked the army for its discipline and organization, but I
found those same elements in smoke jumping.''

''The best of both worlds without lifting a weapon.''
Jim removed his hand from her arm. The intimacy between them was strong and good. If Pepper minded his
touch, it didn't show this time. Instead, she had opened

up, and was talking with gut-level honesty. "We have no backup if we get in trouble." He tapped the walkie-talkie strapped to his waist. "But we can change channels and call for Noah to send the Coast Guard helicopter in."

"They don't carry weapons, either."

"No, not on the chopper." Jim was worried, but he didn't voice the fact. It was one thing on a Recon mission planned to be exactly that. But this mission had too much chance of human contact, and weapons might well be used. He held her clear blue gaze.

"Would you use your weapon to defend?"

"In a heartbeat."

"Good."

"I'm not a pacifist, Jim. I just don't want to kill if I don't have to." She added more softly, "I know if I do, it will haunt me the rest of my life."

He understood only too well. "It's all right," he said gently. "I still get nightmares from what I did in Desert Storm and Panama."

Without thinking, Pepper reached out, her hand covering his injured one. "Somehow I knew you'd understand."

The tremble in her husky voice sent a sheet of longing through Jim. But it was the wrong place, the wrong time. "Help me up. We'll go slowly and take our time circling the volcano to reach Garcia's fortress. We can use the daylight to time the guards and observe the routine."

Somehow, Pepper thought this might end up being a better plan, after all. Knowing the guard's coming and goings and getting a direct feel for the place would help them tomorrow, when they made their raid into the plantation itself. She got to her feet and leaned over, offering Jim her hand. His grip was strong and steady as he heaved himself to his feet with her help.

She watched him for signs of dizziness but saw none. When she'd fashioned a sling for him to rest his right arm in, he went over to his pack.

"There's no sense in me carrying all this weight," he said, bending over it and fumbling with the straps. A left-hander he was not.

Pepper crouched next to him and opened the pack.

"Thanks," he rasped, offering her a crooked smile.

"I'll be your hands on this trip," she joked weakly, as she spread out the items from the pack so he could choose what to take and what to discard. He kept his handgun and its ammunition. At his request, Pepper dug a hole deep enough to bury the items he didn't need. It took nearly half an hour to repack the contents, then he hoisted the pack onto his shoulders.

Pepper opted to continue carrying the full weight of her own pack. If they got into trouble, she could still use the submachine gun to spray the area and protect them.

As the first streaming rays of the sun shot across the ocean and touched the island, Jim and Pepper began heading toward the fortress. He took the lead, since he was more familiar with jungle trekking. Mainly, they had to be careful not to step on branches that could crack or snap, since the sound carried too far for comfort.

Birds had been calling since dawn. As Pepper followed about fifty feet behind Jim, she noticed how he moved not in a straight line, but in one that took advantage of the brush and taller bushes in the area as protection from curious eyes. She could smell smoke from a wood fire in the breeze drifting toward them. Dogs barked now and then, and once she heard children laughing in the distance.

Because they were skirting the volcano, there were few homes, just thick brush that made for slow going. Every once in a while Jim stopped, consulted his compass and map, then moved on. Pepper worried that his arm must be hurting terribly, but she knew he wouldn't complain. Still, she watched him for signs of weakening or fever. The antibiotics should hold him, unless she hadn't cleaned out his wound well enough, which was always a possibility.

Near 0800, Jim stopped. He'd found a fairly thick grove of rubber trees that provided excellent cover, so he dropped his pack and sat down. He watched as Pepper silently came into the circle of trees. Her face had a sheen of sweat from the high humidity coming off the ocean. He was sweating heavily, too, as evidenced by the dark splotches on his utilities.

Taking out the canteen, Jim awkwardly opened it and drank deeply. Pepper joined him, sitting not more than a foot away, after placing her pack next to his. He capped his canteen and watched her drink from her own. She had such a long, slender neck. The greasepaint they wore had streaked off with her sweat. It didn't matter now, anyway. Jim looked around, satisfied that they were fairly safe from natives who might inadvertently discover them. They were miles from any of the dirt or asphalt roads that lined the coast.

Another sound caught his ears and he looked skyward. A helicopter. Pepper was watching the sky intently, too. They knew that Garcia had a helicopter. The *whapping* sounds grew closer. The aircraft was coming in from the west and heading south—toward the fortress. Jim barely glimpsed it as it skimmed by, nearly at treetop level.

Pepper stood, straining to catch sight of the aircraft. "It's a blue-and-white Bell," she reported.

"That's Garcia's," Jim said. He gestured for her to sit down near him. "Let's eat."

Pepper wasn't really hungry. The excitement and danger levels were too high for her to be in touch with something as basic as the need for food. The chance to be near Jim was enough, however, and she sat down next to him, her legs crossed. He handed her an MRE—one of the military's ready-to-eat meals that needed only to be reconstituted with water. She watched in distaste as he showed her what to do.

"At least out on the fire line we get real food," she grumbled.

He laughed softly. "Yeah, MRE's are the pits. I prefer the C-rations we had before they instituted this new stuff." Glancing at Pepper, he saw that some of the fear had left her eyes. Sobering, he asked, "Are you settling into the routine?"

She nodded and picked at her mushy MRE. "Yes, I am." She wrinkled her nose as she tasted the fare. "It tastes like cardboard."

Chuckling quietly, Jim agreed. He tried to ignore the pain in his arm by concentrating on Pepper—which was easy to do. Despite their circumstances, her vibrant inner beauty shone through. Several more curls had escaped from beneath her black knit cap. "You're the first woman I've seen wear Recon gear and look damn good in it."

Pepper's heart thumped once to underscore his huskily spoken words. She glanced up and nearly melted beneath his burning green gaze. Feeling suddenly shaky, she tried to concentrate on eating the unpalatable food. "Sure," she joked, "my face is streaked with that awful stuff, my hair desperately needs to be washed and I stink—some pinup poster I am, Woodward. Maybe you've been out in this jungle a little too long, huh?"

He grinned and spooned some more rehydrated fruit into his mouth. "Do you always parry a compliment, Ms. Sinclair?"

"Probably," she admitted, chewing thoughtfully. "It comes from my hitch in the army. Sexual harassment was everywhere. I got so I hated it, and most of the time I wouldn't take it."

"I don't blame you," he answered. "No one should be subjected to that kind of humiliation."

"Usually, marines are the worst harassers." She watched him laugh at her with his eyes. For the moment, Pepper felt safe, and she relaxed for the first time. Was it Jim? His confident presence? The fact that he'd done this before, and if he was relaxed, she could be, too? Or was it that lazy, warm smile he gave her that automatically made her feel boneless in such a wonderful, thrilling way? Did he realize what his heated look did to her? She was sure he didn't. After all, his heart had already been given to Laura Trayhern. Pepper had no chance with him. Though she knew she should be relieved, a ribbon of sadness wound through her at the thought.

Jim finished his MRE, dug a hole and buried the remains. "Marines are diehards," he finally admitted. "And you're right—they are pretty macho."

"The Tailhook scandal proved that." And the navy and its stonewalling admirals were no less guilty, she thought to herself.

Jim nodded. He couldn't argue the point. Half the aviators at the Tailhook convention had been marine pilots, and word was out that one of the worst suites at the symposium had been a Marine Corps one. Glancing around, keying his hearing, he reassured himself that everything was normal. The birds were singing, a sign that all was as it should be. If they were to stop singing suddenly, he and Pepper would go on alert.

He lay down carefully, using his pack as a pillow.

"Let's rest awhile. We've got three more miles to the fortress."

"Is your arm hurting you?"

"A little," he lied. It was burning, as if on fire. He saw Pepper's eyes change and grow shadowed with worry. "Are you always like this?" he asked.

"Like what?" she asked, leaning against the tree inches from Jim's shoulder.

"A mother hen."

Grinning, she said, "I get accused of that all the time by my team. I guess I am."

"Worrywart is probably closer to the truth," he said, looking up at her. He watched as Pepper removed the black knit cap. Her hair was a mass of curls from the humidity. With her slender fingers, she began to ease them into some semblance of order, and he longed to stroke the dark, wavy strands. She replaced the headset, settling the mike close to her lips, but she left the cap off. He couldn't blame her. The humidity was making him sweat like a racehorse.

Something drove him to get to know her better. He knew he wasn't going to get many chances, and he wanted to take advantage of everyone of them. "Tell me about your growing-up years. Were you a hell-raiser like your mom—a wild woman?"

Laughing softly, Pepper shared a warm look with him. This was the man she wanted to know, and it sent an ache straight to her heart. His green eyes were dark with an emotion she was afraid to define. His mouth was curved recklessly, giving him a boyish look.

"I was no 'wild woman,' as you put it." Tipping her head back against the trunk of the rubber tree, Pepper closed her eyes, suddenly happier than she could recall being in a long time. "Cam, my older brother, might disagree with me, but I never saw myself that way. As I said, we lived in Montana, so we did grow up in the wilds, in that sense. I spent every spare minute hiking and learning about nature.''

''Tell me about it?''

Embarrassed, she shrugged. ''I was just a kid with a high sense of curiosity, that was all. I used to hunt red asparagus berries every fall, collect them and make necklaces out of them. Later, I'd dry and shellac them and give them as Christmas gifts to my friends at school. Or I'd go out with my mother with my flower book and try to identify the different wildflowers that grew around our place, then press and save them.''

''So you were a wood nymph.'' Jim closed his eyes, imagining Pepper as a youngster. ''You must have been a pretty little girl.''

Pepper rolled her eyes. ''No, I wasn't. In fact, I felt awful sometimes because my nose grew larger than the rest of my face, or my lips did. You know how some kids go through that awkward period? Well, I was worse than most. When I was fourteen, I looked in the mirror one day and started to cry. My mom came into my room and found me.'' Her voice went soft. ''My mother, bless her heart, just put her arm around me. I blubbered about how ugly I was, and she said that each part of me was beautiful in its own right, and that one day soon I'd grow into all of them. She assured me I was just going through a gangly stage.''

Jim opened his eyes. ''Your mother is special—like you,'' he murmured.

Flushing, Pepper said, ''I don't know about me, but yes, my mom is special. Cam and I were really lucky. Hearing all the horror stories nowadays really makes me appreciate my parents. I know we weren't perfect kids, and I'm sure we caused them some anxious times, but out in Montana, at least we didn't have problems with drugs and gangs like the big cities do. Anaconda is a relatively small town—a silver- and copper-mining community.''

''I think some of the old-fashioned Western morals and values are still alive and well up there, don't you?''

Pepper was grateful for his grasp of her world. ''Yes, that's why I love living there,'' she said, smiling as a vision of her home flashed before her.

''Western people seem different from Eastern types,'' Jim offered. ''I grew up in Maryland, in a suburb a stone's throw from Annapolis. It wasn't the wide open spaces, but we still learned serious values, it being an Academy community.''

''You were lucky,'' Pepper said. She smiled at him, loving the ease of conversation now that the barriers between them were down.

''Tell me,'' he said, catching her dreamy gaze, ''what are your dreams?''

''What?''

''Your dreams. You've got to have some. What are they?''

Frowning, Pepper ruminated. She drew up her knees and rested her arms around them. ''You'll die laughing, Woodward, if I tell you.''

''No, I won't. Come on, what are they?''

She moved uncomfortably. ''They're nothing special....''

''So? I'd like to hear what's in your heart.''

Pepper tore her gaze from his. Her mouth was getting dry again. She wanted to blurt, *''You're* in my heart, but I know I can't have you.''* Bowing her head, she said instead, ''I have a very common dream, Jim, but it seems to have been taken from me.'' She swallowed against the lump forming in her throat. "Despite my choice of careers, I wanted to find a man who loved me as much as I loved him—one who'd love Montana's mountains and plains as I do. I dreamed of having his babies and of teaching our children, as my parents taught me. I would close my eyes and picture those kids as if they were real— and me showing them the red berries of the asparagus in the autumn, or hunting fresh-water mussel shells along a trout creek. Little things…important things."

Jim eased into a sitting position. He saw the tears in Pepper's eyes. What remained unsaid was that John Freedman had been the man meant to fulfill those dreams. "You'd make a good mother," he said in a low voice filled with emotion. "You're like a kid yourself in some ways." He smiled a little. "That's one of the many things I've come to like about you, Pepper—you're completely adult when you have to be, but there's also a kid inside you that never grew up. I think that's great."

Shaken by the grittiness of Jim's voice, Pepper stared at him. He was so close, mere inches away, and she could feel the heat throbbing between them. The burning look in his eyes rushed through her, making her aware of herself as a woman in every way. The thought that Jim would be a wonderful father himself flashed through her head, and Pepper quickly looked away, afraid he might see a yearning in her eyes. If he did, she'd be mortified. Still, she longed to reach out and tenderly touch his face, though the shadow of his growing beard and the streaked remains of his camouflage paint made him look even more dangerous. What would it be like to kiss his firm mouth again—to feel his powerful form against her heat and need? She ached to reach out and slide her hand across his chest, to absorb his strength. His wonderful half smile tore through her, beckoning to her, and Pepper literally had to stop herself from leaning forward...to meet his mouth and melt against him.

Was she going crazy because of the pressure they were under? Pepper sighed and tried to get a handle on her escaping emotions. Sitting here talking with Jim was opening up her heart in a way she'd thought would never happen again. Clearing her throat, she said, "Fair's fair. Tell me about your dreams."

He chuckled. "They're as pedestrian as yours, Pepper. I want a woman who will love me, warts and all. I want a couple of kids, too. I dream of finding a woman who likes to laugh, who can find humor in even the worst situation. I grew up in a pretty somber family, and I'm afraid I was the joker—the guy who was always playing tricks and then catching hell for it."

Pepper's eyes rounded. "You?"

"Yeah, sure. Why not?"

His grin was devilish, and in that moment, Pepper caught a glimpse of the original Jim Woodward—before the Marine Corps had shaped him to meet their exacting standards. "So, you're a joker?"

"Every chance I get." With a laugh, he said, "Not that I get much chance at the Pentagon. It's one place where you have to watch your every move. There's always someone with a lot more rank watching you—ready to mark you down."

"So when you have a field command, you're different?"

"You bet I am," he exclaimed. Looking up at her he found his gaze caught by her parted lips. Damn, but he wanted to kiss her again. Jim knew she was a woman very much in touch with her needs. She lived too close to nature not to be in tune with herself on those levels.

What was it he could see in her eyes? Desire? Longing? Or was that just wishful thinking on his part?

Hope coursed through him as his gaze continued to probe hers. She was a woman of incredible strengths and courage—the kind of woman he'd been looking for all his life, he thought suddenly. The discovery sent a sheet of heat through him, radiating from his heart. Pepper was as natural as the timeless cycles of the seasons. She had no pretenses; what you saw was what you got.

But even as those thoughts crowded into his mind and heart, reality drenched him. They were sitting in a jungle on foreign soil. Interlopers. The government of Nevis would not be informed of their mission until after Laura was rescued—if she could be rescued. And what made him think he would survive this mission? Or that Pepper would? The threat of death was strong. Jim knew Garcia's guards would kill without a second thought; they'd pull the trigger first and ask questions later. He also was positive that Garcia was on alert, knowing full well that Perseus would attempt to rescue Laura.

"When I was a little girl," Pepper said softly, her voice sounding as if it came from far away, "I used to sit by the trout stream on our property. I had a favorite rock that was large, round and flat. I'd sit there, shaded by the trees and brush, and watch the rainbow and cutthroat trout flash by in the water. I loved the rainbow trout, because when the sunlight caught them, they really lived up to their name. I'd just sit and watch, my legs crossed, my elbows on my knees and my chin cupped in my hands.

"I'd wonder what my life was going to be like after I grew up. What I'd be someday. I used to daydream for hours, trying to imagine myself as an adult and what I'd look like. Then—" her mouth curved gently "—I imagined my children. I saw the color of their hair, their faces,

the color of their eyes. I imagined each of their person-
alities and how much fun I would have with them.

"I saw this two-story white house with a green roof
and a white picket fence around it, too." She laughed a
little. "Actually, it was an exact replica of my folks'
place. Every summer Cam and I would get out there and
paint that picket fence. And we'd help dad on the roof
when it needed new shingles. Mom would plant bright
red geraniums, and I always thought it looked like Christmas in summer with the house's green trim and the red
flowers.

"I guess I'm really pretty simple, Jim. I don't want
much. I don't need much. I just needed a man who would
love me and respect me for what I was—and what I
wasn't. I wanted him to be as excited as I was about
bringing a bunch of mop-haired children into the world,
growing with them and loving them." She turned, gazing
down at Jim's thoughtful expression. "Sometimes there's
an ache in my heart when I remember those dreams," she
admitted. "I'm old enough now to realize it won't happen
that way."

Jim slowly sat up and faced Pepper. He slid his left
hand over hers and held it gently. "Don't ever stop
dreaming, sweetheart. They're good dreams. Dreams that
deserve to be lived out."

The tingling heat that spread from her hand up her arm
set her heart pounding. Looking deep into Jim's darkened
eyes, Pepper saw the desire burning there. His hand was
at once strong and gentle as he held hers. Perhaps it was
the roughened quality of his voice that tore at her the
most, making her long for what she knew could never be
hers.

Without thinking, she found herself leaning toward
him. And almost simultaneously, she saw Jim coming for-

ward to meet her. His grip on her hand tightened, her breath snagged as he bent his head and she drowned in his suddenly stormy green eyes. Her eyelashes swept downward. Never had Pepper wanted so badly to be kissed. Her lips parting, she raised her hand to his shoulder and tilted her chin just enough to meet his descending mouth.

Pepper's world spun dizzily as Jim's lips touched, met and claimed hers with a strength that threw her off guard. His mouth was molten, searching. With a small groan, she submitted to his quest, molding herself against him. She felt the prickle of his beard against her cheek and absorbed the plundering strength of his mouth as she was swept into a river of fire, no longer aware of anything but him—his masculinity, his power.

His mouth moved effortlessly across hers, seeking, tasting and deepening its exploration of her as a woman. She felt his ragged breath against her cheek, pressed herself to his broad chest, her hand sliding up and around his neck. She could feel his heart pounding as hard as hers was, and their breathing seemed to synchronize magically as she opened her mouth to his onslaught. The fragrance of the island flowers and their own natural scents enhanced the euphoria that flowed through her. She felt Jim release her hand, and in the next instant felt his palm against her cheek, tilting her head back even farther, tasting her deeply.

A knot of heat unfolded within Pepper, spreading through her lower body, crying for fulfillment. As Jim's fingers tunneled through the damp, curly hair at her temple, she felt tears of joy coming to her closed eyes. His mouth was at once cajoling and tender now as the overwhelming power of his kiss gentled, and she felt his tongue trace the outline of her lower lip, awakening an ache of pure longing. Never had she been kissed like this, and hungrily she absorbed the amazing sensations his touch evoked.

His hand moved away from her jaw, skimming the slenderness of her neck, sending prickles of fire racing through her. A softened moan was torn from her as his hand ranged farther, finding and cupping the round ripeness of her breast. Despite the rough utilities she wore, she felt his fingers caress her as through the finest silk. Her skin tightened to a painful intensity, and Pepper pressed herself shamelessly forward into his open hand. Her breathing became chaotic as his searching fingers slipped beneath the fabric. Her own fingers opening and closing spasmodically against his taut shoulders, she felt the delicious sensations as he grazed her breast, his thumb feathering across her hardened nipple and sending a keening need through her.

Pepper became lost in a host of plunging, deepening responses as she felt him shift her, bring her more fully into his arms, his hand tugging impatiently at her clothing, to open it more and expose her breasts. His mouth remained strongly on hers, taking even as she gave as never before with her breath, her body, her heart. Somewhere in her spinning senses, she realized this fire that burned so hotly out of control was more powerful and threatening than any forest fire she'd faced. The white-hot need consumed her as his hand fully captured her breast, his touch tentative, as if she were some priceless, fragile treasure. A treasure to cherish....

An overwhelming fear slammed into Pepper. What was she doing? Why was she allowing Jim to touch her, to take her? Her emotions cartwheeled as her reawakened mind screamed that he loved Laura, not her. Tearing her mouth from his, she pulled away. How desperately she wanted to stay in his arms, to continue accepting his caresses. She opened her eyes and looked up into his stormy, slitted ones, which now studied her with blazing passion. That stare made her freeze with the realization that his hunger equaled her own—only she was the one running away. What was she running from? Bitterly, Pepper admitted she knew the answer to that one. Every particle of her being screamed out for the feel of Jim's mouth on hers, for his hands roving across her, inciting her, teasing her, fulfilling her. Her gaze clung to his mouth—to that powerful male mouth that had made her lose all sense of time, direction and rational sense. Her world had narrowed to the breaths of air they'd shared, his mouth conquering hers, his hands scorching her, awakening her to a frenzied awareness of her needs as a woman. Never had Pepper felt like this. John's touches and kisses paled in comparison. Frightened by that knowledge, she simply stared at Jim in the drawn silence.

Shaken, Jim sat back, breathing hard. What the hell had he just done? Fear, curiosity and desire were mirrored in Pepper's widened, lustrous eyes as she stared at him, her lips glistening and well kissed. He raised his left hand and wiped his mouth with the back of it. How could he have allowed his desire for Pepper to overwhelm any rational thought? He'd nearly taken her. He'd come so close. The painful knotting sensation in his lower body cleared his mind. He had to think! They were on a dangerous mission. What business did he have putting them in jeopardy by kissing her, allowing his emotions to take over? None. Absolutely none. But no one compared to Pepper, he admitted at the same time. No one. She'd met him on equal ground in a way that had been startling as well as gratifying. Her strength seemed to emanate from an endless well of femininity he'd never realized existed.

Unexpected tears slipped from beneath Pepper's lashes. Blinking, she continued to look dazedly up at him. His own eyes burned with a newfound tenderness as he lifted his hand, stopped its motion toward her, then hesitantly stroked her cheek with trembling fingers.

"Tears?" he rasped, as he touched their silvery path down her cheeks. Why was she crying? Had he hurt her in his overwhelming desire to take her?

With a choking sound, Pepper eased back and wiped them away. "It's nothing...." she answered in a hoarse whisper.

Jim looked at her intently. "Sure it is, sweetheart. What is it? What made you cry?"

Still dizzied by his branding kiss and the fire his touch had brought to a blaze within her, Pepper tried to look away from the desire she continued to read in his eyes. If only that desire were really for her. She certainly didn't hold any ill will for Laura. The woman probably didn't even realize Jim still carried a torch for her. Despite the passion in Jim's kiss, Pepper couldn't help but believe he'd kissed her in lieu of Laura. Her mind whirling with the tortured observations, Pepper finally tore her gaze from his. How could she tell him her tears were due to the realization that he could never love her—that his heart had already been captured?

She turned away. She had to lie, and she hated herself for it. The truth was she'd enjoyed their exploration of each other. "Don't mind me," she said, her voice strained. "I cry over everything. If you don't believe me, ask my team. I cry when someone gets hurt. I cry at weddings. I cry when babies are born. It's just me, Jim, that's all."

Jim frowned, feeling real frustration. Pepper had turned away, so he could barely see her face. She was embarrassed. Why? Because he'd kissed her? Cursing silently, he admitted that he'd overstepped his bounds. And what a hell of a situation to be in. He could still taste her on his lips. The kiss had been fusing, stirring the deepest parts of himself to such vibrant, throbbing life that he'd barely been in control of his actions.

Jim knew Pepper hadn't answered him honestly about her tears, but he didn't know what to do about it. This mission was all tangled up with Laura, and his heart told him to back off, to have patience and wait. In time, Pepper's reason for tears would be revealed. A part of him still wanted to take her here and now, knowing she was capable of loving him as hotly as he wanted to love her.

What was wrong with him? He'd lost his focus. His reality. With a shake of his head, he reminded himself that that was how powerfully Pepper influenced him by her simple, quiet presence. He would never forget the word pictures she'd painted for him of her dreams as a little girl. More than anything, he wanted to ask her about those children she'd dreamed of so vividly. What color was their hair? Were there any with green eyes like his own? Or black hair? The ache in his throat intensified, and he turned toward Pepper, wanting to speak.

The sad line of her mouth stopped him. She was sitting apart from him, her arms again wrapped tightly around her drawn-up knees. Her tears were gone, and Jim wondered what it had taken for her to jam them back inside. He hadn't realized how easily touched Pepper was until now, and it was an exquisite discovery.

"If we were home, back at my condo," he said, his voice rough with emotion as he caught her startled gaze, "you and I would have a long, heart-to-heart talk. Your tears aren't something to be ignored, Pepper. I care enough for you to want to know what brought them on...."

Chapter Eight

The inky night gave Pepper some relief. After Jim's hot, startling kiss, she had withdrawn deeply into herself. How was she going to manage to stay at arm's length from him? She'd done it with every other man since John had died. How had Jim so easily scaled her barriers? She was thoroughly confused. What did it mean, that he could kiss her like that? She still had no doubts that he loved Laura. She'd seen his eyes take on the darkness of worry as the daylight had waned. Of course, she was worried for Laura, too. She didn't wish for any woman to be in Garcia's clutches. But Jim's responses had once again grown cooler, more disconnected.

As she knelt in the jungle overlooking the fortress, the darkness complete, Pepper knew she had to shove her vibrant feelings toward Jim aside once and for all. The sadness she felt at the thought of never truly getting to know him brought tears to her eyes, but she fought them back. If they could reach Laura and release her, Pepper knew Jim would gravitate back to the woman without question. And whatever wonderful things had sprung up between him and Pepper on this mission would dissolve into the halls of his memory. But she was afraid she wouldn't so easily be able to relegate her recent emotions to the past tense, no matter what she did.

From where they knelt, their packs propped nearby so they'd be unhampered, Pepper and Jim timed the movements of the guards. Luckily, they were upwind of these men and the large, savage-looking Doberman pinschers that walked at their sides on long, thick leather leashes. The map of Garcia's plantation was firmly etched in Pepper's mind. In another few minutes, she would begin spreading the pheromone substance along the wrought-iron fence, away from the area where they wanted to breach it. Luckily the ten-foot barrier was just that. Garcia had put up an ornate fence, seemingly more for show than for actual protection, Pepper thought. There were no spikes or concertina wire, atop it, of the type that could easily cut an intruder to the bone.

Her eyes were well adjusted to the darkness, only vaguely brightened here and there by the quarter moon's light. It was perfect—enough light to work in, but not enough to give them away. Still, they'd reapplied their greasepaint to make sure no hint of pale skin might reflect the watery moonlight. As much as Pepper tried to ignore Jim's powerful presence, she couldn't. She felt his tension and tasted her own. Soon they would scale the fence, with only side arms and knives to protect them. Pepper shivered. She hoped she didn't have to use either one. Right now, her entire focus had to be on getting to the white plantation house with its dark red trim. The red-tile, Spanish-style roof gave it an odd look as far as Pepper was concerned, creating a sort of hybrid between Spanish and Southern-plantation design. Four huge white columns supported a wooden porch roof and every twenty minutes a heavyset guard with a Doberman passed by the south doors, where she and Jim planned to enter.

The night was warm and humid, and the stars had long since disappeared under approaching clouds. Pepper remembered the chance of a hurricane building south of the Windward Islands. She wondered if it would rain. The air seemed heavy, almost pregnant with moisture. Rain would be something they hadn't counted on, but it was a natural defense for any intruder, hiding noise and wiping out scents and footprints. Pepper almost wished it would start raining now.

Jim glanced over at Pepper. She was still and alert, her eyes intent on the fence line. His heart felt as if it were on fire with the need to talk at length with her. Their kiss had rocked his world—his soul. How badly he wanted to impart that to her, but he'd watched her retreat within herself. And he knew why: Captain John Freedman. Though he'd tried to initiate some talk, he had been cut off when some locals had come by, fishing lines in hand, heading for a nearby creek to catch some fish.

Jim had been frustrated, as the rest of their day had been devoted to getting to Garcia's fortress without detection, then to timing the guards' movements. Using long-range binoculars, they'd sat for hours marking down the times and memorizing them. In a way, he was glad they'd had a chance to acquaint themselves with the way Garcia's world ebbed and flowed. It would definitely work to their advantage.

Jim's mind swung to Laura, then back to dwell momentarily on his kiss with Pepper. He'd seen the desire in her wonderful blue eyes—and the tears. Why tears? That had eaten at him nonstop all day. He swore to himself that once they were safe, he would corral Pepper on that very subject, and they would have a long, in-depth talk, whether she liked it or not. Did she think he was one of those men who took and ran? he wondered with disgust, then caught himself. After all, wasn't he? Right now he wasn't at all sure of what might exist between him and Laura.

Scowling at his own confusion, he looked down at the dials of his watch. It was 0200. Time to spread the pheromone. Pepper had volunteered to do it. He would stay, watch and, if necessary, speak to her in a low tone through the headset to alert her of any unanticipated guard activity. So far, everything on the plantation seemed to occur in twenty-minute increments, and Pepper would use that time gap to spread the pheromones away from the area where they wanted to climb the fence. Jim wondered how his arm would handle the physical demands to come. At least Pepper had done a good job of binding the wound tightly so it wouldn't break open and start bleeding.

Jim gave Pepper a hand signal. She nodded, her mouth a tight line as she slowly rose and straightened. With her camouflage utilities and greasepaint, she blended perfectly into the surrounding jungle. The pheromones, Jim knew, were in unbreakable vials in the cartridge belt around her waist.

At the last second, as Pepper carefully stepped by Jim, she felt his hand grip hers. Halting, she stared down at him, shocked by his action. His hand was strong, grasping hers almost painfully. She met his burning, narrowed gaze and swallowed convulsively. She couldn't deny the look in his eyes or the expression on his face. Verbal communication was out at this point, except in dire emergency. But everything about Jim's expression said, "Be careful.'' Pepper nodded and tried to smile, but didn't succeed. Instantly, he released her hand, a satisfied look replacing his searching one.

Her heart pounding hard, Pepper made her way down the easy slope. Though shaken by Jim's unexpected touch, she tried to shove the feeling aside and concentrate on each step she took. Luckily, the brush and trees had been cleared away from the fence, so it was easy to move along it once she arrived at the bottom of the slope. Digging into her cartridge pouch, as quietly as she could, she took out the first container. Moving quickly, avoiding a few small branches, she began spreading the pheromone, placing a drop here and a drop there in an unmistakable path. She knew she had twenty minutes to cover the fence line up to its northernmost point.

Trying to control her ragged breathing, her eyes riveted on each place she set her boots, Pepper continued distributing the scent. Soon she knew she was out of sight of Jim, but somehow she could feel his presence as surely as if he was at her side. It was an incredible feeling, one that gave her confidence to rival her fear, though she knew that one misstep could bring the guards' fire. She could die here.

Jim waited anxiously, his only contact with Pepper the sound of her soft breathing via the headset. He had worried that she might break a branch and cause a snapping sound, but she didn't. An incredible sense of relief overwhelmed him when he saw her move like a shadow back to his position. Sweat glistened on her brow. The humidity was near saturation, and rain was imminent.

Reaching out, Jim gripped Pepper's arm and offered a tight, swift smile to convey his relief, and his pride in her efforts. She reached out, briefly touching his shoulder in acknowledgment, then moved to his side, waiting.

The guard appeared, right on time. Pepper watched with fascination as the Doberman with him picked up the scent of the pheromone. Instantly the big black-and-brown male lunged sharply against his leash—in the direction of the pheromone. Pepper felt like a statue, watching with her eyes, controlling her breathing, not moving a muscle. The guard and his dog headed north. Pepper could see the quizzical look on the guard's face but was relieved to observe he was willing to let the dog follow the scent.

Five minutes passed, and Jim gave the hand signal to move out. The fence was their next challenge, but with Jim at her side, Pepper felt a bizarre sense of confidence. They moved slowly, deliberately, their eyes and ears keyed. A breeze startled the palms, which began to clack noisily. The unexpected sound made Pepper's pulse jump, and she touched her chest in reaction. Jim moved ahead, a mere shadow in the night. She admired his stealth as he approached the fence. But would he be able to scale it with his injured arm?

Despite the fence's imposing height, Pepper saw Jim grab the solid iron bars and hoist himself upward. He groaned softly and stopped. Pepper moved into position beneath his feet, bending over so her back became a platform. When his boots made contact, she grabbed a bar to steady herself. She heard Jim choke back a sharp sound as he made a final lunge, pushing hard against her back. She glanced up to see that he'd made it up and over the fence. Getting down would be easier than hoisting himself up.

As Jim eased himself to the ground, Pepper could see the pain in every line of his face. Her gaze automatically went to his arm, covered by the torn sleeve of his utilities. Had the wound opened? If it had, the bleeding could begin again, and the scent of blood might alert one of the dogs.

As she worried, Jim gave her the hand signal to scale the fence.

Pepper found the iron barrier fairly easy to climb, so she concentrated on remaining noiseless. Jim's hands wrapped firmly around her waist as she slid down on his side of the fence. But as soon as her feet touched the ground, he eased his hands away, and she felt bereft. Did he realize just how much she needed his touch? Pepper glanced up at his shadowed face and found care and anxiety in his eyes. For her? She doubted it, knowing how he felt about Laura, who could soon be within reach.

Pepper and Jim remained close together as they headed into the heavy jungle cover, making their way along the quarter-mile route to the plantation. Luckily, although street lamps lined the white gravel road leading to the house, few lights were placed elsewhere. Jim thought Garcia's arrogance might have given him an exaggerated sense of safety, so that he hadn't lighted up his house. Lucky for them.

Jim's every sense was excruciatingly heightened as he led Pepper through the maze of brush and trees toward the house. The breeze began again, rattling the hundreds of swaying palms growing among the rubber trees. He tensed as he spotted a guard moving slowly past the front of the plantation. Feeling Pepper's light touch on his shoulder, he glanced to his left and saw her glistening features and the fear in her eyes. He understood that fear. They had exactly half an hour to slip inside that house, locate Laura and get her out.

So many questions reeled through Jim's mind. What if Garcia had forced Laura to sleep with him? Then the drug lord would have to be disabled. A blinding, hot anger rose in Jim, and he knew without a doubt he could happily take out the bastard with a shot to the head, if he'd touched Laura.

A sharp, cracking sound emanated from the right. Jim froze, his hand automatically going to his Beretta. The wind had risen, gusting sharply, and the smell of rain surrounded them. He watched as the guard halted, turned and looked in their direction. A limb of a rubber tree fell with a *thunk* no more than a hundred feet from their position. Jim's heart rate skyrocketed, but he didn't move a muscle. The guard started toward them.

Pepper's eyes rounded as she saw the guard move. Oh, no! Luckily, the wind was still in their favor, so the dog with him wouldn't scent them. A second strong gust of wind made another branch crack and give way—on the other side of the house. The guard stopped and looked in that direction. With a shrug, he pulled his guard dog back and continued his normal path around the house.

Pepper closed her eyes, pressing her hand against her heart, which felt like a drum threatening to beat right out of her chest. She felt Jim relax and glanced at him. He was wiping sweat from his upper lip, his eyes remaining narrowed and watchful. She felt suddenly shaky and realized it was the aftermath of an adrenaline surge. Locking her knees, she stood very still, concentrating on not making a sound.

They moved closer. The southern entrance to the plantation was supposed to lead to the kitchen. They moved to that side of the house, protected by the darkness, and moved swiftly toward the door. The information they had from the CIA mole laundress had indicated that the kitchen entrance was the only one with no laser beams or warning device attached to it, because of heavy traffic in and out that door during the day and into the evening.

Let it still be so, Pepper prayed. She saw Jim reach out,

his gloved hand almost caressing the brass knob. Tensing, she waited. Her breath jammed. Her eyes narrowed. Jim slowly twisted the knob. The door opened! Pepper expelled her breath in a relieved sigh.

Miraculously, she found herself inside the darkened kitchen with Jim, who shut the door as quietly as he'd opened it. Looking around, she realized the room was set up like a restaurant kitchen, with huge pots and pans hanging over commercial appliances. Everything was stainless steel, clean and glinting dully in the pale moonlight. Trying to steady her breathing, Pepper followed Jim across the tiled expanse. So far, so good.

Their plan was to take the kitchen stairs to the second floor sleeping area. But were guards stationed inside the house? They didn't know. Pepper watched as Jim drew his Beretta and held it ready in his left hand. Their weapons had muzzle suppressors and silencers, so if they did have to fire, there'd be less chance of detection.

She drew her own weapon, locked and loaded it, and held it ready in an upraised position in her right hand. The door leading out of the kitchen revealed a sliver of dimly lighted, carpeted hallway. Seeing no one, Jim pushed on the door. It squeaked. Pepper froze. Jim eased it open just enough for them to slip through. Watching the hall, the silence in the house deafening, Pepper moved toward the stairs.

Luckily, they were carpeted, too, but the two of them climbed slowly, listening for telltale creaks. At the top, they faced another door. This time Pepper took out a small can of oil and applied it to the hinges. As she stuffed the container back into her web gear, Jim nodded his agreement. He got down on one knee and slowly eased the door open. The expanse of carpeted hall, lined with valuable paintings, was blessedly empty.

In his mind, Jim visualized the blueprint of the second floor. As he moved soundlessly through the doorway, pressing his back against the opposite wall, his gun held ready, he knew that the second door was the one they'd tagged as most likely to be Laura's room. What if it wasn't? What if— He savagely stopped himself. First things first. Try the second door, the prison room.

Pepper joined him, and they inched toward the door. Once there, Jim tried the knob. It was locked. Sweat poured down his body. Outside, he heard the wind rising and the first pings of rain on the roof tiles. Good, it would provide excellent cover—*if* they could find Laura and escape. His breathing was chaotic as he bent down and, ignoring the pain in his arm, jimmied the lock. He heard a distinct click and froze. The sound might waken whoever was inside. He prayed it was Laura.

Pepper swallowed hard against a dry throat. Raising her weapon, she watched Jim straighten. His gloved hand moved to the knob. He twisted it. The door opened! Her heart rate skyrocketing, she kept her focus on the door. Would it creak? Awaken the person inside? Give their position away? Her hands tightened around the butt of her weapon.

The door swung open easily. Moonlight streamed into the room, and Jim saw filmy curtains over windows covered by bars. He slipped into the chamber, every muscle in his body rigid with anticipation. Pepper entered behind him quietly closing the door. Straining to see, he spotted a canopied bed to the right, and his breath caught. Someone was in the bed, all but a twisted sheet thrown aside against the muggy night.

Pepper remained at the door as a guard, watching him move soundlessly toward the bed and its occupant.

Jim moved slowly up beside the bed. His eyes widened.

A lock of blond hair spilled across the sheet. It had to be Laura! He'd recognize that color anywhere. Holstering his weapon, he leaned closer. It was Laura! She lay with her back to them, curled tightly, the sheet up over her shoulders. How beautiful and untouched she looked, Jim thought as he swiftly placed one hand on her shoulder and the other across her mouth.

Laura jerked. Her eyes flew open. Instantly, she convulsed, terror in her expression.

"Ssh! Laura, it's Jim Woodward!" he hissed, his mouth close to her face. She struggled momentarily and he saw the horror in her eyes, felt dreadfully sorry he had to waken her like this. It took a moment for his words to filter through her panic. Then she stopped struggling. The sheet had fallen away, revealing her slender form covered by a long, pink-silk nightgown. Easing his hand from her mouth, he smiled a little.

"Are you okay?" Jim wasn't sure she was. Her eyes didn't look quite right, he thought, and her skin felt clammy.

Laura sat up, fear etched in her expression. She looked at Jim and then toward Pepper, in shadows near the door. Automatically, her hand went to her lips.

"Jim? Is it you?" Her voice trembled. "Oh, God, am I hallucinating again?"

He grinned tightly. "It's me, Tiger. And we're no hallucination. This is real. We're real. We've come to get you out of here." He touched her tousled hair, then her cheek, with trembling fingers. His heart flared with anguish. "Are you okay? Are you hurt?"

Tears welled up in Laura's eyes and streamed down her cheeks. "Jim, it's really you," she quavered. Awkwardly, she threw her arms around his shoulders.

Groaning, he held her momentarily. They didn't have

time for this. "Laura, listen to me," he urged in a low, ragged tone, "you've got to get dressed." His eyes darted to his watch. "We've got twelve minutes before the guard comes around again. Can you walk? Are you hurt?" he repeated.

Laura sniffed, fighting tears. "Y-yes, I'll live." She climbed out of bed, obviously shaken and uncoordinated.

"Get some clothes on," Jim coaxed. He watched her closely. Something was wrong with her. He saw it in the jerky way she opened the drawer, in the terror-filled look in her eyes. The moonlight illuminated bruises on her arms and around her throat. Just what the hell had happened to her? He stopped the questions before he could voice them. Glancing at Pepper, he motioned her over.

Pepper moved swiftly to Jim's side, holstering her weapon.

"Help her get dressed. I'll stand guard at the door," he ordered gruffly.

She nodded. For the first time, she got to meet the woman Jim loved without question. Laura was petite in comparison to her, and Pepper quickly saw how Jim could fall in love with her. In person, Laura Trayhern was beautiful in a delicate, almost-fragile way. Her blond hair, disheveled but still lovely, fell around her face, and her cheeks were flushed pink. But the woman was so obviously shaken that the slacks she'd retrieved from the dresser fell to the floor.

Pepper quickly retrieved them and handed them to her. "Thanks," Laura quavered.

Holding her finger to her lips to warn her not to speak, Pepper saw the woman nod shakily that she understood the silent command. Pepper forced herself to listen for other sounds. The rain was pinging sharply against the windows of the room now, and the wind continued to rise.

Good. All of that was to their advantage. Laura was trying
to hurry, but she fumbled with her clothes. Pepper
grabbed a green tank top, helped Laura pull off the silk
gown and threw it aside. Completely naked, Laura
reached for the slacks.

Pepper glanced over her shoulder. Jim wasn't looking.
All his attention was on the door and the dangerous possibilities on the other side of it. Returning her attention to
Laura, Pepper again could see why Jim would like her.
Despite having had two children, the woman was in wonderful shape. Climbing into the slacks, Laura took the tank
top from Pepper, pulled on a pair of cotton socks and slid
into a sensible pair of leather shoes that Pepper had found
in the walk-in closet.

Jim glanced at them. Nine minutes; it was going to be
close. Maybe too close. As he opened the door, he felt
Laura come up behind him, her hand tentatively touching
his shoulder. Pepper would bring up the rear. Opening the
door, he looked both ways. Nothing. He moved in one
swift motion across the hall to the stairway door. Laura
followed unsteadily. Shoving that door open, Jim moved
sideways, and Laura joined him in the stairwell. Pepper?
He anxiously looked back toward the hall. She was locking the door. *Hurry!* he urged silently.

Pepper turned on her heel and moved quickly to the
door he held open for her. She saw the anxiety in Jim's
eyes, and her gaze automatically went to Laura, who stood
with her arms wrapped protectively around herself. She
was physically trembling, and she didn't look very steady
on her legs. There was more light here, and Pepper could
see an oddly waxen quality to her skin, and dark, almost-
purple circles beneath her lovely eyes. What kind of torture had she endured? Pepper found her anger surging as

she reached out and slid her arm around Laura in support as they made their way down the stairs.

After checking the downstairs hall, they slipped back into the kitchen. Eight minutes. Again Jim took the lead, opening the door to the yard. A gust of wind almost ripped it out of his hand. Cursing inwardly, he used his body to hold it in place, after making sure no guards were around. With his injured arm, he signaled Pepper sharply to come on through.

The rain was falling with stinging force, the wind gusting and ebbing. Pepper kept an arm around Laura as she watched Jim move rapidly toward the rear of the house. Seven more minutes before the guard came by. Breathing rapidly through her mouth, she felt Laura sag against her suddenly. Alarmed, she turned and saw that the woman was semiconscious. With a strangled sound, Pepper again holstered her weapon and grabbed Laura's right arm, pulling it up over her shoulders. She moved her own left arm snugly around her small waist and hitched the woman close against her.

Jim signaled for them to follow him. Luckily, Laura was a featherweight, Pepper thought as she half dragged, half carried her across the lawn to the jungle. Once under cover of the trees, she relaxed a little. Still, Laura's feet were dragging, making noise.

Jim turned at the sound and realized Laura had fainted. Pepper was practically dragging her. Damn! Was Laura drugged? Hurt? Moving back to them, he quickly examined her, discovering several needle marks on both of her arms. Alarm soared through him.

"She's been drugged," he rasped, his voice shaking with fury.

"I'll carry her."

Jim was about to protest, but realized it would be stupid

not to agree to Pepper's plan. Laura probably weighed less than a hundred and ten pounds soaking wet, but he couldn't carry her with his injured arm. He nodded brusquely, signalling that he'd help Pepper lift her over her shoulders in a fireman's-carry position.

Pepper lowered herself to one knee, knowing that that position was the easiest and safest way to carry a person, putting the bulk of their weight across the strength of the carrier's shoulders. But how long could she actually carry Laura? she wondered. There was a vast difference between lugging sixty-pound packs and hefting a live human weighing more than a hundred pounds. Still, she had no choice. She was grateful when Jim helped maneuver Laura's limp body expertly across her shoulders. Now it was up to her.

The wind was strong, slapping at them, and rain slashed at Pepper's face as she slowly got to her feet. Time was of the essence. She knew that a Coast Guard helicopter, flown by a woman lieutenant commander named Storm Gallagher, would meet them on the beach at exactly 0400. It was now 0325. They had to hurry. They hadn't counted on Laura being injured.

As Pepper began to walk with her burden, Jim stayed next to her. The wind and rain covered her mistakes as she moved awkwardly forward. The cold rain fell in sheets, and Pepper shivered despite the heat she was generating with the effort of carrying Laura. Rain dribbled down her face, blinding her, and if it hadn't been for Jim's guiding hand gripping her elbow, Pepper knew she would have fallen.

The fence! Pepper was never so glad to see anything in her life. As they lowered her to the ground, Laura became semiconscious again. Jim moved around and took her in his arms.

"Laura!" he growled. "Laura, wake up!"

Pepper knelt nearby, seeing the anxiety and care burning in Jim's eyes as he spoke. He touched Laura gently, almost like a lover, and it hurt Pepper to her soul. She had been right, after all. Jim loved Laura—still. Pepper tasted salt and realized it was her own tears.

Laura sat up, encircled by Jim's arms. "I'm so groggy," she whispered, touching her brow. "I—I'm sorry. I can hardly think, hardly walk...."

"I know, Tiger, I know. Look, we need you awake. We have to climb this fence. We can help, but you've got to help us, too. Do you think you can do it?"

Laura shivered. "I'm so cold, Jim. And I'm dizzy."

"I understand, honey. But you have to help us. Can you?"

She nodded, her hair tangled and dripping around her face. "I'll try, Jim...."

"That's my Tiger," he said, hoisting her to her feet. She was none too steady, but Pepper was there, helping keep her upright. Jim led Laura to the fence and turned to Pepper.

"Let me use your back to get up there. Once I'm on top, help push Laura, and I'll pull her up and over." He grimaced. "Somehow."

Pepper nodded. She made Laura lean against the fence for support as she waited for Jim to get started up the fence. Once he did, she moved into place beneath him. His muddy, booted feet struck her back, but she stayed steady. With one leap, he made it to the top of the fence, and Pepper was glad for her height. She was able not only to maneuver Laura onto the wrought-iron fence, but to push her upward. Jim caught Laura's outstretched arms, and Pepper knew what it cost him in terms of pain to gently lower her to the ground on the other side.

Laura managed to stand when her feet hit earth, and
Jim slipped off the top, leaping down beside her. Pepper
was next. The wrought iron was slippery from the rain.
She knew any minute now the guard could return and
catch them. Grunting, she hoisted herself up the fence, her
arm and shoulder muscles straining.

A howling bark broke through the rain and wind. Pepper gasped. She heard Jim curse solidly. Scrambling, jerking a glance to her left, she saw the guard—and the dog.
The Doberman had been released and was hurtling toward
her! Anxiety shot through her. She saw Jim push Laura
to the ground and pull out his weapon.

Just as she clambered to the top, gunfire ripped through
the dark night. A bullet struck the iron inches from her,
and sparks flew in all directions. She saw Jim returning
fire, but knew he couldn't aim left-handed, so could offer
only temporary cover at best. She had to get off the fence!
Adrenaline pumping, Pepper had no choice but to leap.
More bullets whined around her. Shoving off, she bent
her legs. She hit the muddy ground off-balance. The soil
gave way. Tucking, she rolled several times to minimize
the force of her landing.

Jim fired again and again keeping the guard pinned
down. The Doberman leapt out, snarling, its white fangs
bared as it tried to bite at them through the fence. Jerking
around, Jim saw Pepper slowly getting to her feet.

"Grab Laura! We've got to make a run for it!"

Pepper spun drunkenly toward them, the carpet of dead
leaves turning slippery beneath her boots. She grabbed at
Laura, who was already heading toward her. Their hands
met, and Pepper shoved her ahead, using her own body
as a protective shield for the woman. Her breath came
in gulps as they scrambled into the dense, surrounding
brush. *Jim!*

Pepper turned momentarily. The firing had stopped. He was hurrying toward them. Good, he wasn't wounded! So many thoughts and feelings careened through Pepper as they climbed the slope of the hill. On the other side was the beach where Commander Gallagher would be picking them up. What time was it? Pepper didn't take even a second to look.

In moments, Jim joined them, gasping loudly from the exertion. He grabbed Laura's other arm, and together they propelled her quickly up the hill. Jim's muscles burned from the exertion. Worriedly, he watched Laura. They were moving too fast for her. Her legs were like rubber. She kept falling, and they could do little more than drag her upright between them. At the crest of the hill he slid his left arm around Laura's waist, and told Pepper to do the same with her right. Together, they could hold Laura firmly enough to prevent her from falling down the slope.

The wind continued gusting, but the rain had stopped. Jim looked back. He thought he heard voices, shouting. He knew the guard had radio communications and was sure the entire fortress was now awake. It wouldn't be long before they were found. They had to hurry! Through the darkness of the trees, he could see the white sand beach. But where was the helicopter?

His mind reeling, Jim realized that if that Coast Guard helicopter didn't arrive exactly on time, they could all be dead. It wouldn't take Garcia long to discover where they were. He heard Laura gasping for breath. Glancing left, he looked at her. She was semiconscious again. Damn! Pepper's face was glistening, her mouth set, her eyes narrowed on their objective. Pride exploded through him for Pepper. What a courageous woman she was. In that moment, he felt such deep, startling emotion that it brought tears to his eyes.

Pepper kept her head, staying cool and calm under some terrible circumstances. Jim expected such a response from himself and from other men under his command, but he realized belatedly that there were women with those necessary ingredients, too. With a shake of his head, he realized how much Pepper was broadening him, awakening him to the huge potential women possessed. Laura's courage was no less impressive, though it came in a different form. She was drugged, maybe beaten, yet she wasn't crying out or hysterical. No, in her own way, she, too, had that bone-deep courage. He felt proud of both of them.

"Look!" Pepper cried, realizing too late that she'd broken the communications silence. Out at sea, she saw the red and green, blinking lights of an aircraft rapidly approaching.

Grinning, Jim nodded. He gave Laura a reassuring squeeze. The slope leveled out, and they hit the white beach at a jog. The sand was thick, sucking, and it slowed them down. But the knowledge that the Dolphin helicopter bearing the white-and-orange colors of the Coast Guard was landing made him dig in and work harder. Pepper did the same.

The wash from the blades kicked up sand everywhere. Bowing his head against its fury, Jim dragged Laura forward. Never had an aircraft looked so good. The door slid open, and a crew member reached toward them. Jim saw the helmeted heads of the two pilots in front. Turning, he released Laura into the capable hands of Dr. Ann Parsons, dressed in a bright orange Coast Guard flight uniform. He glanced back toward the hill. Still no sign of Garcia or his men.

Turning, Jim focused on Pepper, who had helped Laura into the helicopter.

"Get in," he ordered.

She nodded, climbing in swiftly.

Jim was the last to board. As soon as the door was shut and locked, the chopper lifted off smoothly, heading skyward, away from Nevis Island. The cabin lights flashed on and Jim blinked in the sudden brightness.

To his alarm, he saw Dr. Parsons, a helmet on her head, talking rapidly to the pilots. He looked down. Laura was unconscious. Pepper's eyes were wide with fear. Jim frowned. What was going on? He wasn't hooked on the cabin intercom with the pilots and the doctor. His confusion turned to terror as he saw Parsons lift Laura's neck and tip her head back so that she could breathe properly.

"Something's wrong!" Pepper cried.

Jim managed to turn around in the small area. He threw off his own headset and grabbed a pair of headphones patched into the cabin intercom. He moved around until he was on the other side of Laura, opposite the physician.

"What's going on?" he demanded.

Parsons gave him a swift look as she placed her hands on Laura's chest. "She stopped breathing. Do you know CPR?"

Shocked, Jim stared. Laura's face was waxen, her lips parted, her skin so translucent he could see the small veins showing in her eyelids. "I—yes…" *Oh, God, no!* His mind spun as he took a position near her head, ready to breathe life-giving air into her body.

"She's been drugged!" he told the doctor, as she started to press hard and fast on Laura's chest.

"Probably cocaine," Parsons snapped. She turned to the pilots. "Tell them to stand by. I've got a woman with a drug overdose coming in. She's stopped breathing."

"Roger, Doctor," Command Gallagher replied calmly. "We'll alert the *Falcon.*"

Jim bent over, breathing into Laura's slack lips. Of all people, she couldn't die. She just couldn't! Tears leaked into his eyes, ran down his cheeks as he coordinated the CPR with Dr. Parsons. He'd never expected this. Laura couldn't die!

Pepper remained out of the way, an unwilling witness. The vibration of the helicopter warred with her feelings. Jim was crying. In that moment, with Laura's life hanging by a precarious thread, Pepper was stunned by the depth of his emotions. The way he cradled Laura's head, the gentleness of his touch, the wildness in his eyes all confirmed his love for her.

Exhausted and anxious, Pepper could do nothing. She felt ridiculously helpless, but CPR didn't require a third person. Below, the dark ocean kept disappearing behind wispy, low-lying clouds. In the distance, she briefly spotted the lights of a huge Coast Guard cruiser. She prayed for Laura's life. The woman didn't deserve what had happened to her. She looked so fragile, so broken lying on the helicopter's cold, metal deck, her life in the hands of a man who loved her unequivocally, and a doctor whose expression told Pepper she wasn't about to lose her patient.

Chapter Nine

When they'd landed safely on the *Falcon*, Pepper stayed out of the way. She crowded tightly against the bulkhead, allowing a medical team to take Laura off the helicopter. Dawn was barely breaking, a silvery ribbon along the horizon for as far as she could see. Lights flooded the aircraft, making Pepper squint as she crawled out after the others. One of the pilots slid open the small window.

"Hold on, I'll take you down below. They've got officers' quarters waiting for you."

Pepper nodded. The pilot was a woman, and Pepper smiled to herself. It was good to have women in all phases of military life. She watched her disembark after shutting down the aircraft, then followed her across the deck.

Pepper felt incredibly tired and drained. All she wanted was a hot shower and sleep. Her heart was on Laura, though. Would they get her breathing again? Would she live?

"I'm Pepper Sinclair," she said, extending her hand to the woman pilot.

"Storm Gallagher. You look like hell."

"I've been through it."

Gallagher laughed huskily. "Yeah, I know. We monitored your transmissions on the way in. I'll bet Garcia's fit to be tied right now. Serve the bastard right. If that Dolphin I flew came with bombs, I'd dearly love to drop them on him. Come on, we'll go into this hatch."

Pepper followed blindly, barely noticing the activity around her. The roll and pitch of the *Falcon* tipped her off-balance more than once. Waves from the passing storm were three to four feet in height and the sky above them continued to threaten. No sooner had they ducked inside the hatch than the rain began again.

"Where are they taking Laura Trayhern?" she asked as they made their way down a narrow passageway.

"Sick bay. We've got a Coast Guard physician on board in addition to Dr. Parsons. Good thing that woman is an emergency-room specialist. Why do you think Laura stopped breathing?"

Pepper halted when the pilot did in front of a dark brown, mahogany door. "I think she'd been shot up with a drug. Probably cocaine, since that's what Garcia traffics." With a shake of her head, she added, "If she was, I don't know how she managed to get dressed and make it as far as she did before she fainted on us."

Storm nodded gravely. "Adrenaline does wonders."

"You're right." Pepper smiled tiredly at the woman and held out her hand. "Thanks."

Gallagher grinned and shook it firmly. "Any time. I'll let Colonel Woodward know we've taken care of you. I sure hope Mrs. Trayhern makes it. Helluva break. If you get hungry, the chow hall is on Deck Three, just below us.''

Pepper nodded, watching Storm move briskly down the narrow passageway. Opening the door to her quarters, Pepper prayed they could get Laura to breathe on her own. An awful feeling in the pit of her stomach refused to leave. Quietly, she closed the door behind her and looked around. The quarters were small, spare but clean. A set of lockers lined the bulkhead, and another door led to the head, where she was sure a shower was located.

With tired movements, Pepper climbed out of her muddy, rain-soaked gear, leaving it in a heap by the door. Every muscle in her body cried out for sleep. Moving slowly, she found the shower stall and turned on the faucets. In no time, steam rolled through the small area and she gratefully stepped in. The water pummeled her, heating her chilled, shaking body, rinsing off the last of the greasepaint from her face.

Pepper recalled how wonderful a shower always felt after she'd been out for days at at time fighting a forest fire. There was nothing like it. This time, instead of cool water, however, she wanted it as hot as she could stand it. The washcloth lathered with soap scrubbed away at the sweat, the mud and the dirt. Her hair became squeaky clean, hanging limply around her face. Finally, she shut off the faucets. The towel was large and thick. Pepper realized her movements were becoming jerky from letdown. The feeling was familiar—she'd experienced it many times after coming out of a raging forest fire where her life had been in jeopardy.

She dragged herself from the bathroom to the small bunk that served as a bed and pulled back the sheet and light blue spread. The rolling of the ship was lulling her now. With a groan, she towel-dried her hair, lacking the strength even to comb out the tangled strands.

Lying down on her side, Pepper pulled the covers tightly across her shoulders. She could no longer hear the rain, only some distant sounds of the large engines that powered the ship. Her last thoughts as she drifted off to sleep were of Jim and the stark terror carved into his features as he bent over Laura on the deck of the helicopter. His eyes had telegraphed a burning anguish—something she'd never seen in them before. Only true love could wrench such emotion from such a controlled man, Pepper suspected. As sleep closed in on her, she said a prayer for Laura's life.

Jim struggled with bone-deep exhaustion coupled with a drowning array of emotions. He sat alone with Laura, his hand on hers. She was waxen and unmoving, but she was alive, thank God. Dr. Parsons had undoubtedly saved her life in the very room where he now sat. Laura's hand felt cold, and he gathered up her limp fingers, hoping his body heat would somehow transfer itself to her.

His mind was spongy, his feelings clamoring to be acknowledged. As he stared down at Laura's serene features, Jim realized the depth of his caring for and loyalty to her once and for all. But she was a friend, not a lover. Rubbing his face harshly, he wearily took in a breath of air. Maybe he'd underestimated his long-ago feelings for Laura—and maybe he had still been carrying something of a torch when this mission had started. But looking at her now, Jim knew for certain that he didn't love her in the romantic way he'd wondered about.

New feelings crowded his heart now, and they were vibrant and stunning as he sat, pondering them in the silence. Before, Jim had attributed them to Laura, thinking they'd been triggered by her unexpected kidnapping. But now he knew differently. The feelings in his heart had been aroused by Pepper walking into his life.

"You've done all you can," Ann Parsons said wearily, touching his sagging shoulder.

Jim stirred. He straightened a little in the chair and removed his hand from Laura's. Parsons' touch reminded him how exhausted he was. His gaze had never left Laura, who was finally breathing on her own again. The two doctors had battled nearly fifteen minutes to get her heart started.

"I'd rather stay, Doctor."

Ann shook her head. "There's nothing else to be done. We have her on an IV, Colonel. Her heart is working well. Dr. Thompson and I will watch her like hawks, believe me. You need to rest. You look like you're about to fall down."

Wasn't that the truth? "Will she stop breathing again?" he asked.

"I hope not. But we have no way of knowing how much of whatever drug was shot into her. The ship has a small lab, and they're testing her blood right now. I'll know more shortly."

Anger surged through Jim, despite his exhaustion. "I don't know how she managed to get up and dress herself." He searched the doctor's blue eyes.

"I don't, either. Sometimes when your life is in danger, you can override a drug reaction for a while. Laura did. She wanted to escape, to live." Ann shook her head and rubbed her brow. "There are at least five needle tracks in her arms. Garcia must have had her on drugs from the time he captured her."

Jim clenched his fists. Laura still looked wan, but her skin was no longer gray. Even her hair looked washed out beneath the fluorescent lights of the sick bay. Dr. Thompson, a Coast Guard physician in his late thirties, tended Laura, ever watchful. Jim turned his attention back to Ann.

"Thanks for saving her life, Doctor. I'm glad as hell you were out there to meet us."

She nodded. "You weren't too shabby in the clutch, either, Colonel. Come on, I'll show you to your quarters. They're right next to the ones Pepper was assigned, on Deck Two."

Pepper. Jim halted. He scowled and followed the doctor out of sick bay and down a series of passageways that led to a stairway that would take them topside.

"Does anyone know how she is?" he asked as they climbed the stairs. The ship was rolling fairly heavily now, and he had to grip both railings.

"No. I think I'll check on her," Ann said as they made it to the second deck.

Jim glanced out the hatchway window. The rain was coming down in torrents, and the once-azure Caribbean had turned steely gray, with small whitecaps. He drew abreast of the doctor, who was still dressed in the bright, red-orange flight suit.

"Let me check on her, Doctor."

"No problem. If she needs any medical attention, though, call me?"

"I will." Jim saw her point to a door.

"This is yours for the duration of the trip, Colonel. Pepper's cabin is next door."

"Thanks." He watched the doctor move off and saw Commander Noah Trayhern appear at the other end of the passageway. Since he was captain, he had to stay on the bridge, though Jim was sure he wanted to be down in sick bay watching over Laura. He saw the doctor stop and begin to talk with him.

Still worried about Laura, Jim opened the door to his quarters. As he shed his clothes and took a scaldingly hot shower, he felt the last of the adrenaline ebbing away. He dried off and dropped the towel on the bunk. Someone had left him a one-piece, dark blue Coast Guard uniform, and he climbed into it. First he wanted to look in on Pepper, then he'd go get something to eat, check on Laura, then hit the sack.

Stepping back out into the passageway, Jim felt the ship rolling and balanced himself by placing his hands along the bulkhead as he walked. Stopping at the door to Pepper's cabin, he knocked loudly enough for her to hear, but got no answer. He waited. He knocked again. Nothing. Worried, he opened the door and stepped inside. His mouth stretched into a tender line as he saw Pepper in her bunk, sleeping deeply.

His heart started a slow pounding as he shut the door and made his way over to her. Jim lowered himself to one knee, steadying himself with a hand on the edge of the bunk. How fragile she looked in sleep. Her face was pale, much paler than it should be, he thought. All the usual pink had been washed out of her freckled cheeks. And the darkness beneath her thick, lowered eyelashes was obvious. He lifted his other hand and lightly touched her tangled hair. How he wished he could be here when she woke up, to take a brush and smooth those strong, silken strands.

A sudden memory of their heated kisses flowed through him, momentarily easing his various aches and pains. Barely touching Pepper's hair, careful not to waken her, Jim smiled. She lay on her left side, her knees drawn up, the blanket and sheet tightly wrapped around her. The

desire to slide into the bunk with her was almost overwhelming. Right now, he needed Pepper more than he
ever could have imagined possible.

Allowing his hand to fall back to his side, Jim slowly
got to his feet, convinced Pepper was fine. All she needed
was eight to twelve hours of uninterrupted sleep, and
she'd be in good shape. Before he left, he picked up her
dirty gear and took it with him.

Pepper awoke slowly. Where was she? The sounds
were strange. The motion was, too, until she groggily remembered she was on the Coast Guard ship. As she
slowly sat up, every muscle in her body screamed in protest. Shoving her hair back out of her eyes, she sat there,
assimilating her surroundings. The gentle rocking motion
was comforting. As she came fully awake, the memories—the danger—all flooded back.

How was Laura? The question spurred her out of bed.
She located a Coast Guard uniform in the locker and put
it on. Luckily, she also found the toiletry articles she
needed, and quickly combed her tangled hair into some
semblance of respectability and brushed her teeth. Pepper
didn't look too closely at herself in the mirror. But what
she saw, she didn't like. Her skin looked pasty, and dark
circles lay under her eyes. Well, didn't she always look
like this coming off a five-or ten-day fire?

Her heart moved back to Jim, and the pain nearly overwhelmed her. She had to find out how Laura was. Her
stomach growled ominously. Looking around, she found
a clock on the desk that was bolted to the deck. Six p.m.
Impossible! They had landed on the ship at 0500. Had she
slept that long?

Getting directions from a crew member outside her
quarters, Pepper headed directly to sick bay. Looking out

the round hatch windows, she noted it was dusk. The sky was clear, the ocean smooth as glass. She ignored the dramatic red sunset as she moved stiffly down the stairs that would take her to the lower deck. She prayed Laura wasn't dead.

Pepper entered sick bay, a large room in comparison to her quarters, and a corpsman on duty greeted her.

"Mrs. Trayhern? Is she alive?" she blurted.

"Yes, ma'am."

Relief flooded through her. "Thank God," she whispered, touching her heart. "May I see her?"

"Colonel Woodward is with her right now, ma'am. It's a pretty small area, so it gets a little crowded in there."

Pepper hesitated. Her heart bled at the information. Jim was with Laura. What else had she expected? "Oh, okay…" She felt a sense of anguish, mingled with an odd relief. Why? Was she glad that Jim loved Laura? It was just as well he did love her, she told herself sternly. She must have been crazy, allowing herself to get so emotionally caught up with him in the first place. It had to have been the heat of the mission that had allowed her carefully constructed walls to fall into such shambles—that had allowed her to actually consider the possibility of her relationship with Jim going beyond the professional experience they'd shared. Now it was time to get back to reality, before she lost her heart for good. Pepper frowned, hoping it wasn't too late already…. John's unexpected death had taught her the hard way that her heart could never withstand such pain again. Never again would she surrender to such overwhelming emotion without the balance of rationality.

But why had it been so easy to say no and not get involved romantically with men until now? Pepper had no answers. The corpsman was looking at her strangely, so she tried to appear more alert.

"Dr. Parsons doesn't want Mrs. Trayhern to have too many visitors right now," the corpsman continued placatingly. "Perhaps if you went to the galley for dinner and came back after that?"

"Sure." Pepper's hunger was gone. Tears flooded her eyes and she swallowed. Jim was with Laura. As she quietly shut the sick-bay door, she wanted to sob, but didn't. Why was there so much pain in that realization? After all, John had been her life. Her soul. Her only experience with love.

"How're you feeling, Tiger?" Jim smiled and reached out to grip Laura's hand, which lay across her blanketed body. She looked very weak, her skin still translucent, her eyes cloudy.

"Jim...it's so good to see you." Laura cleared her throat, her voice raspy. She tried to squeeze his hand but couldn't muster the strength.

He leaned over and placed a chaste kiss on her brow. "I gotta tell you, you look a little better now than when we found you at the plantation."

"Plantation?"

"Yeah. You remember, don't you? Garcia kidnapped you?"

"Wait..."

Mentally, Jim kicked himself. Dr. Parsons had warned him about hitting Laura with too much information too soon. Sometimes cocaine—which they had verified through lab tests was in her bloodstream—could wipe out certain events in a person's memory. He squeezed her hand. "Let me begin at the beginning," he told her quietly. "Stop me if I give you too much information too fast, okay?"

Laura felt chilled. Desperately, she looked up into Jim's face. "I haven't seen you for such a long time. The last time I remember was when we had lunch in Fairfax, at the Bicycle Club."

Relief raced through him. "Yes, that's right, Tiger, we did." He sat down on a chair and faced her. "Do you recall anything of the last couple days, Laura?"

"I…" She touched her head. The IV in her arm made it difficult to move. She looked around the room and then back at him. "Something terrible happened, didn't it?" Her voice was tremulous.

Jim stroked her hand in an effort to soothe her. He heard a noise behind him and looked around. Commander Noah Trayhern stood there. He was tired, his face lined with worry and his gray eyes burning with concern. Nodding to him, Jim turned and watched Laura carefully. Would she remember Morgan's brother?

"Laura, how are you?" Noah came around to the other side of the bed. He touched her shoulder and looked at her closely.

"Noah." Laura managed a weak smile. "What are you doing here?"

Noah traded a glance of alarm with Jim.

"Her memory will come back," Jim assured him. "As the drug wears off, everything will come back, from what Dr. Parsons said."

"I see." Noah looked down at Laura. "How are you feeling?"

"Awful. I'm cold."

Jim released her hand. "Let me go ask the corpsman where I can get another blanket for you."

"Thanks," Noah said, his voice filled with raw emotion.

Jim returned a few minutes later with two more blankets. The corpsman had assured him that the chills Laura was experiencing would eventually go away. Together, Jim and Noah tucked the warming covers around her. He was relieved to see some of the cloudiness leaving her eyes. How terrible it would be if the drug erased her memory completely. Laura still hadn't remembered that Morgan and Jason had been kidnapped.

Jim felt he should leave. Laura had an established rapport with Noah; he was much more present in her life than Jim was. Besides, it was obvious Noah was upset over the events. Jim moved to the side of the bed.

"Listen, I'm going to grab some chow, Laura. You're in good hands here with Noah. I'll come back later, and we'll talk, okay?"

Sleepily, she nodded. "Sure. Thanks..."

Jim smiled. "See you later, Tiger." As he left sick bay, he wondered if Pepper had slept off the worst of the mission. He'd gotten some solid sleep, but his worry over Laura's condition had forced him up after six hours.

Going down to the galley, he was surprised to spot Pepper there. She was sitting alone at one of the bolted-down tables, a tray before her with a little food on it. She didn't see him. She seemed immersed in looking down at the coffee cup she held between her thin hands. Jim's heart thumped hard to underscore the vibrant feelings she brought out in him. Her hair was combed, softly framing her face. Color was back in her cheeks, and he breathed a sigh of relief. He went through the chow line, loading his tray with food.

"How are you?"

Pepper's head snapped up. Jim's voice was low, intimate. Her eyes widened as she saw him sit down opposite her. His smile was warm, and his eyes burned with that same caring light.

"Jim…"

"Didn't expect to see me?" he teased, cutting up a pork chop.

"Well—I…"

"How are you feeling?" He saw Pepper's cheeks flush red. She couldn't quite hold his gaze, and he wondered why. Her hands fluttered nervously over the coffee cup.

"Like something the cat dragged in," she muttered under her breath.

He pointed toward her tray with his knife. "Have you eaten anything?"

"No…not much."

Between bites of food, he asked, "is this the way you are after coming off a forest fire?"

Touched by his insight, Pepper dabbled with her meat disinterestedly. She should eat, she knew, but her stomach was tied in a terrible knot of grief. Jim looked unscathed by the mission. His hair was clean and combed, his face freshly shaven. His eyes glinted with their usual intelligence.

"Oh…I'm usually worthless for about two days when we come in from a fire," she admitted finally.

"I never realized the demands on you," he murmured. Why was Pepper so nervous? Her fingers trembled when she picked up her spoon and ate a bit of the canned peaches on her tray. Growing serious, he said in a low tone, "You're an incredible woman. I want you to know that, Pepper." They had shared so much in such a short amount of time. Those kisses that had nearly led him into making love to her still burned brightly in his memory, and his body responded to the thought. Now that he'd freed himself of confusion about his feelings for Laura, his uncertainty about Pepper had cleared up. A desperation to let her know how much she meant to him made him hope for an opportunity to talk with her honestly about so many things.

Pepper shrugged, not daring to meet his eyes. His voice, low and gritty, shone through her like blazing sunlight. "We both pulled our share of the load." She glanced up. "How's your arm?"

"Fine. Once Dr. Parsons got Laura stabilized, she checked it out and gave your work her seal of approval."

"How is Laura?" Pepper picked up her coffee, sipping it, and met his eyes for the first time.

"She's going to make it, thank God." Jim frowned. "The only problem is she doesn't remember anything about the kidnapping. Nothing." With a shake of his head, he muttered, "Noah's down there with her now. I think he'll probably break the news to her about Morgan and Jason."

"At least she's going to live. That's everything. I don't know Noah that well, but he seems so gentle. He's probably the right person to break it to her." Sighing, Pepper looked around the room. It was beginning to fill up with off-duty crew. The noise level rose, the laughter in direct opposition to how she felt.

"No disagreement there." Jim saw the shadows in Pepper's eyes but wrote them off as being due to the mission. "You still haven't said how you are."

With a shrug, she took a bite of the chicken on her tray. "Okay."

"I'm discovering that you tend to use that word as a cover-up."

Pepper stared at him. His voice was low with concern. When she looked into his eyes, she was instantly wrapped in that incredible warmth he exuded. Her heart squeezed with such pain that she felt the sting of tears in her eyes. Instantly, she forced them back.

"Well?" Jim prodded.

"I'm just a little sore, that's all," she hedged, her voice huskier than usual. "And tired. I'll be glad to get home."

Jim scowled. "Home meaning Montana?" He wanted time with her, dammit.

"Yes. It's snowing there now. It's a beautiful time of year up in the mountains."

"I see...."

"I imagine Laura's going to need a lot of emotional support and help from friends and family to get through all of this," Pepper said. "I'm glad she has you."

"Yes, she's going to need help." Dammit! Jim dawdled over his dessert of baked apple with vanilla sauce. So much had happened that he hadn't thought much beyond Laura's unexpected health problem. Pepper was right; she would need friends and family now more than ever, and he had every intention of being there in that capacity for her. Worse, Pepper would be leaving.

"What are your plans for returning to Montana?" he demanded.

Pepper heard the slight edge of anger in Jim's voice. Why? "When we get to D.C., Marie will put me on the next plane out."

With her simple words, Jim lost his considerable appetite. The last thing he wanted was for Pepper to leave, but even if she stayed, he'd be too busy to spend much time with her, between his job at the Pentagon and remaining in Laura's life until her husband and son were found. *If* they could be found, he reminded himself grimly. There was no telling what Laura's freedom would mean to Morgan's situation. The drug lords could kill him outright. There were so many unknowns. And no answers.

Looking up, he met and held Pepper's luminous gaze. She looked as if she were going to cry. Frustration ate at him. Those tears again. And again, this wasn't the time or place to ask about them. Damn. "So what does a smoke jumper do during winter? There can't be many fires."

"As a Hotshot team, we're always on standby. Sometimes we get calls from the Southwest—California and Arizona in particular—and we go fight a fire for them." Pepper set her tray aside and grabbed the heavy white mug that contained the last of her coffee.

"What else do you do?"

"We repair our equipment, I put my team through training seminars and, in general, we rest up. There's a lot to do in other ways, believe me. We aren't sitting in Montana twiddling our thumbs."

He grinned a little. "I know you ski."

"Yes, mostly cross-country, anymore." She stopped for a long moment, recalling that it had been a good two years after John's death before she'd put on a pair of downhill skis.

Sliding his own tray aside, Jim sipped at his coffee, deep in thought. "Do you realize we missed Thanksgiving?"

"I know…it's one of my favorite holidays."

"Oh?"

"Yes." She gazed down at her cup. "I always go home for it—to Anaconda."

"Family means a lot to you, doesn't it?"

Pepper lifted her head. "Sure. Doesn't it to everyone?"

He shrugged. "Nowadays, I think a lot of people have

lost their sense of family togetherness. Not that it's anyone's fault. It just happened."

"I'll probably make up for my absence by taking a few days off when I get back and going home to see my parents."

"They can't know anything about this mission. What will you tell them?"

"A white lie. I'll tell them a friend of mine got into trouble on the East Coast and I flew back to help her."

"That's painless," Jim conceded. He ached to have long, exploring conversations with Pepper. "So what are your other favorite holidays?"

She roused herself, trying to fight her inner pain. "Christmas. I love it. I go home then, too. My grandparents live in Billings, and as old as they are, they drive over for the week if there's no blizzard in progress. Cam and Molly and their kids come home, too. We have a great time. I just love seeing the kids, playing with them, building snowmen and stuff like that."

The warmth in Pepper's eyes made Jim want to rail against life in general. Her voice had such a velvet quality to it, and her love for her family touched his heart as few things ever did. He saw new life in her eyes, and he longed to share that with her. If only he could. If only...

"Well, we're due in Miami in two days," he said in a low voice. "I hope we get to share more times like this, Pepper."

Startled, she sat up. "Like what?"

"Talking with you." He frowned. Why did she look incredulous, as if she didn't really believe him? Was the ghost of John Freedman still standing between them? Probably. Jim no longer cared. One way or another, he was going to replace that ghost from her past.

Nervously, Pepper stood up. "If you'll excuse me, I want to go see Laura, if I can."

He nodded. "Okay. I'll see you later."

Laura was sleeping when Pepper stopped to see her. Too restless to go back to her cabin, Pepper went up to the bridge, where she found Noah Trayhern. Though Noah wore the same dark blue uniform as everyone else, it was obvious he was in charge. His carriage, his low, commanding voice and the way the crew members on the bridge responded showed that. Pepper liked the officer. He was easygoing yet firm. She liked to think she was that way with her team, too. It was obvious Noah's crew not only respected him, but liked him—a rare combination.

When he spotted her, Noah stood up and offered her his captain's chair, with the best view on the ship. Huge windows framed the entire area, giving everyone good visibility. "Have a seat."

"Thanks." Pepper slid into the chair. From here, she could see the dark expanse of the Caribbean. Above, thousands of stars seemed quilted into the velvety sky.

"How about a cup of fresh coffee?" Noah suggested, gesturing to one of the crew to get it for them.

Pepper nodded. "Thanks, I could use it. I came up here to find out how Laura is doing. Colonel Woodward said you were just with her."

Rubbing his jaw, the officer leaned against the console and faced her. "She's making good progress physically. Her memory is spotty, though. I just had a talk with Dr. Parsons, and she said that gradually Laura should remember everything."

Pepper took the white mug offered to her, with thanks. Noah took the other proffered mug and sipped the coffee thoughtfully. "I'm just glad the worst is over for her," she said.

"In one way it is, and in another way it isn't," Noah murmured. "Dr. Parsons examined her thoroughly and told me Laura had been raped."

Stunned, Pepper sat very still, the mug resting in her hands. "Oh, God, no…"

Grimly, Noah rasped, "If I *ever* get my hands on Garcia, he's a dead man."

Shaken, she whispered, "That's terrible. She's already got her own private hell she's going to have to deal with."

"Yes, and I just talked to Perseus. They still don't have a line on where Morgan or Jason are." Frustration was evident in his voice. "I'm having a tough time with this whole situation. I knew Morgan going into a security business like this would make him enemies, but I never envisioned it turning into such a can of worms."

"At least," Pepper said hesitantly, "Laura has her family—and Jim."

"Yes, she's got that," he admitted. "I'd like to stay behind and be with her, but I can't. I have a Coast Guard ship to run. I wish I could…."

Reaching out, she touched his broad shoulder. "You've done more than most people could have already, Noah."

He took her hand and squeezed it warmly. "Without you, this mission wouldn't have been a success. Jim told me what happened, how he injured his arm too badly to be of much help." He looked straight into her eyes. "I'm just glad you were in place, Pepper. I have to admit, I had my doubts about your qualifications, but you've convinced me. Jim's right—you're one very special woman. One hell of a role model, to boot."

Pepper felt heat spread across her face, and she knew she was blushing. Noah's hand was warm and strong. She released it and said, "Jim is giving me too much credit. Without his experience, I wouldn't have been able to pull this mission off, Noah."

The captain cocked his head and studied her in the building silence. "No, I don't think he has. I think Jim sees you very clearly. I don't think you always see yourself and how much you accomplish on a daily basis as a smoke jumper."

"Maybe not," Pepper hedged, unaccustomed to all this praise. "I have a job I love. It combines everything I ever learned in life, and I can use it all."

"I know what you mean," he murmured, satisfaction in his tone. "I love what I do in the Coast Guard, too."

"From what I can see, you've got the best of all worlds. You have a wonderful wife who obviously adores you, kids and a great job."

He laughed a little. "I do. I'll be the first to admit it. Kit is something special to me. She's my life, my soul...." He gave her an embarrassed look. "Kit and I met at a real bad time in her life. I fell in love with her immediately, but she was gun-shy of me."

Pepper nodded. "You're a lot like Colonel Woodward, though."

"Oh?"

"He has that same warmth, that humanity about him that you have."

"I guess he does, only he hides it a lot better than I do." Noah chuckled.

Pepper became glum. Somehow, for the next two days, she was going to have to hide how she really felt about Jim. If only she could get off the ship earlier. She knew she had to fill out a report at Perseus, but after that, she was free to resume her life as it had been before—without Jim.

"Noah?"

"Yes?"

"Is there any way to get off the *Falcon* earlier than two days from now?"

"Noah?"

"Yes?"

"Is there any way to get off the island before then? Two days from now?"

Chapter Ten

"Laura? I'm Pepper Sinclair...." Pepper extended her hand to the woman who lay on the hospital bed, covered with blankets. Laura's eyes were half-open, red-rimmed. It was 0700, and Pepper wanted to talk to Laura before catching a flight to Miami with Commander Gallagher. Her heart went out to the pale woman, her skin still translucent. But it was her eyes that most touched Pepper's heart. They were filled with tears. As their hands connected, she felt Laura's cool, damp one weakly wrap about hers.

"Hi..." Laura whispered. "I'm so glad to finally meet you. Jim and Noah have had nothing but praise for you...for helping me, for saving my life. Thank you...."

Pepper squeezed her hand gently and released it. She watched as Laura shakily raised her other hand and brushed the tears away. "I'm glad I was able to help,

Laura.'' She moved uneasily. ''I'm sorry, I've come at a bad time.''

With a half smile quirking one corner of her mouth, Laura whispered, ''No, you didn't. It's just the memories....''

''They're starting to return,'' Pepper said empathetically. She saw the terror in Laura's blue eyes and wanted to help, but didn't know how. Helplessness seized her. ''I just wanted to touch base with you. I'm hopping a flight in a few minutes. I guess I just wanted to wish you the best in an awful situation.''

Laura closed her eyes and sniffed. ''Thank you, Pepper. Wh-when things are better, I want to spend some time with you. I—I don't really remember very much about your rescuing me.''

''You don't have to,'' Pepper whispered unsteadily, her throat closing with tears. The woman's husband and son were still missing, yet she was attempting, despite her own pain and horror, to keep up a conversation. How unselfish she was. Touched beyond words, Pepper gripped her hand gently once again, ''Just get well. Maybe in six months or so, when things have settled down, I'll call you and we'll talk.''

Laura opened her eyes. ''I'd like that, Pepper.''

Releasing her hand, Pepper moved away from the bed. ''Goodbye,'' she quavered, and she turned on her heel, fighting her own tears. Outside sick bay, she halted in the passageway. Quickly wiping the moisture from her eyes, she glanced around, relieved that no one had seen her crying. Her last—and worst—visit was going to be with Jim. He didn't know she had managed to wrangle a lift on Storm's helicopter, which would be leaving shortly. When she'd gotten up earlier, Jim had still been asleep in his quarters.

A part of her didn't want to face him and hoped, as she climbed the ladder between decks, that he would still be sleeping. That was the coward in her talking, Pepper thought, as she moved down the passageway. Of course, part of her very much wanted to see Jim. But what was the use? He'd spent every waking moment in sick bay with Laura. And Pepper couldn't blame him. Laura was a beautiful person—from the heart outward.

Her hands suddenly damp, Pepper stopped outside Jim's cabin and knocked. No answer. Again she knocked. Still no answer. She had no idea what time he'd gone to bed last night. For all she knew, he may have spent half the night with Laura. If so, he'd be sleeping deeply now.

She took a deep, shaky breath. Going to her own quarters, she quickly penned him a note. Fighting back tears for herself—for a future she'd unwillingly gotten a brief glimpse of before knowing with jarring reality that it would never be hers—Pepper finished writing her goodbye. She folded the paper and gently pushed it beneath Jim's door. When he woke up, he'd find it.

Outside, she could hear the helicopter warming up, the blades *whapping* in the early morning air. Hurrying forward with her small duffel bag, she left the main deck of the Coast Guard cutter. She'd seen Noah already and thanked him for his help and hospitality. As she moved outside to the damp, almost-cool morning, Pepper saw the pale pink horizon dotted with a few puffy clouds, but she was in so much personal pain that the beauty of it didn't really register on her senses.

A crew member opened the Dolphin helicopter door, and Pepper climbed on board. She found a place to sit on the cool metal deck behind the two pilots, then leaned against the bulkhead and closed her eyes. She didn't want to say goodbye to Jim. The burning sensation around her heart moved up her throat, and Pepper's hand came up to cover the area. Choking back a sob, she heard the engine of the Dolphin deepen. In moments, the helicopter broke contact with the deck of the cutter, and they were airborne.

Jim stumbled to his feet, his eyes bleary and slightly puffy. What time was it? He glanced down at his watch as he moved toward the head. It was 1000. He'd overslept. With a shake of his head, he twisted the knobs on the shower to get the water running. He'd been up with Laura until almost three this morning. The memories had started to come back, and she had verged on hysteria. There'd been no way he was going to leave her to battle her demons alone.

Jim didn't feel at all good this morning. He needed a long, uninterrupted sleep to recover from the grueling pounding he'd put himself through on this mission. After a hot shower, he shaved and dressed in a clean, dark blue Coast Guard uniform. His heart cried out for Pepper—for her nearness. Because of Laura's continuing crisis, they hadn't had the time together he'd hoped for. If Dr. Parsons hadn't given Laura a tranquilizer at 0300, Jim knew he'd have been up all night instead of just half. He and Noah had arranged to take turns with her as she regained her tortured memories, but the captain had more-immediate responsibilities, so Jim had shouldered most of the load of remaining with her.

Not that he minded, but his heart was torn. He knew the time he spent with Laura now would ultimately help stabilize her and help her cope. Last night, she had recalled the rape with vivid clarity, and he'd cried with her and held her, wanting so much to protect her from that pain but not being able to. Soon enough she would remember the kidnapping—and the fact that Jason and Morgan were still missing. He wasn't sure which would be more devastating to her.

Grimly, he glanced in the mirror long enough to comb his short, dark hair. There were circles under his eyes, which were bloodshot from too little sleep. He looked like hell. He felt like hell. What he really needed was Pepper's company. She had been like a serene angel through all of this. More than once he'd seen her with Noah. She was an easy person to talk to, Jim realized. And in her own way, he acknowledged, she was there for Laura and him—only at a distance.

He made up his bunk and turned to go out into the passageway. First he would get some chow, then he'd visit Noah and, finally, go see Laura. A flash of white on the deck caught his attention as he opened the door. It was a folded piece of stationery. He leaned down and picked it up.

Standing half in his quarters and half in the busy passageway, Jim opened the paper. He frowned and his eyes narrowed as he read the message:

Dear Jim:
By the time you get this, I'll be gone. I knocked twice on your door this morning, but I guess you were sleeping pretty hard. I'm hopping an early flight to the mainland this morning. I wanted to say goodbye, but I guess this note will do.

I don't feel my presence on the cutter is necessary. I'm pretty wrung out by the mission, and right now home looks good to me. It's a place to heal. To forget. Goodbye…

Pepper

"Damn!" He folded the note, turned on his heel and hurried up to the bridge. Noah was standing at the window with a pair of binoculars when Jim opened the hatch door to the area.

"Where's Pepper?" he demanded, slightly out of breath.

Noah lowered the binoculars and looked at him. "She left at 0700 this morning with Commander Gallagher." Glancing at his watch, he said, "They'll arrive at the Miami Coast Guard station after a refueling stop in the Bahamas."

His heart beating frantically in his chest, Jim stood, feeling a terrible pain in his gut. A bitter taste filled his mouth. "Did you see her this morning?" he asked, his voice strained.

Noah placed the binoculars on the console. "Yes." He searched Jim's face carefully. "Pepper finally did get a chance to introduce herself to Laura this morning before she left."

"Why did she leave?"

Noah shrugged and returned his attention to the islands in the distance. "She said she felt useless around here and that it was best if she went home early."

With a shake of his head, Jim crossed his arms against his chest. "I should have spent more time with her...."

Noah cocked his head. "Is there something between you two? Not that it's my business, but—"

"Yes," Jim admitted abruptly, "there is." Or more accurately, should be. "She shouldn't have run...."

"Pepper didn't say much, but as she walked out to the helo deck, she looked pretty upset."

Jim compressed his lips. "How upset?"

"She looked as if she was crying, but I couldn't really be sure," Noah said quietly.

Jim took in a ragged breath. "I've really screwed up."

"Reading between the lines," Noah volunteered as he sat down in the captain's chair, facing Jim, "I think Pepper feels you care a lot for Laura."

"Of course I do," Jim rasped. "She's been a friend for more than seven years."

Holding up his hand, the officer said, "That's not what I mean. Pepper said something odd to me when we were eating dinner in the galley last night." He frowned. "She said she understood why you could love someone like Laura, even if it was at a distance."

Suddenly the conversation they'd had back at his condominium deluged Jim. He was thunderstruck. "Pepper must think I'm still carrying a torch for Laura!" What a fool he'd been. And of course, it would look that way to her. After all, he'd spent every possible minute at Laura's side, helping her cope, being there to support her through her horrible trials. Why hadn't he realized Pepper might see his attention toward Laura differently?

"I guess," he said, pain in his tone, "Pepper could interpret my time with Laura that way."

"Very easily," Noah said. "I didn't help things, either. I told her how close you two were." With a grimace, he added, "I probably helped nail your coffin closed on that one without ever realizing it. I'm sorry."

Frustration ate at Jim. He was even more torn now. "Laura needs continued support. I can't just pick up and leave, even if I want to." He was talking out loud, more to himself than to Noah. "Pepper will probably skip Perseus, grab a flight out of Miami International and go straight home. At lunch yesterday, I could see how much she wanted to get back there. When she spoke about snow in the Rocky Mountains, she got tears in her eyes. And she's looking forward to spending Christmas with her family in Anaconda.''

Jim wanted to cry himself. Pepper had completely misinterpreted his relationship with Laura. Hadn't his hot, branding kiss on the island told her something? His touching her intimately, almost loving her? Had it meant so little to her? No, Jim cautioned himself, he couldn't be angry with Pepper. She might have thought the kiss and his intimacy were due to nothing more than the intensity of the moment. What she didn't know—and what he hadn't ever communicated to her—was that he didn't take what they'd so explosively shared at all lightly. For him, it had been a promise of a future exploration of their relationship. But obviously Pepper didn't know that.

"I just talked to Dr. Parsons," Noah said, interrupting Jim's tortured thoughts. "She gave Laura a mild tranquilizer and is down there with her now." His eyes showed agony. "We've all focused so much on Laura that I think we forgot to check how Pepper was feeling. That was a rough mission, and I'm sure she still has a lot of emotional baggage to sort out from it. I know when my wife, Kit, was an undercover cop, she would go through hell after a dangerous bust. It was important for me to be there for her through those times." He sighed. "I'm afraid Pepper needed us, but we weren't there for her."

"I wasn't there for her," Jim agreed guiltily, a lump in his throat. "You're right—Pepper needed care, too, and I didn't give it to her."

"It wasn't anyone's fault," Noah said, placing his hand on Jim's slumped shoulder. "The situation was unique. I don't think any of us could have done much differently even if we'd been aware."

"We could have done a lot more. *I* could have." Jim felt such a bitter sense of loss that he wanted to sob. Had he lost Pepper entirely? Was there any hope for them? Her note hadn't been signed. "Your friend" or "Love." But what did he expect? He'd practically ignored her since they'd completed the mission. The mistake he'd made was in thinking that their kiss had sealed a promise for their future.

With a shake of his head, Noah murmured. "Ever since this kidnapping, the whole Trayhern family has been in a state of shock. We've been running around like a bunch of lemmings." Scratching his head, he said, "I think we've got to get a handle on our emotions, whether we want to or not. I know my parents are beside themselves over what's happened. My sister, Alyssa, and her husband, Clay, are coming in off a top-secret assignment and they're waiting to hear if Perseus or the Pentagon can get a lead on Jason or Morgan. They're going to take thirty days' leave to be here and help out."

"That's good," Jim said sincerely. But it didn't solve his problem. They had another day-and-a-half sail before they reached Miami. Then he would fly north with Laura and Dr. Parsons. "What are you going to do with Laura once she's home?"

"I've been in contact with a rape-crisis center in D.C., and have been referred to a woman psychologist who will work with her. Killian definitely thinks Laura and her daughter shouldn't go home until after we've located Jason and Morgan."

"Good idea," Jim said. "Ramirez and Garcia could strike again, to get even with us for rescuing her."

"You'd better believe it." Grimly, his eyes narrowed, Noah scanned the nearly smooth expanse of blue-green water. "Garcia and Ramirez have been albatrosses around our family's neck for a long time. Now it's coming down to the wire. It's them or us." His mouth flattened. "And

I'll be damned if the Trayhern family will pay the price again, to this country or otherwise. We've lost so much. We got it back when Morgan returned to us but now it's been taken away again in a different way.''

Jim felt the deep emotion behind Noah's softly spoken words. He saw the anguish in the officer's expression. No one was more aware of the Trayhern history than he, because of Laura's involvement. No, of all people, this family didn't deserve to suffer this kind of attack. ''As soon as we get Laura established, I'll be back at the Pentagon,'' he offered. ''Maybe, with some luck, we'll pick up more satellite transmissions.''

Noah brightened slightly. ''You were responsible for this one, and it turned out to be a good lead.'' He ran a hand through his close-cropped hair and, shifting gears, said, ''It's none of my business, but what are you going to do about Pepper?''

Jim exhaled. ''Wait, I guess. I can't just drop everything and go to her. I was lucky to get leave for this mission. My superiors aren't about to let me go again so soon. Besides, I want to try to locate Jason and Morgan. I think I can do it, given some time.''

''Maybe,'' Noah said, ''time is what Pepper needs right now, anyway. She needs to get some distance on what happened. Hopefully, she'll realize why you had to spend so much time with Laura. It wasn't love but loyalty.''

''I hope,'' Jim whispered, ''she sees exactly that, but I'm not counting on it.''

''Go get some chow,'' Noah urged.

Jim didn't feel like eating, but he knew he had to. Leaving the bridge, he headed for the cutter's bottom deck, but his mind and heart were on Pepper. How was she feeling? What was she feeling? Had he made up this idea of something strong growing between them?

Noah was right, Jim decided. Time could be his friend. But it could be his enemy, too. Somehow, he had to figure out a way to let Pepper know she was part of his life. Some kind of foundation had to be laid so she understood that his kiss had been the seal of a new relationship—not something taken from her in a stolen moment.

"Hey, Pepper!" Joe Conway stood at the door to the cavernous structure where they laid out and folded the smoke-jumping parachutes.

Pepper raised her head. She was at one of the tables, refolding one of her chutes. It was lunchtime and the rest of her team was over at the chow hall. Their smoke-jumping facility was a few miles outside Phillipsburg, next to the small airport there.

Joe looked at her expectantly. "What?" she asked shortly.

"You aren't going to believe it, but in the middle of this snowstorm, a florist truck pulled up. Phillipsburg doesn't have a florist, so this guy must have come all the way from Anaconda, the poor bastard. Bad day to be driving." He flashed her a happy smile and opened the door with a flourish.

Frowning, Pepper saw a man bundled in a heavy wool coat and hat carrying a large, long box under his right arm. He was an older gentleman, with silver in his hair. He removed his hat and thanked Joe for opening the door. Then Joe, her second in command, pointed at her. Joe was tall, brash and only twenty-eight, full of Irish blarney right up to his dancing green eyes and black hair. Was this a trick? He'd been known to pull plenty of practical jokes, especially at this time of year, when things slowed down and got a little too boring around the camp to suit him.

The older man stepped up to her, his hat in one hand,

the mysterious box in the other. He smiled, his brown eyes crinkling with warmth as he nodded at her. "Are you Ms. Sinclair?"

"Yes." Pepper watched him break into a wide smile.

"I got this special order at our shop in Anaconda." Chuckling, he said, "I gotta tell you, the roads are pretty slick out there. That snow's fallin' faster than the plows can remove it." He offered her the large box. "These are for you."

Though completely puzzled and still wary of a trick, Pepper accepted the box and thanked him. When he'd left, Joe wandered over.

"What's inside?" He peered at the box, placing his hands behind his back.

"I don't know." Pepper took a pair of scissors and cut one of the tight plastic straps that held the box together.

Joe raised his thick, black eyebrows. "Secret admirer, huh? I knew something special was going on while you were mysteriously gone that week."

"Quit," Pepper ordered, as she snipped the rest of the straps.

Chuckling, Joe shoved his hands in the pockets of his Levi's and rocked back on the heels of his jump boots. "You were awful down and quiet when you got back." He gestured to the box. "Must have met some dark, mysterious stranger wherever you were and fallen in love with him. Maybe that's why you were so hang-dog lookin', huh?" His eyes glinted with teasing.

Pepper held on to her irritation. Sometimes Joe could make her split her sides with laughter. But today wasn't one of those days. This first week back home had been a special and unexpected kind of hell for her. She had tried to forget Jim's kiss and his words, which haunted her dreams each night. They were torrid dreams, unfulfilled dreams that made her wake with an ache in her lower body. Shooting Joe a dirty look, she growled, "For once your Irish blarney is totally wrong." Setting the scissors aside, she opened the box. Her eyes widened. The fragrance of roses wafted upward, and she inhaled deeply.

"Hmm," Joe murmured, leaning over, "looks like this Irishman is right—again. Too bad I didn't put money on a bet. I could've taken you for a real ride on this one, Sinclair. Red and yellow roses. I'll bet there are two dozen in there."

"Get out of here," Pepper said lightly, matching his teasing tone. Her heart was pounding, not from Joe's prophecy, but from her overwhelming surprise at the gift. Her instincts told her it was from Jim. But was it? Or was it her silly heart in overdrive again, creating wishful, idealistic dreams that would never come true? Pepper saw Joe's mouth draw into a beatific smile of righteous pride. "You're such a know-it-all, Conway," she said dryly, waving her hand at him to leave.

Laughing heartily, he gently patted her shoulder. "Okay, boss, I'll leave you to savor the roses alone." He walked a few feet, then turned around. "By the way, who's the lucky guy? Does the team know him?"

Heat stung Pepper's cheeks. "None of your business, nosy. Why don't you go eat?" She put the top back on the box and went to her office. Joe was like a younger brother to her, but at times he was too curious and got under her skin. He had been especially curious about where she'd gone for a week and what had happened. Of course, Pepper hadn't told anyone, nor would she. As far as her smoke-jumping team was concerned, she'd taken a week's leave to go back East to visit an old friend, and that was all.

Joe raised his hand. "I hear ya, boss. Okay, I'm gone.

I'll eat an extra piece of apple pie for you. I hear Sally made us some. Bless her good Catholic heart. Too bad she's not Irish, but I love her anyway. Catch ya later...."

The door closed.

Pepper shook her head. "You're such a pain in the neck sometimes," she muttered, gently touching the roses. Opening the crinkly paper wider she discovered a pristine white envelope among the blossoms.

The past seven days had been bone-achingly lonely for Pepper. None of her friends, though glad to see her, had succeeded in filling the empty cavity in her heart that they'd once satisfied so easily. If only Jim hadn't branded her with that all-consuming kiss. Somehow he'd touched the depths of her soul and reminded her just what was missing in her life—a man she could love forever. But the price was too high, and Pepper knew it.

Her fingers trembled as she eased the envelope open. Inside was a small white card, which read: *From the heart, Jim Woodward.* Pepper stared at it for a long time, digesting his sentiment. It was vague, but at the same time, it wasn't. Needled, she forced herself to count the roses. Joe was right—there were twenty-four in all. Half were red, the others a buttery yellow. Their fragrance was heady, and Pepper suddenly laughed at the ridiculousness of it all. Here she was, tucked away in some of the most beautiful back country of the Rockies. There were near-blizzard conditions outside, with the temperature in the teens and the evergreens coated with a thick blanket of white snow. And she had two dozen roses. Beautiful, wonderful fragrant roses from a man she'd never dreamed she'd hear from again.

Pepper stopped at the Phillipsburg post office, part of her evening routine after getting off work. She expected very little mail—maybe some catalogs and certainly the perennial bills, but no personal correspondence. To her surprise, a long, business-size envelope lay in her box, thick and heavy. She stood in her colorful Pendleton jacket, a knit cap on her head and her gloves tucked under her arm as she examined the piece of mail. It bore no return address, just her name and address. The postmark, however, was from Washington, D.C. Her heart began a slow pounding of anticipation—and fear.

First the roses, which were out in her truck even now, with the heater running so they wouldn't freeze in this terrible snowstorm. Now a mysterious letter. Pepper jammed the envelope into the large pocket of her jacket, pulled up her collar and put her gloves back on. She would wait until she got home to read it. There was no doubt in her mind that it was from Jim.

As she drove slowly down Main Street, the town already wreathed in near darkness at four-thirty in the afternoon, Pepper tried to contain her wild imagination. She concentrated on driving, careful not to slide off into the ditch as she left the center of town behind. Two miles down the road, she turned left. A mile farther along the rutted, fir tree-lined road, now coated with ice, she was home. Pepper had built the cedar-log cabin herself over three years' time, with a lot of help from her smoke-jumper friends and her family. It had been a weekend project, and many memories of laughter and sharing had worked their way into her home as a result.

The cedar logs were barely visible in her headlights as she pulled into her driveway. Getting out, she tramped through the snow, the wind howling around her as she opened the garage door. Once she'd driven inside, Pepper shut off the engine, got out and shut the door behind her. She felt like a kid at Christmas with the huge box of roses under her arm and the letter in her pocket. Nudging off her boots at the door to the service porch connected to the garage, she went inside.

Her cabin was cool, so she laid everything on the kitchen table and went on into the living room. After making a fire in her Earth Stove, the environmentally benign wood-burning stove she'd installed for heating, she got up, dusted off her hands and went back to the kitchen. First she took the roses out of their box and arranged them in the largest glass vase she had. Inhaling their fragrance, she carried them into the living room and set them on the cedar coffee table.

Standing by the stove, feeling the first tendrils of heat from the newly made fire, Pepper carefully opened the thick envelope. Her heart thumped as she unfolded several handwritten pages. Jim's name, address and phone number were in the upper-left hand corner of the first page. Trying to still her pounding heart, she began to read the letter with an unexpected hunger:

Dear Pepper,

By now, you've got the roses I sent you. It's the least I could do, under the circumstances. When I found your note under my door on the cutter, it jolted me out of my narrow focus. I talked to Noah, and he told me you'd left. To say I was unhappy about your leaving the ship doesn't begin to describe how I felt.

There was so much going down after the mission that I lost my sense of balance. Laura's health, her nearly dying, scared the hell out of me. I was so worried about her that I forgot to think of you and how you might be feeling. I know you weren't wounded in the action, and you came through it with flying colors, but that doesn't matter. I should have paid more attention to your needs, whatever they might have been.

We went through a lot, you and I, in a very short, intense amount of time. And I went from almost disliking you to feelings that I can't begin to explain in the confines of this letter, Pepper. But first I want to say I'm sorry for ignoring you on the cutter. Looking back on it, I should have known better. I know what combat does to a person, and about the necessary letdown period afterward. You took the high ground, and whatever you were feeling, you didn't tell me.

I wish you had. I wish…so much. To say I'm feeling a little guilty is an understatement. We almost died on that island. If it hadn't been for your bravery and levelheadedness, we would never have gotten Laura out safely. And yet you kept to yourself. I asked Noah if you'd talked to him, and he said no. I'm sorry I wasn't there for you, Pepper. I should have been.

The roses are a way of apologizing to you. I wasn't a very good team member for you. Experiences like this bond people for life, and I felt that bonding with you on that island. I dropped the ball when Laura stopped breathing. So the yellow roses are asking you to forgive my all-too-human failings.

The red roses are to ask if there is a future for us. I know I have no right to ask that of you, but I meant what I said on the island. When I kissed you, you cried, and I never found out what those tears were about. I guess it was the wrong place and the wrong time.

I'm pretty busy here at the Pentagon right now. We still haven't got a lead on Jason or Morgan—

yet. I'm spending about sixteen hours a day working with the communications people, trying to ferret out something in all that worldwide traffic via satellite. When I'm not working, I'm exhausted and inevitably, you come to mind. Our conversations are like water to me, Pepper. I'm thirsty to hear what is in your mind and heart. I felt cheated when you left, but I don't blame you for going. I think I understand why you did. Or at least I hope I do.

Some night, if you don't mind, I'd like to call you. But it's your decision, not mine, to make. I've enclosed a self-addressed, stamped envelope. If you want me to call, just mail it back to me. I can't make up for what wasn't given to you, Pepper. Maybe, if you're willing, we can talk. I'd like that very much. I hope to hear from you. Take care.

Jim

Pepper released a small, shaky sigh. Jim's writing was far from legible, but she realized how he must have labored over the letter. There wasn't a single ink smudge, and she smiled a little. Once an officer, always an officer. The fact that he'd handwritten it instead of using a computer meant a lot to her. Fingering the return envelope, she wondered if she wanted to talk to him. After all, what was there to talk about? He loved Laura, not her. He spoke of the future, but what kind of future could there be for them?

Unhappily, she moved away from the stove and gently laid the letter on the coffee table, next to the roses. Her heart couldn't seem to settle down, nor would her flights of imagination. Looking out her front windows, she saw the snow thickening and blowing even harder. How lonely she'd felt until Jim's letter had come. But were his gifts nothing more than a request for atonement?

Turning, Pepper went to her bedroom to shed her dark green trousers and long-sleeved, tan blouse. She'd worn the official Forest Service uniform all day; now she wanted to relax in a far more feminine velour lounger of pale pink. Still, the cabin felt terribly empty, and as Pepper undressed, trading her uniform for civilian clothes, she wondered what it would be like if Jim were here, in her home. The mere thought made her shaky, her feelings raw and clamoring. She had to admit she wasn't sure she could control herself if he was here and kissed her as he had on the island—touched her as he'd touched her then.

With a shake of her head, Pepper wondered if she was getting winter fever early. Tomorrow she might mail back the envelope, but she was still uncertain. It would be a crazy move if she did. A desperate one.

Chapter Eleven

It was Friday night, and Pepper was wrestling with a ton of paperwork, mostly supply orders to replace equipment lost or damaged during the past year's fires. A headache lapped at her right temple and across her forehead, and she rubbed the area as she concentrated on filling out the government paperwork.

Her office was in a small niche within the parachute facility. It was six o'clock, a good hour past quitting time, and her mind strayed, as it so often did, to Jim. She felt nervous and edgy. Telling herself she was chasing a pipe dream, she'd given in and sent the envelope back four days ago, after three long weeks of resisting.

Closing her eyes, she rested her hand against her brow and sighed softly. Her emotions seesawed among euphoria, anger, helplessness and absolute fear. She'd never had this chaotic experience before, so she didn't know how to cope with it. It must be romantic love, she decided—the very kind of love Pepper had made her life-altering decision *not* to experience again after John died. Never again could she risk the pain that came from losing the one she loved. It just wasn't worth it. Her parents had a wonderful marriage—one they worked on continually. Neither of them took it or the other for granted. That was the kind of love Pepper had expected to share with John, but fate had decided otherwise. Now, at thirty, she had to remember why she'd made her decision not to get involved again.

Her office door was open just enough so she could hear the comings and goings of her team. Everyone had left right at five tonight. After all, it was the week before Christmas, and there were parties to attend, gifts to be bought and wrapped, places to go, people to see. Glumly, Pepper opened her eyes and frowned down at the piles of paperwork. The only person she wanted to see was Jim.

Out in the main room the outside door quietly opened and closed. But peering into the shadowy depths, Pepper saw no one. Her imagination?

"Stop it," she muttered, irritated with herself and her unrequited longing. "You are such a stupid idealist. The sooner you get this paperwork done, the sooner you can go home." Home to an empty cabin. Home to the silence. Loneliness gnawed at Pepper as if it had carved a wide swath through her center.

A noise, the sound of footsteps, caught her attention. Frowning, Pepper put her pen aside. Someone *had* come in the door at the other end of the facility. It was fairly dark, save for the emergency lights at the exits, and she didn't want whoever it was stumbling and breaking an ankle. The building was a huge Quonset hut from the Korean War era, made of corrugated aluminum. The floor was concrete, and the whole structure was large and empty, save for the area where parachutes were folded, hung and repaired.

Easing out of her squeaky leather chair, Pepper crossed to her office door and pushed it all the way open, sending a wide path of light into the gloomy building. She saw a shadow—a man, she thought—halfway to her office. Who was it? Pepper could recognize most of her crew by physical build, but this wasn't one of them. Still, there was something oddly familiar about this man, though she couldn't place him. Leaving her office, she moved down the wall to the main electricity supply. She flipped several switches and turned around to face her visitor.

Pepper's mouth dropped open. Her heart slammed against her ribs.

"Jim!" His name echoed oddly through the building.

Jim halted about fifty feet from her and gave her a strained, slight smile. "I'll give you this," he said, embarrassed, "you made me use all of my Recon training to find you." Looking around, his mouth stretching into a wider smile, he moved his gaze back to her shocked features. "This is one hell of a hole in the wall."

She could only stare. Had she gone crazy? Was this some kind of waking dream? Jim Woodward stood before her, a huge pot of bright red poinsettias in his hands. He wore comfortable-looking, dark blue chinos, leather hiking boots and a bright red flannel shirt beneath a well-worn leather jacket. How handsome he looked. How much she'd missed him. Pepper swallowed convulsively, meeting and drowning in his amused green gaze.

"Wh-what are you doing here?" Her voice cracked. Her palms were damp. Her heart was pounding so hard it made her voice wobble off-key. She saw Jim's mouth work into a tense line. Internally, she went on guard. Anger slammed through her, and on its heels, euphoria. Hunger for him, for the feel of his mouth on hers, flowed over her. How badly she wanted to fly into his arms and welcome him back into her life, like a thrilled and trusting child. But she was no longer a child, nor trusting of Jim—or herself.

"I got the envelope back," Jim said simply, slowly approaching Pepper. Despite the mannish Forest Service uniform she had to wear, he thought she looked incredibly feminine. Her dark hair was longer now, touching her shoulders and falling in soft folds around her face. He saw the shock, the denial, in her eyes. Was she glad to see him? He wasn't sure. He'd risked everything by coming to visit. An impending avalanche of fear was poised over his desire for her. Time hadn't dulled his need of her. Like a knife twisting hotly through his lower body, he hungered to kiss her soft mouth, to again slide his hand around the small, firm breast that fit so wonderfully in his palm.

Halting, he lifted the poinsettias. "I decided that what we had to talk about should be said in person, not via a long-distance phone call. Here, these are for you," he murmured. "It's Christmas, and I wanted to bring you something…." Holding the potted plant toward her, he wondered if Pepper was going to take it or not. Her face was devoid of color. Her cheeks, ordinarily pink, looked wan. As he eased out of the shadows, he saw stress around her eyes and mouth that hadn't been there before. Anger flashed in her eyes—toward him. Was the mission the reason for her gaunt appearance and the stress plainly etched in her lovely features?

He held the poinsettias between them. *Please, take them. Take them.* Inwardly, Jim believed that by accepting his small gift Pepper would also at some level be accepting him—even if it was a tentative truce. Rapidly changing emotions flashed through her eyes as she slowly looked down at the flowers and then up at him.

"Christmas—" Pepper choked. She felt justified rage. Jim loved Laura. So what was he doing here? "That's right, it's Christmastime, isn't it?" The poinsettias were large and healthy looking, the flowers bright red among the green foliage. They were beautiful.

"As a holiday, it's kind of hard to forget," he teased huskily. Were those tears in her eyes? The anger in them came and went along with a flash of desire—aimed directly at him. Jim's heart squeezed at the anguish in Pepper's eyes as she wavered, not sure if she should accept the flowers. Her gaze snapped back to his, her eyes wide and incredibly blue, the pupils large and black, belying the gamut of emotions she was feeling.

Jim stood patiently, knowing full well that Pepper could tell him to do an about-face and walk out of her life— forever. The thought was devastating, and every fiber of his being yearned to step forward, set the flowers aside and take Pepper into his arms, kissing her until she melted like hot butter, silkily permeating his body and soul.

Pepper wavered. "I—I just can't believe you're here." Her voice came out tinged with indignation, but her heart cried out for him, for his wildly sensual kisses, the unbridled passion they'd shared on the island.

"I can't, either."

She saw the irony in his eyes and heard it in his voice. It hurt to blurt out the question, but it had to be asked. "Why—why are you here?"

"I couldn't not be here," Jim answered honestly. A little of the anger in her eyes became banked and he saw the desire again, for just a fleeting moment, before distrust replaced it. *She still thinks I love Laura.* The realization was devastating. He lifted the poinsettias a little higher.

"Please take these. There are no strings attached, Pepper."

"I don't believe it," she rattled defensively. Oh, why did she ache for him like this? Need him so much? She couldn't even think of entering a romantic triangle. It was Jim and Laura, not she and Jim. Loneliness was better than heart-shattering pain.

Jim squelched his impatience. Pepper was right; there were strings attached to his gift of flowers. His lower body ached for relief—ached to love her fully. Wildly. With absolute abandon. As he stood, watching her distrust of him grow, Jim knew Pepper was above all a natural woman. She brought out every primal feeling and need he possessed. Right now, he felt more animal than human, longing to obey the impulse to claim her, make her his. The desire ate away at his considerable control like acid. Clearing his throat, he rasped, "The only thing attached to this gift is a dinner invitation." It wasn't a lie, but it wasn't the full truth, either.

"Dinner? That's all?" Pepper hated the waspish sound of her voice and saw the effect it had on Jim. Hurt showed briefly in his eyes before he covered it up with false cheer.

"That's it. Dinner." He urged her silently to take the flowers. If only she would give him a chance....

Robotlike, Pepper reached out and took the plant. The pot was large, and the colorful petals brushed her jaw and shoulders. "This is heavy!"

"I know."

Nervously, voice wispy and strained, Pepper suggested, "Let's take them to my office?"

Jim gestured toward the lighted area. "After you." He saw that the venetian blinds had been pulled to give her some privacy from the rest of the facility. Her personal space was small and cramped, typical of a government-run office, he thought. Several dark green, metal filing cabinets stood at one end. Even her desk was a military-issue gray metal. Opposite it, against the other end wall, was a twin-size bed stalked with several fluffy pillows and covered by an old but much-loved quilt. Jim studied the bed darkly. Pepper probably used it during the summer, when fires were frequent. He could imagine her falling exhausted onto it for a quick nap between fire calls, inundated by the demands on her time in her responsible position as team leader.

The bed appeared startlingly feminine in the confines of the otherwise stark office. The very real desire to reach out, take her hand and pull her over to that bed and love her was nearly Jim's undoing. No one would come into the facility at this time of night, he thought. And the blinds had been drawn for privacy. All he had to do was shut the door, turn out the light and— Savagely he squelched his imaginings. Somehow he had to get control over his emotions. Jim noticed a small group of photos on the wall next to her desk and walked toward them, eager to discover who Pepper was—all of her facets, not just those he'd seen on the mission.

The fluorescent lights were harsh. Pepper nervously placed the plant on top of one of the file cabinets and rubbed her damp hands down the thighs of her trousers. She turned around to face Jim. He had a slight frown on his broad forehead as he studied her bed at the other end of the office. The lightning-bolt realization that all she had to do was take a few steps, reach out and tug him toward the bed shot through her. She could love him until her bruised and aching heart and lonely soul were satisfied. The idea nearly unstrung her and she gasped internally at her unbidden thoughts. Curling her fingers reflexively against her palms, she throttled the desire to reach out

toward Jim. How wonderful he looked! Pepper stifled the
urge to simply walk forward and throw herself into his
arms. His presence was overwhelming to her heightened
senses.

"You've got a real government cubbyhole here," Jim
said, moving toward her desk and taking a quick, perusing
look at the framed photos on the wall. One of them was
of Pepper with her family. She stood next to a man who,
Jim decided, was probably her brother, Cam. They looked
very much alike. The proud, older woman at the end was
as tall as Pepper. No question this was her mother—and
no question that Pepper took after her strongly. Her dark-
haired, tall and heavily muscled father stood at the other
end of the group. It looked like a happy family. Jim's
mouth pulled into a gentle smile.

"Nice family picture." He straightened and turned toward her. Trying to quell his own nervousness, he realized
his voice was strained. Hell, he was scared to death. It
was a kind of fear he'd never experienced before—not
even in combat. It was the fear of being told to leave
Pepper's life—once and for all.

Pepper managed a one-shouldered shrug. "Thanks."

"Going home for Christmas?" Jim didn't know where
to start. Something warned him he couldn't be totally honest about his reasons for being here with her—yet.

"Uh…yes. Home. For Christmas. Sure…" Pepper's
throat ached with tension, and she battled her tears. She
stood helplessly, unsure what to do with her hands. Finally, she crossed her arms over her breasts. The words
begged to be asked: *Why was Jim really here?* Too much
of a coward to press the issue, she cast about for another
topic.

"How's Laura doing?"

Jim pushed his hands into the pockets of his leather

jacket. Small talk. He wanted to do away with it. He wanted to get to the bottom line. The bed behind him beckoned. His imagination was running away with him. Pepper belonged in his arms. Her mouth belonged on his. Compressing his lips, he said, "Surviving. Right now, she's hidden at a condominium that only a few people know about." He shrugged. "The fewer who know, the less chance of slipping up and letting the bad guys find her."

"I see. Yes, that's a good idea."

Jim looked around, desperate. "Susannah Killian, her cousin, is staying with her and helping her with her baby daughter, Katherine. Right now, Laura's mainly trying to recover. She's under the care of a great woman therapist who has plenty of rape-counseling experience." He shrugged, his voice becoming hoarse. "I guess it's the best we can all do for her, right now. I wish we could do more, but healing has to take place from within."

Pepper heard the frayed emotions in Jim's deepening voice and saw the distraught look in his eyes. There was no denying he was suffering for Laura, for her pain. "Rape is murder," Pepper whispered. "My homeopathic-doctor friend, Michaela Ryan, was raped when she was in her early twenties, back at medical school. Even now I see how it affects her. She's lost a piece of herself as a human being, as a woman, and I don't think she'll ever get it back."

Jim scuffed his hiking boot against the drab gray concrete of her office floor and frowned, looking down at it. "Yeah...that's what I was afraid of...."

"Michaela survives okay," Pepper murmured. "I guess...."

Looking up into her grave features, he murmured, "That's what Laura's doing right now—surviving. She's hanging on to hope." He shrugged and added, "At least we've got a lead on Jason."

"Really?" Hope rose in Pepper's heart, and she saw a ruddy flush appear on Jim's cheeks. "You found him, didn't you?"

"Sorta."

"You're too humble."

He grinned sheepishly. "Maybe..."

His smile flowed through her, hot and claiming. It was the first time she'd seen Jim smile like that—a little-boy, embarrassed smile that endeared him to her and momentarily washed away her anger, even as it increased her need of him. "Tell me how it happened."

He took his hands out of his pockets and unzipped his coat, suddenly very warm. But this heat had nothing to do with the temperature inside the facility—it was from being close to Pepper. Did she have any idea how powerfully she affected him? Wrestling with those thoughts, Jim tried to keep the small talk on track. He knew it was a good way for them to adjust to being in each other's presence again. "I worked closely with the CIA on this one, and we got Interpol help, too. Actually, Killian made a lot of the deductions."

Pepper knew Jim well enough to realize he was acting like any good leader—giving his subordinates the lion's share of the praise. "So where is Jason?"

"Maui, Hawaii, we think. It's not confirmed yet, but all the indications are there."

Pepper gawked. "Maui?"

"Yes." Jim shrugged. "It threw me, too, until I contacted the FBI and we started interfacing directly with Interpol." His voice deepened. "Damned if we didn't find out that Garcia flew from Nevis to his *other* home, on Maui. The bastard escaped the Nevis police after we rescued Laura, and went there. It blew me away that Garcia possibly had two of the Trayherns.''

''Do you think Morgan's there, too?''

''I don't know. There are two merc teams coming in right now. One had his partner die on him, and the other's partner suffered a heart attack. The upshot is, Jake is teaming an ex-Israeli army officer named Sabra Jacobs with an ex-marine helicopter pilot, Craig Talbot.''

''Sounds like a good match.''

With a grimace, Jim said, ''Actually, Jake says these two don't get along at all. But he doesn't have a choice. They don't have their regular partners, and he doesn't have another option right now. They've got to move fast on this, because if Garcia thinks we know about Maui, we're sure he'll move Jason somewhere else, and it could take months to pick up another solid lead.''

With a shake of her head, Pepper murmured, ''I'm glad we could do what we did. I don't envy Sabra or Craig. One mission like that is plenty for me.''

Jim attempted a smile. ''No, you're not a mercenary at heart.'' Then he amended his statement. ''You're a warrior when it comes to a cause that means a lot to you, though.''

Heat flooded her cheeks, and Pepper looked away from his intense gaze. ''Yes...I guess.'' She managed a strangled sound. ''I always said I was Don Quixote—tilting at the windmills in life.'' Wasn't *that* the truth? She'd fallen for John, given her heart, her soul, and look what it had gotten her.

Jim forced himself to move forward, closer to Pepper. She looked excruciatingly uncomfortable, and he had no desire to add more agony to her life than he already had. ''Lady, you're the last person I'd accuse of such a thing. You're a passionate person, someone who embraces what she believes fully.'' He forcefully kept his hands at his sides, fearful that if he didn't, he'd reach out and put them on her slumped shoulders.

"Sure,'' Pepper said a little breathlessly, her pulse leaping as Jim came within a few feet of where she stood. "It's called being a right-brained woman.'' She couldn't help herself; automatically, she tensed as Jim took another step toward her. Why didn't he realize it was torture to be with him and not to reach out and touch him?

"No apologies are needed.''

Pepper sobered and cast about for some sane response. "I'm not giving any. I like being a woman, and I like thinking and feeling like one.'' She glanced around her office. "I might be in a man's career, but I don't allow it to affect me as a woman.'' She tapped her chest. "I work strictly off my feelings, gut and intuition. It's saved lives.''

Jim nodded. "I like your fire, your belief in yourself.'' How he wanted to experience that fire again firsthand. She might be cool and calm on the outside, but he'd acknowledged the inner heat that burned deep within her. His aching need of her grew at the thought.

"My confidence was earned the hard way, believe me,'' Pepper said with more than a little fervency. Taking a step away from him, she said, "Let's go to dinner.''

Jim glanced at his watch. "I haven't eaten since noon, East Coast time. I don't know anything about the local eateries, but I bet you do.'' His breath became suspended, because Pepper's face softened for a moment, and he saw her without that mask of anger and distrust she'd been wearing. The expression on her face confused him. For a split second, he saw hope in her flawless blue eyes, followed by fear, then something else he couldn't quite define. Realizing he was holding his breath, he made a conscious effort to expel it.

"Well—uh—sure...if you want," Pepper responded hesitantly.

He'd never wanted anything more, he thought as a surge of joy tunneled through him. He had a tough time keeping a neutral look on his face as she acquiesced to his invitation, even if less than wholeheartedly. "Besides," he murmured, eyeing her desk with a teasing tone, "it looks like you need a break from all this government red tape."

Pepper groaned in response, then laughed. Suddenly, she felt free, euphoric. Going to her desk, she opened the bottom drawer and pulled out her dark brown elkskin knapsack, which doubled as a purse. They were having dinner, she admonished herself. That was all. A one-shot deal. "You ought to know," she countered. "You're in the military paper machine. I'm at the opposite end of the spectrum, but a government-run agency is a government-run agency."

Jim stepped aside, realizing Pepper needed to keep a safe distance from him. Did she have any of the urge to embrace him and kiss him that he felt for her? He wasn't at all sure, but his head cautioned him to proceed slowly, to feel his way intuitively with her. When she straightened and slung one strap of the knapsack over the Pendleton coat she'd donned, he smiled warmly at her.

Pepper felt the hot sunlight of Jim's smile—and the promise that came with it. Again, desire burned in his eyes. For her? Why? He loved Laura. She stepped past him and turned off the light, then closed and locked her office door behind them.

"If you're expecting a five-star restaurant out here, you'll be disappointed," she said as she switched off the main lights to the facility and the place was bathed in gloom once more. She took the lead, knowing the way to the door by heart.

"You choose," Jim told her. Their voices carried eerily through the structure. Pepper opened the door. As the last to leave, it was her responsibility to lock up. The air outside was freezing, their breath visible as they walked through the snow to the parking lot behind the building. Above, the night sky was dotted with thousands of sparkling stars. Pepper felt Jim come abreast of her, his shoulder sometimes brushing hers as they walked carefully along the snow-packed trail to the asphalt lot. A few street lamps lighted the way.

"Man, it's cold here," Jim said, pulling the collar of his leather jacket up around his neck.

Pepper nodded. With her heavy coat, she wore a warm knit cap and a pair of elkskin gloves lined with sheepskin. "Your D.C. gear won't keep you warm in Montana," she agreed. Her heart kept up its rapid beat. She felt like she was floating! All her awareness was focused on Jim, on the fact he was here—with her. As much as she wanted to let down her barriers, Pepper knew she didn't dare. She kept reminding herself of her own past pain, of Jim's involvement with Laura. Two good reasons to keep him at bay.

Giving him a quick, nervous glance, she reveled in the shadowed contours of his strong face. How desperately she wanted to explore it, to explore him. But there was no hope for them, she reminded herself for what felt like the millionth time.

Jim smiled warmly at Pepper, reading a mix of fear and confusion in her darkened eyes. They made it to the parking lot. The only two cars in it were parked side by side. "I can't think of a better place to be right now," he said.

Pepper drove a Jeep, he noted, smiling to himself. The vehicle was obviously old, with a lot of dents and in need of a paint job. He had no doubts that on her days off, she blazed trails in the wilderness of the Montana Rockies, hence the less than mint condition of her intrepid vehicle.

Pepper dug into her knapsack for her keys. Her fingers were trembling—Jim's unsettling effect on her. She saw that his rental car was new and fairly clean, considering he'd driven from Anaconda. It made her wince at her beloved Jeep, which looked like a nag next to the thoroughbred of a car he had rented. Oh, well. He might as well know the real her. *Why?* The word haunted her. Turning at the door to her Jeep, she said, ''There's a diner in town. It isn't much to look at, sort of like my Jeep here, but it serves great home-cooked food. Mandy, the owner, makes the best apple pie I've ever tasted. It's even better than my mom's, and hers is great.''

Jim said, ''Sold. I'm a sucker for a home-cooked meal.''

''Spoken like a true military type. Home-cookin' is hard to get a hold of in the service.''

Jim fished the keys from his pocket, momentarily lost in the laughter he saw flash in Pepper's eyes. How desperately he wanted to know this. Pepper, so comfortable in these giant mountains in their winter raiment and this sleepy town nestled deep in the valley.

''Just follow me. It isn't far,'' she called, sliding onto the cold seat of her Jeep.

Jim liked the old diner. It was straight out of the Depression era, with a mustard yellow interior, its chrome tables topped by red Formica. The place was filled at this time of night, mostly with locals who had been out getting firewood, hunters and townspeople. He noticed a Non

Smoking sign on the door, and praised the owner for her courage in putting it up. Inside, he saw many Pendleton coats, red-and-black checked flannel shirts, knit caps and jeans.

As they walked down the aisle between the booths, Pepper was greeted warmly by the locals. There was no question that she was well liked, Jim thought, as he ambled behind her. Noticing the way just about every head in the place followed them to a corner booth, he smiled to himself. By the way he was dressed and his unfamiliar face, they all knew he was an outsider.

Sitting down across from Pepper, he murmured wryly, "Nothing like sticking out like a sore thumb, eh?"

She shed her coat, cap and gloves. "Don't take it personally. Usually, by this time of year, the tourists have left, and it's just us locals. When we see a dude from the East come in, it's a novelty, that's all."

The waitress, dressed in a white uniform with a black apron, smiled as she handed them menus and automatically filled their cups with coffee.

Pepper saw the look on Jim's face. "Around here, real men and women drink coffee."

"I see." He met her gaze which alternated between warmth one moment and wariness the next. "I'd really get talked about if I ordered hot tea with lemon, wouldn't I?"

She laughed heartily, holding his gaze. How wonderful his sense of humor was. Pepper realized how much she didn't know about Jim—and how much she wanted to know. Joy flowed through her, hot and sweet. Did she dare hope? Dare dream?

"You're really funny."

"Thank you, I'll take that as a compliment." Jim took a sip of coffee. "Whew, this is strong stuff."

Pepper said, "We have a saying about Mandy's coffee—actually, I guess it's a military saying. 'If you put a spoon in the center of the mug, it will stand at attention and salute you back.'"

"That's powerful coffee," Jim agreed, amused. Pepper's eyes cleared of wariness and her cheeks once again blossomed with their familiar pink, making her look excruciatingly lovely. He had to force himself to stop staring into her sky blue eyes. Did she realize how beautiful she was? How he wanted to tell her exactly that! Even more, he wanted to show her. The waitress returned, and Pepper ordered without even looking at the menu, so Jim surmised she was a regular here. He chose a T-bone steak with all the trimmings.

Trying to quell her nervousness, Pepper cleared her dry throat and asked, "How long will you be here?"

Jim became serious, his smile dissolving. He felt renewed tension radiating from Pepper, and he lifted his heavy white coffee mug in both hands. The old jukebox in the corner was playing a romantic song from the sixties, a slow song—one of his favorites. "Well, I got an open-ended return ticket." His throat ached with tension.

"Oh."

He looked up through his lashes. "Really, it depends upon you."

Pepper sat very still. Her heart pulsed powerfully. "With Christmas coming, I imagine you'll want to be home," she murmured nervously.

Shrugging, Jim said, "Home is where the heart is." He looked around the diner and then back at her, his expression growing tender. "I know you go home for Christmas to visit your folks."

"Yes…" Pepper stared down at her coffee mug, her hands clasped in her lap beneath the table. She began perspiring as her mind leapt to a number of responses, none of them seeming appropriate. Out of sheer desperation, she whispered, "The roses you sent were beautiful, Jim. I didn't really thank you for them."

He smiled tentatively, watching her closely. "I wanted to let you know, in some way, how I felt about you. About us…" Pepper, he was discovering, wouldn't look him in the eye when she was nervous. Instead, she stared down or past him. This woman warrior, who had more courage and guts than most of the men he knew, was wonderfully vulnerable in a way that made him want to protect her. There was nothing hard or implacable about Pepper. She was right—she had clung to her femininity and not allowed the male world to strip her of it, as it had so many other women who'd been in the military. Suddenly the love he held for her seemed so incalculably deep and moving that he knew he'd never be able to put it into words. He could only show her—if she would allow him that privilege.

Pepper sat very still, absorbing the huskiness of Jim's voice, the seeming sincerity behind his words. This was not the place, with all the locals who knew her around, to start a highly emotional, personal conversation with Jim. It would have to wait, she realized sadly. When they were done with dinner, she would suggest they go back to her office and talk. It was all they had left between them, she realized lamely. Honest talk. Forcing a pain-filled smile, she made herself look at him. Inevitably, her heart melted, and a little more of her fear with it. Jim's gaze was so direct—fearlessly burning with a warmth that left her breathless and feeling incredibly beautiful.

"I—they were nice. I mean, they were more than nice. I was so surprised," she stammered, opening her hands. "That was only the third time in my life I ever got roses, and I've never gotten that many." She touched her brow and smiled apologetically. "They really were beautiful, Jim. I was just overwhelmed by them, by your gesture."

"I hoped," he said in a low voice, leaning slightly forward, "that it would act as a door to forgiveness."

Tilting her head, Pepper said, "Forgiveness?" She shrugged. "What do you mean?"

"In my letter," Jim said, holding her startled look, "I said how I'd neglected you when we got off the island. Looking back on it, Pepper, I realize I really screwed up. I was overly focused on Laura and her problems."

Shaking her head, Pepper whispered, "Listen, Laura stopped breathing. I'd say you should be concerned. I know I was. I felt helpless. It was a terrible feeling to be sitting on the deck of that chopper, knowing I couldn't do a thing." Frustration ate at her. "I've done CPR before, and I knew how you were feeling. Laura means…a lot to you. I know that." Without thinking, she reached out and briefly touched the hand wrapped around his coffee cup. "And I don't blame you, Jim. Even if you didn't know Laura, you'd probably have reacted the same way. I'm aware of how deeply you care for people."

Pepper was internally aghast that she'd touched Jim, and she quickly withdrew her hand. What on earth was she thinking? Right now she was reacting without thinking—the worst possible thing she could do. Not only that, but in touching him she'd discovered, to her dismay, that she only wanted to touch him more. She wanted to lay her hand on his arm, slide it up beneath the sleeve of his shirt and feel the wiry quality of his dark, springy hair. Wanted to feel the latent strength of his muscles leap and harden beneath her exploration.

The briefest touch of her hand sent a tingle of need flying through Jim, igniting the fire deep within him to a flame that burned with a powerful hunger he couldn't fulfill except with Pepper. "A fault of mine at times," he murmured wryly, holding her warm gaze.

Pepper's fingertips still tingled from her imprudent touch. How strong Jim was, in ways she presently was not. "Never a fault," she rattled, her emotions very close to the surface. "There aren't a whole lot of people out there who take commitment for what it really means anymore—for sticking with a person through thick and thin." With a shake of her head, she rasped, "No, I like your loyalty to people. Your commitment to them, no matter what."

"I wanted to get out here to see you much sooner," Jim admitted, "but I couldn't. Part of it was that Laura needed me, and I was damn well determined to hunt down some or the rest of her family before I left Washington."

"I would have expected nothing less of you, Jim. In some ways, we're alike," she murmured as the waitress brought their salads and a small loaf of hot bread. Pepper was absolutely not hungry for the usually appetizing food. The only hunger she had was for Jim—to love him, hold him and become one with him. Forcing her mind away from her unruly yearning, she whispered unsteadily, "People count with me. I want to make a difference in their lives as much as I do in my own."

"It's called unselfishness—a commodity too long lost in our society, particularly in the past decade," he said wryly. Jim didn't want to eat; he wanted to talk, to explore Pepper—to spend the rest of his life discovering all her wonderful facets. But he forced himself to pick at the salad, occasionally glancing at her. Pepper wasn't eating very much, either, and he struggled to contain his impatience. Timing was everything. He would have to wait until later.

Chapter Twelve

After dinner, Jim knew it was time to get down to serious business with Pepper. Now or never, he thought. Neither of them had eaten very much. As they approached Pepper's Jeep, he reached out, wrapping his fingers around her arm and gently drawing her to a halt. She turned, startled, her eyes searching his.

"We need some privacy so we can have a talk, Pepper."

Gulping, Pepper was wildly aware of his monitored strength on her arm. He was so close—inches away. His breath came out in white wisps as he spoke in a low tone to her. The shadows and light carved his face, accenting its strength as well as its tenderness, from the way the corners of his mouth were flexed to the burning quality in the depth of his serious eyes.

"Okay," she said, a little breathless. "How about my office?" That was safe, neutral territory, she thought.

Jim forced himself to withdraw his hand from her arm. "How about your home, if that's okay with you?" He didn't want to risk interruption once they started to discuss everything. Her silence told him a great deal. She didn't want him there.

Pepper's pulse was fluttering wildly at Jim's softly spoken request. The desire to reach up and slide her arms around his shoulders, to melt against him and feel that strong mouth on her own was nearly her undoing. *Home.* Her home. Her empty, lifeless home, where she'd felt so alone since returning from the mission. Her hands fluttering over the knapsack as she dug for her keys, she said, "Just follow me. It isn't far from town."

Jim nodded. He ached to touch her fiery red cheek, to smooth a strand of precocious hair away from her brow. Pepper was shaken by his request, he could see. But no more shaken than he was by fear over what was to come.

Pepper's cabin was warm, the fire in the stove sending an orangy glow through the living room. Jim fought himself—his need to reach out and touch Pepper. They had gone directly from the garage into the warmth of her living quarters. Pepper stood apart from him, nervously tugging the knit cap off her glorious hair, which tumbled in a shiny cascade about her tense features. Her hands were trembling, he noticed. As she tried to undo the buttons on her coat, his mouth went dry.

"Here, let me help…" he murmured thickly, stepping forward, his hands closing over hers.

Pepper gasped at his sudden, unexpected move. Jim's hands were strong, warm and cherishing on her cold ones. Her head snapped up. Her heart slammed into her ribs. Lost in the darkness of his predatory gaze, she parted her lips breathlessly beneath his tense, silent scrutiny. In less than a heartbeat, she whispered his name. It came out broken, pleading. The look in his eyes changed, grew narrower. Intent.

Without thinking, throwing all caution to the wind, Pepper raised her hands and settled them about his strong shoulders. Instantly, she felt Jim's arms wrap about her like tight bands, drawing her hard against him. The air rushed out of her lungs. She tipped her chin upward. He called her name—a low growl that jagged through her like lightning. His mouth claimed hers hotly, conquering her weak protest. The taste of him, the power of him combined to overwhelm her as she opened her lips farther to drink deeply of his offering. Time dissolved and only his sandpapery skin against her cheek, his mouth taking hers, his ragged breath against her face existed.

Pepper's hands ranged awkwardly across his jacket, finding the opening and moving up across his shirt. She felt the immense breadth of his chest, his muscles bunching and tightening under the skimming touch of her eager, exploring hands. Sagging against him, she returned the raw desire of his mouth against hers, tasting him, sliding her tongue across his. Unable to get enough of him, she pushed the leather jacket off his shoulders, vaguely hearing it drop to the cedar floor at their feet. His hand moved downward, pinning her hips against him in a grinding motion meant to convey his need of her. Instantly, heat exploded within her, and her knees weakened as his fingers curved over her, capturing her even more tightly against him.

Jim tore his mouth from hers. Nothing mattered but now. Right now. To hell with all the reasons—the barriers that stood in their way. This was real. This was what they both needed. Wanted. His arms tightly holding, he lifted

her effortlessly. Looking around, he spotted a hallway and
carried her down it until he found her bedroom.

Fragments of light stole into the darkened expanse. It
was enough. He took her quickly to the bed and laid her
on it, continuing to undress her. Off came her coat, which
dropped to the floor beside the old brass bed frame. The
sultry look in Pepper's half-closed eyes told him everything he needed to know. Thinking was no longer possible. Driven by something so primal he could no longer
control it or himself, he tugged impatiently at the buttons
on her blouse until it opened to reveal the pale pink silk
of her bra. His eyes narrowed upon her breasts, which
were rising and falling in ragged timing with his own
harsh breathing. As Pepper's hands moved upward, pushing his shirt off his shoulders, Jim growled. He was more
animal than man—and more ravenous than he'd ever
been.

Each heartbeat, each touch burned like a brand through
Pepper's skin as Jim's hands ranged up and down her rib
cage. His mouth claimed hers again, and she took his
weight as her slacks and panties were pushed aside. Each
movement of his mouth drove her deeper and deeper into
the fire. The agony in her lower body was like a confla-
gration. As his fingers tunneled through her hair, her
hands slid down to his pants, tugging and pulling at his
belt.

Jim froze as Pepper's hand brushed his hardness, his
zipper opening easily beneath her trembling fingers. Moving to one side, he pushed his chinos off along with his
shorts. He soared inwardly at the sensuous look in her
eyes. Never had two people been so meant for each other,
he realized as he leaned down, again capturing her soft,
glistening mouth.

As he eased down upon her, she arched her hips upward. Air hissed between Jim's clenched teeth as she brazenly brushed against his hardness. She was like velvet, giving and teasing. He slid one hand beneath her hips and felt her breath hitch as he eased his knee between her strong thighs. The look in her eyes was molten, expectant. Her lips parted in a silent welcome. There was such overwhelming urgency that he couldn't wait. Wouldn't wait. Neither would she. Just as he tried to counter the flowing forces careening through him, to ease into her, she thrust upward, taking him, consuming him.

A startled cry of joy burst from Pepper's lips as she felt him plunge into her, filling her. Tipping her head back, she closed her eyes, his name an answered prayer on her lips. Unable to catch her breath, she felt his hand center on her lower back, bring her up hard against him as he rocked deeply into her. A rippling, melting sensation emanated from her core outward. She was dissolving beneath his capturing motion. Each movement was unrelenting, deeper and more consuming than the last. She gripped his shoulders, her fingers opening and closing spasmodically against his skin. The sense of oneness, of flesh meeting and being forged in the fire of something overwhelmingly beautiful and cleansing, tunneled through her. Each rocking movement brought her higher and higher, closer and closer to that ragged cliff of unequaled sensation. As he molded his mouth to her, drinking of her, the movement of his hips thrusting against her triggered an avalanche of molten lava pulsing through her lower body. Her lashes dropped and she surrendered fully to his hands, his mouth, his exquisite body fused with hers, and an intense pleasure swirled through her.

Jim felt the hot, cascading explosion surround him, and moments later he froze against Pepper, their hips locked in a primal union as he spilled richly into her silken depths. His fists locked on either side of her head, his body straining against hers. With each pulsing release, the heat tripled. He felt as if he were being consumed in the white-hot core of a fire, and the only thing that existed in his universe was her.

The moments strung tautly together. Pepper moaned and became limp in Jim's arms. She felt his mouth on her cheek, kissing her lashes, her nose and her parted lips. The smell of him, the dampness of his strong body sliding against hers, were all precious to her. Forgotten sensations from so long ago had been brought to new and vibrant life. She felt his hand move shakily across her hair and she opened her eyes. Pepper drowned in the darkness of his gaze, gleaming with a fiercely tender light. Even now, spent by the explosiveness of their lovemaking, she began to realize just how deeply she touched him. As his hand skimmed her breast, feathering across her hardening nipple, she gasped with pleasure.

He smiled and leaned down, capturing the peak between his lips, suckling her. The sensation was throbbing. Electric. How easily he brought her to ripe awareness of her need of him again. Pepper reached up with her hand, sliding her fingers through his short, dark hair. As he eased his lips from her breast, his eyes glittered with triumph and satiation. Words were too primitive for what she was feeling toward him. How could she have ever thought they weren't meant for each other?

Jim captured Pepper's hand, opening her palm and kissing the center of it, then slowly licking it with his tongue. He felt her move. He smiled inwardly. Pepper was as wild and natural as the earth that had bred her. She was more than a woman of the soil; she was like the majestic mountains that encircled this small town—outwardly beautiful and tranquil, with a roaring volcano of potential beneath that exterior raiment.

Exhaustion ate at Jim, and he slowly eased out of her—the last thing he wanted to do right now. If he hadn't been so tired, he'd have started loving her all over again, but he knew the limits of his body. Without a word, he pulled back the thick, downy quilt, the smooth cotton sheet and eased her beneath them. Pepper's eyes were nearly closed. He understood that she needed sleep, too. Slipping beneath the covers, he contented himself with drawing her into his arms. Gratified as she moved her length against him, he sighed.

"Let's sleep, sweetheart," he murmured near her ear as she settled her head against his shoulder. "We can talk in the morning...."

Pepper nodded, unable to speak. Right now she felt so weak and sated that all she wanted was Jim's continued nearness, the scent of him, the touch of him. Nothing else mattered. As she spiraled downward into a deep, healing sleep, she realized that she'd broken her word to herself: she'd sworn after John's death never to love again. Now she'd not only done that, but she'd loved a man who loved another.

It was all too complicated, and her heart felt satisfied regardless of what the halls of her mind whispered. Right now, only the moment meant anything. Tomorrow would come soon enough.

Jim awoke slowly. For a brief moment, he was lost, until awakened enough to realize he was at Pepper's home in Montana. Opening his eyes, he searched for her warmth. She was gone.... Instantly, he sat up, the covers pooling around his waist. Blinking away sleep, he looked around. The clock on the pine dresser read ten a.m. Ten!

Throwing the covers aside, he located his chinos and pulled them on. Keying his hearing, he recognized the soft crackling of the wood stove in the living room. Classical music—Mozart, he realized—played in the background. The floor was cool beneath his bare feet as he launched himself upward.

Pushing several strands of hair off his forehead, he hurried into the hall toward the living room. He came to a halt at the door. Dressed in an old pair of jeans and a bright red sweater, Pepper was curled up on the couch near the fire, a book in hand. As if sensing his presence, she lifted her head. His heart thumped in his chest as he anxiously searched her eyes. She had such serenity, yet he found a mass of emotions in the depths of her thoughtful eyes. He didn't care if he wasn't fully dressed. What mattered was her—and them.

"Good morning," Pepper whispered, slowly closing the book and setting it aside. How wonderful Jim looked clothed only in the body-hugging chinos. His chest was broad and covered with thick dark hair that emphasized his powerful masculinity. She had loved that wonderful body last night, and the memory sent such a warming sensation through her that she could barely hold Jim's devouring gaze. Still, she saw anxiety in his eyes—and worry? About what? Her? Them? Pepper felt so tentative and uncertain. She sat up, her hands clasped in her lap.

Jim walked over to her, his gaze never leaving hers. When he sat down, his knee rested against her leg. He reached out and gripped her hands. "It is," he said huskily, his voice still filled with sleep.

"You look worried," she observed.

"You weren't in my arms when I woke up." He gave her a partial smile and looked down at her long, spare hands—hands that had loved him last night. Hands that he wanted loving him always. "Last night," he began with an effort, "wasn't planned, Pepper. I swear it...." He held her wavering gaze. It was important that she believe him, he thought, recalling their "no strings attached" conversation back at her office.

Bowing her head, she managed a painful smile. His hands were warm and tender over hers. "I—I know, Jim."

Relief cascaded through him. "Thank God...."

Risking everything, Pepper raised her head and met his searching eyes. "I thought we might go for a snow picnic this morning. A kind of brunch in the snow." She smiled a little wistfully and pointed out the picture window of her cabin. "It stopped snowing last night and the temperature has risen. I've already packed us a thermos of hot chocolate, made some scrambled-egg sandwiches and fried some bacon."

He studied her in the strained silence. Her cheeks were flushed, and her voice wavered with uncertainty. Jim felt her pain. Gripping her hands surely in his, he rasped, "That sounds great. Let me grab a quick shower, a shave and a change of clothes?"

"Sure...."

Pepper had two sets of skis waiting for them in the garage. After helping Jim into his, she easily attached hers to her boots. Jim carried the knapsack containing their brunch, while she led them out into the crisp air and across the deep, white snow. It was nearly noon, and the sun peeked out from behind grayish clouds that hung low around the tops of the mighty mountains surrounding Phillipsburg. The dark green forest contrasted sharply with the pristine snow. Every once in a while, Jim noticed a patch of brilliant blue sky, quickly swallowed up by the swift-moving clouds. But his heart was centered only on Pepper, who moved with such abandoned grace, gliding easily on her skis as she led them deep into the forest.

It was as if she telepathically knew they had to talk, but had chosen the time and place herself. Jim was content with her decision. He knew Pepper had done it to shore herself up against whatever he might say to her. She was noticeably tentative, the wariness observable in her eyes. How badly he wanted to ease her inner pain, but he didn't know how. Maybe after they'd shared an intimate lunch in surroundings that nurtured her, he could finally communicate with her.

A blue jay screeched suddenly above them, startled by their silent approach, sending snow flying off the branch where it had been sitting. The powdery flakes fell around them like stardust thrown by an invisible magician. Jim laughed at the beauty of the sunlight striking the tiny particles, which sparkled around them like miniature rainbows. He saw the appreciation in Pepper's eyes, too, and began to realize humbly just how much she was a part of this forest. She was, for the instant they watched the jay take flight, a child in awe, innocent and filled with the rapture of life. A fierce tidal wave of love flowed through him, and he fought the urge to reach those precious inches with his gloved hand and caress her fiery cheek. Her red cap emphasized her large eyes, and the dark curls escaping from beneath it shouted of her femininity.

"It isn't far," she whispered, smiling at him. How changed Jim's face had become, Pepper realized in that moment. Gone was the eternal stress she'd seen around his mouth and eyes before and during the mission. Gone was the tight line of his mouth. When he smiled, her heart mushroomed with a joy so fierce that Pepper thought she might faint from it. Her, of all people! The tough fire fighter! She laughed at herself, at the momentary appreciation they shared of their surroundings—and each other. Sadness ate at the foundation of her happiness, though, and not wanting to spoil the moment for Jim, she turned away and continued on up the gentle slope of the hill to her favorite spot.

At least a dozen huge cedar trees made a semicircle at the top of the hill, providing a secure nook against the wind, although the breeze was light now anyway. Pepper removed her skis and, with Jim's help, laid a dark blue, plastic-backed blanket on the snow. The sunlight shone strongly now, reflecting brightly off the limitless white expanse. Most of the clouds had moved away toward the east. Pepper felt a contentment here on this knoll as she helped Jim spread out their brunch on the blanket. Finally, she sat down, and he sat less than a foot away, facing her.

"This is incredible," he confided quietly, in awe of the beauty that surrounded them.

Pepper poured some hot chocolate and offered it to him. "Isn't it?"

"You're beautiful," he whispered, taking the cup from her. He saw her blush and look away as she poured herself some in turn.

Pepper set her cup aside and offered him one of the scrambled-egg sandwiches she'd made. "Last night," she began awkwardly, "was beautiful." And it had been. His nearness was pulverizing. Did Jim realize the overwhelming effect he had on her? Was he torturing her on purpose? Reminding her she was a woman with fiery needs that matched his own?

Pepper didn't believe he knew her feelings toward him. Yes, they'd shared wild, hungry passion, but sex didn't necessarily equate with love. How could he know what lay in her heart? He loved Laura with a blind certainty that everyone could see— everyone except him. What did he want to talk about? She nibbled at her sandwich, not really tasting it.

Jim took a deep breath, watching Pepper's lips purse as she stared down at her sandwich. Why did this have to be so painful to both of them? He laughed at himself and considered the question. If he didn't have so much at stake, if he didn't care as deeply as he did, he'd be able to cope much more easily with the potential pain of a rebuff.

As he exhaled, he spoke. ''I've had more than enough time to think about you since we got back from Nevis.''

Pepper turned her head just enough to meet and hold his serious, darkened gaze. A lump jammed her throat, and it was impossible to make a sound. Her heart was hammering.

Jim saw the wariness come to her eyes—along with unshed tears. Damn, those tears! He couldn't stand to see them, and automatically he put his hands on her slumped shoulder and forced her to look up at him. ''Sweetheart, don't cry…please. Tears tear the hell out of me,'' he rasped unsteadily.

His voice tugged at Pepper's heart, unraveling her emotions. His hands had fallen gently upon her and his eyes burned with a tenderness she'd never believed existed in any man—but obviously it existed in Jim. Her lips parted, and a choking sob escaped. Tears burned in her eyes, and she felt his fingers tighten against her jacket. Anguish was in his voice and in the way his mouth twisted with her pain. She felt foolish, as if she couldn't control her feelings in his presence.

''What are those tears about?'' he demanded huskily, reaching up and using his thumbs to remove them from her now-pale cheeks. ''Pepper? Talk to me. When I kissed you on Nevis, you cried, too. It wasn't the time or place to ask why, but it's bothered the hell out of me. Why are you crying?''

Pepper felt her defenses crumbling. ''I—I can't…it's too late,'' she said in a choked voice.

''Too late?'' Jim demanded, his hands upon her shoulders. ''What are you talking about?''

The intensity of his gaze held hers relentlessly. Jim was going to make her say it. Never had she felt so foolish. So helpless. ''I—I didn't want to have feelings for you, Jim. A-after John died, I went into a horrible nosedive. Shock, I guess. I went around like a zombie, not feeling anything. My friends couldn't help me, my family—no one could help. For over a year, I felt numb to living.'' She looked up and blinked away the tears as she gestured to the huge cedar trees. ''See how beautiful these trees are? After John died, I came up here and I couldn't feel anything. Before that, I would feel my heart open, like a flower. I could sit up here, no matter how badly life had treated me, and feel at peace. Feel whole.''

Pepper sighed and shook her head. ''When I came home after John's funeral, I came up here. I stood in this grove and I felt nothing. It scared me. After that—'' she frowned, avoiding his sharpened gaze ''—I plunged into the darkest barrel in the world. The doctors said it was depression. I called it a living hell.'' She touched her breast over her heart. ''Jim, I can't even begin to tell you how awful that year was. Finally, slowly, I began to come out of it. And as I did, I felt pain like I'd never felt before. I never knew that kind of pain existed. Every time I thought of John, of what we'd shared—what we'd planned to share—I felt this knife twisting in my heart. It literally took my breath away. I'd start hyperventilating.''

Pepper put the sandwich aside and gave him a sad look.

"I had been such an active, outgoing person before that, Jim. But suddenly I had no energy, no will to live. It affected my work, my interactions with team members— my family and my friends. It took nearly two years for me to climb out of that hole." She took a deep, ragged breath and looked up at the trees clothed in snow. "I was so afraid of ever feeling that way again that I decided to shut off the possibility of romantic love. I moved my commitment to my job, my family and my friends instead." Shaking her head, Pepper whispered, "I'd learned that love was the one thing that could bring me down—could break me and stop me from living and meeting the goals I'd set for myself. I made friends of any men who wanted to date me. I steered clear of entanglements." She lifted her head and stared at him. "I was successful at it. I had managed to control my life so it wouldn't ever hurt me that way again."

"I..." Jim allowed his hand to drop from her shoulder, digesting her pain and the intimacy of her admission. "Love can be hell," he admitted somberly.

"To say the least," she said brokenly.

"That's why I see so much fear in your eyes?"

"Partly," Pepper admitted rawly. "I never expected to kiss you, if you want the truth."

He smiled deprecatingly. "I didn't, either. But I'm not sorry that it happened, Pepper." When her head snapped up and her eyes widened, he added, "Not ever."

"I—" she struggled visibly with the admission. "—I thought we kissed after you almost fell to your death in that jump because we were happy we'd both survived it."

"And the island?" he asked quietly. "What did you write that off to?"

Wearily, she said, "I wrote it off to the stress we were under, that we could be killed at any moment. I felt guilty for having caused you to be injured in the first place. Guilt and worry—''

''I didn't write either of those kisses off,'' Jim said soberly.

Pepper stared at him, the silence brittle. ''Why?'' she finally forced herself to ask.

Jim felt her tension, saw the grief and terror in her eyes. Now that he was beginning to understand what was behind Pepper's wariness, he rasped, ''A certain woman walked into my life and made me rethink what I wanted out of it.''

Tears stung her eyes. Her voice cracked. ''Y-you love Laura....'' There, it was finally out. The truth.

Jim stared down at her for a very long, painful minute. His hands tightened considerably.

Pepper saw the darkness in his eyes, but her tears wouldn't stop. Frustrated, she swiped at them with both hands. ''I said you love Laura. There's no room in your life for anyone else, Jim!''

Jim assimilated her heated, anguished words. The suffering in her face tore at him. Her lower lip trembled as the tears streamed down her cheeks. With a groan, he called her name and moved closer before she could escape. His hands closed around her upper arms.

''I'll admit my understanding of my feelings for Laura were confused. My emotions ran deeper than I realized. I had fallen for her a long time ago, Pepper, before Morgan entered her life. The truth is I was far more interested in a possible relationship with her than she ever was with me. I was being an idealist about it, putting her on some kind of pedestal—and that was my fault, not hers. When Morgan came into her life, I was bitter for a long time. After a year or so, I got over it, or at least I thought I had.''

Pepper met his suffering eyes. "And when Laura was kidnapped?"

His mouth went grim. "It raised a lot of unresolved feelings I'd buried inside, Pepper. When you and I kissed up on that ridge after I damn near died in that jump, I got even more confused. I liked you, but my worry for Laura and the stuff I hadn't worked through about her was clouding how I saw you." He eased his hands from her shoulders. "I don't love Laura. Yes, she's a good friend who deserves my loyalty, but I never truly loved her." He gently smoothed back several tendrils that clung to her damp cheeks.

Jim's hands were warm, strong and dry against Pepper's face, and she wanted so badly to fall into his arms and be held. Fighting it with the last of her emotional strength, she met his confused gaze. "Back in your condominium I saw how much you cared for her. I challenged you on your feelings for her, but you wouldn't admit anything."

"Yes, I recall now what I said when we had our talk." Frustration cracked his voice. "Sweetheart, that was a long time ago. I no more love Laura now than she loves me. She loves Morgan with every breath she takes. I've never seen two people more in love, more committed, than they are to each other." He touched her wrinkled forehead and her cheek. "I don't love her, Pepper. Please, you've got to believe me. I know I screwed up with you. Badly. So much happened so fast. We had a mission to concentrate on." He pursed his lips, holding her lustrous gaze and seeing some of the pain dissolve from her eyes.

She nodded. "Yes, there was a lot going on," she conceded.

He raised his hands and followed the curve of her soft, dark hair with them. "I knew we'd come to some impasse between us. I felt it before and especially after the mission. Is that why you left the Coast Guard cutter early? You couldn't stand being around me because you thought I was in love with Laura?''

Miserably, Pepper nodded. Each caressing touch he bestowed eased a bit more of her pain. She absorbed his gentleness like a desert plant too long without water. How she thirsted for his touch! The feeling was startling, heated. ''I know she almost died,'' she whispered unsteadily, ''and I didn't blame you for devoting your attention to her. It wasn't Laura's fault. I've never blamed either of you. Sometimes love happens like that. It's no one's fault.''

Making a frustrated sound, Jim pulled Pepper into his arms. At first she stiffened, but then, in increments, he began to feel her surrender. ''Sweetheart, from the moment I set eyes on you, I knew you were special. I admit,'' Jim said harshly, burying his face against her hair, ''that I was a royal bastard at first. Yes, I was upset that Laura had been kidnapped. She's been my friend for many years, and I like her, but that's all. I respect Morgan. I sure as hell don't wish that man any more pain than he's already suffered at the hands of our government. Yes, I was upset when Laura first fell for him. But I'm not an obsessive person, Pepper.'' Jim eased her away from him just enough to place his finger beneath her chin and make her look into his eyes. She had to understand his sincerity on the most basic level.

''When I finally understood that Laura loved Morgan as much as he obviously loved her, I backed off. Maybe I was a bit of a burr under their collective saddle for a while, but after I realized what was going down, I let her go.''

Pepper drank in his dark, intense gaze. He was so close.

So wonderfully close. She could feel the hard beat of his heart against her breast. His arms were strong, supporting, and for the first time in a long time, she allowed her full weight to lean against him. His gaze was probing, and she felt his frustration.

"Laura is like a ghost from your past," she whispered.

"Yes," Jim rasped, "and I've been battling your ghost, too."

Pepper frowned. "What are you talking about?"

"Captain John Freedman," he said, scowling. "I've watched your face change every time you talk about him, Pepper. I saw your eyes fill with tears, heard your voice go soft. What else could I think? Hell, it took every ounce of courage I possess to get up the gumption to fly out here and face you. I felt Freedman still had a claim on your heart."

"He doesn't...not any longer. I—I thought Laura claimed yours," Pepper admitted, embarrassed.

"No more," Jim whispered, touching her cheek. "There's a beautiful, strong, confident woman I'm holding in my arms this very moment. She's the one who holds my heart in her hands."

Pepper reached up, her fingers sliding along the strong line of his jaw. "John is gone," she whispered unsteadily. "And yes, I mourned for him." She squeezed her eyes shut against the pain. "I knew that because I was so different—because I refused to be anyone but myself—I would scare most men away, Jim." She allowed her hand to rest on his freshly shaved cheek and opened her eyes. "John was the only man who loved me just the way I was. He loved my confidence, the job I did in the army, my talents and skills. He loved me. He didn't try to pigeonhole me into what women are supposed to do by society's standards. He didn't care. He loved me for walking my own path in life, and I loved him for allowing me to be myself. There just aren't that many men out there who are confident enough in their own masculinity to let women be all they can be.''

Jim smiled tenderly and brushed her tears away with his fingertips. "I understand," he whispered. "You're a new breed of woman, Pepper. You've been lucky enough to have parents who supported you regardless of gender, and you've been lucky to be born at a time in history where women are grudgingly being allowed to develop fully. That's one of the things that drew me to Laura. She's a lot like you, you know."

Pepper gave him a confused look. "I don't see much similarity between us."

He smiled a little and caressed her damp cheek. "That's because you don't really know Laura. She's held down a man's job in the defense industry for years. She's a noted specialist on defense issues. And like you, she never abandoned her femininity to become 'one of the boys.' Beyond that, Laura is opinionated, stubborn and knows what she knows—just like you."

"I don't think I'm opinionated or stubborn. If I were a man, you'd say I know my own mind and know what I stand for."

Jim grinned a little, feeling some of the tension drain from her, even as it drained away from him. He saw a spark of defiance flare in her eyes along with desire—for him he hoped. "You're right," he amended. "You see, I'm still learning to give ground gracefully to women in general. I'm not as liberated or ahead of my time as John was." He held her gaze. "I wish I were, Pepper. But I'm beginning to understand what kind of raw, continual courage it takes to stay strong within yourself. Laura was the first woman to make me aware of that. Now you. I've

been watching her gather up the shattered pieces of herself, not knowing whether she'll ever see her son or husband again, and she's fighting to heal herself despite that
ongoing trauma. She has guts." Jim leaned down, his
mouth barely brushing her tear-stained lips. "Like you,"
he whispered against them.

Pepper moaned as Jim's strong lips brushed hers. Without thinking, she found her arms sliding around his broad
shoulders, feeling the latent power of his muscles beneath
his jacket, discovering the power of his mouth as he
pinned her against him. He eased her down on the blanket,
the sun warm upon them, and a heated bolt of lightning
seemed to plunge through her as his mouth moved con-
fidently across hers, igniting a fire of such burning need
that it turned her knees to jelly. His mouth was at once
ravishing and tender, and she felt his ragged breath chase
across her cheek as he deepened his kiss, taking her completely.

Pepper was lost to everything except Jim and his mouth
covering hers. Their hearts clamored in unison, their bodies stretching and reaching toward each other, crying for
closeness. As Pepper surrendered against Jim, her breasts
pressing into his chest and the points of their hips grinding
together as their thighs fused, she moaned in pure joy.
The joy of celebration. Jim didn't love Laura! He was
here to see her and only her. Her arms tightened around
his neck, and she felt him tremble with barely contained
need.

"Love me...." she whispered, dragging her mouth
from his. Breathing unevenly, she unzipped his jacket.
The day was perfect, the sky a dark, clear blue, and the
world seemed to be holding its breath. She felt Jim open
her jacket and ease it off her. The jackets became pillows
as they stretched out on the blanket. Pepper's emotions

were alive, illuminating her as if some golden light had been switched on within her very soul. She turned and, with shaking fingers, began to unbutton Jim's shirt. He smiled down at her. It was a very male smile, filled with incredible tenderness as he in turn, slowly unbuttoned her blouse.

Both articles fell to one side, and Jim's fingers lingered against Pepper's warm satiny skin, tracing the outline of her collarbones. She didn't have an ounce of fat on her, just solid, firm muscle shouting of a woman who was strong on so many levels that his heart nearly burst with need. She was his equal in every way, and he savored the discovery as he unbuttoned her slacks. Kneeling over her, he allowed his hands to slide down the length of her firm, long thighs and calves. Helping Pepper out of the slacks, he slowly stood.

The smile on her mouth was dessert in itself for him, as was her look of devilry combined with desire. He admired her boldness and relaxed as she got to her knees, reached up and unbuttoned his Levi's. Her hands were warm and followed the lines of his hardened thighs as she slowly, tortuously, slid his jeans downward. Jim sucked in a deep breath as her hands lingered against the bulging hardness displayed beneath the denim. She caressed him, then pulled the Levi's lower. Jim tunneled his fingers through her hair, gently gripping it for a moment as she returned to caress him again. Heat burned through him, and he nearly lifted her off her feet after he was rid of his clothes. The chill of the air was sharp, contrasting to the heat of Pepper's hands on his skin.

The look in her eyes set him on fire. He knelt down, capturing her mouth, ravishing her soft lips, pressing her hard against him as his fingers sought and found the hooks of her bra and released them. The silky fabric fell away, and Jim broke the kiss, breathing hard. Pepper was so perfect, her breasts small, proud and begging to be seduced—by him.

He felt her hands slide beneath his white T-shirt and slowly push the cotton fabric upward. He surrendered, allowing her to undress him. A look of pleasure entered her eyes as she ran her artistic fingers through the dark hair of his chest. Every touch was like a feathery brand. Groaning, Jim pulled her against him, feeling the soft brush of her breasts. As he slid his hands along her supple spine, he was again aware of how firm and muscular she was.

Laying her back on the blanket, he moved his hands down over her hips. Her belly was softly rounded, ripe for carrying babies, he thought hazily as he teased her silky panties away from her long, coltish legs. She lay before him naked, vulnerable. As he joined her on the blanket, he drew her into his arms.

Pepper inhaled sharply as Jim's hand moved provocatively up her rib cage, caressing, exploring. The hair of his chest teased her nipples, and they hardened. She waited in near frustration as his fingers moved slowly around her breast, shaping it, savoring the feel of her. He leaned down, his mouth capturing the hardened peak, and the warmth and moistness sent a shattering heat streaking through her. In that moment, her world revolved around his strong touch, the power of his body and the trembling control he barely held over it.

She arched against him, begging him to enter her. His smile was primal, as before, but the look in his burning eyes said not yet. She wasn't helpless. He could clearly see that she longed to please him as much as he was pleasing her. Reaching down, sliding her hands along his narrow flanks, she caressed him. A groan ripped from him, and he stiffened against her. She smiled at him this time, and he met her mouth with a growing intensity. Their breath mingled, and she welcomed his weight as he settled above her.

Pepper wasn't disappointed. Jim thrust hard and deep into her, and her wet heat met his plunge as he buried himself in her. A moan of pleasure rippled from her throat, and she threw her head back, feeling his arm slide beneath her neck, bringing her more tightly against him. The rhythm was wild, unfettered. Devouring. She matched him thrust for thrust, moving with him, engaging his powerful movements with her own totally feminine response. Their bodies grew hot and slick, the friction burning them up, consuming them as their mouths clung to each other with frenzied abandon.

Pepper's world shifted, then tilted as he slid his hand beneath her hips, bringing her into irrevocable union with him. Her cry of release was caught and drowned in his mouth as she surrendered herself to him. Seconds later, he stiffened against her, nearly crushing her, squeezing her breath from her as he held her to his trembling, damp body. Moments—golden, heated—spun by, entwining them as tightly as her arms were locked around his narrow waist.

Wordlessly, Jim loosened his grip on her and framed her face, now damp and flushed, as he once again claimed her soft, well-kissed mouth. Her sweetness flowed through him. Tenderly easing his mouth from hers, he brought her down on the blanket. When her fearless blue eyes met his, he smiled gently, still feeling her heat, her tightness—not wanting to give up this sense of oneness he'd never before experienced.

"I dreamed of you every night," Jim whispered, nuzzling her cheek, trailing a series of small kisses downward until he found her warm, beckoning mouth. "Like this. Like now," he uttered, his voice rough with emotion.

Pepper moved sinuously against him, absorbing Jim, reveling in his strength and incredible tenderness. Closing her eyes, she was content to lie against him, their legs tangled, their arms around each other. Fire and ice. The glittering snow surrounded them in its cold beauty while the heat of their recent lovemaking kept them warm. Slowly, ever so slowly, their ragged breathing calmed, as did their heartbeats. Pepper was amazed by their union, which had flown far beyond the physical. Jim filled her with his strength and masculinity in a way she'd never encountered in her life. It was as if she were embracing the sun itself, piercing and brilliant with life.

As he caressed her hair, gently stroking her, Pepper surrendered to him by resting her cheek against his rock-hard chest. The black mat of hair tickled her nose, and she smiled softly. Sliding her hand across his powerful muscles, she whispered, "I never knew this existed...."

Jim smiled tenderly, and he leaned over and caressed her smooth, unmarred brow as he repeated, "I dreamed of this. But I never believed it would happen, either, sweetheart," he admitted. His eyes darkened with haunting memories as he slid his fingers across the warm velvet of her flushed cheek. Her lashes fluttered open to reveal drowsy, fulfilled blue eyes. His smile deepened. "I want to cherish you, Mary Susan Sinclair."

The words, spoken huskily and with such hope, roused Pepper from the golden cocoon she was lying in. Lifting her chin, she drowned in his stormy gaze, which was alive with something she wanted to call love but didn't dare. Her lips parted, and she started to say something, but the words jammed in her throat. His eyes, so steady and intense, held hers, waiting for her answer.

Her heartbeat thumped in response to the magnitude of his statement. What was Jim saying? Did he want to spend the rest of his life with her? Was she imagining this? Had love, an emotion she'd denied herself for so long, made her hear things that hadn't really been said? His smile grew tender, and he moved within her, underscoring how much she wanted him all over again.

He had captured her wrists above the tangle of her curls, his fingers heated against her cool skin. With each slow thrust, she moaned, and the heat fanned out deeply within her.

Words were useless, and Pepper cried out with pleasure as Jim leaned down, capturing her hardening nipple. Arching against him, drawing him deeply into her, she felt his fingers in her hair, pulling her against him until her cheek rested against his damp shoulder. Did she want to spend the rest of her life with him? Yes, a thousand times, yes! Pepper lifted her chin, seeking Jim's mouth, striving to meet and match his power. She wasn't disappointed because in a heartbeat his mouth was plundering her, ravaging her, teasing her, testing her and taking her where she'd never been before.

Each touch trailed liquid fire down her body. Each motion was powerful, riveting. Pepper met his narrowed gaze, recognizing the look of a hunter. She was his quarry—but at the same time she was a hunter, too. Every plane of his body was hard as steel, trembling with bare control as he surged into her, making her his all over again.

Exhaustion lapped at Pepper as they fell into each other's embrace. The minutes fled by, and she was content to remain in his arms. Finally she felt Jim sit up and gather the warm, thick jackets over them. Snuggling against his damp body, she burrowed her face against his neck, her arms around him. Pepper felt his arms tighten, felt his mouth upon her cheek, his warm breath reassuring. Winter's chill would drive them indoors soon enough. But now Pepper would be content simply to go home and spend time with Jim, alone and uninterrupted.

Jim quietly entered the bedroom, a cup of hot tea in hand. It was nearly two in the afternoon. He and Pepper had happily fallen back into bed once they'd returned to her cabin, and had slept like two innocent children in each other's arms. He'd awakened half an hour ago and made them tea. Pepper's cabin radiated with wood-fire warmth, and he smiled tenderly as he eased himself down on the bed next to her sleeping form. Without him at her side, she slept on her stomach, one hand beneath her cheek, the other beneath the goose-down pillow. Sometime after he'd got up to go to the kitchen, the colorful down comforter had fallen to one side.

Now Jim lightly touched Pepper's back, feeling the delicious curve of her spine. He was happy when she didn't stir. He didn't want to wake her; he just wanted to spend this time absorbing another new facet of her. Her hair, once sleek, was curled in disarray around her sleeping features. Her lips were parted, shouting of her vulnerability. Her cheeks had their usual flush, emphasizing her beautiful English complexion.

Frowning, he allowed his hand to come to rest on her satiny shoulder. How many loads had she carried on these proud shoulders? Did she want to assume the load of a relationship—with him? When he'd asked her the question, he'd seen surprise in her eyes, followed by another, unknown emotion. Why hadn't Pepper responded to his question? Perhaps he'd asked too much too soon. By the very fact that she'd loved him twice already, she was showing her courage to reach out and try to love again. He had to be content with that for now. Jim hadn't even guessed at the magnitude of the wall she had erected after John's death. If he had known, he wondered if he'd have been willing to take the chances he had so far with her. Sometimes not knowing could prove to be an advantage, he thought wryly. Moving his fingers gently across her shoulder blade, he again realized just what incredible physical shape Pepper was in—as she had to be to do the demanding work of fighting fires.

A serenity washed over him as he sat on the bed, his hand lightly resting on Pepper's shoulder. He sipped at the lemon-flavored tea he'd brewed. Out in the living room, the soft snap of the fire enhanced his tranquillity. Leaning over, he nudged a curl back from Pepper's temple, and she stirred. Damn, he hadn't meant to wake her. He saw her lashes slowly rise, revealing drowsy blue eyes.

"Jim...?"

"Everything's okay," he said quietly, keeping his hand on her shoulder. She started to rise, but he applied just enough pressure to let her know he wanted her to go back to sleep.

Rubbing her face, Pepper smiled softly. "What time is it?" How dangerous-looking Jim was, she thought sleepily, dressed only in faded Levi's, his chest dark with hair and his shoulders thrown back with natural pride. Her body responded automatically to his quiet presence. His hand was warm against her. The intimacy he'd established with her was powerful.

"Fourteen hundred hours." He grimaced. "My military background is showing again, isn't it?" And he chuckled.

Pepper laughed softly and slowly sat up, the quilt spilling around her waist. She felt no embarrassment as she watched his eyes narrow with appreciation of her.

"I remember my mother making me read the Greek myths when I was nine or so," Jim said as he handed Pepper the cup of tea and rose from the bed. He walked to the closet, found a pink velour robe and brought it back to her. Trading the tea for the robe, he said, "One particular myth involved Diana, the Huntress. She captured my imagination because she did everything the boys did—but did it better. She was an athlete—a prototype, I think now, looking back on it, for the women of today." He enjoyed watching Pepper rise slowly from the bed and slip into the robe.

Placing the tea on the dresser, he went over to her. "You're a modern-day Diana."

It was so easy for Pepper to open her arms and receive him. "I'm not interested in being anyone's role model, thank you very much. I know what I enjoy doing, and that's all that counts. Personally, I just couldn't handle doing an eight-hour-a-day desk job."

Jim leaned down and captured her mouth, sharing her warmth and vulnerability. Then, easing away, he smiled at her. "I didn't mean to wake you."

Pepper smiled and touched his hair. It was thick and silky. "When the man of my dreams wakes me up, why should I mind?"

"I got thirsty," he said, gesturing to the tea. "Want some?"

"At this hour, it's better than coffee."

"Come on," he murmured. Slipping his arm around her waist, he walked her out to the kitchen, where he made her sit down while he brewed another cup.

Pepper propped her elbows on the table and rested her chin in her hands. "Do you realize how delicious you look right now?" she asked huskily.

Jim glanced over his shoulder at her as he stood at the

sink, refilling the old copper teakettle. "No." He grinned and looked down at his bare feet sticking out from beneath his Levi's. "Somehow, I don't think this uniform of the day would make it most places."

"It only has to make it here."

Jim's heart mushroomed with joy at her heartfelt comment as he set the kettle on the stove. He realized that, in his sleepy state, he'd zipped up his jeans, but neglected to button them, leaving his navel revealed. "There's a difference between you and Diana," he teased mischievously, buttoning up. "She was a virgin and refused to let any man touch her."

"I wouldn't like to be Diana," Pepper said decidedly.

Sauntering over to her, Jim stood behind her and placed his hands on her shoulders. "No," he rasped, "I wouldn't like it, either."

Leaning back against him, Pepper gazed up into his shadowed face, its strong planes accentuated by a slight growth of beard. "Am I dreaming? Are you really here? Is this real?" she asked, only half joking.

Jim heard the quaver in Pepper's voice. He squeezed her shoulders and came around and knelt at her side. Facing her, he slid one hand behind her waist and held her hands with his other one. "I'm real. This is real. What we have is real," he said quietly, holding her luminous gaze.

"I'm scared, Jim. Scared as hell."

"I know you are. So am I."

"I worry...." Pepper shrugged. "I mean...I've never felt like I do when I'm with you."

He cocked his head. "What do you mean?" He ran his thumb across the top of her clasped hands. Her skin was firm and soft. Inviting. An ache began building in him again, her mere closeness fueling his desire.

"Something about you touches me so deeply—on such a primal level—that I stand in awe of it," Pepper admitted shakily. "John never touched me in the same way. It was different. With you, I feel your intensity, and you arouse an answering intensity in me. This may sound silly—maybe you'll laugh—but I feel as if you're my wolf mate—the one my soul has been searching for all these years." She gave him a shy look and realized from his expression that he wasn't taking her words lightly.

"Wolves mate for life." He pursed his lips, then lifted her hand and placed a small kiss on it. Raising his chin, he held her gaze. "I think we deserve to spend some time together, don't you?"

His voice was dark, velvety. Pepper struggled against her long-ago promise to herself not to get involved. "Yes…"

Jim smiled a little. "We've had a lot of hurdles to over-come to get this far, sweetheart."

She sat very still. His hands felt almost hot against her own. She saw the commitment in his eyes, heard it in his voice. "How much time do we have?"

"I'm due back in seven days, shortly after Christmas. If Jason isn't in Maui, we'll have to start the search for him all over again. But by that time, this new team, if they get lucky, will probably know one way or another."

"I see…." Pepper knew she'd made a personal com-mitment to Jim simply by loving him. She'd already bro-ken her promise to herself, she admitted. In fact, her heart had ignored that promise from the beginning when it came to him, she thought wryly. Yet Jim hadn't said he loved her. But in fairness to him, she hadn't said it, either. Did she dare call it love? How could she not? Fear warred with her instinctive inner knowing.

Jim got up and embraced her gently. The teakettle was

whistling on the stove. ''I know your relationship with John taught you a lot of good things and bad things, sweetheart. In a way, we have all the time in the world— but I know that hasn't been your experience. You have to trust me on this, Pepper—we've got time. Hang on, I'll get you a cup of tea.''

Amazed that he seemed able to read her thoughts, Pepper watched him putter around her kitchen. Jim belonged, there was no doubt. He looked totally at home here. And she had to admit that she'd never seen him as relaxed as he was now with her. The tea made, he held out his hand and led her into the living room, where they sat down on the large merino rug in front of the stove.

Jim maneuvered Pepper around so that he could lean against the end of the couch and still have her nestled in his arms. The fire crackled in front of them. ''Better?'' he whispered near her ear.

''Much.'' Pepper sipped the tea carefully as they sat in the early afternoon silence, the glow of red-orange flames dancing around the cabin's cozy interior. Outside, it was snowing again, and the windowpanes were frosted with a thick coating of snow. Setting the teacup on her robed thigh, Pepper sighed and leaned back against him.

''So you can stay for a week?''

''Yes.''

''I just never dreamed you'd come back into my life, Jim.''

''I never stopped dreaming of you coming into mine.''

His voice was filled with irony, and she twisted to look up at him. ''Nothing has ever felt so right to me as this,'' she said.

''Me, either.'' Jim inhaled the fragrance of Pepper's hair and enjoyed the feel of her, supple in his embrace. Her robe had slipped off her leg, revealing the length of her calf. He frowned and leaned forward, running his hand across its smooth expanse. "Is that an old injury?" he asked, indicating a ten-inch scar that ran nearly the length of her calf.

"Hmm? Oh, that."

"How did it happen?"

"On the Crown King fire in Arizona a couple of years ago." She shrugged. "If you're a smoke jumper you can expect all kinds of injuries, Jim. That's why I'm glad I met Michaela, with her homeopathic practice. Without her, I'd have been laid up a lot more and a lot longer."

"Where did you get this other one?" He pointed to a scar on her other knee.

Pepper heard the concern in his voice. Setting the tea aside, she turned around and crossed her legs, her knees pressing against his. "What is this? Are we going to compare our war wounds?" she teased with a smile, trying to dispel the worry in his eyes.

"That's a big scar, Pepper."

"So?" She made her eyes large. "You should see the one under my left arm. It's a puncture wound I received at the Patterson fire, just outside of Phillipsburg, as a matter of fact. You remember the Storm King Mountain fire in Glenwood, Colorado, which took the lives of fourteen smoke jumpers?"

He scowled. Who could forget that tragic fire, which had taken so many dedicated and courageous lives? "Yes, I remember it."

"We had a similar situation in the Patterson fire," Pepper said. "It was a hot day—a red-flag day, warning us of high winds. My team and I were moving down into a valley similar to the one in the Storm King fire, and we had a blowout. I had run back down to warn another Hotshot team, because not all of them had radios, when the fire exploded all around us. I got to them and helped them because I knew the woods in this area so well. When a tree fell over, one of the branches gored me. If it weren't for Susan, my fire-team partner, I'd have been dead," she said matter-of-factly. "We were running for it when a burning pine fell across our planned escape route." She raised her arm and pointed to her upper rib cage. "The branch punctured my left lung. I had so much blood in my lungs, I nearly suffocated on the helo ride to the hospital."

Jim captured her graceful hands in his. "I never realized how dangerous your job was," he murmured.

"As if being a Recon isn't twenty times more dangerous, Jim Woodward! And don't give me that pained expression, either. I hope we're not going to have our first fight over our respective careers."

He grinned. "Not a chance, sweetheart. I see enough fighting in my line of work at the Pentagon. I don't want home to be a battleground, too."

Pepper caressed his cheek. "Michaela saved my life when I got that lung puncture. Because we were so close to Phillipsburg, the Forest Service called and asked for her assistance as emergency backup. On the way to the hospital, in the ambulance, she gave me a remedy that stopped most of the hemorrhaging. So you see, I have a homeopathic guardian angel. Too bad you don't!"

Laughing, Jim surrendered to her logic. "Remind me to thank Michaela for giving you the remedy that helped my arm."

"Talk about scars," Pepper murmured, sliding her hands up his newly healed arm. "That was a terrible cut, Jim."

"I had a great nurse—a woman who stole my heart,

then took care of it for me. How could I not get well under her care?''

Pepper digested the sincerity of his tone. "I still think you're a figment of my lonely, overworked imagination."

"Finish your tea," Jim coaxed. "Dreams can't make love. I'll take you back to bed and we'll see if I'm a dream or not. Deal?"

Her lips curved tenderly. "Deal." There was desire in his eyes—and in his touch as he moved his hand slowly up and down her thigh beneath her robe. A new joy, a thread of real hope moved through her. In three days, she would take him home with her to Anaconda for Christmas. What would her parents think of Jim? Her whole family would be there. Suddenly, Pepper felt a wave of happiness like she'd never experienced—and she knew it was because of the man who held her in his arms.

Chapter Thirteen

Jim sat with a cup of freshly made hot chocolate in his hand. Pepper was in her mother's very busy kitchen, preparing the Christmas Eve meal. He looked down and noted the whipped cream and cinnamon sprinkles on his chocolate—a thoughtful touch. A strong burst of love washed through him. From where he sat, he could see Pepper standing at the sink, preparing the stuffing for the huge, twenty-five-pound turkey. To her right stood her aristocratic-looking mother, Mary Sinclair. Though in her fifties, she was almost as tall as Pepper, her short black hair sprinkled with gray. Their laughter was nearly identical, and Jim now knew who Pepper took most strongly after. To Pepper's left stood Molly Sinclair, Cam's wife, who looked tiny in comparison to the other two. Molly was blond and delicately boned; it was tough to imagine that at one time she'd been a navy test engineer on the most modern fighter planes. All three women were laughing and chatting amiably as they worked. Unfortunately, Pepper's grandfather had the flu, so they wouldn't be visiting for the holiday.

Jim smiled and took another sip of the rich, warm chocolate. Happiness seemed to ring through the Sinclair household nonstop. At the moment, Warren Sinclair, Pepper's father, was having a serious talk with Cam by the fireplace. Warren was tall and spare, his hands long and artistic—like Pepper's. He was in his mid-fifties and wore a white cotton shirt topped by a brightly striped red-and-white sweater. Cam was a few inches shorter than his father, lean and obviously fit from his military duties. The navy test pilot had his elbow resting on the mantel, his brow furrowed, eyes intense. Jim smiled to himself. Yes, Cam needed someone like Molly, who was like a cheerful patch of sunlight, to counterbalance his intensity and seriousness.

Molly and Cam's two children, three-year-old Jennifer and one-year-old Scott, played happily around Jim's feet. He leaned over and made sure that blond-haired Jennifer, who decidedly took after Molly, had the coloring book and crayons nearby so she could continue her exploration of creativity on paper. Scott, on the other hand, was the spitting image of Cam, his hair thick and black and his eyes clear, pale blue with a startling intensity to them—just like his father's.

Jim glanced at his watch. It was 1100, and two more families, friends of Molly and Cam, were still due to arrive to spend Christmas with them. Dana and Griff Turcotte were flying in from Pensacola, Florida, where they both worked as instructor pilots. From Miramar Naval Air Station near San Diego, Lieutenant Commander Maggie Donovan-Bishop and her civilian pilot husband, Wes Bishop, were flying in, too.

The Sinclair house was large, a turn-of-the-century three-story Victorian home that had originally been built by Sinclair ancestors when silver mining was at its peak in Montana. Jim had been immersed in the family's stories of the mining era, when the Sinclairs had been among the local elite. But as silver production died off in the 1930s, the family had become destitute like much of the rest of the country. This generation of Sinclairs—Warren and Mary—had turned economic disaster into success. Warren ran a fishing-expedition service with clients from around the world who wanted to fish the state's famous trout streams.

Jim allowed Scott Sinclair to climb into his lap. The boy was tired—he'd been up since six this morning, wanting to touch every bulb and light on the ten-foot-high blue spruce that stood, brightly decorated, in the corner of the expansive living room.

Last night they had all worked together to decorate the tree, and Jim couldn't remember ever having so much fun or laughing so hard. Now Scott snuggled against him, resting his head tiredly on Jim's shoulder and closing his eyes. Jim wrapped his left arm around the boy and watched him drop quickly off to sleep. His gaze returned to Pepper. Again his heart expanded with such joy that it continued to catch him off guard, made him inhale a deep ragged breath as he tried to believe his good luck.

Pepper wore an ankle-length, red corduroy skirt, a dark green angora sweater and comfortable shoes with bright red socks that matched her skirt. Earlier, Molly had placed a sprig of holly and berries in Pepper's hair, and now her cheeks were flushed as she talked animatedly with her mother and Molly in the kitchen. She had pushed the sleeves of the sweater up to her elbows in order to make the dressing. Jim sighed, glanced down at the sleeping tiger he held in his arms and continued to sip the delicious hot chocolate. Life didn't get much better than this and he knew it.

The past three days had been bliss for him and Pepper. Yesterday a brief storm had passed through, dropping another foot of snow, and they'd gone alpine skiing for part of the day. He was sore today from the unaccustomed form of exercise, but it had been a great day. Pepper had packed two thermoses of hot chocolate and a lunch, and they'd shared another snow picnic in the middle of the forest, the towering Douglas firs stately and awe-inspiring around them.

Jim finished the cup of chocolate and saw Cam looking his way. The navy pilot wore Levi's, loafers and a dark green flannel shirt and Jim smiled to himself. He, too, had opted for comfortable civilian clothes: tan chinos, an off-white fisherman's sweater and hiking boots.

"Looks like Scott finally crashed and burned," Cam said as he came over and gently eased his son into his arms. He turned Scott around and allowed him to sink across his shoulder.

"I'd say he's about used up his energy for this mission," Jim agreed as he watched the pilot gently hold his son. It was good to see men who enjoyed being fathers, who weren't afraid to show their full range of emotions with their children—unlike many of the stoic father figures of the past, who'd remained apart from their families in many ways.

"Thanks for baby-sitting," Cam said with a chuckle. He turned, carrying his son down the hall toward one of the many bedrooms to continue his nap. Jennifer quickly got up, leaving crayons and paper behind and followed her dad.

"Playing baby-sitter?" Pepper asked as she wandered

in, wiping her hands on a dish towel. How wonderfully handsome Jim looked, she thought. The cream color of his sweater emphasized his dark good looks, and when he lifted his chin, his green eyes narrowing on her, she felt giddy with joy.

"I think the little rug rat just found any old soft spot to call a pillow," he teased, taking the hand she had extended to him. Pepper came to the side of his chair and knelt down, her hand resting in his lap.

"Rug rats—what an awful term!"

He gave her a nonplussed look. "It's an affectionate Marine Corps term for kids."

"Leave it to the Marine Corps to think that that term shows affection." Pepper sniffed, leaning over to gather up the crayons and coloring book.

"Marines aren't usually in the line of being baby-sitters," Jim drawled, teasing her.

She set the items on the lamp stand next to Jim's chair. As she straightened, she muttered, "Listen, I've been around enough military brats, kids who had to grow up in that sterile, rigid place called the Fortress, and I've seen firsthand how little the military cares about the wives and children. Don't get me started, okay?"

Jim grinned and leaned over, placing a swift kiss on her mouth. "Okay," he murmured.

Pepper sighed and leaned against the arm of the chair, content. "This is so much fun. I just love Christmas."

"It's one of my favorite holidays, too." He placed his hand on her shoulder. "And you've got a great family." He raised his eyebrows slightly. "You really take after your mother."

"Yes. She's something else, isn't she?"

"I was surprised to hear she hikes back into those interior places where the trout are. That's rugged country."

Snorting, Pepper gave him a cool look. "Come on! Women can't be good guides?"

He held up his hands. "Remember? I'm still adjusting to the fact that women can do anything a man can. But I have to admit, I can't see any reason why a woman couldn't know good fishing spots, too."

Pepper shook her head. "You're one of those guys who grudgingly gives up ground to a woman, you know that?"

"Maybe so, but I am trying to adjust," he protested lightly.

"Stick around me and you'll change a lot quicker," she muttered, smiling. Jim's eyes were warm with tenderness, and Pepper felt wrapped in a euphoria she still had trouble trusting. The last time she'd uttered those heartfelt words *I love you,* John had died. In the past few days, she had realized she was genuinely ready to let go of the past and embrace the present. What she felt for Jim more than rivaled what she'd felt for John. But how should she tell Jim? She wasn't sure if he was ready to commit at such a serious level. Did she dare believe that what she experienced in his touch and his kisses and saw in his eyes was love? After all, he'd never said the words to her. Would he ever?

Sighing, Pepper said, "Molly's beside herself. Her friends from Annapolis and Pensacola flight school will be here in a few minutes. I guess this is the first time they've all been able to get leave, meet somewhere and have a great time together."

"Sort of like a college reunion," Jim said.

"Yes. Molly's told me all about Dana and Maggie— how they shared an apartment in Pensacola when they were there to get their navy aviator wings. I'm excited to meet them myself. Molly has told me so much about them, I feel like I already know them. And it will be interesting to see the men they've chosen as husbands. How they compare.''

''Oh?'' Jim took her hand and laced his fingers with hers.

''Well, you know.'' Pepper laughed.

''Is this womanspeak? Some kind of mysterious verbal shorthand we poor males try to decipher, but can't?''

Pepper had the good grace to blush. ''Sorry. Yes, it is. I guess I'm curious about the men from the standpoint that all three of these women are very strong, confident people. It's been my experience that most men get defensive or project like crazy around woman like that. It takes a man who is really comfortable with his masculinity, as a total person, to appreciate women like us, that's all.''

''So you're going to compare Griff Turcotte and Wes Bishop with me?'' He saw Pepper's cheeks grow even brighter red and grinned.

''Not exactly....'' she hedged, obviously uncomfortable.

Laughing huskily, Jim whispered, ''I know I'm not the perfect twenty-first-century male, but I'm trying. And I think that's what counts, don't you?''

Leaning over, Pepper kissed him quickly on his smiling mouth. The heat in his eyes touched her deeply. ''It does count,'' she murmured. ''Besides, you might pick up some good pointers from these guys, especially Wes Bishop. I understand Maggie is a real go-getter. She's one of the first women in the navy to fly the fighters up against the boys—and she beats them on a regular basis.''

''Hmm, maybe I will,'' Jim drawled, holding her laughter-filled gaze, which sparkled with an emotion he wanted to call love. Was Pepper ready to commit to him? To release the past with John once and for all? Jim had seen her seesaw back and forth in the days he'd spent with her at the cabin. Their conversations had tiptoed around the issue. But he'd also seen the deepening of their own relationship. He loved her. Could she put herself out on a limb and love for a second time in her life? Could she do it for him? He still wasn't sure.

The doorbell rang, and they watched Molly fly from the kitchen to the foyer, her long blond hair streaming behind her. Pepper laughed and shook her head. Molly was such a sprite, completely uninhibited, and it reminded her to stay in touch with her own childlike emotions. The woman opened the door, shrieked and flung her arms wide.

Pepper was content to stand at Jim's side and wait until the group shed their coats and gear and came into the living room. Molly's cheeks were pink with excitement, her eyes sparkling with tears as she held the hands of her two dearest friends. She brought them around the room, introducing them to everyone. Pepper and Jim were the last to be introduced.

"Dana and Maggie, meet one of us, Pepper Sinclair. Can you believe it? She made it through Army Ranger school, beat the guys at their own game, was the highest scoring of all of them, and they wouldn't let her graduate? Pepper's a smoke jumper now, for the Forest Service. Pepper, meet my friends."

Laughing, Pepper held out her hand to red-haired Maggie Donovan-Bishop, whose eaglelike eyes seemed to miss nothing. Maggie's handshake was firm, her smile genuine. Dana Turcotte, who possessed an intensity and introspectiveness that reminded Pepper of Cam, shook her hand next.

Pepper was delighted by this unusual chance to meet her "own kind." Though few women had joined the smoke jumpers so far, those who had possessed similar hallmark traits. It was obvious Maggie and Dana had them, too. As Molly introduced Jim, giving a quick sketch of his background, Pepper was able to stand back and observe their reaction to him. Maggie grinned, thrust her hand forward and shook Jim's hand vigorously. Dana was more circumspect, more official, eyeing him with a bit of wariness, or watchfulness, perhaps. Pepper wondered if Dana had had a bad time in general with men, to make her so guarded.

Cam brought the two husbands around next. Pepper liked outgoing and warm Wes Bishop, who was a pilot with United Parcel Service and flew the "heavies," as they called the jumbo jets, all over the world, hauling cargo. Griff Turcotte had a rugged face, a tough exterior, and was more reserved, like Dana. Shaking his hand, Pepper felt Griff was exactly what Dana needed. It was obvious they were happy—she had seen them trade an affectionate glance shortly after the introductions and before Molly had dragged the two women off to the kitchen to give them her late grandmother's recipe for the hot chocolate she'd made for everyone.

Jim went into the kitchen and brought out cups of the famous chocolate for the two pilots. It struck him that the men had formed a loose circle near the roaring fireplace, while the women were in the kitchen, chatting away, laughing and working together on the meal to come. There were differences between men and women, and Jim honored them. He turned his attention to Wes, who pinned him with an interested look.

"Molly said you're a Recon Marine?"

"Yes, a ground pounder compared to you air guys," Jim said, grinning. Everyone laughed. Jim was familiar with the ongoing rivalry between ground troops and the pilots who owned the air above them.

"I won't hold it against you," Wes murmured, his grin stretching wide across his face.

"I'll forgive you, too."

Chuckling, Griff said, "Looks like you have your own tiger by her tail."

Jim stared at him blankly.

Griff motioned lazily toward the kitchen. "Pepper is like Dana and Maggie—ahead of her time, a trailblazer."

"I see…yes, she is."

"How are you rolling with it all?" Griff asked curiously as he sized Jim up.

"It's new to me," Jim admitted. "Sometimes I fall into some pretty pedestrian traps regarding stereotypes."

Wes chuckled indulgently. "Tell me about it. Maggie has changed my language from 'man' or 'woman' to 'person,' and I had to learn very quickly that being a man doesn't give you special privileges."

"At all," Turcotte agreed, chuckling.

"I don't think we deserve special privileges," Jim said. "Pepper has taught me a lot lately about the way women have been held down or kept in what's considered their 'place.'"

Wes Bishop sighed and raised his cup of chocolate. "To our ladies, who have and continue to make us better human beings, gentlemen."

Jim had no problem with that toast and clinked the side of his cup against the others'. As he sipped the chocolate, he enjoyed watching the women in the kitchen. They had such a camaraderie—a closeness men simply didn't seem to foster. He liked the way the women reached out, touching one another on the shoulder or arm, or came over and slipped an arm around each other's waist in a hug before continuing on with their kitchen duties. He was struck by how thoroughly the women worked as a team. They didn't fit into the boss-and-underlings structure that men seemed to insist on.

What was most striking to Jim was the way that, although Pepper had just met Maggie and Dana, she was immediately absorbed into their group. He decided there was a lot to be learned from women. Their ability to become warmly personal and freely show feelings left him wanting to be more open with his own gender.

As he stood chatting amiably with the other men, Jim realized that Maggie, Dana and Molly had already rubbed off on their husbands. These three pilots seemed noticeably more open and personable than the men Jim knew. Even more surprising was the way that Wes or Griff would every once in a while reach out and touch each other's shoulder or arm to emphasize something they were saying.

Jim smiled to himself, liking the discovery and seeing how these self-assured women had influenced the men they loved. Most of all, he was struck by the fact that all three men possessed the ability to be flexible and to compromise—certainly the main component to the longevity of any marriage today. These men weren't lapdogs, nor were they battered males with no egos. Just the opposite. These were highly competent men, with a confidence and assurance that came from within. It wasn't a show, Jim sensed, but a depth of strength they had about their own masculinity that enabled them not only to support the strengths of their wives, but to push them to become all that they could be.

Finishing his cup of hot chocolate, Jim wandered into the kitchen. Pepper was in the middle of the women, her mother at her side, as she finished stuffing the huge turkey. Luckily, the kitchen was large, in keeping with the

old-time kitchens of a bygone era. Jim moved to the end
of the counter that wasn't being used.

Maggie Donovan-Bishop had spare, lean hands like
Pepper's. She worked alongside Molly who was telling
her how to make her grandmother's special recipe for
Jell-O salad. Dana Turcotte stood a little to the side peeling the potatoes that would soon be mashed into a frothy
white mound. Pepper and her mother exchanged warm
looks, smiles hovering around their mouths. Yes, this was
a happy group, indeed.

Pouring himself a third cup of hot chocolate, Jim left
the kitchen and headed back to where the men were standing. His heart was with Pepper. What would she do when
she opened his gift after dinner? The Sinclairs opened
their gifts on Christmas Eve instead of Christmas morning, Pepper had explained, because she and Cam, when
they were very young, had been unable to sleep Christmas
Eve out of excitement. So Mary Sinclair had decided they
could open presents Christmas Eve, instead, to keep the
holiday peaceful.

Jim tried to hone in on the men's conversation, but his
mind and heart were elsewhere. What if Pepper took his
gift the wrong way? He knew she wanted to tell him she
loved him. Hell, he could see it in her eyes, feel it in her
touch and hear it in the tone of her wonderfully husky
voice. But what if his gift backfired? It could create a
destructive split in their new relationship. Should he take
the gift back? Hold it until later? His mind and heart seesawed over the possibilities. Finally, exhausted emotionally from the indecision, Jim decided to fly with his original plan. His spontaneity thus far had gotten him Pepper.
He had to trust his own sense of creativity and honor his
intuition to get him and Pepper to where he so much

wanted them to end up—together. Soon enough, he would know—one way or another. The thought scared the living hell out of him.

Jim sat in an overstuffed velour chair opposite the Christmas tree. Everyone was opening gifts, and the room rang with the sounds of paper being ripped off, children squealing with delight and adults making more-subtle sounds of pleasure as they viewed their gifts for the first time. Pepper sat at Jim's feet, her long legs tucked demurely beneath her skirt, a number of already opened boxes beside her. But Jim was having trouble enjoying the happy scene. His heart was pounding in his chest and his mouth felt dry. What would she think of *his* gift?

Pepper had opened gifts from her family—commonsense items such as a new pair of Levi's to replace her well-worn ones, sweaters to keep her warm during the harsh Montana winter and photos of her niece and nephew to put in her cabin. Jim saw her look back through the packages she'd opened, a puzzlement on her face. Cam and Warren had distributed all the gifts beneath the tree earlier, and everyone had piles of colorfully decorated boxes heaped nearby.

Pepper picked through the surrounding wrapping and ribbons, wondering if she'd overlooked a gift from Jim. She had bought him a Shetland wool sweater in bright red and yellow to remind him of his Marine Corps heritage, as well as a watch to replace the one that had been damaged during the mission. Now, moving the paper aside, the sounds of laughter and surprise still carrying through the large living room, Pepper felt a stab of panic as she riffled through everything once more just to make sure. Jim had gone somewhere two days ago—to Anaconda, he'd told her. He'd been gone all afternoon and hadn't arrived back at the cabin until late that night. Pepper hadn't asked why, figuring that if he wanted her to know, he would have told her. Plus there'd been a look in his eyes that had silently asked her not to question him.

She felt the touch of Jim's hand on her shoulder. Looking up, she met his grave green gaze.

"I think you were looking for this?" he said, his voice low and slightly strained.

Pepper's eyes widened as he placed a small box wrapped in gold foil and a silver bow in her hand. "Oh…"

Jim smiled unevenly, aware that some of the background noise had abated. He looked up to realize everyone was watching them expectantly. How could they know? he wondered, his mouth suddenly dry with nervousness. He squeezed Pepper's shoulder. "Go ahead, open it, sweetheart."

Pepper looked up to see everyone intently watching her. Silence abruptly reigned in the room, except for the soft crackle and snap of flames in the fireplace. She laughed a little nervously and set the small box in her lap. Molly, Maggie and Dana edged closer, grinning and elbowing each other, as if they knew a secret she did not. What had Jim bought for her? Stymied, Pepper grew impatient with the bow, finally pulling it off with strength rather than finesse.

Laughing nervously, she looked up at Jim. "I'm not very good at opening things."

He smiled back. "I know."

His words fell softly, warmly, across her. Pepper took a deep breath and ripped off the gold-foil wrapping. Inside a white satin box was another, smaller box of red velvet Her heart plummeted as she hesitantly touched it. No, it couldn't be. Could it? She gave Jim a look of inquiry, and saw tenderness burning in his eyes.

Touched beyond words, Pepper lifted the box in her left hand and sprung the small, gold latch that raised the lid. A gasp escaped her. The other women quickly crowded around.

"Ohh," Maggie whispered, a wicked glint in her eyes as she looked first at Pepper, then at Jim. "He's serious...."

Dana touched Pepper's shoulder. "It's beautiful," she said in a choked voice.

Molly whispered, "Gosh, what a lovely Christmas gift for you, Pepper. How romantic...."

Pepper felt Jim's hand tighten on her shoulder, as if silently asking her what she thought of his gift. Tears blurred her vision momentarily, and she self-consciously wiped them from her eyes. In the box was an obviously antique wedding-ring set. She lightly touched them with her trembling fingers, not daring to believe they were really for her.

Jim leaned down, his voice a broken whisper. "Those were my grandmother's rings. She was very special to me, to our family. Before she died ten years ago, she asked me to take them, to give them to a woman I would love as much as she had loved my grandfather." As Pepper lifted her chin and looked at him, he felt a powerful wave of joy sweep through him. Her eyes sparkled with tears. Reaching out, he caressed her flaming cheek. The silence was complete around them. Everyone's gaze was pinned on them, on the emotional moment.

"I—they are beautiful, Jim. Beautiful..." Pepper whispered.

"There's no hurry," he rasped, sliding his hand along her cheek, smiling gently down at her. "It's not meant to rush you, or what we have. I just wanted something special for you, for Christmas. I love you, Mary Susan Sinclair.'' He leaned down, caressing her parted lips, which tasted of salt from her happy tears. Her lower lip trembled, and he kissed her deeply, wanting to impart to her just how fiercely he loved her.

The world swam out of view as Pepper surrendered to Jim's long, tender kiss. She clutched the ring box in her hands, stretching upward to meet his questing mouth, to touch him, his heart, his wonderful, thoughtful soul. As awareness that everyone was watching filtered in, embarrassment flooded her. Knowing how private a person Jim was, she realized how difficult it must have been for him to give her these rings in front of everyone, not knowing what her reaction might be. Easing her lips from his mouth, she smiled up into his anxious gaze, touched with his own tears.

"I love you, Jim Woodward," she quavered, sliding her hand upward to touch his clean-shaven cheek. "With my life...."

Much later Pepper sat staring down at the ring box, its lid open. Everyone had gone to bed, and it was past midnight. Jim sat with her on the couch closest to the fireplace, his arm around her shoulders. The house was filled now with a wonderful, peaceful silence. The satisfaction and contentment she felt in Jim's arms had no comparison, Pepper decided. She was dressed in her pink velour robe, her feet bare, though Jim still wore his clothes from the day. She lay back, resting her head on his broad shoulder, and closed her eyes.

"I never thought I could be so happy," she murmured.

"I didn't, either," Jim admitted quietly, looking down at her firelit profile. The house was dark, just the fire offering subtle warmth and light. The shadows dancing across Pepper's face underscored her strength and shouted of her vulnerability. His mouth pulled into a slight, tender smile as he saw her continue to caress the rings in the box. "So you like them?"

"Like them?" She roused herself and faced him, her knees drawn up against his thigh. "I love them." Reaching out, she touched his strong jaw. "And I love you, too."

He met and held her somber gaze. "I didn't expect that from you, you know."

"What?"

"You didn't have to say you loved me earlier this evening. I didn't really expect it, Pepper. I know how you felt about the past. About John and never falling in love again. I gave you the rings because I wanted to let you know the depth of my love for you—the commitment I wanted to work toward, hoping you would want the same thing someday."

With a sigh, Pepper rested her brow against his temple. "I saw how scared you were when you handed me the gift. I couldn't figure out why." Kissing his cheek, she murmured, "Now I know. That was a hell of a risk you took with me. When I saw the rings, I understood."

"You had every right to say no. To give them back to me," Jim agreed, tunneling his fingers through her loose, dark hair.

Pepper eased from him to meet his serious eyes. "With that group hanging around me oohing and ahhing? I thought Maggie, Dana and Molly were going to grab them right out of my hand. Did you see the wistful looks on their faces?"

"Yes," Jim said, "I did. They were happy for you. For us. I saw it in their eyes and the way they looked at us after seeing my grandmother's rings."

"I know," Pepper said with a sigh, sliding her arm

around his neck and placing her hand in his lap. In the light from the flames, the rings sparkled like their own barely contained blaze. "They are gorgeous. Prettier than any I've ever seen."

"I had a hell of a time getting them out here," Jim groused good-naturedly. "You remember I left the cabin that one morning and didn't get back until late that evening?"

"Yes."

"I made a call the day before, after you'd gone to the grocery store, to a friend of mine who's keeping an eye on my condo. I told him what was going on, told him where to find the rings and asked him to send them by overnight courier. Well, I got to Anaconda, and the place that was supposed to have them hadn't received them yet."

"Oh, no…"

"Yeah, well, I was more than a little upset," he assured her. "That snowstorm that hit us a day earlier had grounded all planes coming out of Chicago, and that's where the package was stuck. So I had to wait another eight hours for the plane to finally make it into Anaconda. Luckily, the rings were on it." He shook his head. "I was really sweating."

"No wonder you looked so tired and harried when you got back that night," Pepper soothed. "I almost asked you what was wrong, but that look you gave me told me not to."

"I was a little out of sorts by that point," Jim admitted apologetically, sliding his hand up her arm, feeling the soft, firm warmth of her skin. "On top of that, I wondered if I was doing the right thing. I knew how you felt about admitting your love for me after what had happened to

John. I knew it was rushing things in one way—but in another, I felt it was the right time.''

''Betwixt and between.''

Grimly, he chuckled. ''More like 'caught between a rock and hard place,' if you ask me.'' He picked up the ring box and stared at it. ''Today I felt tortured. I was seesawing between giving them to you and waiting. I was afraid you'd say no. That you'd turn them down.''

''What made you do it?'' Pepper asked softly, kissing his cheek, loving him with a fierceness that continued to amaze her.

Laughing wryly, Jim handed the box back to her. ''The fact that I didn't have another present for you. I mean, I couldn't sit here with everyone trading gifts and not have something for you. I saw how Molly, Dana and Maggie were covertly watching us.''

''Hey, they're old married ladies,'' Pepper teased, ''and we're the new couple on the block. Of course they'd be watching to see what gifts we gave each other.''

Jim chuckled. ''I figured as much. Still, I felt more on a hot seat this evening when you started to open that gift than when my chutes didn't open on that first HAHO.''

''Mmm, that's pretty serious,'' Pepper agreed. She took out the engagement ring. The gold band held five small diamonds. It might not be an expensive ring set from the size of the stones, but they were precious beyond belief to her because she believed family meant everything. How could she help but cherish these special items, handed down from one generation to the next?

She placed the engagement ring in Jim's hand. ''Will you slip it on my finger?''

He sat up straighter and turned. ''You have the most beautiful hands I've ever seen,'' he told her conspiratorially. ''They're so long, capable and slender.'' And wonderful at touching him, making him feel hot with longing, when she caressed his body, he added silently. Taking the lovely fingers of her left hand in his, Jim gently eased the ring forward. "My grandmother was tall and spare, like you. She had work-worn hands with large knuckles, so I figured this ring just might fit you." And it did, perfectly. Satisfaction soared through him as Pepper eased her hand from his and held it out for them to admire. The firelight danced off the small diamonds like rainbows—just as she was his personal rainbow, he thought.

"It's so beautiful," Pepper said with a sigh. She turned, sliding her arms around his shoulders.

"Like you," Jim murmured, meeting and matching the warmth of her lips. She tasted of the wine they'd shared earlier, a toast before everyone, except them, went to bed for the night. Her breath was like the breath of life itself to him. As Jim eased back and met her lustrous gaze, he whispered, "Let's go to bed."

Pepper walked with him, arm in arm, toward the staircase. The house was warm and quiet. Outside, snow fell gently in large, soft flakes, twirling through the darkness of the Montana night. Sliding her hand along the oak banister as they moved up the creaky, carpeted stairs, she smiled gently. The ghosts from the past had finally been laid to rest. All of them. Life wouldn't be easy for them in one way. They still had serious questions to answer about their careers. Jim had twenty years in the corps. Would he want to continue being an officer? Being in the military? And she had to look hard at her career. What did she want? Pepper knew that in another five years she would probably be relegated to a desk job instead of jumping out of planes. The physical demands were just too extreme, and by thirty-five, most smoke jumpers were taming desks instead of forest fires.

She leaned languidly against Jim as they topped the stairs and turned down the carpeted expanse to her room at the end of the hall. Their room. The ring felt natural and right on her hand. Never could she have dreamed that she would meet a man like Jim on an unexpected mission that came out of the blue. When she'd lost John, she'd barricaded herself against loving. It had been the wrong decision, Pepper now admitted, but she understood why she'd done it. Still not believing her own fortune, she knew that no matter what, she and Jim had their love to help them compromise and work out their life together. Forever.

* * * * *

MORGAN'S SON

Chapter One

"Jake, who do we have to rescue my son?" Laura looked at him steadily, struggling to keep her voice even and low despite her excitement at Jason's being located. To Jake's right and left at the War Room's familiar the oval table sat Wolf Harding and Sean Killian, their faces kind but impassive. Jake's brow furrowed.

"Well," he rumbled hesitantly, flipping through some reports before him, "we've got one member available from each of two different teams that have just come out of the field."

"It isn't a good idea," Wolf said, looking across the table at Laura. "Putting members from two different teams together to create a new, untried team."

Laura felt her throat closing up with tears at Wolf's pronouncement. Since her own release from the hellish prison on Garcia's Caribbean estate, she seemed to burst into tears easily and often unexpectedly. Her therapist,

Pallas Downey, assured her that her response was normal for anyone who had been drugged, raped and had her family kidnapped. Holding tightly to a delicate, embroidered handkerchief beneath the table, she tried to focus calmly on Wolf's concerns. "Why not?" she asked quietly.

With an apologetic shrug, Wolf said, "Teams are teams, Laura. Team members have adjusted to each other's quirks and foibles, so to speak."

"Team members often know intuitively what their other half is going to do," Jake offered. "If you throw together two people who don't know each other, it can be detrimental to a mission—especially one as complicated as this rescue attempt for Jason."

As tears clawed their way up her throat, Laura turned to Killian, whose face remained unreadable, as always. His green eyes glittered as she looked into them. "What do you say, Killian?" In spite of his taciturn nature, Laura knew Sean's depth of experience was something they could all count on.

"I say it depends on the individuals concerned."

"Well," Jake said slowly, "that's true."

"Who are they?" Laura asked, trying to blot her eyes as inconspicuously as possible.

"We're lucky," Jake said. "The woman is Sabra Jacobs. She's been with Perseus since Morgan started it. She's got time in grade, she knows the system and she takes only high-risk assignments."

"Sabra?" Laura whispered the name, hope springing to life in her breast. "Why, Jason knows her! Between assignments, Sabra lives here, near us. She's baby-sat for us many times. Jason loves her. He calls her 'Auntie S' because he can't quite pronounce her name yet."

Jake held up his hand. "I know it sounds like good

news, Laura. But unfortunately, Sabra's partner, Terry Hayes, suffered a heart attack overseas. We can't ask him to climb out of his hospital bed and join us.''

''Who's the person on the second team?'' Laura demanded, hope spiraling crazily through her despite Jake's words of caution. Sabra Jacobs was one of the most dependable, solid women she'd ever met. If there was anyone who could rescue Jason, it was Sabra.

Jake grimaced. ''A merc by the name of Craig Talbot. He's only been with Perseus six months. He's an ex-marine helicopter pilot who came to us after Desert Storm.''

''That sounds like a wonderful combination!''

''Laura, I wish I could be as enthused as you are,'' Jake warned, ''but Talbot has been involved only in low- and medium-risk assignments.''

''So what?''

''So, he doesn't want any high-risk assignments.''

Laura sat there assimilating Jake's words. ''But why?'' she managed to ask after a moment.

''I don't know.'' Jake glanced at Wolf. ''All we know is that shortly after Desert Storm, Talbot, who was a captain, resigned his commission from the Marine Corps to knock at Perseus's door.''

''Do you have Mr. Talbot's personnel file?''

''Yes.''

''I want to see it.''

''Laura, the first thing we have to do is find out if these players are willing to take this assignment. Sabra no doubt will jump at the chance, because she has a personal stake. She's close to you and your children.''

''Is she here?''

''Sabra should be here in about half an hour,'' Wolf said, looking at his watch.

"And Craig Talbot?"

"He's still in the air," Killian muttered. "We've sent someone to the airport to pick him up. We should be able to talk to him in about an hour and a half, if traffic cooperates."

Laura looked at her watch. It was shortly after noon and she should be hungry, but even the thought of eating these days made her nauseous. Her therapist assured her that, too, was a normal reaction after what she'd experienced. Still, she had to keep up her strength. She would have to force herself to eat.

"I want to be here when you interview them, Jake."

"Of course," he said, picking up his nearly cold cup of coffee and taking a swallow.

"Are they well rested?"

"Sabra is, but Talbot's just coming off an assignment that should have been labeled high risk."

"What happened to his partner?"

"Died in an auto accident. Talbot wasn't with her. He was tailing one of two suspects in Vienna, Austria. Jennifer Langford, his partner, was tailing the other one."

Laura felt her heart squeeze. "Oh, how awful...."

Jake slowly rose. "Laura, I really don't think you should be here, under the circumstances. You're still too raw from your own ordeal, and sitting in on team debriefings won't do you any good. You're white as a sheet."

Shamed, Laura touched her cheek, then stood. "I know you're right, Jake, but I can't help myself. My son, my husband... It's so hard to stay home, to go through the motions of my day...."

Jake came around the table and placed his arm gently across Laura's drooping shoulders. "I know how hard this is on you," he rasped. "We're doing everything humanly possible to locate Morgan."

Laura looked up into his dark, worried features. "I don't know what we'd have done without the three of you," she said solemnly. "You've held Perseus together. I—I'm so grateful." Then the hot tears spilled from her eyes and down her cheeks. Managing an embarrassed, apologetic laugh, she eased away from Jake and wiped at her eyes. Then she took a deep breath and again leveled her gaze on Jake's.

"Please let me stay for the interviews and assignments, Jake. Then, I promise to get out of your hair and leave you to the unpleasant realities. Okay?"

"That's fine, Laura," Jake said gently, his harsh features softening. "Come on, let's all go get something to eat. When we get back, Sabra should be here and, with any luck, Talbot about an hour after that."

"I'm just so glad Sabra is coming," Laura whispered. "So glad."

"She's one of the best," Jake agreed, guiding her toward the heavy oak door.

"And Jason knows her," Laura said, walking with him. "I feel that's so important."

"Yes," he agreed, "it's a lucky break for us."

Laura waited as Jake opened the door. Then, clenching the now-damp handkerchief in her left hand, she walked out into the spacious reception area, where Marie was working at her computer. Laura smiled warmly at Morgan's assistant, who had so ably taken on a much-larger area of responsibility in the wake of the kidnappings. Her mind rushed back to the fact that Killian and the CIA had stumbled on information about Jason's whereabouts. That was the best news yet, she reminded herself as she worked to shore up her broken, scattered emotions—an improvement on the numbness that stalked her lately, between brief periods of euphoria and gut-wrenching fear.

But if anyone should be on this assignment, it was Sabra. Laura was grateful for the woman, for her loyalty not only to Perseus but to the Trayhern family. A trickle of real hope entered her heart. Yes, with Sabra heading up the team, Laura just might actually get her son back—safe and sound.

Sabra entered the Perseus office at exactly 1300, the time she'd promised Jake she'd show up. Marie looked up from her desk and smiled.

"Hi, Sabra."

"Hello. Where is everyone?"

"They went to lunch." Marie looked at her watch. "But they should be back soon." Standing, she said, "May I get you some tea while you wait for them in the War Room?"

"I'd love a cup, thanks."

"Earl Gray, right?"

"You never forget anything, do you?" Sabra smiled and shook her head. She liked Marie immensely. The gray-haired woman was the soul of efficiency.

"Well," Marie said with a worried chuckle as she opened the War Room door for Sabra, "I try not to, but with the way things are now, I'm afraid I sometimes am forgetful."

Sabra lost her partial smile. "What do you mean?"

"It's not for me to say, Sabra. Jake Randolph will want to fill you in himself," the woman replied in a low voice, motioning Sabra to take a seat at the oval table. "Jake is heading up Perseus for now, with Laura's blessing. Wolf Harding and Sean Killian are assisting him."

Raising her eyebrows, Sabra nodded thoughtfully, wondering where Morgan was.

"Do you know any of them?" Marie asked.

"I know Killian, but I've only heard of Harding and Randolph through the grapevine, so to speak." Sabra took a seat, propping her elbows on the table's highly polished surface.

"I'll get your tea," Marie offered. "Have you eaten?"

"Yes, tea will be fine. Thanks." She watched Marie shut the door. The War Room felt comfortable to her after all these years. It was where Morgan had given her and Terry every one of their assignments. The expanse of oak, shining from the obvious care given it, stretched before her. Ten chairs surrounded the table, but the room seemed ominously quiet. Sabra knew the entire room had been shielded with a thin, space-age metal to prevent eavesdropping by any spying country. Reports could be made and assignments given with full confidence here.

Absently, she ran her fingers across the table's smooth surface. Wood had such a warm feel, almost like skin. But then, Sabra wryly reminded herself, she was always close to nature. Was it her Irish heritage through her mother, born to a fishing family on the seacoast? she wondered idly, as she had so often before. Or the French grape-and-wine-country ancestry of her Israeli father, now a general in the Mossad? Both her parents had soil in their souls, and she was glad of it. Sabra frequently used her thirty days of rest between assignments to visit either her mother's parents, who still lived in a thatched hut by the wild Irish Sea, or her own parents, in Jerusalem. In Ireland, she reveled in the endless green carpet of grass. In Israel, she felt the ancient gnarled strength of olive trees that surrounded her parent's desert home.

Sabra placed her small leather purse on the table. Greenery and desert. What a dichotomy. But then, she supposed, so was she. How did one reconcile the richness of Ireland with the arid desert of Israel? A half smile curved her lips, and she absently smoothed the cinnamon-colored silk skirt that draped around her nearly to her ankles. She had inherited her mother's rich black hair shot through with red highlights and her father's large gray eyes, patrician nose and square face. Her lips and tall, fluid build were her mother's again.

At thirty-two, Sabra often felt as if she were a citizen of two entirely different worlds. Part of her was thoroughly Irish, and that wild nature had led her to join the Mossad after getting a degree in biology, despite her mother's protests against the dangerous work. Somehow Sabra seemed to thrive on the terror that became a very real companion in her undercover spy work. Her father had wanted a son, and she had to admit that that knowledge, too, had affected her decision. She'd wanted to prove to her father that even though she was a woman, she could compete and succeed in his world.

A soft sigh escaped Sabra, and she folded her hands in her lap. Her father had tried to curtail her Mossad activities. Her skill had garnered her many high-risk assignments. But with her father a general, influential in case responsibility, Sabra had found herself getting fewer and fewer of those toughest jobs. Luckily for her, she had found Perseus and slipped from beneath her father's huge shadow. At Perseus, she was free to use all of her considerable talents and skills—at her own discretion.

Sabra's thoughts ranged back to her dear friend and partner, Terry. Quite suddenly and without warning, he'd suffered a heart attack, that had prevented them from completing their recent assignment. Terry was only forty-five, and no one had been more shocked by his attack than she. They'd been a team for five years, and they shared the kind of good chemistry that was absolutely essential in their kind of work.

Who would she be teamed with now? Sabra wondered. And what was this unexpectedly urgent assignment? She was glad that Perseus wasn't giving her the usual month of leave between assignments. She felt unfulfilled by the aborted mission with Terry. She wasn't the kind of person not to complete something she started.

The War Room door opened. "Here you are," Marie said pleasantly, placing in front of her a small tray holding a fine china cup and teapot, a spoon and napkin. Cream and sugar waited in gleaming silver receptacles.

"Thank you, Marie." Sabra smiled. "I see you've put my favorite cookies on there, too, just in case…"

"Just in case you were a mite hungry," Marie agreed, smiling back at her.

A small plate of Oreos sat next to the steaming tea on the silver tray. Touched by her thoughtfulness, Sabra picked one up and bit into it. "I hope someday, when I get married, I'll have a husband who will spoil me like this."

Tittering, Marie straightened. "When my husband was alive, he made it his business to know my likes and dislikes. He spoiled me, but I spoiled him, too."

"Marriage is a two-way street," Sabra agreed, enjoying the taste of the chocolate cookie and creamy frosting. "I don't think there are many men who would want me as a wife, though."

"Nonsense, Sabra. You're a beautiful, poised young woman, with everything to offer a man. You have brains and strength."

"Not many men are looking for that combination," Sabra said dryly, pouring tea into the waiting cup. "They may see the beauty, but that's all."

"Hmm, well, yes, there are those types out there. I won't disagree with you. But my late husband, Alfred, always said that somewhere on this globe, he knew the perfect mate was waiting for him. When he saw me, he knew it was me.''

''He knew?''

Marie smiled fondly in remembrance. ''I was eighteen. He was twenty-five and in the diplomatic corps here in Washington. I worked as an assistant to a senator. Alfred came in to the senator's office one day, angry and upset. He said he saw me sitting at my desk and forgot everything—even his anger.''

Sighing, Sabra said, ''I wish love were that easy. That uncomplicated.''

''I know it is.'' Marie frowned. ''Today's generation has grown up making it far more complicated than it needs to be, you know. Love is about being the best of friends. Of course, there's sexual chemistry, that's a given. Love means being a team and working off each other's strengths. I think if the children of today understood that, there wouldn't be so many divorces. Alfred and I were married thirty-two years before he died of a stroke. It was a wonderful marriage.''

''Listening to you makes me want to get married.''

Marie laughed and walked to the door. ''Now you're teasing me. You're one of this generation, you know. Always reading so much into things—perhaps being too realistic for something as magical as love.''

''I don't have to worry about it,'' Sabra said with a grin. ''I don't exactly have any men looking at me as marriage material.''

Shaking her finger, Marie said lightly, ''Mark my words, when the right man walks into your life, you're going to know it.''

Sadness filtered into Sabra's heart. Marie knew a great deal about her because of her position in Perseus. But she didn't know everything. "I think the man I could have loved has come and gone, Marie. I realized too late, I guess."

"That's because you let your head get in the way. I've always said this generation works too much from the head and not enough from positive emotions."

"Maybe that's so," Sabra agreed, her voice lowering with feeling.

"You enjoy your tea, dear. Jake and the rest should be back any moment."

The door shut quietly, and Sabra held the cup of tea in both hands, its warmth like a balm to the old anguish that lingered in her heart. *Joshua.* The name still brought her pain. She'd tried to forget about him. About her love for him—too little, too late. Was Marie right? Did her generation see too much of the harsh reality of life and let it prevent them from getting involved? She certainly fit that particular bill of goods.

Sipping the tea, hoping to ease the ache in her heart, she tried to close the emotional door that had been flung open unexpectedly by Marie's well-meaning counsel. Captain Joshua David had been a fighter pilot in the Israeli Air Force. One of the best—destined for a career of military greatness. He had been everything Sabra was not: extroverted, a joker who teased her unmercifully, in love with life. He'd lived solely in the moment—and he'd wanted her to do the same—to live with him.

The sugar she'd stirred into the tea was sweet against the bitterness of her memories. She'd been shy and introverted in comparison to the outgoing, ebullient Captain David. He'd swept her off her feet, wooed her without apology, and all she'd done was back off, finding reasons not to date him, not to open up to him. Josh had been so emotionally open that it had scared the hell out of Sabra.

She still wondered how he had been able to do that. She'd suffered too many hurts, too many disappointments over the years to parade her vulnerability about as he had. The hare and the tortoise. He'd always accused her of being the turtle in their on-again, off-again relationship, which had ended suddenly. Shockingly.

Biting down on her lower lip, Sabra closed her eyes and felt the rending loss. Felt the old pain that somehow never quite went away. After that, she'd left Mossad. Left Israel. Perseus had become her new life—like a second family. And bless Terry, her older, more-mature partner. He'd been forty when she was teamed with him, and she'd been an injured, disillusioned twenty-seven. Terry had been more father than friend to her, if she was honest about it—everything she'd ever wished her own father would be. In five years, Terry had in his own safe way helped her to heal. He'd treated her with respect, as an equal—something she'd always wanted from the men in her life but had never before experienced.

Sabra knew Terry would retire now, and she would miss him terribly. He was an introvert like her, philosophical and quietly worldly. He'd been a mercenary all his life, and he'd noticeably mellowed over the years. Terry had been able to impart the wisdom of his life experience to her; and to her own credit, Sabra had assimilated it, had grown from his lessons. He'd taught her to be a risk taker, within reason—not going off half-cocked with some half-baked plan. He'd taught her the importance of attending to details, meticulous details that could save their lives. But his caution and common sense didn't make him a coward. If a risk had to be taken, Terry would be out in front of her, his life on the line as surely as was her own.

Slowly opening her eyes, Sabra felt the ache in her

heart deepen. Terry had been more than a partner. He was part sage, part mentor and mature beyond his years. She already missed him terribly. And until this moment, she hadn't realized just how much she'd relied upon his experience and wisdom.

Well, whoever they teamed her with now she wouldn't dare compare to Terry. He'd been called the Old Man in the merc business, and he had the scars—both physical and emotional—to prove it. What would her new partner be like? Would he be older? Sabra hoped so. She had an easier time getting along with older men than with those in her own age group. They lacked the sort of maturity she'd learned to rely on.

The door opened unexpectedly. Sabra set her teacup back on its saucer and stood up. Instantly, her intuitive side was awake, picking up fragments of impressions, assessing body language and facial expressions. The big man dressed in a wrinkled, white short-sleeved shirt and dark brown chinos was the leader. His scowl was set, and his eyes missed nothing. His gaze pinned hers.

"Sabra Jacobs?"

"Yes."

"I'm Jake Randolph. Welcome."

He extended his large, scarred hand, and Sabra felt an immediate liking for his directness and warmth. She gripped his hand firmly. "Hello. Where's Morgan?"

Jake turned and stepped aside. "We'll get into that in a moment." He gestured for the rest to enter.

Sabra felt her eyes widen as Laura Trayhern entered the room after the two other mercenaries.

"Laura!"

Laura smiled wanly. "Hi, Sabra." She opened her arms.

Caught off guard by her unexpected presence, Sabra

gave a hesitant hug to the smaller woman, then pulled back a step. "What are you doing here?" Sabra's radar was going off; she'd never seen Laura at Perseus, and she knew, as all the operatives did, that Morgan didn't want his family involved in his company—for a lot of good reasons.

"Sit down," Jake invited, as Wolf Harding closed the door, "and we'll fill you in."

Stymied, Sabra slowly sat. She was shocked by how pale and thin Laura was. The small-boned woman, who slipped into the chair opposite her, looked haggard and drawn. Sabra's heart began to pound a little faster, with dread. Something had happened. But what? She pursed her lips to stop herself from blurting out her troubled questions. She watched warily as Jake sat at the head of the table—in Morgan's habitual seat.

Obviously Morgan wasn't here. Sabra's glance cut to Laura. Although she was dressed in a navy suit and white silk blouse, her blond hair neatly in place as always, falling in soft curls around her shoulders, the lipstick coloring her mouth seemed almost garish against her unhealthy pallor. Sabra clenched her hands, picking up on an incredible grief surrounding Laura. The other woman's eyes, usually shining with life, were dark and shadowed.

Never had it been harder to keep a hold on her always-limited patience. Sabra had hoped that as she got older, her patience would grow with her, but so far she wasn't having much luck. Her mother was terribly impatient, and Sabra seemed to have inherited that family trait with a vengeance. As her gaze skittered from one face to another, she realized how grim and somber they all were. But she was especially disturbed by Laura—by the unknown tragedy written clearly across her tense features.

"We're glad you're here," Jake said heavily. "And

what we are going to share with you doesn't leave this room. Is that understood?"

"Of course," Sabra murmured, frowning because Morgan would never question her confidentiality.

"Good." Jake opened his hands. "I'm going to make a long story very short for you, Sabra, because time is of the essence. About a month ago, Enrique Ramirez, the Peruvian drug lord Perseus has been battling off and on for the past five years, kidnapped Laura, Morgan and their son, Jason."

With a gasp, Sabra nearly came out of her chair, then caught herself and forced herself to sit back down. Her gaze was riveted on Laura, her senses reeling. "My God…"

"We had no teams available when we managed to trace Laura's whereabouts, so we brought in two outside people for her rescue. Thankfully, they were equal to the task, and we owe them a great deal of gratitude. Now you've come in off a busted assignment, and we have got another team member in. Thanks to Killian here, and the CIA, we've managed to pinpoint where Jason Trayhern is being kept, or at least where we *think* he is."

Jake got up and crossed to the wall, pulling down one of the many well-used maps—this one of the Hawaiian Islands. Punching his finger at the map, he said, "We have reason to believe that the boy is on Maui. Killian intercepted a cryptic message via satellite relay, suggesting that Jason is being held on the island. After a lot of investigation, we discovered that Ramirez has a well-concealed, multimillion dollar investment in condominium holdings on Maui.

"As you may know, one of Ramirez's right-hand men is Garcia, and the CIA was able to provide documents showing that Garcia has a hideaway near Kula, a small town in up-country Maui, on the side of the big, inactive volcano, Haleakala.''

Sabra sat very still, her fingers wrapped around the arms of her chair as if to hold back her surging emotions. No wonder Laura looked so ill. The darkness in her eyes *was* grief—her husband and son were prisoners.

"Is Morgan there, too?"

"No. We're still working twenty-four hours a day covering satcom links, trying to get a clue to his whereabouts, as we did with Jason. The Maui police will be helping you. We've got full approval from the state, and they will provide us with whatever we need. But they can't get a warrant to enter Garcia's estate because no one has actually seen Jason."

"So all of this is circumstantial?"

"Yes, I'm afraid so. We're asking you and your new partner to go into Maui posing as a husband-and-wife team, there on assignment to photograph the flora and fauna of Haleakala. You'll set up on the hillside and covertly watch Garcia's estate until we can confirm whether Jason is there. We've cautioned the police not to put Garcia under surveillance, because we don't want to raise his suspicion. If Jason is there, we don't want Garcia to panic and move him. If he does that, we could spend months trying to locate him."

"I see," Sabra whispered. She turned her head to hold Laura's tragic gaze. "I'm so sorry, Laura. So sorry...." And she was. She loved Jason and Katy almost as if they were her own. And she knew how much Laura and Morgan loved them. Family meant more to Morgan than anything, and Sabra had often seen his children pull him out of one of his dark moods. Their innocence and enthusiasm were like sunlight to him. And no one was a better mother than Laura. Sabra hurt deeply for her friend, almost unable to believe that a terrible tragedy had once again cast its pall over the Trayhern family.

Laura managed a brief, wan smile. "What I'm thankful for, Sabra, is that it's you who will be on this assignment. Jason loves and trusts you. If anyone should be there to rescue him, it's you."

"Yes," Jake agreed heavily, "it's definitely in our favor for the boy to know one of the team members."

"Do we know anything of Jason's condition?"

"Nothing."

Sabra looked at Laura. "What did they do to you?"

Laura shrugged. "They drugged me...."

Sabra turned her attention back to Jake. "Jason could be drugged, too."

"Yes." Jake glanced at Laura, a worried expression on his face. "They nearly killed Laura with an overdose of cocaine. We're concerned that Garcia might do the same with Jason."

Anger chilled Sabra as she met Jake's concerned gaze. "I had a run-in with Garcia three years ago. He's an ugly little man with a depraved mind. If I know the bastard at all, his idea of getting even with Morgan and us would be to make his son an addict."

"Oh, dear..."

Sabra turned at Laura's small cry of alarm.

"Laura," Jake said quickly, "we don't know that." He gave Sabra a warning look, obviously telling her to say nothing more.

Sabra gazed down at the table. She should have kept her mouth shut. Laura had turned even paler, if that was possible. Looking back up at Jake, Sabra said quietly, "Laura, I don't think you should be here. You need to go home and rest. It won't help you to hear the details of this mission—a lot of them 'what-ifs' that may never happen. You've been through hell. Don't sit here and keep hurting yourself.''

"I think that's a good idea," Jake rumbled. "Come on, Laura, Sabra's right. Her remark was only a possibility, but all these ideas have to be put on the table and discussed. And it's only going to tear you up to hear them. Come on, let's go...."

Sabra felt terrible as she watched Jake help Laura to her feet, then walk her to the door. As he opened it, Laura turned back toward her.

"Promise me you'll see me before you go, Sabra?"

Sabra nodded. "I'll see you."

"I—I have Jason's favorite toy, a little gray squirrel. If—if you could take it with you, maybe—"

"Laura, she'll come by and see you," Jake reassured her gently, placing his hand on her arm and leading her out of the room.

"My God," Sabra whispered as the door closed. She looked up at the two remaining mercenaries. "I didn't...I didn't know...."

"It's okay," Wolf grunted, placing his hands palm down on the table. "Laura should never have been in on the planning anyway, but she insisted."

"She's too wounded to hear all of this," Killian rasped.

"I should have kept my mouth shut," Sabra murmured.

"Don't blame yourself," Wolf insisted.

"Jason. Jason's kidnapped. But why him? Why hurt a child?''

"We think," Wolf offered, "that Ramirez took Jason because he's Morgan's only boy. You know how South Americans emphasize the importance of the oldest son."

Closing her eyes, Sabra felt the shock moving through her. "And Jason is such a sweet, curious little boy. He's so trusting...."

"Too trusting," Killian said. "Garcia will use that against him."

"What a horrible thing," Sabra whispered bitterly. "Those drug lords will stoop to any level for revenge."

"That's why we've removed Laura from her home. We're afraid of further reprisals," Wolf answered. "She's staying at a safe house we've arranged, with Killian's wife, Susannah—her cousin. Just for your info, Laura is on tranquilizers and seeing a therapist twice a week."

"She looks so fragile. No wonder…"

"We're all worried about her." Wolf grimaced. "What you don't know yet is that Laura was repeatedly raped by Garcia."

Pressing her fingers to her lips, Sabra stared at Wolf in shock. A combination of revulsion, anger and hatred twisted through her. It took her several minutes to wrestle the explosion of feelings back under control. Until then, all she could do was stare at Wolf's dark features.

Jake entered the room and quietly shut the door behind him, his mouth set in a grim line. "Marie is going to take Laura home. She'll be better off there."

Sabra nodded. "Jake, I—"

"Don't apologize," he said, sitting back down. "You're walking into this mess cold. Laura knew the risks when she came to this table. She's not dumb."

Bowing her head, Sabra whispered, "I know how much Jason means to her. If we can't get the boy back…"

"One step at a time," Jake cautioned, holding up his hand. "First we need to introduce you to your new partner. Then we need to do some detailed planning. The Hawaiian police are waiting for you, but I don't want to go into the details of the mission until Talbot arrives." Jake glanced at the clock on the wall. "Marie got word that he landed. He should be on his way."

"Talbot—is he my new partner?"

Jake opened a dossier and slid it across the table toward her. "Yes. Craig Talbot. He's been with Perseus for six months. Study his file while we wait."

Sabra felt their interest, on her reaction to the information on Talbot. She looked down at the open folder and was greeted by an 8-by-10 color photo of her new partner. True to her training, she carefully masked any overt reactions, but inwardly, her heart gave an unexpected thump. Talbot's oval face featured a strong jaw and a hawklike nose. What drew her, though, were piercing, dark blue eyes with large, intelligent black pupils, eyes that made him look more like an imperious eagle than a man. He looked in his early thirties—near her own age—and something about his mouth, a thin slash that seemed to be holding back so much, touched her heart. On the left side, a scar at least six inches long extended down his lean cheek, and that whole side of his face had an unusual shiny quality.

His hair was black with blue highlights, cut military short, and his black brows straight, emphasizing the glittering eyes that even in a two-dimensional photo seemed to miss nothing. Sabra hid her initial reaction. Talbot was neither good-looking nor bad, but he had seen perhaps too much in his relatively short life. He was deeply tanned, and though he'd obviously shaved, a darkness shadowing his jaw gave him a dangerous look—and a dangerous appeal.

Sabra had met many mercenaries in her years of service with Perseus, and she was familiar with military men and their demeanor, but this man put her on guard. She stared at the photo, trying to keep her brain at bay and allow her feminine instincts to tell her why. Talbot possessed an animal-like quality, as if he lived life on a very thin edge that could crumble at any moment. The set of his mouth, his compressed lips, hid a great deal. But what was he hiding? The scar on his left cheek appeared fairly recent.

All Sabra could receive intuitively was that Talbot was unsettling to her on every level. But why? Was it the frosty challenge in his bold blue stare? The secrets protected behind that well-shaped mouth? The boxerlike set of his jaw, defying anyone to try to hurt him? Sabra was sure he had been hurt.

The crow's-feet at the corners of his eyes reminded her of Josh. Aviators always had crow's-feet from squinting against the sun. She sensed a hidden vulnerability to Talbot, though when this photo was taken, he'd obviously been doing his best to camouflage it. As she stared into the eyes, she saw a darkness there, just as she had in Laura's eyes. Grief, perhaps? Pain? The feeling around Talbot wasn't inspiring Sabra to any greater insights. He was a man of many secrets—unlike Josh. Unlike Terry.

Forcing herself to casually push the unexpectedly provocative photo aside and look at his personnel record, Sabra saw that Talbot was thirty-two—her age. His birthday was May 22, making him a mere two months older than she was. He'd been born in Fort Wingate, New Mexico.

Before joining Perseus, he'd had a career as a marine helicopter pilot. Her heart skipped a beat: he'd been a pilot just as Josh had been. Her heart aching, Sabra compressed her lips. Talbot was single. Why had he resigned his commission shortly after Desert Storm? Sabra had a lot of questions, but decided to hold off on them until he arrived.

When she realized that he took only low- and medium-risk assignments, she lifted her head and looked at Jake, surprised. "This is a high-risk assignment. He doesn't have the background for it."

Jake's mouth became a slash. "Yeah, we know." He opened his hands. "We don't have a choice in this, Sabra. Talbot's the only person available for the assignment right now. It takes all three of us to stay on top of things here— I don't know how Morgan did it alone. We're scrambling just to keep communications open between the State Department, the CIA, Interpol and the FBI on these kidnappings. If we could, one of us would go with you, but it's not possible.

Sabra frowned. "He's only got six months with us, in low- or medium-risk missions. There's no comparison between those and a high-risk assignment."

"Talbot is ex-marine. He knows how to handle himself and weapons."

"I'm sure he does," Sabra said, her voice deepening with concern. "But we're going undercover. Has he ever done that?"

"No."

Frustrated, she looked at Jake for a long moment. "So you're saddling me with a green team member. Talbot might as well have walked in off the street."

"He's not our ideal pick," Jake admitted heavily, "but Sabra, we don't have a choice. Right now, it's most important that we verify that Jason is on Maui, don't you think?"

"Of course," she said. "But if we do verify it, Talbot and I will have to go in after him. I don't know Talbot, and I don't know how he'll react if and when we're faced with a potentially life-threatening situation." She took a deep breath. "I'd rather do the assignment alone than with a rookie, Jake. I really would."

"I understand your concerns, Sabra. But Talbot has the

capacity to live up to our expectations for this mission. We've just never asked him to do it before.''

"Does he know he's being asked to do it now?'' she asked, sarcasm in her voice.

Jake glanced away. "Not yet. He will shortly.''

She glared at him. "This really smacks of loose planning, Jake, and I don't like it. I don't mind risking my life to find Jason, but I'm not about to add the burden of teaching someone who isn't prepared for this kind of assignment.''

"Why don't we wait and see?'' Wolf pleaded. "None of us knows Talbot. After all, he went through Desert Storm as a combat helicopter pilot. That says something doesn't it?''

"Yes,'' she conceded unwillingly, "it does.''

"And he was in the Marine Corps since graduating from Annapolis, so the man must have tactics and strategy training down pat,'' Jake reasoned.

Sabra stood up. "Maybe I'm jumpy,'' she murmured in apology. "I mean, if Jason wasn't involved, I probably wouldn't be so concerned about my teammate's qualifications.''

Jake nodded. "I feel,'' he said gently, "that because you know and love Jason, your emotions are clouding your judgment.''

Sabra sighed. "I won't disagree with you, Jake. I'm terribly upset. And you're right—I love Jason as if he were my own son. I've baby-sat that kid since he was born. I've taken him to the zoo....'' Helplessly, she shrugged. "Maybe I am blowing things out of proportion. But I die inside every time I think about Jason being with Garcia. I want to cry....''

"We all do,'' Jake assured her, his voice rough with emotion.

"You have to realize we're going to help you every way we can," Wolf vowed. "Talbot is the unknown in this. Aside from his file, no one here knows anything about him. You're being thrown into an off-balance situation with him, we know. But we believe that with your time in grade with Perseus, and your background, you'll be able to take charge and find Jason."

Sabra glanced at Jake. "I'm in charge of the mission?"

"That's right."

She stood a long time without moving. Terry had always been the team leader. Now the shoe was on the other foot and she was in charge. Of what? A man she didn't know, who lacked the experience to work with her at the level she had to demand.

Releasing a long sigh, she whispered, "I reserve the right to say whether or not Talbot goes with me after I've had a chance to meet him and assess his abilities."

Jake scowled. "No, Sabra, you don't have the privilege of that decision."

"I demand it."

"No."

"It's my life on the line," she said hotly. "And Jason's! I'm not going to take on someone who may not have the guts to get close to Garcia to rescue Jason. What if Talbot is squeamish? What if he can't pull a trigger to defend himself? Or me? In high-risk missions we have to be concerned with that question. I know Garcia," she added, her voice trembling with emotion. "I know what the bastard is capable of doing. He raped and drugged Laura. He may have drugged Jason. If he catches me or Talbot, we're as good as dead. How do I know if Talbot has what it takes? Can I trust him? Why is he a merc in the first place? Can he shoot to kill? Would he? And is he really a team player?"

Pacing the length of the room, Sabra muttered, "I reserve the right to decide whether or not Talbot goes, and that's all there is to it."

Jake slowly stood up. "Then you're off this assignment, Sabra."

She halted and jerked around, her mouth falling open. "What?"

"You heard me." He frowned. "Under any other circumstances, I'd probably agree with you. But we don't have that luxury. All our other teams are out in the field, and it's too late to try to recruit from outside Perseus. The government isn't about to loan us a SEAL team or Delta Force. We're on our own with whatever we have at hand. We have you, we have Talbot. Look at it as a marriage of convenience. You don't have to like this guy, you just have to work with him on one mission. I hope we find Morgan alive and that he'll return to get Perseus back on line. Until then, this organization is reeling. We're all off-balance. We've been caught off guard in the worst kind of way.

"Sometimes," he added, a note of pleading entering his voice, "we have to settle for seconds. Nobody likes it, Sabra, but that's all we've got. That's life."

Shaken, Sabra said, "Where's Talbot's partner, then?"

"She died in an auto accident two days ago."

"Are you sure it was an accident?"

"As sure as we can be. It was a low-risk assignment."

Eyeing him angrily, Sabra muttered, "That's just great. Talbot's going to be upset about losing his partner on top of everything else. Do you really think he's got the emotional stability to hop from that into something like this?"

"We're all going to find out the answer to that together," Jake stated firmly. "Now, are you in or are you out?"

Glaring, Sabra said, "And if I'm out, what will you do?"

"Assign it to Talbot."

"You're crazy!"

"That's the choice we're faced with Sabra. You've been here five years. You know how the system works."

"You can't put someone like Talbot on this assignment alone. That's guaranteeing failure."

"Then agree to be the leader of the team."

Frustrated, she raked them with an angry look. "I don't like this, Jake. I don't like it at all."

"Give yourself some leeway, Sabra. Wait until Talbot comes in and we've had a chance to talk to him about it. Assess his responses."

"What if he doesn't measure up in your eyes, Jake?" Sabra challenged. "What then?"

"Then," he said heavily, "I'll ask you to go alone. I won't like it, but I'll do it."

She smiled grimly. "That's the better of two evils in this case. At least with me, you know what you're getting."

"I don't disagree."

There was a knock on the door. The room fell silent. Sabra turned, her fingers resting on the oak tabletop. It had to be Talbot. Her heart was beating erratically, and she tried to calm it—tried to calm herself. Jake was right: she was personally and emotionally involved in this assignment in a unique way. Since Jason's birth, she'd fed him his bottle, changed his diapers, watched him learn to crawl, then walk. Jason was like the son she'd always dreamed of having—the dream that had died five years ago with Josh. Whether he knew it or not, Jason had eased her pain simply by being himself. Sabra could live the dream of having a dark-haired little boy with beautiful gray eyes, though she would never admit it to anyone else. Jake had no idea exactly how close she felt to Jason—and why.

Moistening her lips, she whispered, "I'll stay on the mission."

Jake nodded. "I'm glad, Sabra. Thank you." He walked to the door and twisted the polished brass doorknob. "Come in," he said gruffly.

Sabra's eyes widened. Her heart contracted. Automatically, her hand went to the top of her chair, and she gripped it, feeling suddenly dizzy in the wake of Craig Talbot's silent, lethal entrance.

Chapter Two

Craig halted wearily in front of the War Room door. No one had been at the reception desk, which was highly unusual. Marie was such a calming, constant presence at Perseus. Exhaustion pulled heavily at him, and he ran his hand across his jaw, the prickly whiskers there reminding him he'd been without shower or shave for forty-eight hours—since the tragic loss of Jennifer.

His heart gave another twinge of guilt as her young, eager face danced once more in front of his smarting, bloodshot eyes. He shouldn't have allowed her to tail the suspect by herself. He should have listened to his gut instead of allowing her to talk him out of his decision. Once again he'd been a leader—and once again, he'd gotten someone killed.

His mouth tasted bitter from too much coffee on the flight from Europe, and he wiped it with the back of his hand, then knocked on the door again. Where was everyone? If he wasn't so damned tired, his internal radar might be picking up on something.

The door swung open, and he stared at the tall, burly man standing there in a white shirt and dark chinos. "Where's Marie?" Craig demanded.

"She's on an errand. I'm Jake Randolph, one of the Perseus mercs. Come in, we've been expecting you."

Confused, Craig stepped through the door. Two other mercs nodded greetings from the other end of the table, their faces set and unreadable. Although his senses were muddled by changed time zones and lack of sleep, Craig swung his attention to his right. His eyes widened slightly. There, on the other side of the table, stood a young woman of incredible exotic beauty. Craig stared at her. She was dressed in a silk T-shirt patterned with cinnamon, dark blue, lime green and black flowerlike colors. A cinnamon skirt draped her long thighs revealingly and hung gracefully around her slender ankles and sandaled feet.

Impressions of her assailed his numbed senses. Was it her large gray eyes, framed by thick black lashes, that entranced him? Or the soft set of her lips, unmarked by lipstick. She wore no makeup, but she certainly didn't need any. Her skin had an olive cast and her wide-set eyes were slightly tilted at the corners, giving her an exotic Egyptian quality. She reminded Craig of a statue of Queen Nefertiti he'd once seen in a museum.

Tearing his gaze from her, he followed Randolph into the room. One of the other mercs got up and quietly closed the door behind them. Randolph pointed to the chair next to him.

"I imagine you're tired, but have a seat. We've got a crisis at Perseus and I'm afraid you're one of only two mercs available for the assignment."

Stymied, Craig sat, his joints aching in protest as they

always did if he had to stay too long in one position, ever since— He coldly squashed the rest of the paralyzing thought. Trying to push the threatening past from his mind, he watched as the operative who'd closed the door came around the table and sat opposite him. The woman also took a seat. Who was she? His mind was mushy, and thinking was difficult. All he wanted was sleep, but he didn't dare doze off here, so he fought to remain awake.

"Killian, would you mind getting Talbot some coffee?" Jake asked, understanding tinging his voice.

The Irishman rose in one fluid motion and left the room.

Jake jerked a thumb toward the door. "That's Killian who just left, and this is Wolf Harding."

Craig nodded, but his gaze was pinned on the woman across from him.

"And this is Sabra Jacobs."

"A merc?" He heard the disbelief in his voice. As soon as the words were out, he was sorry he'd said them. Her slightly winged, thick brows drew down in displeasure, her eyes mirroring irritation. Despite her expression, he liked the way her thick, black hair fell gracefully around her proud shoulders. A strand dipped prettily across her brow, further emphasizing her oval face and high cheekbones. For a moment, her cheeks flushed a dull red at his unfortunate comment, and the flash of anger in her eyes stunned him. Why did it surprise him that her emotions would be revealed in them? Maybe, somewhere in his Neanderthal mind, he thought beautiful women were always poised and never showed their true feelings. Craig almost laughed at the absurdity of his clashing thoughts. Like every other man in the military, his ideas regarding women had come under fire. He was trying his best not to look at them in terms of their relative beauty of body or face, but it was nearly impossible not to appreciate Sabra Jacobs on that level.

Disgusted with his weaknesses, which were many, he disengaged his gaze from hers and returned his attention to Randolph, who seemed to be in charge. "What's going on? Where's Morgan?" Morgan always greeted returning teams, no matter what time of day or night they came in from a mission. It was one of many things Craig admired about the man—a sign of his abiding loyalty to his people. Not many bosses felt that level of care and responsibility toward their employees.

Jake opened his hands. "Talbot, a lot has happened in the past few weeks. Ramirez, a Peruvian drug lord, sent a team up here and kidnapped Morgan, his wife, Laura, and their son, Jason. The good news is we pulled an outside team together to rescue Laura, who is back home with us. Now we've got a lead on where Jason might be."

Craig sat up, stunned. His mouth dropped open. He snapped it shut. Though he remained silent as Jake filled him in on the kidnappings, his weary eyes betrayed his shock.

When Jake had finished the initial briefing, he gestured to Wolf, who leaned forward and shoved a sheet of paper across the table. "This is Garcia's estate. We got a fax of the floor plan from Honolulu FBI. Every developer that builds there has to apply for a building permit and submit a copy of the plans. This place is situated on roughly three acres of rich Maui real estate on the side of an inactive volcano. You been to Hawaii?"

"No." Craig blinked his burning eyes and tried to focus on the paper in front of him.

"Sabra's been there," Jake said, "so that's good. Anyway, we want you two to fly there, take up residence at the Westin Kaanopoli, then drive to Kula, set up your long-range cameras and keep watch. We need confirmation that Jason is there, which may mean manning cameras twenty-four hours a day on a hillside near Garcia's estate. We've got the necessary credentials in order, including confirmation of the assignment by Parker Publishing in New York, should anyone get snoopy.''

Craig looked up at Randolph. "So say we spot Jason—then what?''

"Then you'll go in and rescue him.''

Scowling, Craig said, "I don't do high-risk missions.''

"I know that's usually the case," Jake said steadily, "but what you have to understand is that all the high-risk teams are tied up with assignments. We can't break any of them free. Sabra is a high-risk merc, but her partner isn't available. You're the first person to come off the line. We're sorry about Jennifer's accident, and I'm sure you're as upset about her loss as we are. But right now we're operating under emergency conditions, Talbot, and you're the only merc we've got.''

Craig sat straighter, feeling his gut begin to tighten, a rolling, painful sensation. He wanted to lean forward to ease the pain, but all eyes were on him, the gazes seeming to eat into his raw emotional state. "So, you want to pair me with a high-risk merc for a high-risk mission?''

"If Jason's there," Jake said reasonably. "He may not be, and if he isn't, then this is classified a medium-risk assignment. You may not have to do more than sit on a Hawaiian hillside and watch through a lens. There's no danger in that.''

"But if we spot the kid, we go in," Craig persisted.

Jake nodded, watching him warily. "We have grave concerns that Garcia might shoot the kid up with cocaine and hook him on the drug as part of getting even with Morgan. When we rescued Laura, she was drugged so heavily that we nearly lost her. If we hadn't had an emergency medical team standing by on that Coast Guard cruiser, she would have died. The boy is in danger.''

Running his hand around the smooth surface of the heavy white coffee mug, Craig tried to think coherently. The part of him that wasn't injured wanted this mission. He'd always had a soft spot for kids. ''The son of a bitch shouldn't be hiding behind a little boy,'' he muttered angrily.

''Only a drug dealer would,'' Killian intoned.

''Normally,'' Jake said, ''you don't interface with drug dealers as the high-risk mercs do, Talbot. Believe me when I tell you from personal experience that Ramirez and his worldwide cartel are just about the worst kind of human beings you'll ever run into.''

''I've had dealings with Garcia,'' Sabra interjected, ''and he's like an Israeli viper—lethal.''

Craig looked up at her, surprised by the sudden change in her face from utter serenity and confidence to emotional intensity. She was leaning forward, her elbows on the table. Again he was struck by her beauty, the black hair framing her face to emphasize her slim nose, soft mouth and riveting eyes.

Reluctantly returning his gaze to Randolph, he said, ''Who would be in charge of this team?''

''Sabra would.''

Craig frowned.

''She's got five years of experience on high-risk assignments,'' Jake said.

Craig looked at her. ''And has she headed up a team before?''

''No,'' Sabra said steadily, ''I have not.''

''Well, I have.''

''Look,'' Jake said more firmly, ''Sabra will be in

charge. She has knowledge of Hawaii and of high-risk assignments.''

''Then I'm not taking the mission.''

Sabra gasped and stood up. ''You'd let the fact of a woman in charge get in the way of a little boy's life? Where are your morals?''

Craig glared at her. ''Lady, my personal integrity is none of your business.'' He hated his own icy, defensive tone. If he hadn't been so tired, so emotionally beaten by the sudden loss of Jennifer, he might have handled this situation better. At least, he wanted to. But, as usual, he was a miserable failure; the thought wounded him as nothing else could. He saw her mouth snap shut, her gray eyes blazing with hurt disbelief. She stood tensely, tall and proud, and he could find nothing to dislike about her, even in her anger and disappointment. Sabra took his breath away, though it panicked him to admit it, even to himself. Why *was* he turning down the assignment? Fear of dying? Yes. A fear of her? He sighed. Yes. Or, more accurately a fear of himself—his naked, raw response to her. That was the truth, and that was one thing Craig still had; his honesty with himself, even when the truth hurt.

Sabra felt as if she'd been stung. She halted just across from her would-be partner, who glared up at her with a defiance that made her want to slap his insolent face. ''Admit it—you don't like having a woman for a boss,'' she challenged.

''That's part of it.''

Her heart wouldn't stop pounding. She wanted to hate Craig for his decision. In her book, no one worthy of being called human would turn away from saving a helpless child, whatever the risk. ''How can you?' she demanded. ''How can you sit there when there's a vulnerable boy at the mercy of a bastard like Garcia? Have you no heart? No soul?''

Fury shot through Craig, and he slowly stood, holding her blazing glare. Her cheeks were bright red, flushed with righteous anger. Sabra was at least five feet seven, maybe a little taller, and probably weighed around a hundred and thirty pounds, if he was any judge. She was tall, graceful and defiant. No matter what she did, he couldn't dislike her. She was too beautiful, and maybe that would prove to be his Achilles' heel. ''Look,'' he rasped unsteadily, ''I'm sorry Jason got kidnapped. I don't like it any more than you do, but—''

''Then come with me on this mission!'' Sabra said huskily. ''Forget that I'm a woman. Just hold this boy's plight in front of you and know that you're doing it for him.''

The urgent plea in her low voice tore at Craig. He could feel it—and see it in her large eyes, her huge black pupils ringed by a thin crescent of gray. She held her hands in front of her, clasped to her small breasts.

He looked away from her. ''I've never been on a high-risk mission. I'd be a detriment to this assignment, and everyone here knows it,'' he said, struggling to keep the bitterness from his tone.

Jake sighed and asked Sabra to sit down, then returned his attention to Craig. ''Please take a seat,'' he entreated him in turn. ''Yes, there are problems in pairing a high- and medium-risk merc. But we don't have the time to wait for another high-risk team to come in, Talbot. I know it's not the best of all worlds, but Sabra is right—there's a little boy who is completely blameless in this whole thing, standing in the middle. Can't you put aside your personal prejudice for his sake?''

Craig gripped the coffee mug, staring down at the black contents as he mulled over Randolph's plea.

Sabra sat very still, holding her breath, praying that Talbot wouldn't take the mission. She knew she could do this on her own, and she would rather work alone than with someone whose priorities were so mixed-up. Yet, as she stared at Talbot's darkly bearded face, saw his brow kneading, his mouth compressed as if to hold back pain, she recanted her feelings. Despite the aura of animal danger he projected, a part of her wanted him on the mission. The feral quality in his shadowed blue eyes told her he would miss nothing—that he possessed an extraordinary sentience about him that would work in their favor.

Torn, Sabra kept her mouth shut. She wanted to tell him to forget it, to go home and get some sleep. That tomorrow was another day, a safe day. Her heart told her differently. Talbot appeared excruciatingly bare emotionally as he considered Jake's request. She saw the man in him, the warrior, but she also saw vulnerability. A crazy urge to lean across the table and smooth those rebellious, dark brown strands of hair off his wrinkled brow caught her off guard.

Wrestling with a turmoil of feelings that seemed too much like an out-of-control roller-coaster ride, Sabra stared hard at Craig, hoping to find the reason for her uncharacteristic confusion. She'd never experienced this strange combination of uncertainty, giddiness and challenge. What was going on?

Talbot was obviously exhausted. She saw the darkness beneath his bloodshot eyes, and the way his broad shoulders slumped—shoulders fully capable of carrying very heavy loads.

Forcing herself to disconnect from him emotionally, she looked at him through new eyes. Talbot was at least six feet tall, with a lean, cougarlike body. He was pure muscle, fit and trim. She took in his navy long-sleeved shirt—

then suddenly noticed a lot of small scars on his large-knuckled fingers, and some angry pink skin that covered the backs of his hands and disappeared beneath the cuffs, as if he'd been badly burned. As her gaze ranged upward, she saw a sprinkling of dark hair peeking from the neck of his shirt. His masculinity was powerful—and beckoning.

Sabra swallowed and found that her throat was constricted. Talbot wasn't pretty-boy handsome. But the photo in his file didn't do him justice, either, because as he sat opposite her, she felt a powerful, swirling energy emanating from him that was utterly masculine—and utterly compelling to her senses as a woman. She was shocked by her unbidden desire to lightly run her fingers across his arm and feel that latent power. Talbot sent her senses spinning as no man had ever done before.

Reeling at that revelation, Sabra sat back in her chair, more confused than ever. What she saw in Craig and what was in his personnel file seemed diametrically opposed. The man sitting here was all-warrior. So why did he take only the lower-risk missions? And something else was missing. Sabra sat up as she realized that it was his confidence. Yes, he looked strong and capable, but he lacked that gleam in his eyes that she'd seen in other warriors—a look of utter assuredness about themselves and their abilities.

She told herself that he had jet lag, and that his partner had just died—enough to snuff out, at least temporarily, any person's confidence. Sabra knew how close she was to Terry. Had Talbot been that close to Jennifer? Or perhaps emotionally involved on an even deeper, more-personal level? Sabra had heard how from time to time a man-and-woman merc team would fall in love. Studying Talbot, she could understand how any woman might be drawn to his rugged looks and those dark blue eyes that burned with inner torment. Any woman might choose to know him—to explore him like a dangerous hidden treasure.

Finally Killian leaned forward. "I think you have to separate your personal feelings from what's important, Talbot. The target is a boy. He can't protect himself. He can't escape. He's too young to realize what's happened. I'm sure he wonders where his father and mother are, but Garcia could lie to him and make him believe anything. If we don't get someone in there to help Jason, the boy could be lost to us even if he's allowed to live. I don't think you want that to happen."

Sabra released her held breath. She didn't know Killian very well, but she agreed with his bottom line. This wasn't about Talbot. He had to look to what was really important: a lone, defenseless five-year-old. She moistened her lips, exchanged glances with Jake, then covertly watched Talbot. His expression had changed instantly with Killian's statement. The anger in his eyes was doused and replaced with—fear? Sabra started to lean forward, but caught herself, forcing herself to sit back and appear relaxed. She knew the value of body language, and Talbot was feeling penned in anyway, without her silent challenge to hurry up and decide.

But why the instant of fear in his eyes? It seemed an odd response to Killian's reasonable statement. She saw Craig's mouth work as his hands caressed the mug in front of him. She had to admit he looked absolutely tortured. But couldn't he put his personal demons aside for the sake of a little boy? Sabra knew she could. A child in jeopardy spurred her to an instinctive, fierce desire to protect. She had to remind herself that almost any woman would respond similarly because it was genetically programmed into them, while some men, she knew, didn't care much for children. Was Talbot one of them?

Finally, she could stand the tension and silence no longer. Reaching slowly across the table until her fingers were bare inches from the cup Talbot held, she whispered unsteadily, ''This mission is more than that for me, Craig. I helped raise Jason. This is personal. I happened to be coming off a task as Laura gave birth to Jason, and I got to hold him shortly afterward. Over the years, I've baby-sat him, and later Katy, their daughter. Jason knows me. He calls me 'Auntie S'....'' Tears stung her eyes, and her voice cracked as she said, ''Please, put aside whatever personal feelings you have toward me. Jason is what's important, not you or me or the ghosts we carry with us.''

Talbot's head snapped up, his eyes narrowing danger-ously. Sabra felt the intensity, the heat and the torture instantly as his gaze met and locked with hers. She was shamed by the tears that leaked from her eyes and began to trail down her cheeks, but she no longer cared. ''I— I'm begging you, as one human being to another, to come with me on this mission. It's true, I've never led a team, and I'll value your experience and input. Whatever you have to offer to help us get to Jason.'' She stretched her fingers toward him. ''Please....''

Shock snaked through Craig as he stared down at her outstretched hand. His throat went dry. His mouth tasted bitter. The instant he looked into her lustrous, tear-filled eyes, it was as if she'd torn a layer out of his heart. He *felt* her pleading. For two years he had felt little, as if caught in an imprisoning cocoon, cut off from his emo-tions. But looking at Sabra's begging eyes, as the deep honey of her voice flowed through him like light in the darkness of his agonizing existence, seemed to pull him— if only for a moment—out of his personal hell.

He gripped the mug hard, feeling all eyes on him. Sabra's fingers were long and beautifully shaped, the nails blunt cut and without nail polish. If nothing else, she was herself, and Craig respected that discovery. She was confident enough in herself that she needed little outside adornment, he realized, slowly raising his head. As he met and drowned in her lustrous gaze, he felt such an incredible warmth flow through his heart that it startled him— as if the look in her eyes was capable of melting the glacier of ice he'd been trapped in for so long. The past half hour in this room with her had made him feel like living again, reviving a trickle of hope he'd believed destroyed forever.

Craig had no idea how Sabra had unlocked his heart, but he had to acknowledge that she wielded some kind of power. Did she realize her effect on him? No, not judging from the haunted look in her eyes that tore so effectively at him. Was she using her exotic beauty to persuade him? He didn't think so. There was nothing coy or flirtatious about Sabra. She was bold and straightforward in a way he could admire—and respect.

More than anything, Craig found her diplomacy appealing. She could have acted like a man and told him that whatever she said went, since she was the leader of the team. Instead, she had appealed to him on a personal level, asking for his help and counsel.

Craig delved deeply into her gray gaze, trying to ferret out her reasons for the diplomatic invitation to share her power. But all he found was grief—a plea for a child's welfare. His instincts told him she wasn't the kind of person to put on an act.

"I think," Jake said, rising slowly, "we ought to leave you two alone for a few minutes."

The other men rose and left the room. The door shut

behind them. Sabra pulled her hand back to her side of the table and sat, watching Craig in the gathering silence. He was burdened by something so terrible that he couldn't get past it to make a decision. She had no idea where that knowledge came from, but she trusted her senses.

Quietly, she said, "I know high-risk missions can be life threatening, Craig. I don't know if this one will be. There's so much we don't know yet about Garcia, or where Jason is, or how he might be guarded. I can use your help and experience on this. I—I had a wonderful mentor for five years—Terry Hayes. He was in his forties, and he'd kicked around the world for years as a merc before coming to Perseus. He taught me his craft and he taught me well. I'm not sitting here saying I know it all, because I don't. Terry taught me a whole new version of teamwork. We talked over every detail of our plans together. He listened to my ideas, and I listened to his. Sometimes—" she spread her hands as Craig slowly raised his chin and pinned her with his gaze "—I knew something from my past in the Mossad that we could use. Sometimes Terry's past would be of help."

"I don't question your sincerity about enlisting my help or experience in this mission," Craig said roughly, breaking his long silence.

Sabra stared at him, puzzled. "Then what's stopping you from saying yes? I can feel you wrestling with something—something almost insurmountable...." She held his angry, confused stare and watched his generous mouth become a dark slash against his face.

"My past is none of your business," he said in a grating tone. "None of it."

"I wasn't trying to pry...."

Shaken by her insight, Craig felt anger temporarily replace his fear. "Is there flying involved in this mission?"

Sabra reacted to the unexpected question as if he'd physically struck her in the face. Reeling from his sudden fury, she stammered, "Well—yes, the flight to Hawaii."

"What about once we're there?"

"I...don't know. I've been on Maui. Kaanopolis is at the west end of the island and Kula is to the east. A rental car should be sufficient."

"No helicopter flights?"

"Why—no...not that I know of. At least not right now."

Craig pushed the chair back and stood, glaring down at her. "Good, because I *refuse* to fly a helicopter. I refuse to even climb in one. You got that?"

Stunned, Sabra stared up into his tortured, stormy features. "Y-yes, I've got that." *Why?* Her mind spun. He'd been a helicopter pilot in the Marine Corps. Why would he refuse to even ride in one? And she hadn't asked him to fly a helicopter—it wasn't in the plan.

"Perseus owns a Learjet," she said, rattled. "That's all."

Craig paced the length of the room, his hands behind his back. "I don't like being squeezed into this mission. I can't help it if the kid got nailed by Ramirez and Garcia." He stopped and twisted to look at her over his shoulder. Sabra's face was filled with desolation at his statement. "Don't play on my sympathies about kids, because it won't work. I don't like high-risk missions. There's too much that can go wrong."

"Yes," Sabra said in a strained voice, "there's no question of that. It will no doubt require a lot of creativity and flexibility on both our parts, but I feel you have that. So do I."

"You know what your problem is, Ms. Jacobs?"

Sabra blinked once, feeling the full force of his intensity, which rattled her as nothing ever had. "Excuse me?"

He gave her a lethal look. "Your problem is that you're one of these gung-ho types that goes around saving the world. You've got confidence. You've got a lot of experience under your belt. There's one problem though—you've never hit bottom. You've never paid the price for what you do."

"What are you talking about?" she demanded throatily. "I've paid plenty of dues working with Perseus! Do you think I see my job as a game? As fun?"

He shrugged and placed his hands on his hips. "I don't know, and frankly, I don't care. You're a fresh-faced kid to me. I see the excitement in your eyes over this mission. I hear it in your voice. What worries me most is that you'll do something foolhardy just because you're personally close to Jason. Being a merc means being disconnected from everything." He jammed his thumb into his chest. "I'm about as disconnected as I can get, but you aren't. And don't sit there and tell me you can put your feelings for this kid on the back burner and behave rationally when the chips are down. You won't be able to, and you'll jeopardize us because of it."

Anger surged through Sabra, and she stood suddenly, nearly tipping over the chair. She caught it, set it firmly back on the carpeted floor and whirled toward him. "Who do you think you are? You think you know me so well, but you don't know me at all! And disconnected? I've never been disconnected from any mission I've undertaken. You're dead wrong about how that plays out in me. It makes me careful, and it makes me care."

"*Care*—" he spat the word savagely "—is going to be your undoing, Ms. Jacobs. And I'm sure as hell not going to be there to see it happen."

Sabra felt the heat rush into her face as she stood, shaking in the aftermath of his attack. "How dare you," she whispered hoarsely. "How dare you think you know me and my heart, or the kind of care I put into every mission. I didn't join Perseus because I was running away from something, Talbot. I joined because I knew I had certain talents and skills, and I cared one heck of a lot about people in trouble. I love my job, because it's about my heart and my concern for others. That's why I do it." Her nostrils flared, and she walked to the end of the table, stopping within a foot of him. He was glowering down at her, and she glared back.

"Your reasons for being a merc are obviously very different from mine," she continued warningly. "I work from my feelings, my intuition. Evidently, you're just the opposite. While we're on the topic of why we're here, why don't you tell me why you joined Perseus."

"That's none of your business," he insisted doggedly.

"Oh, yes it is. If we're going on this mission together, I have every right to know."

Breathing hard, Craig turned away from her. "It has nothing to do with this mission."

Choking back her fury, she whispered, "What are you running from, Talbot?"

He spun around, eyes blazing. Sabra stood like an avenging angel in front of him. It was the look in her eyes, lustrous with compassion and the need to understand him, that was nearly his undoing. Something deep inside him moved, cried out. He squelched the sudden desire to tell her exactly what he was running from. But the compassion in her eyes was genuine. She was concerned about him. About his ghosts. A bitter bile coated his throat and mouth. "You don't want to know," he rasped harshly.

Without thinking, Sabra reached out, wrapping her fingers around his lower arm. His skin felt chilled, as cold as the look in his eyes, the sound of his voice. "I don't care what you tell me. It won't change my mind about you." She tightened her warm grip on his arm as he tried to pull away. "No! No matter what you say, I know you care about Jason, about this mission! Come with me, Craig. Please. Maybe somehow I can help you with your past—with your fears, whatever they are. A team is only as strong as the trust two people share. You know you can trust me—I see it in your eyes. You know I won't let you down, and I know you're the same way. I trust you, even if you don't trust yourself."

With a snarl, Craig wrested his arm from her grasp. "That's the trouble," he said in a shaking voice. "You've never been hurt in the line of duty, Sabra. It makes you starry-eyed, idealistic and full of hope." He jabbed his finger at the map of the islands on the wall. "I'm gonna tell you something—this mission could get us both killed. Drug dealers place no value on life. Jason could already be dead, for all we know. You're waltzing into this situation like Joan of Arc on a charger, thinking you're going to save the day." His mouth tightened as he grabbed her arm and gave her a small shake. "The hell with the idealism. Forget wanting to save the world. I won't go in there with you unless you let me call the shots. You're a risk taker, and I'm not. I've been shot at too much, seen too many men die around me. I don't want to end up that way, and I don't want my partner ending up like that, either."

He monitored the amount of strength he used on her arm, Sabra noted through reeling senses. Craig's eyes were wild looking, haunted, the past overlaying the present and their situation. She stood very still, intuitively understanding how deeply shaken he was by whatever nightmare he'd experienced. Sweat stood out on his furrowed brow, his voice trembled with emotion and his hand was damp against her skin.

"I won't," she said in a low, steady tone, "jeopardize you or myself, Craig. I don't see myself as saving the world. I've had one partner for five years on high-risk missions, and neither of us has ever been hurt. I think that says something, don't you? How many partners have you had since joining Perseus?"

He released her, fighting the urge to simply throw his arms around her, drag her against him and hold her, as if doing so could keep at bay a world that was closing in on him. Craig looked down, startled by the calm in her husky voice. Just her firm, steady nature was pulling him back from that uncontrolled emotional edge that haunted him, especially in the dark hours of the early morning. Swallowing hard, he honed in on her voice letting it soothe him, tame his frantic fears, release him from the grip of his sordid past and the debilitating shame that accompanied it.

"I've had four partners." He saw the shock in her eyes. "Look," he said defensively, "how many partners you have says nothing." It did, but he wasn't about to admit it to her. In fact, Craig was surprised and pleased to hear Sabra had had only one partner. It told of a good, reliable, steady relationship. Something he'd never had with any of his partners.

"Why don't you have a partner now?" he demanded.

"Terry had a heart attack in Prague. He's alive, and he's going to recover, but he'll never be able to work again, at least not in our business."

"I see...." Craig turned away and took a deep, shaky breath.

Sabra waited in the silence, feeling the tension, seeing

it in every line of Talbot's body. He stood like a man already beaten. Why? She had so many questions for him, yet she knew she didn't dare ask. Right now, her only concern was to get him to agree to the mission, though a huge part of her was afraid of him. How could she stay in the same hotel room with him, night after night? Being close to Craig was unleashing every emotion, good and bad, she'd ever experienced, and that was frightening to Sabra. But she knew she had to forsake her own misgivings and put Jason's life first.

"Do you have brothers or sisters?" she asked softly.

"What?" Craig looked at her warily.

"I just wanted to know about your family, whether you had siblings."

"Do you?"

She accepted his challenge. Okay, if Talbot wanted her to open up first, she didn't have a problem with it. "I'm an only child. I never had brothers or sisters, though I wanted them. What about you?" she persisted.

Craig stared down at his leather shoes and shrugged. "I have an older brother and a younger brother."

"Oh, you're the middle child." She smiled a little, hoping to disarm him. "So were you the mediator?"

"I don't know."

"What does your older brother do?"

"Dan is a captain in the Marine Corps. He's a legal officer." Craig pulled out a chair. His knees were shaky, and he felt as if he was going to fall. He sat down heavily.

Sabra walked to the chair opposite him. She sat down slowly, smoothing the cinnamon silk over her thighs. "An attorney. That's impressive. What about your younger brother?"

"Joe runs the family trading post and grocery store on

the Navajo reservation,'' he said darkly, picking up his now-cold coffee and taking a slug of it.

"So, two of you went into the Marine Corps?"

"Yes. So what?"

"My father is a general in the army, and when I was young, I realized he wanted a son to follow in his footsteps. As I got older, he transferred into the Mossad. Shortly after getting my degree in college, I joined the Mossad, too. My father wasn't very pleased about me entering the spy business, but I wanted him to be proud of me.'' Sabra smiled sadly as Craig lifted his head to stare at her. "I spent three years there, but he kept influencing my assignments, so I quit. I came to Perseus because I liked Morgan's philosophy that getting the work done was what counted, not the gender of the worker. I've been here five years, and I nearly lost my life three different times. Maybe I'm lucky, I don't know."

Craig snorted. "Everyone's luck runs out eventually in this kind of work," he muttered, his anger dissolving in spite of himself beneath her soothing voice.

"Yours did, didn't it?"

He nodded, unable to give verbal acknowledgment to the truth. Her eyes were large with sympathy, and he felt as if he wanted to drown in them, to pull her to him and absorb her natural strength and confidence. "Someday," he said, "you'll hit bottom. It happens to everyone. It's inevitable."

"I've never denied that fact," Sabra said quietly, holding his tortured gaze. "I know that what I do could kill me."

"Then why do you do it?"

"Because people need help. Right or wrong, Craig, I feel I have something to offer Perseus as a mercenary. I'm good at what I do, but I'm not arrogant about it, nor do I fool myself into thinking I'm impervious to a bullet, which could take my life at any time.''

He shook his head tiredly. ''This is a crazy world. We're crazy.''

''I don't think so. I'd like to think that what we do is important, if only to the people we help and to the families waiting for their safe return. We aren't in the line of killing. Our job is to save.''

''It doesn't matter,'' he said flatly, all the life draining out of him. ''Nothing matters much anymore.''

''I know you just lost your partner. I'm very sorry.''

He grimaced and looked down at his cup. ''Yeah, so am I. She was a sweet kid. Idealistic. *Like you.*''

Sabra refused to be baited on that point, realizing that he was slowly giving in to the idea of taking the mission. It wasn't like her to rub salt in anyone's wounds, and it was obvious Talbot was not only wounded, but hemorrhaging from something that had happened in his past. That was why he felt so disconnected from the world in general. Her father had been the same way after the war.

''Will you help me?'' Sabra asked gently. ''Will you come with me on this mission, Craig?''

His mouth contorted. His hands tightened around the mug. The silence deepened. Finally, he lifted his head and held her warm gaze. ''If I had an ounce of sense, I'd tell you no.''

She managed a grateful look. ''Then I'm glad you don't have that ounce of sense.''

Sitting up, Craig squared his shoulders, trying to throw off the weight that perpetually saddled them. ''Don't be. If Jennifer was alive, she'd tell you the personal hell I put her through.'' His eyes darkened and his voice dropped in warning. ''I'm hell on everyone, Sabra. You'd better protect yourself from me, because if we go in together, you'll come out of this either wounded or dead.''

Chapter Three

Badly shaken by the warning, Sabra said nothing as Jake knocked lightly on the door. She saw Talbot pivot, breathing hard, his fists locked at his side. Jake looked at Talbot as he entered, then at her, and halted in the doorway.

"It sounds like a damn war going on in here," he muttered. "What have you decided?"

Talbot glared at Randolph. "I'll go."

"And you can follow Sabra's orders?"

"I'll follow them as far as I think they should be followed."

Jake grunted and walked into the room, Killian and Wolf behind him.

Sabra swallowed hard, wishing her heart would settle down. They had no more than closed the door and sat down when the phone rang. The unexpected sound shattered what was left of her nerves. Talbot was back in his place opposite his shadowed gaze trained on her. He made her nervous and frightened yet strangely excited at the same time. Why this crazy quilt of feelings. She had no time to seek an answer. Jake answered the phone.

"Laura? Yes, we've got a team in place. No...I don't think you should meet with them. You're fragile enough under the circumstances. Yes, Sabra is going—it's as we discussed."

Sabra saw Jake's scowl deepened. "Laura, I don't think—" He slowly settled the receiver in its cradle and looked gravely at them. "Laura is coming over. She wants to meet and talk with both of you."

"She's just hurting herself all over again," Sabra whispered in a strained tone.

"That's what I tried to tell her," Jake said irritably, waving his hand in frustration. "She says she has something Jason will want."

Instantly, Sabra realized it was Jason's favorite stuffed toy, the gray squirrel she had mentioned earlier. "Maybe it's better this way," she said.

"It's not," Talbot retorted sharply. "Morgan never allowed his wife into his affairs at Perseus—and with good reason. I don't want to see her. What are we supposed to say—don't worry, we'll get your son back? We can't promise that, and that's what she'll want to hear."

Glaring at him, Sabra said, "We can promise we'll try."

"Promising anything is bad news and you know it."

"Laura isn't a client. She's the owner's wife. I'd say it's a little different this time around." Again, Sabra wanted to slap his insolent face. How could Talbot be such a jerk? The last thing she wanted was him hurting Laura—she'd been hurt more than enough by this tragedy already.

"It doesn't make a difference," Craig muttered, glancing at Jake. "We promise nothing."

Jake cleared his throat and moved uncomfortably in his chair. "He's right, Sabra. When Laura gets here, don't raise her hopes. The woman's walking an emotional tightrope that's ready to shred at any moment. Just let her talk. We can only be sounding boards for her fears."

Chastened, Sabra nodded. "I understand, Jake." She didn't like it, but she understood the wisdom of his request. Still, she smarted at Talbot's harsh take on life.

"Look, why don't you two go get some coffee? The rest of us will sit here and discuss a few details of the upcoming mission for a few minutes," Jake suggested.

Sabra was more than ready to leave the tension of the room. "Fine." She was at the door before Talbot had even gotten to his feet. Outside, she drew in a deep breath of air and headed to the women's rest room. Right now, she wanted to be alone. Her feelings were raging like an unchecked flood within her and she had to try and figure out why. Maybe washing her face in cold water would bring her back to reason again. Besides, with Laura coming in, Sabra wanted to be under full control. Now was not the time to show weakness; it would only make Laura worry more.

As she walked down the long, quiet hall, she wondered if Talbot was going to be an ogre to Laura. Would he give her a good dose of his version of reality, or leave her with a shred of hope? Knowing the bastard, she suspected he wouldn't give her an inch to cling to. Anger surged in her again at the thought as she entered the rest room and turned on the cold faucet at the sink in front of the mirror.

By the time she wandered back toward the War Room, Marie had returned to her desk. Sabra's heart skipped a beat as she realized Talbot was there, too, talking with her. Marie was smiling and gesturing at whatever he'd said. And to Sabra's surprise, he was smiling back! Old Sourpuss Talbot was smiling! Sabra cautioned herself not to hold such immature thoughts. This wasn't the time or place for them. She might be angry at him for attacking her on a personal level, but she couldn't afford to hold a grudge. Jason's life was at stake, and rescuing him was all that mattered.

"Sabra," Marie called in greeting, "look what Craig brought my grandson, Chris." She held up a T-shirt depicting a boat on the canal waters of Venice. "Isn't that sweet of him?" She turned and said, "You're always so thoughtful this way, Craig. You didn't have to do it, you know."

Sabra frowned. Talbot had bought a gift for Marie's four-year-old grandson? She couldn't hide her shock. Talbot flushed under Marie's warm, genuine praise, avoiding both their gazes and choosing instead to stare down at his shoes.

"How nice," Sabra said in a choked voice.

"Every mission Craig has been on," Marie said, carefully refolding the T-shirt, "he brings back some small gift for Chris."

"That's interesting," Sabra murmured. The words came out with more sarcasm than she'd intended, and when Talbot snapped a look in her direction, she realized she'd hurt his feelings. Damn! Why was she behaving like an immature teenager? She had never done so around Terry. Never, for that matter, around anyone. What was it about Talbot that drew her full range of emotions?

"Actually," Marie continued, "Chris and his parents were in here on a visit one time, and Craig happened to meet them." She turned to him and smiled. "I believe that was right after Morgan hired you, wasn't it?"

"Yeah, something like that," Craig said uncomfortably, wildly aware of Sabra's renewed interest in him. Her face had lost a lot of his sarcasm as Marie explained the circumstances. A huge part of him felt it was none of her business.

"Chris was three and a half at the time, Sabra, and he went flying toward Craig as he came out of the War Room. That little guy took to Craig like a duck to water." Marie chuckled and reached out, touching his arm. "Your first assignment was to Germany, and you brought Chris back that teddy bear. My grandson just went crazy over the gift," Marie said in a confidential tone. "Ever since then, Craig's always brought some little gift for Chris when he comes in with his report." Her eyes filled with tears. "You're so special, Craig. I hope you know how happy you make my grandson."

Craig wanted to escape Sabra's interested gaze. He squirmed inwardly as she studied him curiously. Her face had softened considerably as Marie had continued the story. Why? Had she thought he was some kind of unfeeling monster who hated children? Apparently so—until now. He saw confusion and then understanding come to her eyes. He turned to Marie.

"I really don't think Ms. Jacobs is that interested in all this, Marie."

"On the contrary," Sabra said smoothly, walking toward them. "I'm very interested."

Just then, Marie's intercom buzzed. She leaned over it. "Yes, Jake?"

"Are Talbot and Jacobs out there?"

"Yes, they are. Want me to send them in?"

"Would you, please?"

Marie nodded to them. "Go on in."

Relieved, Craig was the first to the door. Out of habit,

he opened it for Sabra. Old ways died hard, he reminded himself. In the Marine Corps, an officer always opened a door for a woman. Times were changing, but he didn't care. Noticing the surprise in her eyes, he smiled slightly.

"What's the matter?" he taunted.

She slowed and turned to him. "I'm surprised, that's all."

"Get used to it."

Sabra held his challenging stare and started to give a flip answer in return, but decided against it. Jake and the others were listening, and she had no desire to continue to dig at Talbot. It was time to put her responses toward him away and get on with the business at hand. She seated herself and watched as Talbot shut the door, then reclaimed his seat.

Jake folded his hands in front of him and looked gravely at each of them. "We've got some real reservations, and I think we should put them on the table for discussion."

Craig waited.

Sabra frowned.

"We feel there's a lot of antagonism between the two of you. That's not good for the mission. I'm worried, frankly, that you aren't going to listen to Sabra, Talbot. Tell me I'm wrong, will you?"

Craig shrugged. "I said I'd follow her orders. If I feel there's a different way, a better one, we'll discuss it."

"Sabra, how do you feel about that?"

"I don't have a problem with communicating, Jake. It's absolutely essential on a mission like this. I want to talk everything out beforehand."

"All right," Jake said, his features reflecting a degree of mollification. He turned to Talbot. "We all have the impression you don't really like Sabra."

Craig smarted at Jake's statement. "Then you're wrong," he snapped. "I neither like nor dislike her."

"Something's eating you about her," Jake prodded. "You tell us what it is."

Wrapping his hand around his cold cup of coffee, Craig said, "I don't like her high level of confidence. It could get us killed."

Sabra glared across the table at him. "My 'high level of confidence' has often kept me and my partner from getting killed, Mr. Talbot. I think you've got this all wrong, frankly." Damn! Why couldn't she just stick to the facts? Why keep rising to his bait? Sabra closed her eyes for a second. When she opened them, she held up her hands. "Hold it. We've got to stop this bickering. I have to stop making digs at Talbot." She opened her eyes and held his blunt stare. "I don't like it that you seem too careful. That can hurt our efforts as much as going off half-cocked."

"Neither of those ways will serve you," Jake warned darkly. "You two are going to have to talk at an impersonal level with one another and hash these things out. Sabra, you're right—you can't afford to pick at Talbot. He has a different operating procedure than you do, is all. That's not to say his way is bad. It's just different from yours."

"I know that," she said irritably. "And I promise to make the necessary compromises to ensure this mission is successfully completed and Jason is returned to Laura. That's all I want, Jake."

"I know," he murmured. "What about you, Talbot? Do you think you can compromise with Sabra, if it comes down to that? Or are you going to shove your way of doing things down her throat?"

Talbot's mouth quirked. "I'll compromise, Randolph."

"Then we have your word on this—both of you," Jake said, relief now evident in his voice.

A light knock sounded at the door. He scowled. "It's probably Laura." He looked at them darkly. "Keep your war between yourselves. Show her your best side. I don't want her worrying any more than necessary."

Craig stood as a small, thin woman with blond hair was ushered into the War Room by Marie. He was shocked by her haggard appearance—and felt an unwanted pang at the sight of the small blue blanket and stuffed squirrel she clutched to her. When Jake introduced him, Laura gave him such a warm, grateful smile that he temporarily forgot everything. Her blue eyes swam with tears as she reached out toward him.

"Marie says you're wonderful, Mr. Talbot," she whispered. She gripped his hand. "I'm so grateful you're taking on this mission. Here, I wanted to give you this. This is Jason's 'blanky.'"

Craig gently took the very worn, obviously much-loved blanket from her. The figure of Winnie-the-Pooh was embroidered into one corner of the soft blue fabric, though it, too, had lost some of its color over the past five years. "Sure," he whispered, touched by her intense emotions, "we'll take it with us, Mrs. Trayhern."

"Oh…" Laura choked, pressing her fingertips against her lips and reaching out to touch the blanket one last time. "I pray you'll be able to give it to him. How upset he must be by now. Jason waited every night until his father got home. They are so close, Mr. Talbot. If—if you can give Jason this blanket, I just know it will help him. I know it…"

Sabra came around the table and gently placed her hands on Laura's frail shoulders. "We'll do our best, Laura. No one loves kids more than we do, believe me."

She saw Talbot shoot her a dark look. Well, maybe he didn't like them as much as she did. Still, she felt intuitively that Craig loved children more than he let on. Why else would he keep bringing home gifts for Chris? He was such a strange, quixotic mixture of qualities, she had to admit she couldn't really read him. Talbot was highly complex—a man with a lot of secrets.

Sniffling a little, Laura patted Sabra's hand. "I know you'll do everything you can to bring Jason back to me. I know how much you love him, Sabra. Here's his favorite toy."

Sabra felt tears in her eyes and swallowed against a lump as she held the stuffed toy in one hand and gripped her friend's shoulders more firmly. "We'll bring him back, I promise you."

Embarrassed by her tears, Laura whispered, "I'm sorry, Jake. I—I know I shouldn't be here, but I had to meet Sabra's partner. I—I had to be sure...."

Jake nodded and eased Laura out of Sabra's grasp. "We all understand, Laura. You can see that Sabra and Craig are the best people for this mission."

Taking a handkerchief from the pocket of her suit, she dabbed at her eyes. "Y-yes, I do see that."

"Come on, you need to go home now, Laura. You need to rest." Once again Jake led her out of the room. Killian and Wolf followed.

The minute they were alone, Craig rasped angrily, "You had no right to promise her anything!"

At the intensity of his whispered words, Sabra felt as if she'd been struck. His eyes blazed. Taking a step back, she retorted, "It's too late to take it back, isn't it?"

Craig gripped the small blanket in his fist. "You've set her up. You know that."

"For what?" Sabra flared huskily. "I just wanted to reassure her."

Bitterly, he thrust the blanket at her. "All you've done is foolishly raise her hopes. What if we can't get Jason? What if he's already dead? How have you helped her by being Miss Goody Two Shoes?"

"I was trying to help her, that's all!" Sabra's heart was pounding furiously in her breast. "I'm not the ogre you are, Talbot. Maybe you don't believe in hope. Well, I do! And I'm damn well glad if I can give some to Laura."

"It's one thing to offer hope," he snarled, "and it's another to promise something we may not be able to deliver. You crossed that line, Ms. Jacobs."

Breathing raggedly, Sabra held his stare. In that moment, she realized she was coming up against the hard-bitten warrior—a man who wasn't about to back off. In some ways, his harsh response was reassuring, because Sabra wondered if he had the guts to remain staunch when a situation demanded it. On high-risk missions, that kind of endurance counted. She turned the blanket in her hands. "Okay," she whispered, "maybe I did go overboard. Laura is more than an employer to me. She's been my friend for five years. I love Jason as if he were my own boy...."

Craig placed his hands on his hips and watched her face soften, heard her voice went low with pain. "I hate it when missions involve children."

Sabra looked up and was shocked to see his undisguised anguish. The change was as startling as it was breathtaking. No longer was he the avenging warrior, anger blazing in his eyes. Looking down at the blanket and touching it softly, she whispered, "I'm so scared, Craig."

Craig frowned. His hand twitched with the need to

reach out and touch her. But he stopped himself. "Of what?" he demanded hoarsely.

"Of—" Sabra risked everything and looked up at him as she crushed the blanket to her breast "—of failing. Oh, God, I know how much Laura loves Jason. I know what the boy means to her and Morgan. What if—what if he's dead?" She searched Craig's stormy eyes for an answer she knew he didn't have.

"Look," he said roughly, placing his hands on her shoulders, "you can't flail yourself with that stuff. Just shut it off. We've got work to do." He gave her a small shake. "You can't blame yourself, whatever happens." He stared deep into her moist eyes. "You know that, don't you?"

Sabra felt the bite of his hands on her shoulders, felt his courage, his steadiness, for the first time. It was shocking, his touch, which communicated strength as well as gentleness. She hadn't thought Talbot possessed those qualities. As she forced herself to look up into the deep blue of his eyes, she recognized in him a unique type of strength that was different from—and complementary to—her own. His hands were warm against her blouse, and she felt their heat radiations through the silk to touch her frightened heart.

"I—I want you to know," Sabra said brokenly, "that this is the first mission I've been on that I've had a personal stake in. I've never had a connection with the people on a mission like I do with Jason...with Laura. I felt for the families involved, of course, who hoped we could help them. But this is different, Craig."

"I know," he murmured wearily. Forcing himself to release her, because if he didn't, he was going to do the unthinkable—wrap his arms around her and crush her tightly against him—he allowed his hands to slip away.

The need for Sabra, for her raw strength and courage almost overwhelmed him. Craig took a step back. "Look, I'm rummy with exhaustion. I can barely stand, and I sure as hell can't walk straight anymore. I need to get over to my apartment in Fairfax, shower, change clothes and shave."

Sabra felt bereft when his warm, strong hands lifted. She stood, swaying slightly, the child's blanket pressed tightly to her. The look in Craig's eyes startled her. Heated her. For just a moment, there had been a change from darkness to gold in their depths as he'd looked down at her. Her mouth dry, she stammered, "Why—why don't I drive you? You're too tired to drive yourself. Everything I need is here and I've had two days' rest. Maybe when we get on that flight to Hawaii, you can sleep."

His mouth twisted, and he rasped, "Planes and I don't get along, remember?" With a shake of his head, he added, "Let's saddle up. You'll drive my car for me?"

"Sure," Sabra said, gently folding the toy up in the blue blanket.

Craig was too tired to think or feel anything. "I'll give you directions. Let's go."

Sabra stood in the living room of Craig's small, one-bedroom apartment and looked around. Yes, he had furniture, but somehow the place felt empty. She spotted a couple of photographs on the television set and went over to look at them. As she leaned down to inspect them, she felt someone else in the room. Turning, she saw Craig watching her darkly. He'd come out of a quick shower, a towel wrapped haphazardly around his waist.

Sabra straightened, her pulse bounding. She hadn't been wrong about Craig Talbot looking dangerous. His chest was covered with a mat of dark hair, emphasizing

his primal, animal side. His shoulders were thrown back
with natural pride and grace. Her mouth went dry as she
realized that the stark whiteness of the terry-cloth towel
dipped provocatively below his navel, hugging his narrow
hips. In a physical sense, he was beautiful, lean and very
fit. Her gaze went to his arms. The pink burn scars were
not only on the backs of his hands, but claimed at least
half the skin up to each elbow. She wondered what terrible fire he'd been in and somehow survived. If he realized she was staring at him, he didn't show it as he rubbed
at his dripping hair with another, smaller towel.

"Those are my brothers," Craig said, walking toward
her. He told himself to stop—to turn around and leave.
Sabra stood like a tall, graceful willow in his apartment—
so wonderfully alive. He couldn't decide whether it was
her exotic beauty, the sudden flush on her cheeks or the
shyness in her eyes that drew him. As he realized she was
blushing over his dress code—or lack of it—he smiled to
himself. Should he tell her he walked around draped in a
towel after every shower? That it was one of his many
eccentricities?

The look in Sabra's eyes spoke of more than shyness;
he saw a pleasure in them, that made him feel powerful
and good. It was nice to be admired—especially by her.
Still, he was touched by that shyness. Despite her many
strengths, Sabra was vulnerable, he discovered. How did
she balance that against the cruel realities of their work?
A desire to sit down and talk with her at length overcame
him as he walked toward her. She was the kind of woman
he usually liked—intelligent and her own person, with a
good sense about herself as a human being.

Sabra tore her gaze from Craig's beautifully sculpted
form. The ache to reach out and touch him, to see if he
was real—if he was as dangerous as her spinning senses

told her he was—was almost her undoing. Gripping her hands together in front of her, she forced herself to turn back to the photos. She could literally feel him coming toward her as a strange, flooding warmth enveloped her like a blanket, triggering her senses. Merely standing and waiting for his approach was excruciating.

Craig draped the smaller towel around his shoulders and picked up one of the gold-framed photos. "This is my older brother, Dan, and his new wife, Libby."

He handed the picture to Sabra, and as their fingers touched, she inhaled sharply. If Craig noticed her reaction, he didn't show it. Holding the photo, she tried to concentrate on it. Dan Talbot wore his Marine Corps dress summer uniform; his beautiful bride was dressed in a pale blue suit. "They look very happy," she murmured.

Craig managed a nod of his head, wildly aware of her closeness. He picked up the faint, lingering scent of her perfume—spicy and tantalizing, like her. "Dan deserves some happiness. He went through hell with his first wife, who turned out to be a closet cocaine user for seven years of their marriage."

"Oh, no…" Sabra spun toward him and was caught by his blue eyes, which were banked with some unknown emotion as he studied her. A wild sensation bolted through her and she momentarily lost her train of thought at his smoldering inspection. How close she was to him. She merely had to lift her hand and reach out a few scant inches to tangle her fingertips in the dark mat of hair on his chest. She exhaled shakily. This man was virile in a way she'd rarely encountered.

Craig forced himself to talk. If he didn't, he was going to reach out and stroke that wonderfully rich black hair tumbling across Sabra's proud shoulders. Would it feel silky? Warm, like her? "Dan didn't know it when he mar-

ried her," he said stiffly instead. "He discovered it after
they'd been married a year. He went through hell and
back for her. I told him there was nothing he could do to
change her if she didn't want to quit. He got pretty angry
with me when I advised him that the only recourse was
to divorce her. But eventually he was forced to see I was
right."

Sabra fingered the gold frame, trying to concentrate on
the photo. She could smell the fresh pine fragrance of the
soap he'd used and feel the natural warmth of his body
because he was standing so close. Her voice went unin-
tentially husky as she said, "A dose of your usual blunt
realism?"

He slid his fingers through several damp strands of hair
plastered to his brow. "You could say that, I guess."
Craig saw unexpected panic in her eyes. Over him? Was
he too close? Consciously, he stepped back, creating a
safer distance between them. He longed to study her face
as minutely as a scientist looking through a microscope,
but didn't dare.

"Have you always had this hard sort of realistic take
on life?"

"Yes." He stared down at her clean profile. Sabra had
the most beautiful lips he'd ever seen. They were soft,
slightly full and gently curved at the corners—and he had
this wild desire to touch them with his own, to explore
and savor the taste of them. Would she be pliable and as
hot as he suspected? The insane urge to find out nearly
unstrung him. Craig took another step back, pretending to
dry his hair some more, desperate to keep his hands
busy—and away from Sabra.

He cleared his throat. "My brothers are idealists, like
you," he said dryly. When Sabra snapped a look in his
direction, he smiled a little. "It's only a comment."

"You make it sound like a disease."

Shrugging, he said, "Sometimes it is."

She turned, holding his still-amused gaze. "I couldn't live the way you do," she said honestly. "If I didn't have some hope, some idealism, I don't think I'd survive."

"The world is made up of realists and idealists." He poked a finger at the photo. "My brother's idealism made him hang on to that marriage and suffer for nearly seven years before he got a reality check."

"He must have loved her," Sabra said simply. "That's different from idealism. You don't just bolt and run when your partner has a problem."

"I won't argue with that. But Dan's idealism prevented him from forcing her to get help or do something that could have saved the marriage. He dragged his feet, hoping that talking with her would help. It didn't, of course."

"It sounds as if, in his place, you'd have dropped the marriage in a heartbeat."

With a shrug, Craig said, "I don't believe in wasting time where I'm not wanted. His ex-wife wanted her habit more than she did him. Dan didn't want to believe that. His idealism got in the way of reality."

Sabra set the photo down and picked up the other one. "So who's this? Your younger brother?"

"Yeah, that's Joe. Our folks retired to a small place called Cottonwood, Arizona, and he stayed on to run the family trading post and grocery store at Fort Wingate. It's on the Navajo reservation in New Mexico."

"You two look a lot alike," Sabra said, studying the man dressed in a pair of well-worn jeans and a blue-and-white-checked cowboy shirt, a black felt cowboy hat pushed back on his dark brown hair. He stood by the store, smiling broadly, a border collie at his feet. But despite his similar features and coloring, Sabra realized Joe actually looked very different from Craig—both brothers did. What was the difference?

It took her a moment to realize that Craig looked battered in comparison to his siblings, as if he'd been beaten down by life more brutally. It was only conjecture, but Sabra instinctively felt she'd hit upon the truth.

"Joe's the joker of us," Craig said as she placed the photo back on the top of the television. "He's the wild cowboy from New Mexico."

"And he never went into the military?"

"No, not him. He doesn't do well with too much discipline and organization around him. I think he inherited our mother's love of the land and earth. The Navajo people love him, and he's worked hard to see they have a better quality of life."

"He sounds very humanitarian."

"As opposed to me?" He saw her flush at his insight. "Well...I meant—'

"It's okay," he told her, turning away. "I'm used to being the heavy in the family. Once, Joe was engaged to an Anglo." He stopped and twisted to look at her. "Anglo is how the Navajo describe a white person. Anyway, Joe fell head over heels with this Anglo teacher, Rebecca, on the res. He fell for her hook, line and sinker. When she told him she was pregnant, I laughed."

"Why?"

"Because the woman was pregnant when she met him, just looking for some idealistic jerk to marry her so she could have security and money. I happened to be home on leave, and I saw her coming a country mile away."

"Did Joe?"

"No." His mouth twisted. "She turned on her arsenal of charm, and he fell for it. I asked him if it was possible to really fall in love that fast. He said he thought so, but

I warned him she wanted something from him. Something she wasn't telling him.''

''So what happened?''

''I was around for thirty days, so I did a little investigating. I knew all the locals, since I'd been born and raised there. Old Doc Conner, an obstetrician from Gallup, came out to the res to see someone. On a hunch, I asked him if Rebecca was one of his patients. He said he'd been seeing her for three months, so I told Joe. He might be blind when he's in love, but he's not stupid.''

''How did he take it?''

''At first he was angry with me for suggesting she was pregnant with some other man's child. We got in a fistfight over it and both ended up with broken noses. But eventually, he went to her and she spilled the truth. He broke their engagement.''

''He must have been devastated,'' Sabra murmured.

''Yeah, he was. He really thought he was in love with Rebecca.'' Shaking his head, Craig said, ''Love doesn't happen overnight. It takes time.''

''Not always,'' Sabra challenged.

His eyes glittered. ''There you go again—your idealism is showing. You think love is that easy?''

''I didn't say it was easy,'' Sabra retorted. ''But my folks fell in love the moment they set eyes on each other. They've been married over forty years now, and they're still happy.''

His smile was cutting. ''Don't pitch one experience against the statistics, Ms. Jacobs. One out of every two marriages fails within a couple of years of tying the knot.''

''Well,'' she said tightly, ''that doesn't mean people can't fall in love quickly.''

''That's romantic love, not the real thing,'' he drawled.

Stopping in the doorway, he said, "As soon as I shave, I'll pack some clothes and we'll leave."

Sabra stood in the middle of the room feeling angry and cheated. Craig was so sure of himself when it came to love. Well, what the hell did he know about it? Very little, she was sure. With his kind of attitude, he'd probably never been involved with a woman beyond an occasional one-night stand when it suited his needs.

Sabra shook her head. That wasn't fair of her and she knew it. Wandering around the living room, she finally sat on the overstuffed couch and crossed her legs. She felt bothered by Craig's harsh view of the world. Yet his vision had helped his younger brother avoid entering a marriage based on a lie—and helped his older brother get out of one.

Maybe she was too used to Terry's easygoing ways. Terry was a realist, too, but he didn't rub his viewpoint like salt into an open wound. Talbot had so many hard edges to him. She wondered if they were edges life had placed there through experience, or ones that life hadn't yet knocked off. Either way, she felt under fire from his unyielding view. But somehow she was going to have to deal with it—and him. She rested her head in her hands. On a purely physical level, Talbot was incredibly male, a teasing masculine to her feminine desires. Yet on an emotional level, he was abrasive. Complex. Craig Talbot was highly complex, and she hadn't a clue how to handle him—or how to adequately defend her vulnerable emotions against him. What was she going to do?

Chapter Four

Sabra got up and wandered nervously around Craig's apartment. Shaken by the masculine power he exuded, she wondered if she'd assessed him correctly. Even nearly naked, he was a man no one would trifle with willingly. She shook her head, mystified by his many contradictions.

The apartment was pitifully decorated, if you could even use that word for this starkly utilitarian place. The living room held one sofa and one overstuffed chair, in an early American style, while the glass-topped table and chrome-legged chairs in the kitchen were strictly contemporary. Worse, the kitchen windows had no curtains. *Barren.* That was how the apartment struck her. The only evidence of life were those two photos on his television set.

Forcing her thoughts back to the essential business at hand, she walked back into the living room: Marie had given her a large manila envelope containing a great deal of information. The airline tickets were in there, and their hotel confirmation. Two passports gave their own first names with ''Thomas'' as a last name. Even driver's licenses in the new names, issued from the State of New York, were there. Automatically, she began organizing the credentials into her purse. Then, digging to the bottom of the big envelope, her hand touched something else, and she pulled out a small, white envelope.

What was in it? As Sabra carefully opened it, her heart dropped. Inside were two plain gold wedding bands— sized for a man and a woman. What would it be like to be married to Craig? The unbidden thought sent a spasm of panic through her, coupled with an unwanted surge of heat and desire. No question, the man appealed to her on a strictly physical level. But in every other way, he was enough to confound the wisest of women.

''Those the wedding rings?''

Sabra jumped. She'd been so intent on the rings in her palm that she didn't hear Craig approach. Angrily, she turned, upset at allowing herself for allowing her to lose the outer awareness she took pride in—and depended on. If she continued in this unaware mode, she could easily get one or both of them killed.

''I—uh, yes, they're wedding rings.'' Swallowing, Sabra tried not to stare as Craig came around the end of the couch. He wore a casual, short-sleeved navy shirt with white chinos, the blue of the shirt emphasizing his dark looks. Shaven, he looked less threatening, but that potent animal power still swirled around him. *He even walks like a cougar,* a little voice inside her whispered.

Craig saw shock and anger ignite briefly in Sabra's eyes. He took a seat on the couch about a foot away from her. ''Well, like it or not, we're married,'' he said, taking up the larger, thicker gold band from her palm and slipping it onto his left ring finger. "Hmm, Marie did a good job of picking the size." The ring fit snugly, but moved onto his finger easily. Looking up, he saw that Sabra still held her ring, betraying emotions flickering in her shadowed gray eyes. He gave her a cutting, one-sided smile. "Don't worry, this isn't for real. Go ahead, put it on. It won't bite."

Sabra's palms were damp. Grimacing, she slipped the ring on. It fit perfectly.

"Not bad," Craig murmured, reaching out for the long, slender hand sporting the shiny new band. Her skin felt warm and slightly damp as he captured her fingers, admiring the ring. Her gaze snapped to his. What lovely eyes she had. Suddenly he wanted to tell her that—wanted to express her the pleasure that touching her, even briefly, brought to him. Did Sabra realize the island of calm she offered in his chaotic life? Probably not, judging from the panic in her eyes.

"You look like a woman who just walked in front of an oncoming car," he noted wryly, releasing her hand. She snatched it back and quickly got to her feet.

"It's not that," she whispered nervously, smoothing her silk skirt.

"You've gone undercover before, I'm sure. You said 'Terry' was your partner's name?"

Sabra stood a good distance away from Craig, still feeling like a target beneath his hooded gaze. She felt stripped before him, as if he could look inside her heart and read her fear—and her crazy longing for him. "Yes," she said, her voice clipped with wariness.

"I'm sure you posed as man and wife many times."

"We did."

"This won't be any different, Sabra. Quit looking at

me like I'm some kind of monster who'll make you come to bed with me.''

She stared at him, openmouthed. ''I—I didn't think any such thing!''

His smile was sad as he rose. ''Really?'' he taunted softly. ''I know you don't like me, Sabra. That's all right. A lot of people hate my guts. So what's new? You can add your name to a very long list.'' He held out his hand. ''Where's our dossier?''

Hurt by his remarks, Sabra pointed to the envelope on the couch. ''In there.''

''Okay,'' Craig murmured. He pulled some papers out and studied them intently. ''I suppose you've got your part memorized already.''

''I'm Sabra Thomas, wife to Craig Thomas,'' she recited. ''We're professional photographers on assignment from Parker Publishing out of New York City. They want a book on the flora and fauna of Haleakala, Maui's inactive volcano.'' She pointed to the envelope next to him. ''Your driver's license, passport and credit cards are in there.''

''This is new to me,'' he admitted, looking over the information. ''On my assignments, we've always kept our own identities.''

''In high-risk,'' Sabra murmured, ''we never put our real identities in jeopardy.''

''No doubt,'' he agreed, sliding the new driver's license into his wallet and taking out his own.

She crossed her arms over her chest. ''Our cameras and other equipment will be waiting for us at the airline desk.''

He looked up. ''Do you know much about photography?''

''Not really.''

"I'm surprised. You strike me as a woman who could do anything."

Sabra glared at him. "And I suppose you're a camera expert?"

"Only with your basic, all-American snapshots." He saw the pain in her eyes. "I didn't mean to hurt your feelings, so stop looking at me like that."

Sabra stood very still. Was she that readable? Scrambling internally, she muttered defiantly, "I'm not hurt."

But she was, Craig knew and he tried to modulate his tone of voice. "I'm exhausted, Sabra. I've been two nights without sleep, and I'm a little raw around the edges. Sometimes I say things that wound other people."

His apology—as close to one as he probably ever got—soothed her. "I—it's okay. I understand."

He glanced at her. "You're awfully forgiving. Are you always like this, or is it part of your wifely act for the mission?"

Tempering her sudden anger, Sabra moved to the couch and picked up her shoulder bag. "It's me. Like it or not."

He caught and held her mutinous look. His mouth pulled into what he hoped was a smile. "I like it." He liked her—way too much. Taking his various papers from the folder, he wadded up the empty envelope. "Let's saddle up. I've packed a bag. We need to get going."

Sabra walked to the door. "I'm ready." But was she? Keeping Jason's plight in front of her, she tried to ignore the reality of her situation. Once they left the safety of his apartment, they would assume the demeanor of husband and wife. She watched Craig walk down the hall to his bedroom to retrieve his single piece of luggage, tucking his ticket and passport in an outer pocket. When he returned and met her at the door, she said, "I need to understand our married relationship."

He set his bag down. "In what way?"

"Well…" Sabra hesitated. "Are we a couple that's close or distant? In the dossier, it says we've been married five years." She cleared her throat and had a tough time holding his amused gaze.

"What's comfortable for you?"

"Uh, maybe holding hands in public from time to time?"

He shrugged. "Okay."

"What about you?"

Craig placed his hand on the brass doorknob. He could see the depth of wariness in Sabra's eyes. "My parents held hands in public, kissed a little here and there and made no apology for the fact that they loved each other very much." The panic in her eyes mounted. "But," he said, "judging from your reaction, I might as well be the Hunchback of Notre Dame, so I'll keep my distance. Occasional hand-holding it will be, Ms. Jacobs."

Avoiding his gaze, Sabra whispered, "I don't think you're the Hunchback!"

"Really? You look scared to death of me, Sabra." He lost his smile. "Don't worry, I'll keep my hands off you. If there isn't a second bed or couch in our room, I'll be more than happy to sleep on the floor. That way, you can feel safe from your frightening husband." He opened the door, gave her one last penetrating look and stepped into the hall. "Come on, Mrs. Thomas. We have a plane to catch."

Sabra was quiet, mulling over a number of apologies as they sat in the first-class section of an airliner speeding across the country. They'd been in flight for over an hour and had been served food and drink. The first-class section was nearly empty, and for that she was grateful. No one sat near them, and when the flight attendant had passed, Sabra leaned over and said, "I'm sorry."

Craig had been pretending to read a magazine. He lifted his head and met her gaze. "For what?"

She licked her lips. "For what happened at the apartment. I don't think you're ugly, and I'm not uncomfortable around you. Okay?"

He saw the sincerity in her eyes. "Don't fix what isn't broken, Mrs. Thomas."

"What does that mean?" Sabra's voice was very low and taut.

Craig picked up his glass of wine and took a sip. "It's okay to admit you don't like me. I understand."

"But I don't dislike you!"

"Really?" He set the glass aside and devoted his full attention to her. Sabra had changed clothes and now wore a loose, light green silk top with dark green silk pants— completely tasteful, yet provocative as hell on her, Craig thought. She really didn't seem aware of her stunning beauty, or the grace that had made nearly every man in the airport twist his head for a good, long look at her. She had caught her hair up in a French roll with soft, wispy bangs across her brow, making her look very cosmopolitan and accentuating the emerald green earrings in her delicate ears. He had a mad urge to caress her flushed cheek as she leaned closer, her shoulder barely touching his.

"It's just that—well, I don't know you."

"I see...."

"No, you don't!" Her eyes flashed. "You don't make anything easy, do you, Craig?"

"I've been accused of that," he said agreeably. Deliberately, he reached over and picked up her left hand, then pressed a light kiss to the back of it. Her skin was soft and fragrant and suddenly he wanted to turn her hand over, run his tongue provocatively across her palm and watch her eyes grow dark with desire. Laughing at his own unexpected idealism, he released her hand as shock registered in her eyes.

Sabra jerked back her hand, her skin tingling wildly where he'd kissed it. Of all things! She looked at him angrily, her hands rigidly clasped in her lap, and saw the laughter in his eyes. He'd known full well she would overreact to his deliberate kiss. But she'd seen a pleasure in his stormy eyes, too, as he'd touched his lips to her skin. She wondered what it would be like to feel that strong mouth against hers, to explore those lips with the one corner turned slightly upward in a sad, sardonic expression.

Her heart was pounding in her breast, and she absently raised her hand to her chest, realizing belatedly that she was blushing furiously. She heard Craig chuckle and snapped her head toward him.

"What's so funny?"

"You." He smiled a little. "You don't like my touch, Sabra. I wanted to see if you were lying, and now I know the truth."

"You are infuriating!" she said through gritted teeth. "You have no idea how I feel toward you."

"The way you jerked your hand back," he rasped, leaning forward till his mouth was mere inches from her ear, "told me more than any words could ever do."

"I hope," Sabra rattled under her breath, "that you don't use the same kind of faulty judgment once we're on Maui, or we'll both be dead."

Craig eased back into an upright position, pondering Sabra's words. But if she liked his touch, why jerk her hand away? And why should he care one way or another?

Something in him wanted to goad her. She invited that response, and Craig found himself wanting to kiss her again—only this time on the mouth. Well, she was right about one thing. He had to pull his attention away from her and stay head's-up on this mission. Once they got to Maui, the games would stop and they'd get down to business. And when they got on the jumbo jet in Los Angeles, he could try to get some sleep—maybe.

Sabra tried to pretend indifference to Craig when they'd boarded the second jet. But no sooner had the jumbo jet taken off from L.A., heading out over the deep blue Pacific, than he pulled a prescription bottle out of his shirt pocket. Unlike the other flight, the first-class section on this one was completely filled. Sabra watched out of the corner of her eye as Craig opened the bottle and dropped two capsules into his palm.

Leaning over, she whispered, "What are those?"

"Sleeping pills." Craig saw the surprise in her eyes. "You got a problem with that?"

"Yes, I do."

He snapped the lid back on the bottle and slowly put it back into his pocket. "Why?"

"What if I need you? You'll be out!"

He looked around the cabin. "It's a five-hour flight. Unless there's a hijacking, I think we're safe up here."

Sabra gripped the arm of the chair between them. "Craig! Don't take those pills. Can't you sleep without them?"

He gave her a deadly look. "At one time I could. But now I can't." He popped them into his mouth and took a slug of water. The fury on her face was real. "Don't be so damned judgmental," he rasped. "I need to sleep. I'm dead on my feet. And don't you or the flight attendant touch me or try to wake me after I go to sleep. Understand?''

Sabra frowned. "No, I don't."

"I can see that." He kept his voice very low. "Look, Sabra, if someone touches me while I'm sleeping, I'm liable to strike out. I don't want to hit you or anyone else by accident. Now do you understand?"

The anger Sabra had felt dissolved. She saw a shadow in Craig's eyes, the nameless horror that stalked him. The use of sleeping pills—or for that matter, any prescription drug—was condoned by Perseus, but sparingly as the individual situation necessitated. As tough as Craig was, she felt a sudden compassion for his plight. "You have a bad time sleeping?"

He put the seat back and tried to get comfortable. "That's an understatement. Just leave me alone, Sabra. I'll wake up before we land, on my own. Whatever you do, don't touch me."

"Okay...." Sabra was glad he had the window seat and she was on the aisle. What was it that haunted him to the point of sleeplessness? Worriedly, she glanced at him. Craig had turned to his right, facing the bulkhead after lowering the window shade against the evening light. He had crossed his arms over his chest, his back to her—to the world. Holding at bay, perhaps? Chewing worriedly on her lower lip, Sabra felt more concerned than angry. He was right, of course, that they were relatively safe on this flight. Still, what if something did happen? Craig would be too groggy to deal with it.

While the professional part of Sabra was irritated over Craig's less-than-stellar response to her concerns, her human side ached at the thought of a suffering so deep he couldn't sleep without the use of drugs. How long had he been using the pills? she wondered. She knew they became addictive at some point. And he'd drunk wine on their earlier flight. Sleeping pills and alcohol didn't mix. *Slow down,* she cautioned her cartwheeling mind. He'd had only one glass of wine.

Curiosity ate at Sabra. When she looked over at Craig, he seemed to be asleep, but she couldn't really tell. The fabric of his shirt was stretched taut across his shoulders, revealing their latent power. A hour after he'd taken the pills, a flight attendant came by with a blanket, and Sabra quickly snatched it from the woman with a smile of thanks. She set the blanket aside, afraid to place it over Craig for fear of waking him and having him come out of his drugged stupor swinging.

The noise of a chopper droned into Craig's exhausted slumber. He frowned as he heard the faint, familiar sound. *No. Not again. God, please, don't let me see it again.* He groaned, the sound moving through him like an earthquake, but the whapping blades grew closer. *Oh, God, no....* The darkness was complete. He was sitting at the controls of his helicopter, his copilot to his left, his helmet heavy on his sweaty head, as if his neck were being shoved down through his aching, tense shoulders.

His hands were slick with sweat through his gloves, and they ached and cramped as he gripped the controls. The reddish glare of the instrument panel glowed up at him as they flew through the night. Craig's copilot, Brent Summers, was droning off numbers. They were fifty feet above the desert floor, skimming swiftly through the night. SCUD missiles were everywhere and nowhere. At any moment their aircraft could be shot down by a rocket launcher from an undetected Iraqi force below. No one knew where the enemy forces were hidden in this godforsaken desert.

The helicopter shook around him. The safety harness bit deeply into his shoulders, holding him snugly against the seat. Shaking. Everything was shaking. Craig was trembling inwardly, his guts so shaky that he wanted to cry out with the fear that raced through him like a spreading, deadly disease. Two teams of Recon Marines were in the rear of his helicopter, trusting his flying abilities, trusting their lives to him. It was so dark, dark as the pit of hell. And below...the enemy below was just waiting for them to fly close enough so they could blow them out of the sky, waiting behind some camouflaged sand dune, their rocket launchers aimed.

Groaning, Craig felt a clawing sensation snake upward from his tightly knotted stomach into his constricted throat. Closer...they were getting closer.... *Oh, God, please...no, not again...not again....* He felt his throat tighten. He couldn't breathe. Struggling for air, he turned, gripping his throat and panting. The darkness was complete. He was lost. And then the screams began....

Craig sat bolt upright, gasping. He dug at the collar of his shirt with badly shaking hands and gasped for air. Sweat ran down his temples. He could feel dampness at his armpits and sweat trickling down the center of his chest.

"Craig?"

A woman's voice. *Who?* He was completely disoriented, caught up in the nightmare and groggy from the pills he'd taken. Again he heard his name. The voice was husky with concern, but he could see only darkness. Were his eyes open? Was he asleep? Awake? A hand tentatively touched his shoulder, and he squeezed his eyes shut, honing in on that gentle touch. His senses were spinning out of control. He wanted to scream along with the cries reverberating inside his head. Doubling up, he pressed his hands to his ears.

"Craig!" Sabra leaned over, sliding her hand along the expanse of his shoulders. His shirt was soaked with his sweat. He'd bent over, his arms wrapped tightly across his belly, his head shoved between his legs. Alarmed, she sat up. Three hours had passed, and he'd seemed to be sleeping deeply. Then he'd started to toss a little and had turned over suddenly onto his back. Sabra had seen the sheen of sweat on his frozen features and had heard the animal-like groan that came from deep within him. He'd started breathing hard.

Anxiously, she unbuckled her seat belt and scooted forward, leaning over him, her arm tight across his shoulders as he remained in the bent-over position. Luckily, the cabin was in near darkness, with most of the passengers asleep. Craig gasped for air. More alarmed, Sabra gripped his shoulder with her other hand.

"Craig? Craig, answer me! Are you all right?" She realized her voice was raspy and off-key. He was soaking wet! Feeling him trembling, she held him even more tightly.

"Can I be of help?" the flight attendant asked, bending over, worry on her face.

"N-no," Sabra said, "he's having a bad dream, that's all."

"I see." She straightened. "Perhaps some water?"

Desperately, Sabra nodded. "Yes." She was afraid Craig would scream or strike out, as he'd warned. But as the flight attendant left, his breathing began to even out to a series of ragged gasps. Slowly, he eased from his hunched position, his arms loosening from around his stomach. As he leaned back, Sabra released her grip on him. The look on his face terrified her. He was utterly without color, his skin shiny with sweat, his eyes open but vacant looking as he stared into the air above him, his head tipped back against his seat.

Gulping, Sabra reached out again. Would he strike her? She had to take the risk. Her fingers barely touched the scars on his forearm. She felt the tautness of his skin beneath her fingertips. Even the dark hair, which grew in uneven patches, was damp with perspiration. "Craig? It's Sabra. You're all right. You're safe," she crooned unsteadily. Her eyes never left his frozen, twisted features. The shocking change in his expression tore at her heart. She increased the pressure of her touch, gently running her fingers across his arm in a soothing motion. At least she hoped it was soothing.

"Craig?"

Craig blinked rapidly, sweat running into the corners of his eyes and making them smart. *Sabra.* It was Sabra. The nightmare slowly released him as he honed in on her husky, tremulous voice. Still, he saw nothing but darkness in front of his open eyes. He struggled valiantly to hear her voice over the shrieking screams echoing crazily inside his throbbing head. The moment she touched him, he reeled internally from the contact. Her hand was warm and steadying on his arm. As she tightened her grip, he was able to pull away from the virulent nightmare holding him captive in its unforgiving talons.

He squeezed his eyes shut and opened his mouth, taking in great drafts of lifesaving oxygen. He heard another woman's voice, but things became confused in his head as he lay there, breathing raggedly. A warm cloth touched his forehead, and his eyes flew open again. He jerked upright, pulling away from the unexpected contact.

Sabra gave a small cry and watched as Craig wrenched away, pressing himself against the bulkhead and staring at her with dark, unseeing eyes. The flight attendant had brought a warm cloth, and stupidly, Sabra had followed her suggestion of laying it on his brow. Handing the cloth back to the attendant, she told her to leave them alone, that Craig would be all right in a few minutes. But would he?

Sabra turned back to him. In the low lighting, the shadows emphasized every frozen line in his tortured face. She saw him close his eyes again, still breathing in gulps through his mouth, his hands clenched into fists against his stomach. Softly, she began speaking to him, realizing belatedly that her voice had a soothing effect on him.

"Craig, it's Sabra. You're all right now. You're safe. I want you to just sit quietly. Try to control your breathing. Breathe in and out. In and out. You're safe…safe.…" Without thinking, she reached out, barely touching his cheek. His skin was clammy beneath her palm. Even as she touched him, she froze, preparing for him to lash out at her. Instead, her touch had a mollifying effect, and she saw him sag heavily against the bulkhead, his head tipping back. She maintained the contact.

She continued talking to him in a low voice, no longer caring what anyone thought; her focus was on Craig. Eventually, he opened his eyes once more. This time he looked at her. She tried to smile. "Craig?"

"Yeah…" he said roughly, his voice trembling. Sabra's touch was steadying. She kept caressing his cheek, and he absorbed her tentative strokes like a man starved for touch. Well, wasn't he? Craig wanted her to never stop touching him. She made the nightmare recede—her touch had made it let go of him a hell of a lot sooner than usual. He felt the perspiration dribbling down the sides of his face, smelled the fear sweat bathing his body. Craig hated that powerful, raw odor. Through it all, Sabra's voice remained low with genuine concern. Clinging to her dark, anxious gaze, he drowned in her eyes, savoring her life, her touch, like a greedy thief.

Slowly, Sabra eased her hand from Craig's cheek. She briefly touched his left shoulder, her fingertips trailing down his left arm until she tangled her fingers with his. He was shaking like a baby and the urge to throw her arms around him nearly undid her. She remembered his warning about touching him. Did she dare risk it? Looking deep into his nearly black, stormy eyes, Sabra didn't think so. Instead, she kept talking in a low tone, gripping his hand to give him a point of reality to concentrate on.

Gradually, his breathing calmed, and the perspiration on his face began to dry. Sabra could smell the fear around him, and her heart opened at the unknown torture he'd seen or endured. Memories of her father slammed into her, and she wondered if Craig had suffered some terrible event as he had. When Craig raised his hand to wipe his face, she released his fingers. Sitting uncertainly on the edge of the chair, she clasped her hands in her lap. The flight attendant had left a glass of water, and Sabra picked it up.

"Here," she offered, "drink this. It might help you feel better...."

Craig stared at the glass and at the hand that held it. Sabra had such lovely, slender hands. He slowly reached for the glass, his fingers curving around it, curving around hers. Her skin was warm with life, while his was cold with death. For a long moment, he gripped her fingers and the glass, holding her worried, compassionate gaze.

His mouth was gummy, with a bitter, metallic taste that reminded him of the taste of blood. Sabra eased her hand away, and he brought the glass slowly, jerkily, to his lips. The cold water was shocking to him, but he gulped it down like a man who'd been in the desert far too long. He laughed at himself. He was a man in the desert all right. A desert called hell.

Closing his eyes, he handed her the empty glass, then sank against his seat. "Just leave me alone. I'll be all right in a little while," he heard himself rasp. Though he had shut his eyes, he could feel her nearness, smell the faint fragrant scent of her skin. How Craig ached to simply turn over, slide his arms around her, draw her against him and hide from the world. His need for Sabra was so great that he felt like crying. Crying! Hardly appropriate for a marine. This was the first time since the crash he'd come even close to wanting to cry.

Craig hid in the darkness behind his tightly shut eyes, his hands gripping the arms of the chair, for a long time. Every muscle in his body was screaming with tension, the ache in his shoulders and neck particularly severe. Sitting up at last, he turned to her.

"Would you mind massaging my neck and shoulders a little?" It was the first time he'd ever asked for help. The first. He saw the care in Sabra's eyes. Her lips parted, and he knew she would do that for him. Slowly, he turned his back toward her, anticipating her healing touch. Craig knew she didn't realize just how much he needed her hands upon him. It didn't matter.

Sabra gently settled her hands on Craig's back. His shirt stretched tightly across its breadth, damp beneath her palms. She had wanted to do something, anything, to help him. But no one could be more surprised at him asking for help than she was. She moved her fingers in a light, caressing motion up his spine, then slid them across his shoulders. His muscles were rigid. Concerned, Sabra began to realize the true depth of the nightmare's effect on him.

"Just try to relax," she whispered unsteadily, her lips near his ear. "Lean back on me and I'll help you...."

Biting back a groan of pleasure, Craig surrendered to her touch as her strong, sure fingers eased the pain and tension he carried. Every stroke wreaked a magic on him he'd never experienced. As she worked the knots from his shoulders, he groaned softly.

"I'm sorry...."

"No," he rasped, "it feels good. Damn good. Don't ever stop...."

Heartened, Sabra continued sliding her hands across his shoulders, kneading and coaxing the tension out of them. Just being able to touch him quelled her worry. It was on the tip of her tongue to ask him about his nightmare, but she realized it would be poor timing. She couldn't believe that he'd taken two sleeping pills and three hours later was completely awake. What kind of nightmare could rip him out of a drugged sleep that way?

Biting her lower lip, Sabra concentrated on loosening the dream's hold on him. With each stroking sweep of her fingers, Craig leaned a little more heavily against her. He was trusting her, and that knowledge sent a shaft of hot, sweet discovery through her. Craig didn't trust anyone, she'd realized early on. But now he was trusting her—with himself. A euphoria flooded her, chasing away her fear and anxiety. Touch was underrated by Americans, Sabra had realized many years ago. Human touch was healing, and Craig was allowing her an intimacy she would never have dreamed of.

Chapter Five

"Is there anything I can do to help Mr. Thomas?" the flight attendant asked as she leaned over and smiled, her eyes trained on Craig.

"Uh, no," Sabra said, "it was just a bad nightmare, that's all." Craig was sitting up, his elbows planted on his thighs, his face buried in his hands, unmoving.

"Are you sure?"

She strengthened her voice and put an edge in it. "I'm very sure. Thanks for your help."

The flight attendant nodded and left, disappearing into the gloom of the cabin.

Sabra sat tensely, her hands clutched in her lap. What else could she do? Reach out and try to comfort Craig? Say something?

"Craig?" Her voice was low and unsteady.

Craig opened his eyes and savagely rubbed his face with his hands. Shame wound through him, along with the remnants of the horrible nightmare. Despite Sabra's ministrations, he could hear the screams echoing faintly. Feeling as if he were going insane, he rasped, "Talk to me. About anything. Just talk to me...."

Sabra swallowed hard, her mind whirling. She twisted her head and looked around the cabin. Anyone who might have been awakened seemed to have gone back to sleep. She riveted her attention on Craig who remained in the same rigid position.

"When I was a little girl," she began huskily, unsure it was something he wanted to hear, "my mother would take me to Dublin to visit my grandparents. I have wonderful memories of being in their home. They really didn't live in Dublin proper, they lived outside of it on a small plot of land that had been in their family for six generations."

She looked around, then concentrated on him again. As she spoke, she saw him slowly begin to relax. "Since I was an only child, my grandparents doted on me. I remember my grandmother, Sorcha, teaching me how to knit. She was a wonderful crocheter and knitter. I used to sit by the hour on an old footstool at her feet. She would knit in her wooden rocking chair, her fingers flying, and I would struggle with a pair of small knitting needles my grandfather, Kerwin, had made for me."

Hesitating, Sabra went on, beginning to relax herself at recounting the happy memories. "Grandfather Kerwin had been a potato farmer, like his father and grandfather before him, until he hurt his back. Then he turned to carving and making furniture. He became locally famous for his rocking chairs. I remember his hands—large, with a lot of little scars on them, much like yours. I would stand in his small garage and watch him for hours as he took a piece of fruit wood and shaped it. I was amazed at how gentle he was with a carving knife or a rasp. The wood seemed to melt to his will.'' Sabra moistened her lips, glanced apprehensively at him and went on.

''My mother loved visiting her family. Israel is desert dry. In Ireland, she always said she felt reborn.''

''How often did you go?''

Craig's voice was rough, and Sabra checked the urge to reach out and touch his sagging shoulder. Somehow, her story had helped bleed away his tension. ''Well...'' She hesitated, not having expected him to ask questions. ''We went when we could afford it. My father was in the army, and the paychecks were small. But my mother was a wonderful seamstress. People hired her to make dresses, and she saved her money until we had enough to fly to Ireland.'' Lifting her hands, Sabra murmured, ''I think we visited about every two years.''

''Where were you born?''

''In Jerusalem.''

''And did you have your mother's love of Ireland?''

Delighted that Craig was taking an interest in something other than his nightmare, Sabra said, ''I was born in a hot, dry place, but I feel, in my soul, I'll always love Ireland's moist greenness. I never saw much rain until I started visiting my grandparents. I have this memory, when I was about three, I think, and it was raining outside my grandparent's home. I toddled outside, and my mother panicked because she couldn't find me.'' Sabra chuckled, the memory still strong. ''There I was—standing outside in that pouring rain, my little hands stretched skyward for all they were worth, my face upturned, laughing. The rain was wonderful, and I felt like a thirsty sponge. My mother, of course, was upset to find me soaked to the skin and shivering, but I was oblivious. That rain just felt so good.''

Craig took a deep breath. Sabra's voice was like an
angel hauling him out of hell itself. Finally, he had the
strength to lift his head and sit up. He could feel the cold
rivulets of sweat still trickling down the sides of his rib
cage, the dampness of the fabric now making him chilly.
He shivered, unable to hide the response.

"You're cold," Sabra whispered, getting up.

Before he could say or do anything, she opened the
overhead compartment and retrieved a blanket. In the
shadowy gloom, he saw concern burning in her eyes as
she leaned over and settled the blanket around his shoulders. Unable to look at her, he turned away.

"Thanks," he muttered roughly. Pulling the ends of the
blanket tightly about him, Craig wished he had a warm
shower to climb into. That's what he did after every nightmare, letting the water drive out the last of the inner trembling that kept him in its poisonous grip. Well, he didn't
have that luxury this time, and he was feeling confused
and groggy from the damn sleeping pills he'd taken earlier. Usually, when he took the pills, he could grab four
or five hours sleep—enough to survive on. Tonight it
didn't work, probably because of the stress of the mission
and the flight.

"Better?" Sabra asked, sitting down and rebuckling her
seat belt.

"Yeah," he said. "Thanks."

She stole a glance at him. "Would some coffee help?"

The corners of his mouth cut upward. "Coffee? No. A
nice warm shower would, but that isn't available."

"Oh…" She laced her fingers together nervously. "I
remember my father getting nightmares when I was growing up. Before he transferred into the Mossad, he was on
the front lines, protecting Israel's borders. I think I was
fourteen when he started having these horrible nightmares.

My bedroom was down the hall in our small apartment, and I used to wake out of a sleep and hear him screaming."

She gave Craig a sympathetic look, noticing how bloodshot and exhausted looking his eyes had become. "The first time it happened, I leapt out of bed, thinking someone was attacking us. I ran down the hall and into my parent's bedroom and saw my mother holding my father. He—" she grimaced "—I had never seen my father cry before. I just stood there in shock, watching him weep, hearing terrible animal sounds tearing out of him. It was awful...."

Craig saw the pain in Sabra's eyes. "Anyone who fights in a war gets that way eventually," he muttered, wiping the sweat off his brow and allowing his elbows to rest on his long thighs. He felt weak, with even the effort of talking draining him.

"At the time, I didn't realize that," Sabra admitted quietly. "My mother, bless her heart, told me to go back to bed, that Father was all right and that things would be fine. The next morning, before I went to school and after my father had left for work, she tried to explain what had happened. I remember crying because I was so frightened."

Craig twisted his head to look in her direction. "And despite that, you joined the army."

"In Israel, everyone has to join the army for a period of time. I served at a kibbutz as a communications specialist. Kibbutzim are like outposts, and the work wasn't dangerous."

"Did you want it to be?' Craig's gaze clung to her soft, shadowed features. How beautiful and calm Sabra looked. He wanted to turn and bury his head against her breasts and just be held—if for a little while. She fed him strength—something that had never happened between him and any woman before. Stymied, he kept his hands where they were.

"No, not really. My father's nightmares were many, and over the years, I learned to sleep through them, because my mother was always there to help him when he woke up from them."

"You don't have nightmares?"

Sabra raised her eyebrows. "Not often."

"I would think with high-risk missions, you would."

"Maybe it was because of my partner," Sabra offered quietly. "Terry was a wonderful teacher. One of the first things he taught me was to talk about anything and everything that bothered me. If I was scared, he wanted to know about it. I think he realized that talking helped bleed off some of the adrenaline that built up over the stress of whatever had to be accomplished."

"He was older?"

"Yes, he was forty when I was teamed with him."

"You were like a baby to him."

She smiled a little. "I'm sure I was. He used to tease me that I was awfully green around the edges."

"Was he a merc all his life?"

"Yes. He told phenomenal stories of his adventures before joining Perseus. Originally, he'd been in the British Army, part of a very secret and elite commando troop. After that, he kicked around the world, getting hired out by small countries, and I'm afraid he did a lot of killing."

"Have you?" He held her startled look.

"No."

"And yet you're in high-risk."

"Usually that means we're liable to get shot at or killed, not that we're doing the killing, Craig. I couldn't do that. That's why I like Perseus so much—we're in the business of rescue, not murder.''

He stared at her. "Have you been shot at?"

"Yes, a number of times.'' She held up her hand and pointed to a small, round scar on her forearm. "A bullet went through me there. I was lucky. It could have hit a bone and shattered my arm.''

"How did it happen?"

"The first year I was with Terry we were trying to rescue an American child from kidnappers in Italy. He was the son of an American diplomat. The U.S. government called Morgan and asked for help, though the Italian police and the CIA were trying to locate the son, too. Terry was very good at finding local contacts. He speaks at least eight languages fluently, including Italian. An old man in a village outside of Rome gave us reliable information. We found the child at a villa owned by a mafia leader in that country. Under cover of nightfall, we scaled the walls and saved him. During the escape, the guards discovered us and started shooting.'' She shrugged. "I took a hit climbing over the wall.''

"What did you do?"

"Nothing, at the time. I felt a sting on my arm. I was carrying the boy and Terry was behind me, returning fire. We made it down a hill to where our car was hidden in an olive grove, and took off. It was dark, and I was so concerned about the boy's safety that I honestly didn't think anything about my arm until much later. By dawn, we reached Rome and returned the child to his parents. It was only afterward, when Terry pointed to my arm, that I realized I had been bleeding.''

"Did you go into shock then?"

"Actually,'' Sabra whispered, avoiding his gaze, "I did something very embarrassing.''

"What?"

"I fainted."

"Not an abnormal reaction."

"I guess not, but can you imagine? I'm supposed to be this tough mercenary, and I take one look at my bloody sleeve and drop like a ton of rocks to the floor." Laughing quietly, Sabra added wryly, "I found out later that Terry picked me up and carried me to a chair and plunked me down. They called an ambulance, and I remember waking up in it on the way to the hospital. Terry was with me, holding my hand, reassuring me I wasn't going to die. Later, I found out it was little more than a flesh wound, and I was embarrassed by my reaction. At the time, it seemed a lot worse to me."

"Experience teaches you to minimize or maximize your reaction."

Sabra nodded, absently rubbing the small scar on her arm. "That's what Terry told me. I was in the hospital, and when he came to visit me the next day, I started to cry. I mean, this was no small amount of weeping. I felt horribly embarrassed at my lack of control over my emotional state, but Terry just laughed. He assured me it was a healthy reaction and encouraged me to keep on crying as hard and long as I wanted."

"He sounds like a good man."

"He is. I hope," Sabra murmured, "you can meet him someday."

"Maybe," Craig muttered. "First we have to survive this mission."

Nervously, Sabra picked at her slacks. "Craig?"

He turned, seeing the question on her face. "Look, I'm not the talking type. I don't want to discuss what happened to me."

"But—"

"No."

She saw the flat glare in his eyes; the warning was clear. "Then answer me this—do you have to take sleeping pills every night in order to sleep?"

"Yes. So what?"

Her lips curved downward. "You can't do that on this mission, Craig. From the time we land on Maui, we have to be alert. If you take those pills, you might not hear something that could save our lives. I can't be expected to stay up and be alert enough for both of us. I'm going to need your help."

"I don't think we've got to be on guard twenty-four hours a day. We have to be heads-up when we check out the estate, but not back at our hotel room."

"You're wrong," Sabra said forcefully. "If Garcia even suspects us, he could send his men there to kill us."

Holding up his hand wearily, Craig rasped, "Let's discuss this later. Right now, all I want to do is try to get a little more sleep."

Chastened, Sabra realized belatedly it wasn't the right place or time to discuss the issue. She knew better. Terry had taught her the importance of timing talks. "You're right."

Craig lay back in his seat. "I hope I don't wake up like I did before. If I do, just talk to me, okay? It helps."

She managed a strained smile. "Sure...." Sabra watched him turn on his side again, his back to her, the blanket wrapped tightly around him. She felt such an urge to lean over, gently stroke his tousled hair and reassure him that everything would be all right. But she couldn't do that. Worriedly, she leaned back in her chair, wrapped her arms around herself and closed her eyes.

Sleep wouldn't come. Part of her waited for Craig to have the nightmare again, while another part of her searched frantically for the reasons behind his responses. Something terrible had happened to him, and judging by the violence of his reactions, not too long ago. Did the burn scars on his hands, arms and cheek have anything to do with it? The scars still looked relatively fresh. Sabra sighed and tried to clear her mind. In two hours, they would land. Perhaps the magic of Hawaii's ephemeral beauty would ease his pain. She hoped so.

A policeman in civilian clothes—a bright Hawaiian print shirt and white cotton slacks—met them shortly after they'd retrieved their luggage. Sabra had spotted the man immediately as they'd walked to the luggage area to wait for the items. He appeared Chinese in heritage, with short black hair and dark brown eyes that were constantly roving, missing nothing. Craig was groggy, and Sabra walked closely at his side, remaining alert for both of them. They had no weapons, because it was against the law to carry them onto the islands.

The crowd of tourists who had been on the flight milled around them. Children cried from being awakened too early. Jet lag was compounded by the fact that it was 3:00 a.m. Hawaiian time, and Sabra felt exhaustion pulling at her, but forced it away. The warm dry air of Hawaii felt good, almost reviving, to her.

As soon as they'd retrieved their luggage, the same man she'd noticed made a beeline toward them. Automatically, Sabra went on guard, unsure if he were friend or foe, and put herself in front of Craig. She felt him stiffen and become intent behind her.

"What?" he demanded.

"That man," she said in a low voice, keeping her eyes on the approaching figure, "is either a cop or a hit man."

Craig squinted against the lights, groggy and not at all

alert. Gripping Sabra's arm, he forced her to step aside. What the hell was she doing, putting herself between him and potential danger? He used enough force to let her know that and saw the anger leap to her eyes as he drew her aside.

"You're not my shield," he growled.

Sabra rubbed her arm where he'd gripped it. Before she could say anything, the man stopped in front of them.

"I'm Detective Sam Chung." He dug out his badge case as inconspicuously as possible and held it open to their inspection. "You're from Perseus, right?"

"Yes," Sabra said, "we are."

"Great. Come with me."

Sabra gave Craig a glare and jerked up her single piece of luggage, hefting photographic equipment in her other arm. He glared back at her and did the same. Together, they braved the crowds of excited tourists and headed outdoors. Maui's early morning warmth struck her full force. She inhaled deeply as she hurried to keep up with the short, wiry detective. Overhead, stars twinkled in a soft ebony sky. Palm trees hugged the asphalt road around the airline building, starkly silhouetted against the glare of the area lights.

Chung opened the trunk of his car. The parking lot was comparatively empty this time of morning as they settled their luggage in the compartment.

"Once we get in the car, I'll give you weapons that are registered with us," he told them in a low tone. "Then I'll drive you to the car-rental area, where you can pick up your vehicle."

"Good," Craig said, shutting the trunk. "Let's go."

Sabra climbed into the rear seat, while Craig sat up front with Detective Chung. The policeman was in his forties, but he looked much younger, a toothy smile in place as he turned and laid his arm along the back of the seat to speak with both of them.

"We still don't have conclusive proof that Jason Trayhern is at Garcia's estate. We haven't tailed any of Garcia's men, because we don't want to arouse suspicion." He reached into his pocket and handed Craig a piece of paper. "Here's a detailed map of Garcia's estate and suggested locations where you can set up your camera equipment to watch for the boy. There are two hills you might use. One is pretty steep and rolling, with lots of eucalyptus trees and tall grass to hide in. The other hill is pretty brushy, with shrubs and fewer trees, so you'd have to be more careful. Both are about a mile from the estate, right off the Kula Highway. Most of the traffic stops at nightfall, so you don't have to worry too much about headlights interfering with your infrared equipment."

"Does Garcia have any idea we're around?"

"No," Sam said, shaking his head. "We know who his guards are, and there's been no unusual activity. We're fairly sure Garcia isn't on to the fact that we know something. We've deliberately stayed away from his area. We have a police cruiser that normally drives the road to Kula daily, so we've maintained that schedule but nothing more." He reached into the glove box and handed Craig an envelope. "There are photos in there of Garcia's hoods, the boys who do the damage, as well as some of his chauffeur, the maids and other people in his employ that we've managed to photograph over the years. His hit men have criminal records, so their photos are real clear. The rest tend to be surveillance shots, so they can be a little fuzzy."

"It's good to have these," Craig said.

Sabra leaned forward. "Is Garcia at his estate now?"

"As far as we know. If he leaves by jet, we know it."

"How?" Craig demanded.

"Garcia keeps a Learjet at this airport. He uses it to fly to Honolulu on the island of Oahu, then takes a commercial flight from there to the Mainland or wherever he's going."

"I see," Craig said.

"But," Sam added, "Garcia also has a helicopter with long-range fuel tanks. So he could fly from his estate to any of the other islands, leaving his Learjet behind. We may or may not know about those flights."

Frowning, Craig said, "By federal law, he has to file a flight plan."

Sam chuckled. "Listen, there are so many interisland flights here, the FAA can't track all of them down. Yes, the small airline companies do file flight plans, but these helicopter businesses don't. Most of them have commercial trade. For instance, there's a helicopter service in Kula that offers flights up to the Haleakala crater and the rest of the island. They don't file flight plans."

Sweat broke out on Craig's brow and he wiped it away with his fingers. "Do you have a photo or ID on the helicopter he uses?"

"Yes. It's all in there. You'll probably see it on Garcia's private landing pad at his estate, anyway. If you want my opinion, I think it's going to take you three or four days of surveillance to find out anything."

"I don't disagree," Sabra murmured. "Sam, can you take us to the rental agency? We're really exhausted."

"Sure." He pulled two weapons in leather holsters from beneath his seat. "You're going to need these. Both are registered with our department. When we get your luggage out of the trunk, I'll give you some boxes of ammunition." He frowned. "Garcia jets between Maui and his Caribbean kingdom frequently. He's been here for a week this time. Usually, after two weeks at the most, he'll fly out of Maui, then return a month or two later. If the Trayhern boy is with them at Kula, you may not have much time.''

"If Garcia tries to take the boy on his Learjet, will we have your help to stop the flight?" Sabra asked as she carefully checked out her weapon, making sure it wasn't loaded. She saw Craig handling his similarly.

"Of course," Sam said. "We'd like to nail him on kidnapping charges and put his rear in prison for a long, long time." He handed Sabra a radio. "This will put you in touch with us twenty-four hours a day. The thing is set on a special frequency, so transmissions between us can't be detected. If you see anything, call it in. We have a special SWAT team unit standing by in case you need help."

"If things go as planned," Craig said, slipping on the shoulder holster and positioning it beneath his left arm, "we'll break into Garcia's estate, grab the boy and get out without detection."

"Good luck," Sam snorted. "Garcia's got goons carrying submachine guns all over his estate. Look, I'm not saying you can't do it, but if you see the boy and can't get to him, we'll get a search warrant and go in."

Craig nodded. "Fair enough. Let's get going."

Sabra was too tired to appreciate the beauty of the Westin Hotel at Kaanapoli. It was a sumptuous place, with expensive Oriental carpets and a huge waterfall right outside the registration area, nearly empty at four in the morning. She stood fighting off tiredness, looking around the deserted place as Craig checked them in, but saw only a few hotel clerks.

"Aloha, Mr. and Mrs. Thomas," the desk clerk said with a smile. "We'll have your luggage taken up—"

"No, we'll carry it," Craig said tersely, picking up the plastic key card for their room. "Thanks." He turned to Sabra. Shadows lingered under her glorious eyes. He forced a smile he didn't feel. "Let's go, sweetheart."

Sabra nearly choked on the endearment, but forced a returning smile as she picked up the photographic equipment. "Of course, darling."

The carpeted hall was filled with expensive sculptures and paintings from around the world. Sabra felt as if she were in the Louvre in Paris than in a hotel. The brass elevators at the end of the hall ran quietly. Craig punched the button, one of the doors whooshed open and they quickly stepped in. Once the doors had shut, Sabra leaned wearily against the wall as the elevator sped upward.

"I'm so tired I could sleep on my feet," she muttered.

Craig nodded. "You take the bed."

She nodded. The doors opened and they stepped out on the twelfth floor. The halls were eerily quiet, all the guests asleep. Craig slid the card key into the door and opened it. The room was a suite, with a huge picture window facing the Pacific and overlooking the hotel beach. The aqua curtains were filmy looking, part of a decor comprised of soothing pastel colors. Sabra placed her luggage on the huge bed.

Craig dropped his luggage in the smaller room, which sported a couch, a coffee table, two overstuffed chairs and a refrigerator.

"Why don't you take a shower?" he suggested, walking back into her bedroom.

Sabra put her finger to her lips. First she wanted to check out the room for electronic bugs. She moved from lamp to lamp, checking them out, top to bottom. Then she crossed to the phone and unscrewed the receiver. She ran her fingers along the window, but found nothing. She saw Craig frowning at her, as if disapproving, but she didn't care. First things first—she had to make sure there were no hidden devices, including cameras in the ceiling, watching them. She wondered if Craig had ever made such a search, because he just stood there and watched her as she made her efficient rounds.

The bathroom seemed clean, too. Craig entered and shut the door behind him, then gripped her arm and moved her to one side while he leaned into the shower and turned it on, full force. The sound of falling water filled the huge, tiled room.

"What are you doing?" Sabra demanded, wresting her arm away.

"What are *you* doing?"

"Checking the place out. What did you think I was doing?"

"I could have done that. Why don't you get showered and go to bed?"

"It's my responsibility, Craig, to make the place is safe for us." Sabra was relieved to see Craig knew enough to turn on the shower to create noise to cover their conversation if there were bugs. She saw his face darken.

"Okay, so it's checked. So how about getting that shower and going to bed?"

She hesitated. "What are you going to do?"

"Reconnoiter a little. I'll be in and out of the room for a few minutes. I want to check where the emergency exits are—things like that."

"Okay...." She slipped past him and opened the door. Just being with Craig in such a small space made her feel unaccountably panicky. She'd seen the burning look in his eyes as he'd studied her, and despite her best intentions, her gaze had lingered too long on his strong, male mouth. Swallowing hard, she fled into the main room.

Dawn was barely crawling up the horizon, revealing the still-dark Pacific Ocean, as Sabra closed the drapes to prevent morning light from spilling into the huge bedroom. She'd taken a hot, relaxing bath, washed her hair and pulled on a pale pink silk nightgown that fell to her knees. She'd loaded her pistol and placed it beneath the pillow next to hers. She could hear Craig in the next room and had deliberately left the door open. She heard his suitcase unzip and realized he was unpacking.

Walking to the connecting doorway, she saw him throwing his folded clothes into a dresser near the couch.

"Craig?"

Craig turned. His eyes narrowed. Sabra's hair fell in glossy waves around her shoulders. Recently washed, it glinted in the low light, framing her face. His heart sped as his gaze moved downward. Her silk nightgown lovingly outlined her every contour. He started to take a step forward, but forced himself to remain where he was. He could see the swell of her small breasts outlined by the smooth fabric, the front of the nightgown curving in a graceful scooped neckline to reveal smooth skin. An ache filled him. He longed to walk over, slide his hand across those finely outlined collarbones and trail a series of hot kisses downward until he met the softness of her breasts.

"*What?*" The word came out harsh.

"I—I'm done in the bathroom." Nervously, Sabra said, "I'm leaving the door open between our rooms. I don't think it's a good idea to shut it, do you?" She felt the smoldering intensity of his gaze burning through her nightgown, scorching her breasts. The look on his face was primal. His eyes burned with desire—for her. Unconsciously, she touched the nightgown. She hadn't meant to tease him. Terry had never given her this kind of look. Her mouth went dry as she plainly read the hunger in his face. Shaken, she whispered, "I'm sorry. I should have worn my robe...."

"No," Craig whispered thickly. "It's all right." He turned away, forcing himself to stop staring at her tall, slender form. The ache in his lower body intensified to a painful level. Every inch of her spoke of beauty and grace, and she wore the silk nightgown like a lover's hand. He wanted to run his own hand over her hills and valleys, experience her softness, her giving way beneath his exploration. Savagely, Craig reminded himself his feelings were a one-way street. Sabra didn't desire him as he did her. Somehow he had to quell his need of her.

Feeling the familiar flush flow into her face, Sabra turned and fled. Her body seemed heated wherever his gaze had touched her. Switching off the light, she quickly crossed to the bed and threw back the covers. She heard the door to the bathroom open and close. Sabra took a long, unsteady breath. What was going on here? Why did she feel so trembly every time Craig looked at her? She slipped into bed and turned her back toward the door, embarrassed at her stupidity. She had a robe. Why hadn't she worn it when she went to talk to Craig? Obviously, he was upset with her.

As exhausted as she was, Sabra couldn't fall asleep right away. She heard the shower being turned on full force. At least Craig would get the shower he'd wanted so desperately. Her heart twisted with compassion. He was a man chased by invisible demons—and how badly she wanted to comfort him. Turning onto her back, she stared up at the darkened ceiling, a bone-deep weariness finally forcing her lashes closed. How much she'd wanted to kiss him! The thought was heated, filled with promise and panic. Turning angrily onto her side, Sabra pulled the covers up over her shoulders and sighed loudly. Not since Josh had she thought of a man this way. For so long, men had ceased to exist in her life—until now. Until Craig.

The thought sent Sabra sitting bolt upright in bed. Clenching her fists in her lap, she released a ragged breath. What was wrong with her? She pushed several thick strands of hair away from her face. She was acting like a lovesick teenager. But her feelings were real and vibrant and clamoring to be heard and acted on. Even Josh had never made her feel this way, she admitted grudgingly. No man had.

Great, all she needed was to be attracted to trouble like Craig Talbot. And he was trouble with a capital *T*, no doubt about it. He wasn't anything like Josh. In fact, he was the opposite, closed up tighter than a proverbial clam. He was an introvert, going beyond her own range of shyness. He wasn't a talker, and he was abrasive to her feelings. He was a man on the run, and she had absolutely no experience with someone like that. Josh had had goals in life, dreams he wanted to fulfill and he'd known exactly where he was going. Sabra didn't think Craig had any dreams—or hopes.

Maybe she was wrong, Sabra chastised herself as she lay back down on her left side. Just because she'd seen hunger for her in his eyes didn't mean he liked her. A man could want a woman on a purely physical level. The idea that Craig might not really like her—probably didn't, when it came right down to it—made her feel pain as never before. She had an attractive body and face—that's where his interest lay. Well, that was hardly an excuse to give in to her own desire for him—which went beyond physical superficialities.

He did have such a wonderful mouth, though, with strong, well-shaped lips. She wondered again what it would be like to press her mouth to his. Would he kiss her hard? Claim her as if he owned her? Or would it be a gentle kiss, filled with exploration and tenderness? Groaning, Sabra put an end to her wild fantasies. It was time to go to sleep and stop thinking about the difficult, complex man in the room next door.

Craig slowly walked toward Sabra's bedroom. He'd taken the longest shower of his life. Water dripped from his hair, and he absently toweled it off as he halted in the doorway. From the light that came from his room he could see Sabra sleeping, a pale blue sheet draped across her hips and waist. Her hair pooled around her, and he had to fight an urge to walk in and look more closely at her as she slept. Checking his idiotic desires, Craig turned away. He couldn't have Sabra anyway. He'd seen the revulsion in her eyes.

Switching off his light, he dropped the damp towel on the coffee table. The other towel rode low across his hips as he padded over to the sofa. He'd found a blanket in the closet and a spare pillow. Now he threw them on the couch in a makeshift bed, then went to the door and made sure the dead bolt was engaged. His eyes stung from lack of sleep, and his head ached as if hammers were pounding his temples. Sleep. Precious sleep. That was all he needed—and the last thing he was likely to get.

Ambling back to the couch, he loosened the towel and allowed it to drop to the carpeted floor, then tugged on light cotton pajama bottoms. Sitting down, he shook out the blanket. His pistol lay on the coffee table. Leaning over, he took it out of the holster, fed a bullet into the chamber and put the safety back on. Placing it gently on the carpet near his head, he lay down.

Everything was quiet. Sabra had opened the window in her bedroom earlier, and he could hear the waves crashing on the beach outside the hotel. The sound was lulling, and he closed his eyes. If only he could sleep. If only... Now was not the time to take any more sleeping pills. Sabra was right: Garcia could already have staked them out— could be watching and waiting for the right moment to nail them. His eyes drooped closed, as if weighted. Without the pills, he knew he'd spend hours tossing, turning, moving between raw wakefulness and the terror of the nightmare. God, if only he could get up, slide into the bed and draw Sabra to him, he was sure he could sleep for the first time in two years. She could give him the solace to surrender to the darkness.

Craig's mouth tightened, and he turned onto his side, burying his head in the soft pillow. Maybe if he pretended Sabra was in his arms....

Chapter Six

By concentrating on the image of Sabra's face and recalling her soothing voice, Craig found an element of comfort in his usually chaotic night. Soon his fear of the nightmare returning had dissolved, and he plummeted into a deep sleep. He'd always been a vivid dreamer, but this time his dream visions were of something beautiful: Sabra. Her expressions fascinated him—the quirk at the corner of her mouth when she was irritated or didn't quite agree with him, the lowering of her thick, black lashes when she was shy, and, more than anything, the changing of her gray eyes from light to stormy and dark.

He was lost in her small gestures and the way she used her hands when talking. Moment by moment, he reexperienced her touching him, massaging the tension from his shoulders and back. She'd been strong yet gentle, monitoring the pressure as she coaxed the rigidity out of his muscles....

On some far boundary of his peripheral senses, Craig heard the blades of a helicopter. No. It couldn't be. In his sleep, he struggled to shut out the approaching sound, which sent an icy shaft of fear through his gut. Sabra's touch, her face, began to dissolve, to be replaced by the *whap, whap, whap* that grew louder, closer with every passing moment.

Groaning, Craig turned over. *Not again. No...* The sound intensified, and he began feel the tiny tremblings a helicopter pilot experiences when his bird starts up. The vibration began in his booted feet and, like small currents of electricity, moved up his legs, into his thighs. As the blades whirled faster and faster, he could feel his whole body swinging in time with them, until he became a part of the machine and it a part of him. Where did flesh and blood leave off and cold steel begin?

Craig felt sweat running down his temples from beneath his helmet. He was gripping the controls through wet Nomex gloves. He always sweated on a dangerous mission—everyone did. Lieutenant Brent Summers, his copilot and one of his best friends for three years, called off their altitude.

It was dark, so dark out. The reddish glow of the control panel glared up at him, while before him stretched endless desert.

"We're in Iraqi territory," Summers warned.

"Indian Country."

Summers laughed, but the sound was strained. "Yeah. Got to watch for those arrows, buddy."

Wasn't that the truth? Only this time the arrows were rocket grenade launchers. Craig compressed his lips, feeling moisture form on his upper lip. He had a wild urge to scratch at his temple, where the sweat tickled unmercifully. He couldn't, of course. Both hands were fully involved on keeping his aircraft straight and level.

The machine vibrated around him, vibrated with him, and he felt the heart of it beating in time with his own pounding heart, which was throbbing with unleashed adrenaline and fear. Behind him was their precious cargo: two marine reconnaissance teams they were to drop close to the enemy line. Their mission: to destroy their defenses and put such a scare into them that they'd hightail it and run. What Craig had heard about the elite Republican Guard was that they weren't cowards; they'd stand and fight.

They flew lower, and Craig strained his eyes, trying to focus on the screen located at the front of his helmet, revealing through a series of radar images the rolling desert dunes, now dangerously close. He could hear Summers's altitude information, the twenty-five-year-old's voice tighter than usual. This wasn't a practice run. No, this was for real. They'd already made one run—and had a harrowing close call—but had managed to drop their human cargo at precisely the right place and time.

This was the second run, different and more dangerous, as far as Craig was concerned. He knew the men of these recon units. They had come from Camp Reed, where he was based, and he'd trained nearly a year with them— dropping them off, picking them up. Always before they'd been training runs, with no real danger beyond him screwing up at the controls and crashing them into a hill. It was his greatest apprehension—his only one. Still, he was known as the pilot in his squadron who took the most chances.

He'd been the only pilot willing to dangle his chopper dangerously close to some high electric power lines in order to rescue a Recon who had busted his leg in the middle of nowhere. He'd hung in midair as the man was hoisted to safety, then had flown him to medical help at the nearby base hospital.

Craig concentrated so hard on the all-terrain monitor in front of him that he felt as if his head might explode with pain. The hills of Camp Reed were far different from the shifting sand dunes of Iraq. The winds here were haphazard, constantly changing the dunes' height and size. There was no such thing as stable terrain in this war, he thought as he felt the harness bite deeply into his shoulders, his hands cramp as he gripped the controls. Desert Storm was a crap shoot, in his opinion.

His mind shifted back to the cabin and his precious cargo. He'd gone drinking and carousing with these Recons. The man who had broken his leg last year was Captain Cal Talbot—not related, but since they shared a last name, Craig had volunteered for the rescue. It had been a windy day, and a gust could easily have thrown his chopper into the high-tension lines. After the delicate rescue, his friendship with Cal had begun. Now they were closer than brothers, and Cal was back there with his men, greasepaint concealing their white skin, wearing the most technically advanced equipment in the world, ready to be dropped behind enemy lines.

Cal was married. Craig had visited him at the Camp Reed hospital when Cal's wife, Linda, had delivered their second beautiful red-haired daughter. Craig had stood outside the window of the maternity ward with Cal while his friend cried and laughed, pointing to the tiny girl wrapped in a pink blanket. He'd stood, big hands pressed against the glass, smiling with pride and telling Craig they were going to name her Claire, after Craig's mother, with the middle name Lynn, after Linda's mother.

Craig had been dumbstruck that Cal and Linda would

name their new baby in his honor. But Cal had laughed, brushed the tears out of his eyes, and put his hands on Craig's shoulders and told him they'd wanted to do something to thank him for rescuing his miserable neck that day he'd broken his leg and nicked an artery out in the bush.

"But," Craig rasped, shaken, "I didn't do anything anyone else wouldn't have done."

"Hey," Cal chided, sliding his arm around his friend's shoulder and pointing to the baby in her crib, "if it hadn't been for you, Talbot, I wouldn't have been here to make that kid, much less see her born. No, Linda and I wanted to surprise you. We can't name her Craig, but when I found out your mom's name was Claire, we thought it was the next best thing." Cal turned, tears in his eyes. "To remind us of the man who risked his life to save mine."

Craig stared openmouthed at Cal, not knowing what to say or do. "Well...no one has ever done something like this for me..."

Patting him on the shoulder, Cal released him. "That's okay, pardner. In my book, you're the best damn leatherneck pilot there is. There are three things I love more than life in this world, and that's my wife and my two daughters." He poked a finger at the window, becoming very serious. "Craig, you don't get it, do you? You're standing there with that funny look on your face again. There are pilots and there are *pilots*. I've flown with you nearly two years now at Reed, and you're the best. Why shouldn't I honor you in some way? That little girl will know why she's named Claire when she can understand it all. She'll be proud, too, the way Linda and I are of you."

Craig felt embarrassment mixed with a deep satisfaction

as he stared down at the tiny baby with the thick thatch of red hair. Cal stood by him, sharing a profound, awed silence as they watched his daughter sleep.

"You know," Cal said in a low, off-key voice, "I was never much one for kids. At least, not until I met Linda and married her. I came out of a pretty rugged family— my folks got divorced, and I was a pawn between two war camps after that. I told Linda I was afraid to have children, but she convinced me otherwise. She came out of a real stable family, just the opposite of mine. She was one of six kids. Can you imagine? Six kids?"

"No, I can't," Craig answered.

"Big family," Cal said with a laugh, "and a happy one. When Linda got pregnant with Samantha, I freaked. I was afraid I couldn't be a good father. I was afraid I'd end up like my old man, a kind of absent shadow, you know? Linda just laughed at me. I remember the first time she took my hand and pressed it against her belly to feel Sammy moving. I was kneeling next to the couch, and I just busted into tears, of all things. I mean, to feel that little thing inside her moving around... Man, it was a miracle or something."

Craig stole a look at his friend's somber profile. "What do you mean?"

Chuckling, Cal said, "From the moment I felt Sammy kicking, I began to lose my fear. Linda had a lot of long, serious talks with me. Yes, I'd be absent from time to time because of my Recon work. But at least I'd be home after my watch. By the time Sammy was born, I wasn't panicking anymore."

Propping his hands on his narrow hips, Cal grinned proudly. "Linda helped make the transition from wild bachelor to father easy for me."

"That's saying a lot," Craig teased. He knew Cal had

been known by the nickname Wild Man, earned in his earlier years in the Corps.

Sighing, Cal pressed his hands against the glass again. "Look at her, Craig. Isn't she tiny? So perfectly formed? Isn't she a miracle? Claire lived nine months in Linda and look at her. She's so pretty."

It had been hell on Craig to watch Linda and Cal kiss one last time at the Camp Reed airport before he and his team had boarded the transport plane that would eventually take them halfway around the world to a staging area in Saudi Arabia. Craig had been part of that deployment, and he'd hugged Linda goodbye, too, feeling very much a part of her and Cal's extended family.

"Bring him back home safe to me, Craig," Linda had whispered as she released him, tears in her eyes. "Please take care of him—for all of us."

Choking back tears that lodged in his throat, Craig rasped, "Don't worry, Linda, I will."

"Here, kiss the girls. You're practically their uncle." She lifted two-year-old Sammy into his arms.

Craig smiled at the carrot-topped little girl, who was a spitting image of her mother.

"'Bye, Uncle Craig." She'd thrown her small arms around his neck and hugged him as hard as she could with her tiny strength.

"'Bye, sweetheart," he'd whispered, kissing her on the forehead and blinking back tears as he gently set her down next to her mother. He didn't dare look into Linda's tear-swollen blue eyes as he eased three-month-old Claire from Cal's arms. The tiny pink bow in Claire's hair made her look even more feminine.

"Say goodbye to your goddaughter," Cal had said, slapping him on the shoulder.

Babies, Craig had discovered, always smelled good.

Sometimes they smelled of baby powder; sometimes their skin possessed a sweet fragrance like a newly blossomed flower. He never got over that fact, and he loved to hold Claire close, to inhale her special scent. Claire was wide-awake. Though she had Linda's red hair, she had her father's big green eyes and gorgeous smile. Craig couldn't help smiling back as the baby reached up with one of her pudgy little arms, her fingers opening and closing against his shaven face.

"She's going to be a beauty," Craig confided in a strained voice.

"Just like her mama," Cal murmured proudly. "A real heartbreaker."

Craig pressed a soft kiss to Claire's ruddy cheek. Her skin was so delicately soft, so unmarred by life. He carefully returned the blanketed form to her mother's waiting arms. Turning on his heel, he'd whispered goodbye to Linda, unable to stand the look of anguish in her face any longer. As he walked toward the ramp of the plane, he knew Cal was holding her, saying goodbye to her one last time. He felt the weight on his shoulders, knowing that Cal's life, and that of the other Recon teams, would be in his hands once they got over there. The fear of losing them, of destroying families' lives, ate at him....

The shuddering, shaking of the helicopter continued to vibrate through Craig. He hated the darkness. He hated even more the unknowns of this second mission. The two teams were to be dropped very close to Republican Guard lines—much closer than the first teams. They were nearing the drop zone. The muscles in his body were so tight with tension that Craig felt like one huge, painful cramp. He kept praying that nothing would happen. *Let them land safely. Let them—*

"Look out!" Summers shrieked, gesturing to the right in warning.

Craig had only seconds to react. Out of the corner of his eye, he saw a flicker of light, the illumination of one of the thousands of sand dunes surrounding them. A grenade launcher! They were flying at five hundred feet, dipping up and over one dune, down into the valley then up and over the next. Called "flying by the nap of the earth," it required hard, tense maneuvering. Crashing was always a possibility, and Craig counted on avoiding that by sheer concentration, flying as he'd never flown before. But the one thing he couldn't avoid, and couldn't allow for in advance was a direct enemy attack.

The grenade hit the chopper even as Craig jerked the controls, sending his aircraft up and away. *Too late.* An earsplitting explosion sounded above him, and he knew the grenade had struck the main rotor. He heard a sharp cry from Summers and the copilot slumped forward, held in place by the array of harnesses. Craig felt pain, shut his eyes and jerked his head to one side, away from the main explosion. Hot metal tore through the cabin, shredding everything in its path. The aircraft jerked upward, mortally wounded. And then it began to spiral, tail first, toward the desert below.

Frantically, despite the fires igniting all around him, igniting on his protective clothing on his arms, Craig tried to stop the flailing fall of his aircraft. He heard shrieks in his earphones. He heard Cal's voice booming above the rest, yelling at his men to prepare for a crash landing. The bird tumbled out of the black sky toward the black ground. Wildly, Craig tried to use the controls to stop the tail-first slide toward the sand. It was impossible! The grenade had not only shattered the main rotor above them, but shrapnel from the explosion had cut through the cables that would have allowed him some control over the wounded bird.

Craig was jerked violently from side to side. He felt the bird inverting from the tail, falling slowly over on it's port side. He heard the shrieks and screams of the men in the rear. They had no safety harnesses on them; they merely sat on nylon web seats, waiting, just waiting. He knew they were being thrown around in the cabin like marbles being thrown into a huge, empty room.

Below, he saw the fire highlighting the sand here and there. He saw hot pieces of metal plummeting down before them, lighting their way. Craig knew he was going to die. They were all going to die. In those seconds before the helicopter crashed into the three hundred foot sand dune, his entire life ran past his widened eyes, as if in slow motion.

Everything slowed as Craig tried to brace himself for impact, screaming at the others to do the same. The aircraft struck the sand on its left side. Craig was jerked violently downward, but the harness held him in place, probably saving his life. They had a lot of fuel on board for the long haul to the target drop zone, and it exploded on impact, hurling liquid through the rear cabin. In an instant, fire raged all around them.... The windows on the bird shattered inward, into the cockpit, sending glass projectiles hurling like bullets through his cabin. Droplets of fire rained down on him. Frantically, Craig tried to find the harness release. It was jammed! The heat in the cabin was intense. He heard the screams of men being burned alive all around him. The helicopter was still sliding downward, on the steep side of a large dune.

His Nomex gloves had been burned off his hands as he attempted to jerk the harness free. The heat and odor of fuel choked him. He gasped. The heat funneling up his

nose into his mouth burned him. Both arms of his flight
suit were on fire. Craig tried to think, but it was impossible. Out of instinct, out of hours of training, he reached
for a boot knife that he always kept strapped to his right
leg. Gripping the handle, he jerked it upward and laid the
large blade against the harness that now held him prisoner.
He had to get free to help Cal! The screams of the marines
were pounding against his ears. The roar of the fuel fire
was spreading. The heat was intense.

The aircraft jolted to a stop, and then slowly pitched
over so that Craig was thrown upside down. It rested on
its top, the metal wreaking and tearing as the weight of it
sank downward. The fire engulfed everything. Sobbing,
Craig sawed against the straps. One by one, they freed
beneath the sharpened blade. He fell hard. Frantically, he
worked to get Summers free. The heat was terrible, driving him out of the shattered cockpit window. Somehow,
he got to his feet, ran around the copilot's side and began
to saw at the harness that still held Summers. The copilot
was unconscious. Maybe dead. He didn't know. He heard
screams in the chopper. Heard men pounding against the
metal skin and trying to escape.

Once he dragged Summers free of the cockpit, Craig
drunkenly ran around the chopper to the door on the other
side. The dune was steep, sucking at his boots, slowing
down his forward progress. He heard men crying and
screaming, banging on the door that had been jammed
shut. The main fire was between the cockpit and cabin,
stopping any escape attempts from it through the shattered
windows of the cockpit. Sobbing for breath, Craig saw
the burned, twisted metal that had once been the door.
The grenade had landed between the door and the rotor
above it.

Just as he launched himself forward to try and pull the

door open, the second fuel tank exploded. There was a tremendous whoosh of heat, the sound of the explosion breaking his eardrums, and a feeling of being hurled bodily through the air. Craig remembered nothing more as he was slammed into the side of the dune, unconscious from impact.

He regained consciousness maybe fifteen minutes later. He felt very weak, disoriented, and his skin feeling like it was on fire. Barely raising his helmeted head, Craig saw his helicopter burning brightly down below him, like a torch in the darkness. A cry ripped from him as he sat up. When he tried to stand up, to run back down the slope to try and help his comrades, he fell flat on his face and lost consciousness again. Much later, he regained consciousness—only this time, it was at a field hospital behind the safety of American lines in Saudi Arabia.

Craig thrashed about on the couch, twitching feverishly. He felt a horrible fist jamming through him, and the need to cry was overwhelming. He'd never cried after what had happened. Once, after he'd gotten out of the hospital, he'd gone to see Linda and her children....

He retreated into a fetal position, the continuing *whap, whap, whap* of helicopter blades threatening to drive him insane. Why wouldn't the sound stop? Why? *Oh, God, just let me die. Release me. Stop the pain. Stop the remembering....*

In the midst of his tortured anguish, Craig felt a cool hand on his sweaty shoulder. He wrestled out of his tormented state, the sound of the helicopter still in his ears. He could literally feel the vibration of it, it was so close. Had his nightmare of the crash taken a turn for the worse? He heard a woman's voice, low and husky, calling his name. Despite his disorientation, Craig realized the voice belonged to Sabra.

He concentrated on her touch, her cool hand sliding gently back and forth across his sweaty shoulder. A whimper escaped his tightly shut lips as he fought to disengage from the past and hone in on the present. He would have done anything to give up the nightmare, to bury his memories of the crash forever. Sabra's touch was healing, helping him stabilize. *Just let Cal get out of it. Please, let me go. Let me survive....*

Sabra sat on the edge of the couch where Craig lay wrapped in a tight fetal position, his blanket twisted and knotted around his drawn-up legs. It was almost noon, and light was leaking in around the edges of the drapes. She'd been awakened by a helicopter flying very close to the hotel, just outside their window, along the beach. Then she'd heard a cry from the other room—Craig's voice. It had sent her flying out of bed.

Thinking he was under attack, she ran into his room, her pistol in hand, the safety off. Shocked, she saw Craig flailing around on the couch, as if fighting an invisible enemy. He kept clawing upward, reaching for something, then making slashing motions across himself. Realizing there was no intruder, Sabra put the safety back on her pistol, laid the weapon on the dresser and hurried to his side.

Though she vividly recalled his warning not to touch him, she couldn't help herself. He was in a tight knot, his arms wrapped around himself, his knees drawn upward toward his chest. He wore only light blue pajama bottoms. As full awareness surged through her, abruptly wiping away all sleepiness, she realized the cotton fabric was soaked, sticking to him like a second skin. His face looked tortured, his mouth contorted as if in a silent scream as she lowered herself beside him, her hip barely making contact with his knees. Even in the gloomy light, she could see his burn scars. They had reddened considerably during the nightmare. Lifting her hand, she reached out, her fingertips barely grazing his damp flesh. Craig was trembling, caught in the vise of something only he could see.

"Craig?" she whispered.

She saw the effect of her voice on him. His mouth eased, and he seemed to respond peripherally. Heartened, Sabra continued talking in a low voice. She wasn't sure what she said, so caught up was she in his pain. She just continued stroking his shoulder, offering him a point of reassurance within his nightmare experience.

Slowly, ever so slowly, Craig stopped trembling. His arms loosened slightly, and his knees were no longer frozen in such a locked position. Sabra pushed her hip against his thigh, forcing his long, powerful legs to stretch downward and release the rigid tension that had gripped them. She had never been able to stand seeing someone in pain. Maybe that was a weakness, but she didn't care. With her right hand, she increased her area of contact, softly caressing his bunched shoulders. There was such terrible tension in him. She placed her left hand over his badly scarred forearm, so in case he lashed out unexpectedly, she could parry the movement somewhat.

Strands of his hair stuck against his furrowed brow, and his eyes remained tightly shut, his spikey lashes flat against his drawn, pale skin. His breathing was ragged, gasping, and his body convulsed from time to time. Sabra leaned forward, her face close to his as she slid her arm around his shoulders to cradle him. To her utter surprise, the movement worked. As she curved her arm around him, Craig huddled against her, his damp face pressing against her nightgowned body.

Gently, Sabra allowed him to find her. His head nuzzled

against her; one shoulder pinned her thigh. She tightened her arms, just holding him. Words continued to slip from her. How many times had her mother held her, and soothed her this way as she lay crying, searching for protection?

Something old broke loose in Sabra's heart as she leaned forward and rested her lips against Craig's damp, short hair. He needed to be held, to be protected. She had no idea against what, but that no longer mattered. Even in the throes of his tortured sleep, caught in the predatory claws of the nightmare, he'd sought her arms and the safety of her embrace like a hurt child

Craig nestled more deeply into her lap, and in that moment, Sabra felt an incredible joy fill her pounding heart. As she continued speaking in soothing tones, her lips close to his ear, she felt him relax further, his arm unwinding to follow the curve of her hip and waist. A soft smile touched her lips as his arm encircled her and tightened. He was holding her back, his face against her belly, his breathing much less chaotic now.

Minutes ran together as her world became his. With each stroke of her hand up and down his strong spine, she felt his muscles respond. The sound of the helicopter receded, replaced by the happy noises of people at the beach. The salt breeze mingled with the scent of sweat from his body. Sabra saw color return to his face, his dark beard maintaining his dangerous look even now. Out of instinct, she leaned over and placed another soft kiss against his temple. She tasted the salt of sweat tangled in the strands of his hair. His breathing became more regular, and she closed her eyes and kissed his cheek. Something miraculous was occurring, and she didn't question it as she moved her lips against him.

This time, Sabra felt Craig move, his arm tightening

even more around her. She had kissed him to ease his pain, an offering of solace and love. As she trailed her lips downward, his head moved. In moments, she felt his fingers touch her jaw and guide her down—down to his mouth. Heat purled within her as his lips, strong and hungry, slid against hers. His breath brushed her cheek and his fingers tightened, drawing her down, drawing her closer. Every place her body touched his was like wildfire to Sabra. Vividly aware of his strong, guiding hand at her cheek, Sabra surrendered to his hungry, searching mouth.

She lost all sense of time and place. The sounds of the ocean crashing onto the sandy shore, of children laughing and playing, dissolved and melted into a startling awareness of Craig moving his lips powerfully against hers. His mouth was electric, molding and stamping her with his taste, his strength. A soft sigh escaped her as she felt him turn onto his back, both of his hands now framing her face, drawing her down over him. She felt the rise and fall of his chest, the thick mat of hair tantalizing her breasts through the thin silk barrier of her gown as she rested more surely against him. His mouth was demanding, and she acquiesced, understanding on some instinctive level, that he needed whatever she had to share. There was a desperation to the feel of his lips on hers, and she allowed him to drink deeply of her, taste her and take her as she'd never been taken before.

For lingering, molten moments, Sabra lost all awareness of her surroundings. When reality finally intruded on her spinning world of light and heat, she drew back, out of his grasp. Her eyes flew open and she stared down at Craig, her ragged breathing in time with his. His eyes were open, smoldering, watching her, and Sabra saw the terror in their depths—and the desire for her overlaying those fears. She felt his hands clasp her arms, as if to stop her from leaving. His face glistened with sweat, but his cheeks were flushed with life now, not drained to the pallor of death. His mouth… She groaned to herself. Craig's mouth was wonderful. She could still taste him on her lips, a tingling sensation lingering in the wake of his branding, possessive kiss. She had been right: he was a man who claimed and took the woman he wanted. He was primal—part animal, part man.

Shaken, she stared at him, a sudden sinking feeling in her stomach. What had she just done? She shouldn't be kissing Craig. He was her partner. They had a dangerous mission to accomplish. A little boy's life was at stake. With a small cry, Sabra pulled free and stumbled to her feet.

"I—I'm sorry," she whispered. She turned and fled from the room, her hand pressed to her parted lips to stop the cry that threatened to tear out of her.

Craig slowly sat up, still caught in memories of the past that were tangled with the surprising, molten present. What the hell had happened? Confused, he tried to sort out the events. He'd relived the crash. In the distance, he could still hear a helicopter. Was it his imagination? Shaking his head, he rubbed his face savagely and sat very still, his head cocked. No, there was a helicopter nearby. Had it flown near the hotel? Was that what had triggered the nightmare?

Looking around, he slowly realized where he was. He'd just been kissing Sabra. But how had it happened? Small fragments of memory started flowing back to him. His body ached like fire itself. He'd wanted Sabra—all of her—in every possible way. He wanted to lay her on the carpet, cover her with his body, plunge deeply into her, take her, love her and make her his. It was craziness!

Rubbing his face again, Craig wrestled with his demons—past and present. He could hear Sabra moving around in her room, but he was unable to see her from this angle. Without thinking, he got up, the twisted tangle of blanket falling to the carpet. He stepped over it and headed to the doorway between their rooms. Just as he got there, he heard the bathroom door shut. Grimacing, he stood, hands hanging helplessly at his side. He'd kissed her. He'd done more than kiss her, he realized as he slowly walked to the windows and pulled back the drapes. He'd taken her. Claimed her. As he stood there, bathed in the bright noontime sunlight, he looked with unseeing eyes over the turquoise Pacific and yellow sand beach below.

The room seemed suddenly stuffy, so Craig slid open the glass door and walked out onto the small balcony. Before him stretched hundreds of bright hibiscus bushes, exploding with a profusion of color, and palm trees swaying gracefully in a slight breeze. Birds sang melodically. Frowning, Craig leaned on the wrought-iron balcony railing. Families and couples moved around below, following a number of concrete paths that connected at least ten different pools within the hotel's expansive grounds. White and black swans swam in one huge pool, next to a man-made waterfall. In a smaller pool, children played on a water slide. Ducks swam in other pools. The hotel seemed to be part zoo, part water park, and definitely aimed at entertaining the hundreds of guests who could afford what it had to offer.

Craig's emotions remained elsewhere, however, hovering sweetly on his kiss with Sabra. Her mouth... He groaned and shut his eyes momentarily, reliving their wild, hot exchange. Her mouth was like a ripe, red hibiscus blossom, opening to him. She had tasted sweet and delicious, her lips sliding across his, allowing him to brand her with his essence. She had surrendered to him completely, he realized, as he opened his eyes, a stormy mix of emotions tunneling through him. Sabra had entrusted herself to him. He laughed sharply and straightened, throwing back his shoulders as if to throw off the weight he carried.

· Sabra had no business trusting him. No one did—but especially not her. Why had she been sitting on the couch where he slept? Had he screamed? Called out? Grimly, Craig turned, stared into the room and leaned back against the balcony railing, his arms crossed over his bare chest. Somehow, he had to apologize for his actions. He'd seen the sorrow in her eyes as she pulled away from him—and the terrible regret. Compressing his lips, he sighed, unlocked his arms and walked back into the suite.

He could hear the shower running as he walked through the bedroom to the smaller room. Picking up the phone, he ordered breakfast and coffee. Then he picked up his blanket, folded it and placed it with the pillow on the sofa. Always, he kept his hearing keyed. What was he going to say to Sabra? The truth? No, he could never speak the truth of that horrible tragedy to anyone. Somehow, he would find a way to apologize to her.

Sabra felt the beat of her heart pick up as she quietly opened the bathroom door. She had towel dried her hair, and it hung in damp strands against the pale green blouse she'd put on. The mirror was covered with steam, and she deliberately turned back and wiped a small clearing on the fogged surface with her palm. For the first time, she dared look at herself. She felt so different after Craig's crushing, heated kiss. Leaning closer, she touched her lower lip, seeing its lush, well-kissed look. Craig's kiss had been startling. Unexpected. Wonderful.

Why was she trying to deny the good feelings that ran through her? She studied her eyes in the mirror, seeking an answer and finding none. Her cheeks were flushed a rosy color that made her look innocent. But she was hardly that. She was old enough to know what had gone down and honest enough to admit her role in it. Bluntly, Sabra told herself it was her fault the kiss had occurred in the first place.

Determinedly, she left the bathroom, her nightgown and robe over her arm. She looked around before stepping into the bedroom. Where was Craig? Hearing nothing, she moved to the bed.

"Sabra?"

She gasped and whirled around, her nightgown spilling off her arm and falling to the carpeted floor. Craig stood between the rooms, frowning, his arms crossed over his broad, masculine chest. All words fled from Sabra's mind as she helplessly surrendered to his dark, smoldering gaze. Desire was banked like hot coals in his eyes. Was she crazy? Too long without a kiss? When had she last kissed a man? *Joshua.* That had been two years ago.

She leaned down and picked up the fallen nightgown. "You startled me," she whispered, straightening, the silk gripped in her tense fingers.

"I didn't mean to," Craig murmured, walking toward her. He had changed into a short-sleeved white shirt and a faded pair of jeans. He was still barefoot.

Gulping, Sabra took a step back as he halted within feet of her. She tore her gaze from his mouth—the mouth that had claimed her, heart and soul, in one breathtaking kiss.

"I have to apologize," he said, opening his hands in a gesture of friendship. "I don't know what happened. I was asleep, and the next thing I knew, I dreamt you were there beside me, kissing me." He ran his fingers through his hair. "It shouldn't have happened...."

Sabra bowed her head and held the nightgown tightly against her. "I—I'm sorry, too. It was my fault...all my fault." She shrugged helplessly and whispered, "I heard a noise and went to investigate." Getting up enough courage to look him in the eyes, she said in a strangled tone, "I thought someone had broken into our suite."

"That's why your pistol is on my dresser?"

"Yes...I—I saw you on the couch. You were using your arms, swinging them around, as if trying to hit someone or maybe escape. I don't know. Anyway," she rushed on breathlessly, unable to stand the sudden warmth in his gaze, "I came over, thinking you were having that nightmare again, the one you'd had on the flight...." Sabra turned and went to the bed, dumping her robe and nightgown on it. She felt herself trembling. Why was Craig looking at her like that? She couldn't stand that unexplained warmth in his eyes. Wrapping her arms around herself, she turned back toward him, strengthening her voice.

"I—I did a stupid thing. I know you told me not to touch you when you were having a bad dream. I sat down and—and slid my arm around your shoulder. You seemed so tortured, Craig." She bit her lower lip and looked away. Finally, she forced the words out. "I tried to hold you, that was all. When I put my arm around you, you were still caught up in your nightmare, I think. You crawled into my arms and I just held you until...well, I felt so awful for you. You were like a hurt little boy, and I hurt for you. I leaned down and kissed your cheek...."

Craig rested his hands on his hips, studying Sabra in the uncomfortable silence. She was flushed, her gaze darting to him and away again. Feeling her nervousness, he took a step forward. "Look," he rasped, "you didn't do anything wrong. I'm not saying that. I can't separate nightmare from reality when I'm caught up in it. I thought I heard your voice. I thought…" He grimaced. "I felt your hand on my shoulder, and I thought it was some kind of crazy overlay to the nightmare." He managed a twisted smile for just a moment, the corners of his mouth deepening. "To tell you the truth, when I went to bed last night, I didn't think I'd sleep. So I replayed the words you spoke to me on the plane and remembered your touch." He shrugged. "I fell asleep. It's the first time in a long time I've dropped off that fast." He halted, realizing he was saying too much. Clearing his throat, he added, "So, you see, I thought you were a dream. I didn't know it was real, not until later…."

Rubbing her brow, Sabra whispered, "You don't have to make excuses for me—"

"I'm not trying to, Sabra." He saw the wariness in her lovely eyes and had the urge to reach out and touch her long, damp hair, to tame away some of her nervousness. "I'm just trying to tell you what happened at my end of that…kiss."

Heat flared up into her cheeks, and Sabra died inwardly. She hadn't blushed like this in years! Craig's gentle tone was undoing her, just as his mouth had unfastened the gates to a cauldron of desire hidden deep within her. She'd had no idea of the power of her desire for him until that moment, and it frightened her. "It was a stupid mistake, that's all," she found herself rattling. "Let's just forget it, okay?" But how could she? She saw amusement lingering in his gaze. The man was going to drive her to distraction with looks like that! Did he realize his impact on her? She didn't think so. What hurt most was that he was apologizing for kissing her! If he'd meant to kiss her, he certainly wouldn't be apologizing like this.

"It's forgotten," he said huskily. He pointed to the other room. "Listen, I ordered us a late breakfast. It's here. Do you want to eat something?"

Touched, Sabra shrugged. Her stomach was in knots. Her lower body felt like it was on fire. She wanted only to throw her arms around his broad, capable shoulders and kiss him until they melted into each other. Moistening her lips, she said, "I could stand some coffee."

He allowed his hand to drop to his side. "Good. Come on."

She followed at a distance, but not because she didn't trust him. Oh, no—it was herself she didn't trust. With his day's growth of beard, Craig looked devastating, and now that she'd encountered the power of his kiss, she had to be careful not to respond to his looks, to any accidental touch. Her throat aching, she tried to put her turmoil and desire aside as she stepped into his room. Breakfast had been set out on the coffee table, and Sabra realized Craig must have done it. The coffee was already poured, her toast buttered, with jam slathered across it, waiting for her.

She sat down hesitantly at the opposite end of the couch, as far away from him as she could get. "You didn't have to do this," she murmured, motioning to the toast.

"Old habits die hard," he said wryly, trying not to stare at her too long or too much. Sabra's mint green blouse lovingly outlined her contours. Her white silk pants were as loose and flowing as her glorious dark hair. Once again, Craig was reminded of a graceful willow.

"What do you mean?" Sabra asked as she picked up the toast, barely noticing its whole-wheat flavor or the rich strawberry taste of the jam. Craig's powerful presence mere feet away from her was overwhelming.

He picked up his cup of coffee. "Back home in Fort Wingate, it was my job to butter the toast and put jam on the table for everybody." Giving her a slight smile and holding her shadowed gaze, Craig said, "Everyone at our house was assigned chores. Dan made breakfast, Joe set the table and I made sure the toast was buttered and the juice poured."

Relieved to be discussing such a safe topic, Sabra took a sip of the fragrant Kona coffee. His voice sounded low and intimate in a way she'd never experienced from him before. His face appeared totally relaxed for the first time, and she was in awe at the difference in him between their first meeting and now. How much of himself had he been hiding from her? Had their kiss made this difference? Flushing hotly, Sabra put her cup back on its saucer and stared down at the toast in her other hand.

"You said," she began, trying to keep things light between them, "that you were raised on an Indian reservation?"

"Yes. All three of us boys were born at Gallup, New Mexico, about sixteen miles from the family trading post and grocery store on the Navajo reservation. We kids were more or less adopted by neighbors of ours, the Yazzies. Alfred and Luanne Yazzie had a pretty big family of their own. I think we were lucky growing up in the wilds of the New Mexico desert with the Navajo people."

Sabra nodded and forced herself to swallow another bite of toast, then take another sip of coffee. Silence descended on them, and she scrambled mentally for some safe response. But what came out of her mouth was anything but safe. "Do you think the nightmare will come back again? Tonight?"

Craig's hands stilled on his thighs. He saw the worry in Sabra's eyes and heard it distinctly in her voice. "No," he said, "I hope not." Giving her a sad smile, he added, "You've really been lucky. Usually, the nightmare only hits about once a week. The rest of the nights I'm just restless. I toss and turn a lot, but I don't remember..." His voice trailed off.

"Maybe you're upset over losing Jennifer?"

He nodded, resting his elbows onto his thighs and clasping his hands between his knees. Avoiding Sabra's gaze, he rasped, "I'm more than upset."

"Were...you two close?"

He caught the inference. Looking up at her, he shook his head. "She was a good teammate, nothing more. We'd been on assignments together the past couple months." His mouth turned down. "I guess what hurts is that Jenny was engaged to be married as soon as we got off this last mission." Running his fingers through his hair in an aggravated motion, he muttered, "If I hadn't let her tail that suspect alone, she'd be enjoying her wedding now."

"Maybe," Sabra said quietly. "Maybe not. You can't predict future events any better than anyone else. You didn't know she would get in an auto accident."

He nodded, staring at the floor beyond his hands. "Maybe..."

Sabra set the cup down. "I could walk out of here and be nailed by a car crossing the street, Craig. It could happen to anyone."

He snapped his head up, glaring at her. "I've lost people twice in my life to things like that. I'm not about to lose you the same way."

Chapter Seven

Stunned by his sudden emotional intensity, Sabra stared at him, her cup frozen halfway to her lips.

"Look," he said angrily, "I've lost people I've loved before. Good people who didn't deserve to die. I'm like a black cloud, Sabra. Bad things happen when I'm around." He avoided her compassionate gaze and rubbed his hands together slowly, feeling the pain of the admission. "I know you're supposed to be the leader on this team," he croaked. "My head knows it, but my heart doesn't. I just lost my partner. I'm feeling damned guilty about it." He raised his chin, his eyes stormy. "I'm not going to lose you, Sabra. You're too special…too—"

Craig caught himself and snapped his mouth shut. He'd said much more than he'd intended. Much more. Sabra set her cup down and clasped her hands in her lap. He felt her gaze on him, and heat swept into his face. "There's no sense in you trying to give me any arguments,'' he told her irritably, meeting and holding her gaze. *''None.''*

Gently, Sabra reached out, her fingers barely grazing his arm. She felt the tautness of muscles beneath her fingertips, felt the same heat as when he'd been in the grasp of that virulent nightmare. ''Listen to me,'' she pleaded softly, ''I'm not your past. I'm your present, Craig. You keep forgetting, I've been through a lot of scrapes and lived to tell about them. I'm not going to do anything stupid, trust me on that. I'll look both ways before I cross the street. I always drive defensively.'' She released his arm, though it was the last thing she wanted to do. Taking a shaky breath, she added, ''If it makes you feel any better, you can drive when we go up to Kula to start snooping around.'' The look of relief on his face was telling, and the suffering in his eyes when she'd reached out and touched him was heartbreaking. She'd seen tears in his eyes. Or had she?

Craig sat for a long moment, battling his emotions. He picked up his cup, because if he didn't, he was going to slide over and put his arms around Sabra. She invited that kind of intimacy, and right now, he felt exceedingly vulnerable to her—more than ever before, because of the nightmare striking two times within a twenty-four-hour period. ''Thanks,'' he rasped, and took a gulp of the hot coffee.

''Why don't we get going?'' she suggested softly, looking around the room. Though the suite was large and spacious, she suddenly felt trapped.

''Good idea,'' he muttered, rising. ''Let me grab a quick shower and shave. Get the map and the car keys?''

Sabra breathed a sigh of relief and stood. ''Yes, I'll get them.'' Perhaps the tension that vibrated between them would dissolve if they were out on the road doing something to keep their minds occupied. As she went to retrieve her purse, she laughed at herself. No matter what she did with Craig, she would always be highly aware of him—of the charismatic power that swirled around him and of the danger he presented to her as a woman.

Opting not to wear the shoulder holster, she placed her pistol in her purse. Wearing the holster meant covering it with some kind of jacket, and with the temperature in the eighties, that was the last thing she wanted to do. Craig headed into the bathroom to shower.

"I'll go get the car," she called from the door.

"Fine, I'll meet you there."

Good. She had something to do. Opening the door, she saw a number of people, mostly families, in the hallway. She noticed both Japanese and Americans, and she heard a smattering of German from a couple ahead of her. Hawaii drew people from all over the world. And with good reason, she thought, as she took the elevator to the main level.

In the lobby, Sabra began to appreciate the unique beauty of the hotel. A huge, concrete pool stretched half the length of the place, with a man-made waterfall cascading noisily into it right outside the registration area desk. Below the falls, graceful swans and various species of ducks swam. All around the pool, hotel guests took photos of the extraordinary place, or tossed bread crumbs to the birds.

Just getting out the room helped Sabra start to unwind. She hadn't realized the tension she carried in her shoulders until she walked into the spacious lobby filled with antiques and art. Outside, a valet approached, but she waved him away, deciding to get the car herself. The sky overhead was a pale blue, with fluffy fragments of white clouds. In the distance, she could see the velvety green

slopes of Haleakala. Once it was classified as a dormant
volcano, but recently, she had read smoke had been spotted in the bottom of the crater, so it had been taken off
the dormant list and upgraded to inactive status. More
clouds circled the top of the ten-thousand-foot peak, Sabra
noted as she stepped onto the asphalt driveway in front
of the hotel.

The Westin was a very busy place, with a row of lim-
ousines, plus a number of Mercedes Benzes and BMWs,
speaking to the wealth of the visitors. As Sabra made her
way to the parking lot, she enjoyed the high, dark green
bushes that surrounded the hotel. Hibiscus bloomed in
colorful profusion, like miniature rainbows. Bougainvillea
climbed walls here and there, and palms trees, for which
Hawaii was famous, were scattered around the huge parking lot.

Sabra's instincts took over as she approached space
121, where they'd parked the white Toyota Camry they
had rented. Dredging up her knowledge of car bombs, she
carefully knelt down and checked under the car, especially
around the doors. Sometimes terrorists placed bombs to
go off when a car door was opened. She found nothing.
Moving to the hood of the car, she visually inspected the
opening, then ran her fingertips beneath the hood area,
searching for any unusual wires.

Next she carefully lifted the hood and inspected the
engine. Most car bombs were placed either in the engine
compartment or on the fire wall, near the ignition.

Her gaze ranged knowingly across various areas where
the plastic explosives might be placed. Though she found
nothing, Sabra never relaxed her vigil as she checked under hoses and cables, sliding her fingers along them, just
in case. C-4 was completely pliable and could be taped
anywhere.

Finally satisfied, she gently closed the hood and went around to the car door, noting the new-car odor that lingered in the vehicle as she slid into the driver's seat. Inside, she automatically checked under the dash and in the glove box, where someone could have planted a bug to pick up their conversations. Leaning over, she visually inspected both areas. A bug could be put almost anywhere, and she knew that although she was trained to find them, one could be hidden in the light above her, or under her seat. Or in the trunk.

Popping the trunk lid open, Sabra got out and inspected the area. Often, a transponder device could be attached beneath the trunk lid, so a car could be followed with ease—either by road or by air. Finding nothing except the spare tire and tire iron, she closed the lid and relaxed a little, enjoying the warmth of the noonday sun. The wind was sporadic, tugging at strands of her hair.

Just as she was about to get back into the car, she spotted Craig walking purposefully toward her, their camera equipment in a huge canvas bag over his shoulder. His hair was dark and sleek from its recent washing, and his face was scraped free of the dark shadow of beard. He wore the same clothes as before, but with a light blue jacket to conceal his shoulder holster. To her surprise, he held a lei in one hand.

Sabra reopened the trunk. Craig met her there and stowed their equipment.

"Here," Craig said gruffly, "this is for you," and he lowered the lei over her head, settling it against her neck. "It's plumaria. I liked the smell of it and thought of you...." He saw the pleasure in her eyes as he gently pulled her hair away from the flowers. Just as he'd thought, her hair was not only thick but fine, like strong silk. Though he ached to thrust his fingers through the mass of it, glinting with reddish highlights in the sun, he resisted.

"Thank you," Sabra murmured, touching the waxy petals of the fragrant white blooms.

Craig stood for a moment, watching a blush spread across her cheeks. Her eyes shone with such beauty that he forced himself to turn and slam the trunk closed. "Come on," he said. "Let's go."

Once they were in the car, heading down the long, palm tree-lined lane that would eventually take them to the highway, Craig asked, "Did you find anything?"

Sabra shook her head. "No...nothing."

Quirking his mouth, he braked at the stop sign. The only highway that traversed Maui was busy this afternoon. He wasn't surprised. Making a right turn, he accelerated until they were moving with the rest of the traffic, heading east toward what was commonly known as up-country Maui.

Craig knew that although Sabra had no doubt gone over the car with a fine-tooth comb, there still could be a bug present, so they couldn't risk talking about anything that might make them suspect. His gaze ranged from the cars ahead of them to the ones behind, particularly alert for any that might seem to be following them.

"What do you feel like doing today, sweetheart?"

Sabra smiled a little, realizing Craig was pretending for the benefit of a possible bug. "Oh, I don't know. Part of me would love to go shopping, but the other part says we should drive around and look for photographic sights for our book." She deliberately stretched her arm across his seat and touched his shoulder. The contact was pleasurable, and she watched his mouth part slightly at her unexpected contact. Well, they were married, and such touching was expected, Sabra told herself. Only Craig reacted far differently from Terry, when they'd had to play such a role. She wondered if Craig's response was real or feigned.

"Lahaina isn't far from here," he suggested.

"Mmm, let's just sort of be whimsical today. Go where our spirits take us."

He smiled a little. "Okay." Sabra's soft touch against his shoulder again set his skin to tingling. But it was all an act, he realized, chastising himself unhappily. She wouldn't be touching him otherwise. Despite the pleasure of her company, he concentrated on the traffic around him. At the last moment, he turned off onto a side street that would lead them to Lahaina, one of the huge shopping areas on Maui. No cars followed. He went down a few blocks, made a left turn and headed back out to the highway. Again on the main thoroughfare, he continued to keep watch.

Sabra couldn't relax despite the excellent job Craig was doing driving and watching. She shifted her arm off the back of the seat and clasped her hands together in her lap. The beauty of Maui was evident everywhere. Once they'd gone beyond the main business area, the four-lane highway narrowed to two lanes. On the left rose volcanic hills of reddish black lava. On the right stretched the turquoise waters of the Pacific. As they climbed in elevation, Sabra could see a good portion of eastern Maui ahead of them.

Craig remained silent on their forty-five-minute drive to Kula, a small farming community roughly four thousand feet above sea level on the slopes of the magnificent Haleakala crater. Besides the local farmers, tiny Kula boasted its share of million-dollar estates for the rich and famous. In addition, the rare flower known as protea grew in the rich volcanic soil around Kula. The foliage was thick, and the many silver-barked eucalyptus trees that lined the narrow highway leading to Kula reminded him of Australia.

Proteas poked their huge, pincushion-shaped heads up here and there in people's front lawns bordering the highway. Craig glanced at Sabra, who had pulled out a map and spread it across her lap. Without a word, she held up one finger, meaning it was one mile to Garcia's estate. He nodded and slowed down a little more. Traffic through Kula was mainly tourists, coming from or going to Haleakala, which rose above them.

Garcia's estate sat about fifty feet off the highway on their right. Craig noted that the surrounding black, wrought-iron fence was at least ten feet tall, covered with red, pink and orange bougainvillea. Palm and eucalyptus trees grew near the iron fence, both inside and out. He didn't dare slow down too much and draw attention. Sabra had raised her camera and was clicking away as they passed the huge estate. Up ahead, he saw a small road and turned left, following it. The road was dirt and very rutted. Slowing to a crawl, they climbed its dusty expanse. Slopes of knee-high green grass bracketed them, interspersed with numerous eucalyptus trees, which dominated the rolling landscape.

Finally, after nearly a mile, Craig pulled the car to the side of the road. The slopes rose around them, all part of Haleakala's lower skirts, which flared outward to encompass most of eastern Maui. Climbing out, he opened the trunk, pulled out the canvas bag and slung it across his shoulder. He saw Sabra locking the car. Their eyes met, and he signaled her to follow him up the grassy knoll, thickly covered with eucalyptus.

The day was warm and breezy, the dark green leaves of the eucalyptus swaying in the wind. The grass was tall and thick and tangled easily around Craig's feet as he carefully made his way up the slope. The rich, black soil was composed of volcanic matter ground away over millions of years. He felt Sabra move up beside him. The climb was steeper than he'd realized.

"Did you see how secluded Garcia's estate was?" she asked, slightly out of breath.

"Yeah."

"Still," she said, continuing to look around and study their position, "it's accessible."

"Maybe." Craig halted at the top of the knoll and grinned at her. "We've got a good view."

Sabra pushed strands of hair away from her face as the breeze swirled around her. Her heart was pounding from the climb as well as the elevation, but a smile tugged at her own mouth as she stood there. A thousand feet below, the road ran like a narrow ribbon, and directly across from it lay Garcia's elaborate, multimillion-dollar estate. From here they could see not only the iron fence that completely enclosed the grounds, but a huge Olympic-size pool to the left of his sumptuous house, the helicopter landing pad to the right.

"Whew," she said, wiping her brow, "that's quite a climb."

"We'll adjust to the altitude in a couple of days," Craig said, kneeling down and opening the canvas bag. "Come on, help me get this equipment up and running."

For the next half hour, they worked together in silence. The photographic equipment was state-of-the-art. When it was assembled, Sabra could see every movement on the estate as if it were mere feet away, through the lens of the high-powered camera she'd secured to a sturdy tripod. Craig anchored the tripod to prevent the gusting wind from knocking it over. They'd placed it next to a huge eucalyptus tree that provided partial cover for them and the camera. There was no doubt in Sabra's mind that the sentries would constantly check the surrounding hills for eavesdroppers such as themselves.

Finally, everything was done. Dancing sunlight slanted across the thick green grass. Craig sat down near Sabra's feet, his back against the tree, as she peered through the lens at the estate.

"We're going to have to pull half-hour watches," he said, opening his notebook and resting it against his drawn-up legs.

Sabra slowly panned the camera. "I know."

"Give me a verbal on the exterior layout."

Pleased at his efficiency, she said, "An Olympic swimming pool, regulation size, lies to the left of the house, completely enclosed by a white, wrought-iron fence. A number of lounge chairs and some tables with red-and-white-striped umbrellas surround the pool, but no people are visible."

"Good," Craig exclaimed, writing down the information and beginning to make a detailed map. "What else?"

Sabra moved the camera gently, panning to the right. "Wait…I see a man, probably a guard. Yes…he's carrying an assault rifle…no, it's a Beretta 12 submachine gun."

"I'm not surprised," Craig muttered, writing down the information.

She followed the progress of the guard, who walked slowly around the entire pool area. "I'm not, either. I was just hoping otherwise."

"That Beretta submachine gun can do a lot of damage in a hurry."

Sabra's heart pumped a little harder as she watched the guard. "This guy is about six feet tall, one hundred and eighty pounds. He's got black hair, brown eyes and a swarthy complexion.''

Craig looked up. Sabra's mouth was compressed. The breeze tugged at her silk blouse and pants, outlining one side of her lithe form. She was beautiful no matter what she was doing or wearing, he decided. Tearing his mind off such things, he said, "Do you see any other guards?"

"Not yet. I want to time this guy."

"I'll do it." Craig set his watch.

"He's circled the pool, and now he's heading toward the rear of the estate, toward the fence."

"He's got a circuit he's walking. Let's find out how long it is. If we get lucky, Garcia won't have too many goons on the perimeter fence."

"Maybe," Sabra murmured. "This guy is good. He walks a few feet, then waits and listens, looks around and then moves on. He's trained well."

"See any dogs?"

She sighed. "Not yet. I hope he doesn't have any, if you want the truth." Dogs made it much tougher to enter an area undetected.

"Jake said Garcia had them at his Caribbean-island estate. Why wouldn't he have them here?"

"He probably does. I just haven't seen them yet."

For the the rest of her half-hour shift, Sabra watched, giving verbal reports to Craig. To their relief, there appeared to be only two guards on duty, each walking one side of the estate. Both were heavily armed. She'd spotted no dogs, but that meant nothing at this stage of the game.

Craig closed the notepad and reached into the canvas bag. "Hungry?"

Sabra came and sat down opposite him, the huge trunk of the eucalyptus hiding them completely from any prying eyes at the Garcia estate. "A little."

He pulled out two sandwiches wrapped in plastic. "I got these at the deli at the hotel. They're both chicken."

Her fingers touched his as she took one sandwich. Sabra found herself wanting excuses to touch him. "Thanks," she murmured, unwrapping the whole-grain bread. Crossing her legs, she began munching and looked upward.

"This tree is so beautiful."

"Like you." Craig frowned. Now where the hell had that come from? He saw Sabra's eyes widen over the compliment. Just as quickly, he saw her avert her gaze. "You've always reminded me of a willow," he said gruffly, trying to cover his faux pax. "You're graceful, like this tree."

Sabra chewed on the sandwich, no longer tasting it. "I've never been compared to a willow before, but it's a nice compliment," she said softly.

"When I first saw you, I wondered if you'd taken ballet lessons or something." Craig couldn't help himself. He wanted to know more about Sabra on a personal level. He had no right—no business asking, but it didn't matter. For the moment, they were safe, and they had gotten useful information.

"I never took ballet," she said. She enjoyed watching him lean back fully against the tree, his long legs sprawling in front of him. "But I love to dance."

Craig believed it, feeling his body tighten with desire at the thought of moving with her in his arms.

"What about you?" she asked, studying him. "Do you like to dance?"

He snorted softly and took another big bite of his sandwich. "I've got two left feet. It goes downhill from there."

Chuckling, Sabra set her sandwich aside and wiped her

mouth with the paper napkin he'd provided. "I don't believe it. I think you're like a lot of men—just shy about dancing."

"It's more than that."

"Prove it, then."

He raised his head and stared at her darkly. "What?"

"If things are slow tonight, and we don't find anything to act on, will you take me dancing?"

Was Sabra playing her role of wife? Or was she sincere? He probed into her wistful eyes and found nothing coy in them. Rubbing his jaw, he muttered, "Out here, you can drop the wifely pretense."

"I wasn't pretending," Sabra said. If only Craig realized how much she valued his touch. She was sure he didn't know, and the playful, bold part of her wanted more. Right or wrong, she felt something driving her to want Craig on any level she could have him. They were both single, and it was obvious he had no one in his life at the moment. Working with him, she could see he was just as professional as she was at intrigue and espionage. Whatever doubts she'd had on that score were quickly being laid to rest.

"Oh." He swallowed the last of his sandwich and threw the wrapper back into the canvas bag. A huge part of him was hungry for any reason to be with Sabra. The idea of holding her close on the dance floor was excruciatingly tantalizing—it was the ideal excuse to hold her tight and feel her contours against him. His mouth went dry as his thoughts turned to more torrid and burning possibilities.

Trying to swallow her disappointment, Sabra realized that her attraction was only one-sided. He was frowning, settling his gaze anywhere but on her as he mulled over her invitation. With a sigh, she got to her feet and brushed off the seat of her pants.

"Forget it," she said as lightly as possible, "it was just a thought. I'm not going to hold you to it, Craig." Forcing herself to move, she went back to the camera, to begin once more monitoring activity at the estate.

Stung, Craig sat where he was for a moment, feeling pretty damned foolish. He had acted like some green, tongue-tied teenager asked to his first dance by a cute girl he had a crush on, but unable to believe she could like him enough to ask. The hurt in Sabra's tone needled him. She'd offered herself to him, and like a fool, he'd frozen....

It was nearly 10:00 p.m. when Craig said, "Let's close up shop for the evening."

Sabra was sitting next to the tree, her arms wrapped around herself against the evening chill. "Good," she said through teeth that chattered. "I didn't realize how cold it would get here at night."

Craig took the camera off the tripod and knelt near the canvas bag. "Me, neither. Tomorrow night we're bringing jackets and blankets. We're going to have to time the guards' watches from dark to dawn."

"Yes," she agreed, getting up to help him with the equipment.

It took far less time to break it down than it had to set it up. In no time, Craig was slinging the bag across his shoulder. Sabra was obviously cold, her arms wrapped around herself in an effort to keep warm. He reached out, placing his free arm around her shoulders. "Lean against me," he said. "It will help warm you up."

Surprised by his sudden gesture, Sabra found herself drawn up against his bulk. "You're so warm!"

He nodded, carefully feeling the terrain beneath his feet as they started down the steep slope. "Yeah, I'm pretty warm-blooded." Hot-blooded would be more like it, but he didn't want to get into that. Sabra fell into step with him quickly, and he bit back a groan of pleasure as she flowed against him. Her arm went around his waist, and he smiled to himself. How good she felt against him, strong and supple and inviting.

It was very dark, with only a small slice of moon in the starry sky above them. Craig balanced the weight of the equipment on his shoulder, keeping Sabra tucked beneath his other arm. All too soon, they were off the grassy slope and back on the dirt road. Reluctantly, he eased his arm from her shoulders.

"Thanks," Sabra whispered, going to open the trunk. Her heart was fluttering rapidly in her breast, and her skin tingled pleasantly from the feel of his body against hers. She stepped aside so that he could put away the equipment.

"Are you warmer now?"

"Yes…"

"Get in the car and start the engine. You're still shivering."

She was, she realized, but it wasn't from the chilly evening—it was from Craig unexpectedly claiming her once again. Getting into the car, Sabra started the engine and waited for him. As he came around the driver's side, she slid into the passenger seat, deciding to let him drive.

Once in the car, Craig said, "How about we grab something to eat at the hotel?"

"Fine," she answered.

"Are you tired?"

Sabra shrugged. "Bored maybe, but not really tired. What about you?"

"Bored." He turned the car around and eased it down the road without turning the lights on. Craig didn't want to risk detection by Garcia's people. He'd wait until they were entering the main highway before he turned on the headlights.

She laughed a little. "In our business it's hours and days of boredom punctuated by moments of terror. At least, that's the way it's been for me."

Craig was focusing on the road, not wanting to run off it. Realizing that Sabra had forgotten their playacting, he said, "Sweetheart, if you're so bored, what do you say we go dancing? I think the photos we took today of the flowers are going to be pretty spectacular. Let's celebrate."

Damn! Sabra realized her laxness and, despite the darkness, gave Craig an apologetic look. What was wrong with her? She knew better. She never lapsed with Terry. Disgruntled and embarrassed, she forced a brittle laugh. "Oh, darling, I'd love to go dancing!"

"Good, we'll do it then."

Sabra knew there were so many types of bugs available that their conversation could be easily recorded from almost any distance. Fortunately, Craig hadn't blown their cover as she almost had. What must he think of her now? She was behaving like an inept beginner in a world that didn't forgive mistakes.

"I love you," he said, picking up her hand and kissing the back of it. Craig hated himself for playing the charade. Wanting to kiss her wasn't a lie, of course, but Sabra didn't know that. He heard her swift intake of breath at his gesture. And where had those words come from? Angrily, he released her hand and turned onto the asphalt highway. Switching on the headlights, he reentered the flow of traffic, which was very light at this time of night.

Sabra sat still, her fingers resting over the spot Craig had kissed. The words, *I love you,* rang in her mind and vibrated wildly in her heart. It was all a charade and she knew it. Or was it? Craig's voice had lowered to such an intimate level when he'd spoken the words, as if an animal growl—as if he were an alpha-male wolf claiming her as his mate. Shakily, she touched her brow. She was being silly. Craig had pretended in order to cover her faux pax, that was all. When she stole a look at his profile, her pulse bounded unexpectedly.

His face was rugged, his mouth deliciously firm beneath his strong nose and those hooded eyes that could look straight into her. Sabra took a deep, ragged breath. She couldn't help herself; driven by her own needs, which Craig was completely unaware of, she leaned over and placed her arm around his shoulders. ''I love you, too,'' she whispered, kissing his cheek.

If Craig was surprised, he never showed it. As Sabra eased back, releasing him, she watched him closely. His mouth had compressed, almost as if with displeasure. Wounded, she fell into silence. It was pretend. That was all. Closing her eyes, she realized she wanted Craig's genuine attention, wanted to know how he honestly felt about her, but it was an impossible wish to fulfill under the circumstances.

Sabra knew the routine for when they got back to the hotel. They would have to scour their suite for bugs again. And even if they found none, they still couldn't be sure they weren't being monitored. It was pretend there, too. She longed for the freedom to really talk to Craig. To find out, one way or another, if he truly liked her. She wanted to tell him how his touch affected her, how his kiss was indelibly stamped upon her lips and that she longed to kiss him again.

Miserably, Sabra sank into a well of sadness. What was wrong with her? Craig was only doing his job. Desperately, she searched for a way to talk with him—honestly and openly. But they could be followed and never know it. Someone who looked like a tourist could really be one of Garcia's hit men. Sabra knew the drug cartels had sophisticated equipment that could overhear conversations anywhere. A laser beam could be aimed from miles away to pick up the vibrations of their voices through the glass of their hotel windows. Even on a dance floor their conversations could be monitored. Somehow, she would have to swallow all these vibrant, wonderful emotions. She'd thought her feelings were dead since Josh had been torn from her life. But now Craig was bringing her to life in a way she'd never experienced before.

Though Sabra yearned for time to talk with Craig, she had to be realistic. A little boy's life hung in the balance. Her mind seesawed between worrying over Jason and wondering if he was really at the estate at all. Today they'd seen no sign of him. Still, they would need to carry out surveillance twenty-four hours a day for the next couple of days before they could say for sure.

"Look out!"

Craig's voice broke into Sabra's meandering thoughts.

A set of headlights swerved, aiming directly at them. Slamming on the brakes, he yanked the steering wheel to the right, tires squealing. The lava bank loomed close. Craig felt the car skidding against the gravel of the berm. The other car suddenly veered back to its own side of the road, as their Toyota slid to a stop a few inches from the sharp lava bank.

"Sabra, are you okay?" Craig turned, gripping her shoulder. In the oncoming headlights he could see the terror on her face.

"I—yes, I'm okay." She slid her fingers upward across her right cheek. "Oh, dear..."

"What?" He unsnapped his seat belt and turned to get a closer look at her. "What is it?"

Sabra grimaced. "It's all right. It's just a little blood. I think I hit the window, that's all."

Worriedly, Craig slid his hand along her jaw. It was hard to tell much of anything in the darkness, but he could make out a small rivulet of blood trickling down from her hairline. "Yeah, you've got a cut or something. Hang on. When we get back to the room, I'll take a closer look at it."

Closing her eyes momentarily, Sabra absorbed the roughened touch of his hand against her cheek. His voice was low and urgent, filled with genuine care. Or was it pretense? Her head seemed to spin. Opening her eyes, she pulled away from him.

"Are you—"

"I'm fine!" she assured him. Shakily, he released her. "Damn good thing we wear seat belts."

Touching her brow, she whispered, "Yes."

"Stupid jerk," he muttered, putting the car back into gear. "Probably drunk or something."

Sabra wasn't so sure. She bit down hard on her lower lip as he eased the car back into traffic. Was it an accident? Or had it been intentional?

Chapter Eight

Sabra pressed her hand to her aching forehead. The darkness was complete, broken only by occasional headlights flashing by as they drove down the main highway toward Lahaina. Had it really been an accident? She couldn't voice her fears for fear of electronic eavesdroppers. Every once in a while, she felt Craig's intense gaze fall upon her for just a moment.

Just as they reached the outskirts of Lahaina, she heard him suck in a breath of air. She twisted to look in his direction. Too late! Sabra's eyes widened enormously as she saw a car race up beside them on the four-lane highway. As it deliberately swerved toward them, she clung to the door handle and tried to brace herself for the coming impact. The first attack had been no accident! Fear shot through her. All she could do was watch through horrified eyes.

Craig yanked the steering wheel to the right. Fortunately, traffic was light, and he took the car onto the side-walk, where it groaned and clunked, one set of wheels higher than the other. Glass shattered around them. The other car was firing at them!

"Get down!" Craig roared, wrenching the wheel to the left. The light had just turned red, but if he braked, they were dead. He heard the *ping-ping-ping* of submachine-gun bullets stitching along the side of the car. More glass shattered inward. Hunching over, he jammed his foot down on the accelerator, and the car leapt through the light. The speedometer needle rose rapidly to fifty, sixty, seventy miles an hour. He wove between the few cars, jerking a look into the rearview mirror. Were they following? He had to assume they were.

Luckily, it was night, which made them harder to tail—unless a bug had been attached to their car so they could follow it by remote control. His head spun with options. He risked a quick look at Sabra. She had bent down, her hands covering her head.

"Sabra?"

"I—I'm okay. You?"

Craig said raggedly, "I'm okay."

She sat up and twisted to look out the shattered rear window. Her breath was coming in ragged gulps. Bits of glass tumbled out of her hair and down her front as she turned back to face the road. Her heart was pounding hard in her chest. She looked over at Craig. His profile was hard and set, and sweat stood out on his face, gleaming in the oncoming headlights.

"What are we going to do?"

"They're on to us. Whoever they are," he rasped. Slamming on the brakes, he turned the car down a dark-ened side street to the right. Flicking off the headlights, he guided it down the rutted, dirt road in near blackness.

Houses flashed by on either side of them. Ahead, he spotted another small road, and steered the car onto it.

"See anything?" he demanded.

"No," Sabra said, watching out the rear window. "Nothing."

"We've got to ditch this car."

"Yes."

Savagely, he jerked the steering wheel, aiming the vehicle down another meandering lane with very few homes along it. Pulling into a grassy area off the road, he left the keys in the car and climbed out.

"Come on," he ordered, hurrying to the trunk.

The night air was cool and still. Craig's hands shook as he pulled the trunk open and grabbed the canvas bag. He felt more than saw Sabra reach his side as he hefted it over his shoulder.

"Where—"

"Let's get away from the car," he said raggedly. Grabbing her arm, he said, "This way." He led them up a grassy knoll toward a stand of darkened trees at the top— probably eucalyptus. Right now, he wanted good, thick cover. If those were Garcia's henchmen, they'd certainly have night goggles or infrared scopes on their weapons that detected body heat. If necessary, he and Sabra could dig shallow holes, cover themselves with dried leaves and wait it out.

Sabra dug her toes into the damp, moist earth of the hillside. She felt dizzy, but shook it off, trying to keep up with Craig. The hill was steeper than she'd thought, and by the time they'd scaled it, she was breathing hard from the exertion. Following Craig into the heart of the eucalyptus grove, she looked back, but could see no one coming down the road toward where they'd left the car.

"Over here," Craig called. He gently placed the canvas

bag on the ground and with his hands raked up a bunch of leaves to hide it. "Get down and start digging a shallow grave to lie in."

Sabra nodded and fell to her knees. Her fingers felt numb; her head ached. She dug quickly, finding the soil loose.

"Do you think—"

"I'm assuming they've got night goggles," he rasped, rapidly digging his own shallow trench. "Maybe infrared. We're going to have to wait them out. We can't talk, either. They may have sensing equipment that can pick us up a mile away."

Sabra steadied herself and nodded. "I'm going belly down in my grave. Cover me?"

Craig leaned over and quickly placed dirt and leaves across her legs, back and shoulders. "I'll be close by. If you see anything, just nudge me lightly with your foot. I'll do the same. I don't know how long we'll have to stay here."

Already shivering in the damp ground, Sabra said nothing. Craig had dug his trench close enough to her that if she stretched out her right foot, her toe could make contact with his arm. Trying to steady her breathing, she studied the streets below. A dog barked somewhere in the distance. She could see the lights of Lahaina not far away, the main shopping area that was lit up in carnival-like colors.

Craig was covering himself the best he could. Night goggles allowed a person to see into the night as if it were daylight, magnifying whatever light was there, so that everything looked light green or yellow. If Garcia's men had body-heat detectors, they could find them even if they missed them with the night goggles—providing Craig and

Sabra were above ground or moving around. If they remained silent, they had a chance of surviving.

His mind whirled with questions. What had given them away? Had they somehow compromised themselves by their position on the hill earlier today? A bug in their suite? Was there a leak in the police department? Had the detective, Chung, given information to Garcia, acting as a paid informant and mole? Craig didn't want to think that. Sam Chung didn't seem the type. But how had Garcia found them?

He ticked off the possibilities, among them that someone at the hotel could have become suspicious. But how? Their cover was intact, as far as he was concerned. Someone in the airline watching for flights out of D.C. to Hawaii? That was possible, but not high on his list. No, Garcia's guards must have spotted them earlier today. Damn!

His mouth grew dry as he saw a vehicle make the turn off the main highway and take the same dirt road they had. It was moving deliberately, as if searching for something—or someone. He felt Sabra nudge his arm with her toe. She'd seen it, too. At least they were armed; but Craig didn't want a shoot-out. He frowned, squinting as he watched the car crawl up the road. Its headlights stabbed through the darkness, and it slowly turned onto the smaller road where he'd parked their Toyota.

To his surprise, he saw the lights of a police cruiser suddenly switch on. It was the cops! Watching warily, Craig saw the vehicle pull over next to their car. He felt Sabra nudge him strongly. Could they trust the police? Should they go down and tell them what had happened? Sweat trickled down his temples as he watched. But how did the cops know about this? How could they possibly know he and Sabra had parked there? Perhaps someone in the sparsely populated neighborhood had called the police because the two of them had been tearing around at high speeds on back roads late at night. There were so many possibilities. But right now, Craig instinctively mistrusted the police.

Anxiously, he watched as two uniformed policemen got out of the cruiser, their flashlights on, and started investigating the bullet-ridden car. They were too far away to hear their voices, but from time to time he could pick up snatches from the police radio in the cruiser. He felt Sabra move. No! Risking everything, he slowly reached out and wrapped his hand around her slender ankle. Giving her flesh a long, slow squeeze, he tried to impress on her that it was vital not to get up, not to move. Would she remain still?

Slowly, ever so slowly, he felt the tension in her leg dissolve beneath his hand. Good. She was going to stay put as he had silently requested. Slipping his fingers from her ankle, he brought his hand carefully back against his side. Chances were the cops would check out the car, then call a wrecker to impound it. Releasing a slow breath, Craig knew they had at least another hour of hiding in store before they could escape.

Sabra tried to stop her teeth from chattering. The wrecker and police cruiser had come and gone. Their car had been hauled away. The road was again clear of any traffic. Her head ached, and she felt the muscles of her legs drawing up from the dampness, wanting to cramp. Just when she thought she could take it no longer, she heard Craig slowly rise from his trench. Leaves fell around her, then she felt his hands upon her body, brushing the leaves off of her. Slowly, she turned over and sat up.

"Come on," he said, holding out his hand to her.

She gripped it and felt herself being pulled upward. Dizziness assailed her, and Sabra felt herself falling forward. Before she could cry out, Craig's strong arms wrapped around her and brought her against him. Without a word, she sank into him, her head hurting so much she couldn't speak for a moment. Instead, Sabra placed her arms around his shoulders and allowed herself the momentary luxury of resting against his strong reassuring bulk. How could he feel so warm? Right now, she was cramping and shivering, her teeth chattering.

Craig groaned softly and held Sabra tightly against him. She'd flowed against him like sunlight. He was surprised at how strong and supple she felt beneath his hands. She was shivering, and he realized she was very cold. Beginning to rub her back briskly with his hand, he rasped, "Just lean on me. I'll get you warmed up in a minute."

Sabra closed her eyes and surrendered to Craig. No longer did she try and fight what her heart wanted. She felt the slow, powerful beat of his heart against her breasts, felt the warmth of his breath against her cheek and the side of her neck as he ran his hands firmly up and down her back, encouraging her circulation. A soft smile touched her lips as she nestled her head against him. How wrong she'd been about Craig. If anything, he'd acted far more professionally in this crisis than she might have. Knowing that made her trust him even more. His hand felt good, and she automatically tightened her arms around his neck, steadying herself against him.

Craig forced himself not to pay too much attention to Sabra's nearness. It was close to impossible, though their circumstances were precarious at best. A few minutes later he felt her stop shivering and gently eased her away from him, enough to look down into her dark, shadowed eyes.

Even in the dim light, he could see the dried blood along her right temple, where she'd struck her head earlier. Not only that, but he saw tiny nicks on her neck and shoulder where the exploding glass had cut into her beautiful skin.

"We need to get help," Sabra said in a low voice. She was glad Craig didn't let her go. Instead, he wrapped his arm around her waist and kept her leaning against him.

"First, we need a room somewhere." He pointed to Lahaina below. "There are a lot of motels along the main road. We need a room for the night."

Sabra nodded. "We can't go back to the Westin. They're probably waiting for us there."

He frowned and nodded. "We can't trust anyone, Sabra," he warned. "Not even the police."

"I know," she said sadly, searching his dark, hard features. "We need to get to a pay phone, something they can't trace, and alert Perseus."

"First things first," he rasped, leading her to where he'd hidden the canvas bag. "Let's get a room, and I'll make the call. You can wash up, get some sleep, and we'll figure out what our next move will be."

Sabra moved away from Craig as he leaned down to pick up the bag. Her knees felt wobbly. She and Craig had almost died. The rush of adrenaline had long since left her. Now, she felt weak and shaky, and she wanted to cry. She knew the reaction was a normal one for her. She saw Craig hold out his hand toward her.

"Come on," he entreated softly. He saw the surprise in her eyes and managed a twisted smile. "Whether you like it or not, we're hip deep in trouble. All we have is each other right now."

Sabra lifted her hand and slid it into his. Amazingly, Craig seemed to be unaffected by the chaos and danger of the last few hours. He must be hiding his feelings, she thought, as they carefully made their way down the slope. Right now, they had to remain alert for any possible complications. Garcia's henchmen could still be around. The cops might be looking for them.

Moving through back alleys, slipping between houses, Craig got them to Lahaina. A small motel, the Dolphin Inn, displayed a vacancy sign out front, glowing bright red in the darkness. Craig cautioned Sabra to remain in the shadows of the hibiscus bushes with the canvas bag at her feet. He brushed off his shirt and chinos the best he could before heading into the office. Sabra stood unmoving, her back against the wooden wall, well hidden by the lush greenery growing around her. It was three in the morning, and fog was rolling in off the Pacific, beginning to blanket Lahaina. She shivered, desperately wanting a hot shower. It was the kind of cold that went to her bones, and she knew she would take hours to really warm up.

She heard the door to the office open and close. Holding her breath, she watched the corner of the building. Craig came around it as noiselessly as a shadow.

He held up the key. "We've got a home." Picking up the bag, he walked back the way he'd come. Sabra followed warily, her gaze pinned on the driveway and highway in front of the small motel. There was hardly any traffic now, most of the island deeply asleep. He led her down to the end of the L-shaped motel.

"We're lucky," he said as he opened the door. "It was the last room he had."

She stumbled into the darkened room and flipped the light switch. Squinting against the sudden brightness, she put her hand up to shade her eyes. The room was dingy, with yellow paint peeling off the walls, the drapes old and thin, and the carpet scruffy-looking. But Sabra didn't care.

In the middle of the small room was a double bed covered by a bright red quilt with white hibiscus flowers on it. Yellow and red. Not a great color combination, but at this point Sabra's only care was for plenty of hot water. She headed into the bathroom.

Craig closed the door and laid the canvas bag on the floor near the bed. He saw Sabra go into the bathroom. Taking out his pistol, he put a bullet in the chamber, flipped the safety back on and jammed the gun back into the holster beneath his left arm. Glancing at his watch, he saw it was 0300.

First things first. He went to the bathroom doorway. Sabra was testing the temperature of the water with outstretched fingers. Her hair sparkled with bits of glass still scattered among the thick strands. The left side of her neck was pockmarked with a number of tiny cuts.

"I'm going to locate a phone to call Perseus," he told her.

Sabra straightened. Seeing the darkness in Craig's eyes, she realized he was as exhausted as she was. "I can do it, if you want."

"No, you stay here." He smiled briefly. "You've got a nice goose egg on the right side of your head, did you know that?"

Frowning, Sabra touched it. "Ouch."

"Take your shower and get into bed. I'll be back as soon as possible. I think I saw a pay phone about two blocks away."

"Be careful?"

"Count on it." He gestured to the door. "Keep the lights out. When I come back, I'll knock three times. You let me in."

Exhaustion was sweeping over her. "Okay...."

Craig reached out, grazing her bloodied cheek with a

finger. "Just take care of yourself, sweetheart. It's been one hell of a day."

Shaken by his unexpected warm, brief touch, Sabra watched him turn and disappear from view. The motel door opened and closed. Automatically, she forced herself back out into the room to slide the dead bolt into place. Next she dowsed the room lights. Craig was taking a huge risk of being spotted by going to the pay phone, but Sabra knew it was necessary. The sound of running water beckoned to her and she headed back into the bathroom.

The hot water pummeled the tense, sore muscles along her neck, shoulders and upper back. As she washed her hair, so many shards of glass fell out that she ended up cutting her feet on them. But the fear sweat was washed away and, with it, the last of her shivering. By the time Sabra finished, she felt unbelievably tired. She wanted only sleep.

She towel dried her hair. Then, looking at her soiled silk pants and blouse, she put them into a sinkful of cold water, glad she'd chosen washable silk. She wrapped a towel around herself, then scrubbed her clothes clean. These were the only clothes she had for now, and come tomorrow, she couldn't afford to have them looking soiled or bloody. For the next fifteen minutes, she washed them carefully, then rolled them up in a towel to press out the moisture. Finally, she found the room's lone closet and hung them on hangers.

Worriedly, Sabra looked at her watch. It was 0330; half an hour had passed. Craig should be back by now. A sudden lump formed in her throat as Sabra considered the possibilities. She stood in the center of the room, gripping the front of the towel that covered her, fear snaking through her.

Three sharp knocks sounded at the door. Gasping, she moved to the door. "Craig?"

"Yeah. Let me in."

Sabra breathed a sigh of relief and slid back the dead bolt. Her heart pounding, she opened the door, and Craig quickly slipped inside.

Craig stared down at Sabra. Her clean hair lay in damp strands against her face and shoulders. He saw the fear and worry in her eyes as he closed the door behind him and twisted the bolt. The white towel emphasized her olive coloring, and he had a tough time not staring. He'd never realized exactly how long limbed she was until now, her beautifully shaped calves and firm, curved thighs extending below the terry cloth.

"Did you reach them?" Sabra asked, breathlessly aware of Craig's hooded look, of his power as a man. Automatically, she stepped away.

He took off his jacket and shrugged out of the shoulder holster. "Yes. They don't know what went wrong either. Jake is sending the jet over with Killian and two FBI agents—they're going to join us."

"Good," Sabra whispered, relieved. She sat on the edge of the bed, watching as he unbuttoned his shirt. Despite everything that had happened, Craig looked unruffled with only a few tiny cuts on the left side of his neck to show for it. "It's a miracle we survived tonight."

"Tell me about it," he said gruffly, throwing the shirt on the bed. He started to unbuckle his pants, then hesitated. Sabra's eyes had widened, but it didn't look like fear. His mouth flattened and he allowed his hands to drop from the buckle. "I'm going to take a shower."

Gulping, Sabra nodded. "Go ahead. We can talk afterward." As she watched him turn and disappear into the bathroom, it suddenly hit her that they were going to have to share this small bed. Her fingers worried the top of her towel. She had no nightgown—nothing. And neither did he. Looking around, Sabra felt her heart picking up in beat. What could she do? The room was so small. There was no sofa, not even an upholstered chair—just a table and a straight-backed chair in one corner.

Her emotions were at war, a huge part of her wanting Craig's closeness and the sense of protection he gave her. She remembered how strong he'd been on the hill earlier. He seemed invincible. Whatever horror and nightmares he carried from his past certainly didn't interfere with his ability to act professionally in the present.

Sabra felt groggy. Her head hurt so much that it was troublesome to move. After a few minutes, she gave up. They were both so tired that it really didn't matter. Sleep was the priority, or they'd never be alert enough to cope with whatever was coming next. Slowly she pulled back the covers. The only light in the room was filtering through the thin, faded drapes. But it was enough to see by, and Sabra lay down. After tightening the towel around her the best she could, she pulled the covers up over her shoulders.

She closed her eyes and listened to the water running in the shower. Her heart pounded briefly at the thought that very soon, Craig would join her in bed. Or would he? He was as exhausted as she was. He couldn't sit up the rest of the night in that chair. Thinking of what it would be like sleeping in his arms, Sabra spiraled into a deep, healing sleep.

Craig emerged half an hour later after wrapping a towel around his waist. Shoving damp strands of hair off his brow, he quietly opened the bathroom door, allowing the steam that had built up to escape. Shutting off the bathroom light, he allowed his eyes to adjust to the gloom. Sabra was in bed, the covers drawn tightly across her. She lay on one edge of the small bed as he approached soundlessly on damp, bare feet.

Tonight he needed her. Desperately. Was she awake? Uncertain, he sat carefully on his edge of the bed. The springs creaked in protest. The clock on the nightstand read 0400, and Craig felt tiredness claw at him. He wanted to hold Sabra. He needed her. He removed the pistol from its holster, took the safety off and laid it on the floor next to the bed, where he could reach it in a hurry if he had to.

Turning, he sighed and carefully inserted his long legs beneath the covers. Sabra didn't move. The bed creaked again, but he no longer cared as he stretched his length across the lumpy mattress. The motel was seedy, not a place he'd stay if he had a choice. But right now, despite the lumps and sagging springs, he had to admit this bed felt damn good. Pulling the covers up around him, Craig turned onto his right side. Sabra's back was to him, and he smiled to himself as exhaustion dragged him smoothly toward sleep. Well, he'd wanted her close. Now she was mere inches away. He could feel the natural heat of her body and longed to reach out and slide his arm beneath her neck, to gently turn her till she fit snugly against him.

Dreams. All dreams, he told himself wearily as he shut his eyes. Tonight, he knew, the nightmare wouldn't strike. Tonight he could sleep. It was one of the few times in two years that Craig could know that for sure, and he knew it was because Sabra was next to him. She offered him protection in a way he didn't understand, but gratefully accepted. He was a man on the run. A man with a terrible past and no future. Yet she was here—next to him. Somehow, fate had been kind to him for once.

* * *

Craig didn't know what wakened him. Maybe it was the sunlight pouring through the dingy drapes. His groggy attention shifted and he became aware of someone lying against him, of warmth and soft breath caressing his chest as he lay on his back in the bed.

Sabra. Her name flowed through him like hot honey. He realized that, as they'd slept, they must have naturally gravitated to each other. Keeping his eyes shut, he savored her length against him. One of her arms was thrown across his belly, her cheek resting in the crook of his shoulder. She was still asleep, he realized, monitoring her slow, steady breathing. Absorbing her nearness, he felt one of her long legs stretched across his. His arm was under her neck, curled around her shoulders to hold her close. His other arm lay across her, his hand resting on her upper arm. They were tangled together like two perfectly joined puzzle pieces.

Slowly, Craig senses awakened. His nostrils flaring, he caught a breath of her sweet scent. Her skin was firm and velvety against him, and a few dark strands of her hair tickled his cheek and nose. The rest of her hair cascaded over his shoulder and across his chest, surrounding her head like a halo. Her breasts were pressed against his chest and her hip seemed melded to his. She was only a few inches shorter than he was, and he marveled at how well her feminine curves fit against his harder planes.

Heat began to purl in Craig's lower body. The fragrance of her skin encircled him entrancingly, and he inhaled it like a dying man. He moved his hand gently against her shoulder, feeling the pliancy and warmth of her skin beneath his fingertips. The urge to tuck Sabra even closer and love her flowed through him. It was more than a thought; it was a powerful, primal urge. For the first time in two years, he'd slept deeply, without interruption, free of the screams that so frequently haunted his hours of darkness.

Carefully, Craig eased away just enough to raise himself onto his elbow. He stared down at Sabra's sleeping features. Her lips were parted, her face without tension. In sleep, she looked innocent—and vulnerable. Her hair was softly tangled around her face, and he lifted his hand to touch those thick, silken tresses. He hadn't meant to touch her at all, but he couldn't help himself. They'd nearly died last night, and the only thing he'd remembered through that hellish escape was the importance of his feelings for Sabra.

The panic he'd felt for her safety, the fear that she could have been killed, collided within him. These were crazy, stupid thoughts, Craig realized as he gently stroked her hair. She didn't even like him! As he'd huddled in that shallow trench, all he'd thought of was her. Even now, they were in danger. They could die at any moment—he knew it with a certainty that shook him to his core. Every protective mechanism in him as a man was emerging; the urge to keep Sabra safe was paramount. But that, too, was stupid, since he knew she was just as capable as he was, and probably better at surviving this sort of situation because of her greater experience. For him, yesterday marked the first time he'd been shot at since Desert Storm. The feeling was ugly. Invasive.

Lifting a strand of her hair, he leaned down and pressed his face against it. Her hair combined softness and strength as she did. There was a faint scent of plumaria, one of the lei flowers of Hawaii, to her hair and he realized that she'd washed it last night with that small bar of soap that had the same fragrance. Gently, he laid the strand back across her shoulder. The covers had slipped off during the night, revealing the swell of her breasts,

and the towel she'd worn to bed had long since dropped
away. They were naked, lying together, sharing their body
heat.

Craig watched as Sabra took in a slow, deep breath.
She moved slightly, pressing against him, as if realizing
he'd moved away from her. The corners of his mouth
pulled up in a soft smile. Leaning down, he touched his
lips to her smooth, high cheek. He became lost in the
fragrance of her, his fingers tunneling gently through her
hair, easing her back just enough so he could find her
parted lips. In the midst of his spinning senses, Craig
heard himself say *no,* the word repeating in his head as
Sabra moaned beneath him, her lips opening to receive
his questing kiss.

His dreaminess turned to heat as he felt her awaken
beneath his exploring kiss. Her lips parted, soft and pliant
against him. Sliding his hand around the back of her head,
Craig brought Sabra's mouth fully to his. She smelled of
heady plumaria, her breath was coming raggedly in time
with his own. Unable to stop himself, he closed his eyes
and deepened the kiss, his lips moving against hers. This
time, he wanted to do more than take; he wanted to share
with her. In moments, he'd eased Sabra onto her back and
framed her face with his hands. As he opened his eyes,
Craig saw the smoky gray of hers looking up at him—
filled with a smoldering desire. Desire for him. Nothing
else mattered right now. Only her. Only them.

"I need you," he rasped unsteadily, moving his hand
down over her collarbone to the ripe curve of her breast,
feeling her skin tighten beneath his exploration. He
waited, not wanting to force himself on her, not willing
to take unfair advantage of their dangerous situation. He
could see the sleepiness in her wonderful eyes, along with
unmistakable fire. His mind swirling with new and con-

fusing feelings, Craig hesitated, trying to focus on the harsh reality: people just didn't fall in love this fast. Or did they? He remembered Sabra telling him how her parents had fallen in love the first time they saw each other. Briefly, Craig wondered if these feelings could be something like that. Then he forced the crazy thoughts aside. Whatever the possibilities for other people, he knew he wasn't worthy of being loved that way.

Easing his hand around her breast, he saw her lashes flutter closed. Her lips parted even more, and she arched against him. Good. She wanted this as much as he did. Craig wasn't sure of Sabra's reasons, but he didn't want to talk right now. All he wanted to do was worship her, let her know in his own male way how much he needed her. She was offering herself to him, whatever her reasons, and he humbly accepted the gift.

The scorching touch of Craig's fingers as they caressed her breast, finding the tightly raised nipple, made Sabra gasp with pleasure. When his moist mouth covered the hardened bud, suckling her, she gave a small cry and pressed herself hard against him, locked in the strength of his arms. She had awakened out of a torrid dream of him skimming his hand across her naked body, igniting heat and urgency though her. Where did the dream end and reality begin? It didn't matter to Sabra. She'd only wanted Craig to hold her, to love her.

Never had she felt this kind of urgency. Never had a man's touch made her cry out with need, as she pleaded with him to complete her. She clung to his demanding hardness as he suckled her, twisting beneath him as his hands ranged downward, his roughened fingers leaving a trail of fire in the wake of his exploration. An ache built intensely within her, and Sabra moaned. As his hand slid between her damp thighs, she opened to his continued exploration. A wild, tingling sensation exploded through her at his gentle touch. Then she felt him move above her, his knee guiding her thighs farther apart. Never had she wanted a man the way she did him.

Sabra's ragged breathing caught and held deep within her as she felt Craig settle his weight upon her. Mindlessly, she thrust her hips forward. A powerful sensation filled her, and a small cry escaped her throat. She threw back her head, aching to meet him and take him deeply within her. His sliding heat filled her as she began to rock with him, melding into a oneness that left her sobbing and clinging to him. His mouth plundered hers as he thrust hard and deep into her, taking her, claiming her, making her his in all ways. Their bodies were moist, sliding against each other as his powerful thrusts went deeper. Her legs caught and tangled with his.

The fire in her culminated. Sabra felt Craig stiffen against her, his arm crushing her to him. A cry began somewhere deep within her as she tensed against him, feeling the heat unfurl rapidly through her. A wild, dizzying sensation held her captive as a hot river of pleasure coursed through her. She felt Craig's brow press against hers. He groaned, his hands digging into her shoulders as he pinned her against the bed.

A broken smile pulled at Sabra's lips as she relaxed within his grip, absorbing his weight, strength and power. The moments eddied and swirled around them, and she weakly rested her arms across his shoulders.

Ever so gently, Craig took her lips, testing them as if they were some treasured, fragile possession. Undeniable joy flowed through her, along with an overwhelming sense of protection. Barely lifting her lashes, she saw Craig looking down at her through hooded, smoldering eyes. His face glistened with sweat, his mouth strong, his gaze tender as he regarded her in the silence. She smiled a little, then closed her eyes and sighed, content to be in his arms.

She felt his fingers tunnel through her hair and gently begin to massage her scalp in a sensation as wonderful as it was unexpected. He trailed a series of small kisses from her brow to her nose, over her cheek finally coming to rest on her lips. This time his kiss was long and slow, filled with reverence. Sabra returned his kiss with equal heat and felt him smile against her mouth. Before she could ask why he was smiling, he'd eased away from her and brought her on top of him. The smile in his eyes told her everything as she relaxed against him. She placed her hands on his chest and rested her chin on top of them, caught in the unrestrained joy dancing in his dark blue eyes.

Craig tugged the covers back up and over them, then rested his hands on her upper arms. The light he saw in Sabra's eyes was clearly happiness, not regret, and for that he was thankful. Running his fingers across her silky shoulder, he collected her damp hair and smoothed it behind her graceful neck.

"You have the most beautiful hair," he murmured. "And you're just plain beautiful."

He grinned a little. "I've been called a lot of things in my life, but 'beautiful' wasn't one of them."

Sabra luxuriated in her position atop him. Feeling his returning strength, she pressed her hips more firmly against his, to show him her appreciation of him. The change in his eyes was instantaneous; then became hooded with desire once more.

"When I first saw you, that was the word that came to mind," she said, her voice a little breathless. She slid her fingers across his brow and gently tamed several rebellious strands of his hair back into place.

"I won't tell you what I thought."

She grinned, caught up in the moment of shared intimacy. "You can tell me. I'm a big girl."

"I know you are," he murmured appreciatively, absorbing her fleeting touch, "but my thoughts were purely X-rated, believe me."

"Hmm." Sabra leaned down, caressing his mouth and feeling his immediate response. His hands ranged downward beneath the covers, outlining her ribs, waist and hips.

"You are incredible," he rasped against her lips. "Beautiful, warm and incredible."

Sabra reveled in his low, husky voice, feeling his words thrum through her as if she were a drum being struck. Every movement of his body, every breath he took she took with him.

Craig brought her close, pressing her against his length. She rested her cheek against his chest, and as he moved his hand slowly up and down her arm, she thought she'd never felt so content in all her life.

Craig took a deep breath and released it. Gently, he eased Sabra to his side and rested his chin against her hair. He knew it must be near noon and they had to get up, though it was the last thing he wanted to do. He wanted to spend the day here, with her in his arms, loving her all over again. Outside the motel room, traffic noise told of the ceaseless coming and going of tourists. The motel was right next to the Lahaina shopping district, where they all came to spend their money.

"Last night," Sabra whispered, gently moving her fingers through the thick tangle of hair on his chest, "I thought we were going to die. I was so afraid, Craig. More afraid than I'd ever been.''

''Because of me?''

She eased away just enough to look into his dark blue eyes. ''No.''

He grazed her lower lip with his teeth. ''What then?''

Her lip tingled beneath his butterfly caress, and it took her a long moment to collect her scattered thoughts. ''I was caught off guard last night, Craig. I wasn't reacting the way I should have. You took over.''

He smiled a little and slid his hand along her flushed cheek. ''You sound amazed.''

She had the good grace to blush. ''Let's just say any doubts I might have had about you are gone.''

''You didn't do anything wrong last night, Sabra.''

She frowned and slid her hand over his. ''I know. I guess…the nightmares you had, Craig, made me question whether you could handle the stress of a life-threatening situation.''

''You had every right to question me.'' Easing into a sitting position, Craig brought Sabra into his arms and pulled the covers up. ''Settle back against me, okay?''

She nodded, surrendering to his embrace. Was life really this good? Taking a deep breath, she whispered, ''Please, tell me what happened to you, Craig.'' She stroked his beard-stubbled cheek and saw the pain come back to his eyes. ''So many times, I almost asked you,'' she continued quickly. ''I know you didn't want to tell me. But we're in danger here, and we may not make it Craig. Let's share ourselves with each other. I'm not the type for a one-night stand.''

''I know that,'' he said gruffly, capturing her hand and kissing it gently. He felt as if he was drowning in Sabra's compassionate eyes. "Do you know how you make me feel?"

"No," she breathed.

"Like I want to live again," he whispered unsteadily, touching her hair, smoothing it away from her shoulder. "What I have to tell you is pretty bad, Sabra. You may not want to be with me after I tell you all of it."

She shook her head. "No. I'd never feel that way."

He looked down at her grimly. "We'll see. I've never told anyone about it. I was too ashamed, I guess." His mouth quirked, and he looked up at the ceiling, holding her a little more tightly against him. "After I tell you, I know you'll leave me...."

Chapter Nine

Craig hesitated. Once Sabra realized just how much of a coward he'd been, she'd surely leave his side, her eyes filled with accusation and disgust. Still, the gentle touch of her fingers grazing his jaw suggested otherwise. It was a chance he was going to have to take, he decided. As he forced the words between his lips they came out in a rasp.

"I was stationed at Camp Reed three years ago," he began. "A Marine Recon, Lieutenant Cal Talbot, busted up his leg on one of those rocky, cactus-strewn hills during war games. I was at the weather desk at Ops when the call came in. The wind was really gusting—maybe thirty or forty miles an hour—coming in off the Pacific. Talbot's team was calling for immediate pickup because he was bleeding to death. He'd not only broken his leg, he'd cut into an artery. They'd applied a tourniquet trying to stop the worst of the bleeding, but the situation was grim.

"I volunteered because his last name was Talbot, like mine. My copilot, Brent Summers told me we should do it—that it wasn't every day I could save one of my relatives out in the field." Craig scowled, nervously running his hand up and down Sabra's velvety arm. "He wasn't a relative, of course, but Summers and I tended to be high risk takers, so we went for it. When we reached the area, I realized the high-tension electric lines were too close to the pickup area. I couldn't land, because they were on the side of a very steep hill, and we could see that the Recons couldn't move the officer to better ground."

Sabra frowned. "What did you do?" She wasn't a pilot, but she knew the risk of strong gusts of wind. It chilled her to think that they could have been blown into those power lines....

"I ordered my crew chief to drop the litter basket we carried for such rescues. My helo was dancing all over the place, and Summers was watching out the window, telling me how close we were to the wires." He shook his head. "We had so many close calls that day, I lost count. Finally, we managed to rescue Cal. We flew him to the base hospital and saved his life. That evening, I went to see how he was doing. That's when I met his wife, Linda, who was pregnant then with their first child, Sammy."

Sabra heard Craig's voice drop, and she slid her arm around his waist, squeezing gently. "They are very lucky to have you for a friend. You didn't have to go find out how he was."

"I've always been that way," he muttered, absorbing her touch.

"Something happened, though?"

"Yeah," he whispered roughly, releasing her and pushing himself into a more-upright position against the wall.

The covers pooled around his waist, and Sabra moved close, her hand on his blanketed thigh, her eyes soft with compassion. Glancing down at her, Craig said, "It happened during Desert Storm." He almost choked on the words.

Sabra's hand tightened on his tense thigh, and she held his grief-stricken gaze. "I thought it might have."

He studied her a moment. "How?"

"Terry had seen action in Vietnam, and he warned me the first day we teamed up not to touch him to waken him—just like you did."

"I see...."

Sabra reached out to captured the hand that lay against his belly and tangled her fingers with his. "It's a symptom of posttraumatic-stress syndrome. I know I'm not telling you anything new. But Terry sat me down and we had a long heart-to-heart talk about what he'd seen during the war and how it affected him." Sabra shrugged, saddened. "I'm pretty used to what you think might be terrible to tell others, Craig. In the past five years, Terry has had some nightmares as bad as the ones you've had. I remember the first time he had a night terror, and I ran into his room to help him, like an idiot." Sabra touched the side of her jaw. "I forgot what he'd told me, and he nailed me with a right cross that sent me flying halfway across the room."

Craig's eyes narrowed.

"I had it coming," Sabra said wryly. "It broke the skin but didn't break my jaw. I was young and idealistic then, thinking I could change things." She studied his scarred, burned hand against her own perfect-looking one. "Terry taught me a lot about PTSD, Craig. I understand that it's hard for you to communicate what happened because you're ashamed." She fought back tears, her voice drop-

ping to a husky, uneven whisper. "I see no shame in
what's happened to anyone who's been in a wartime situation. I don't think less of you for crying out. For wanting to cry, even if you don't...."

Craig tightened his fingers around her slender ones.
"So you knew all along..."

"In a way, I did. I didn't want to make assumptions,
though. I felt it was only fair to wait and let you share
with me when you were ready, Craig. Terry taught me
that everyone reacts differently to any given situation.
One thing you have in common, though—the trauma is
like baggage."

His mouth flattened and he managed a twisted smile.
"Yeah, that's for sure." His terror dissolved a little more
at Sabra's understanding look, and he felt more emotionally stable with her holding his hand. He placed his other
hand over hers. "I haven't been giving you very much
credit, have I?"

"You remind me of Terry in some ways," Sabra admitted softly. "So it's easy to allow you the space you
need. But it would help if you could share what happened."

Craig hung his head and concentrated on running his
fingers across hers. Sabra's skin was so smooth and unmarred, unlike his own. But scars went beyond the visible
ones; he carried the worst ones inside him, where very
few people could see them. Struggling to speak, he said,
"I...tried to talk to Linda about it, thinking she'd understand..." He shook his head, then rasped, "After that experience, I didn't talk to anyone again. Ever."

Sabra changed position, sitting next to him, capturing
his hand and holding it firmly between her own. "We
share something very special," she quavered. "I hope you
can trust me enough to tell me, Craig. Whatever it is, it's

eating you up alive. I see it in your eyes when the nightmare's got a hold on you. I saw it earlier tonight.''

He closed his eyes, tipped back his head and rested it on the headboard, glad of Sabra's steadying touch. ''No one knows what happened. Not even the widows and children who were left behind,'' he whispered, his voice barely audible. ''I was flying my second raid of the night. It was windy, very windy, and I was flying 'nap of the earth.' Brent was copilot, and in back, I had two more Recon teams to drop close to the enemy lines. We were responsible for the first assault, before the rest of the forces engaged.

''It was so dark that night, and I've never sweated like I did then. My flight suit was wringing wet. My gloves were so sweaty they were slippery on the controls, and I worried about losing my grip, and sending us crashing into one of those dunes. Cal Talbot was there. He and his men made up one of the Recon teams. We carried a total of ten men....''

Craig opened his eyes and stared up at the ceiling as the scene rolled out as if on film before him. ''We were all nervous—except Cal. He came over just before the mission, slapped me on the back and told me how lucky he felt having me as the pilot on this mission. I remember saying I didn't feel lucky that night. I was scared. I'd just come back from the first drop, and the damn wind was so bad it had nearly knocked us into a high sand dune. Luckily, Summers saw it and warned me in time. We'd had three grenades launched at us, too, though we'd managed to avoid them somehow.... Still, my hands were shaking like leaves, and my knees were so weak I sat in my chopper for fifteen minutes before I had the strength to get up and walk out of there.

''Cal thought I was joking. He'd never seen me scared.

He pulled a small plastic bag from his pocket. In it was a lock of hair from each of his daughters. He told me he carried it for good luck and gave it to me to hold onto for this trip. I said no, that he should keep it, but he just laughed and stuck it in my left sleeve pocket. He laughed and said that if we crashed, I'd survive.

"I stood next to my bird while they were refueling, just shaking. Cal went back to check his team before boarding, but I had this knot in my gut. Finally I ran away from the lights and the crews and puked my guts out. That's how scared I was."

"With good reason," Sabra said unsteadily. All the fear Craig had worked so hard to control was alive in his eyes as never before. Did he realize how strong he was? How brave he was to try to behave normally in society while carrying these awful memories?

With a shrug, he muttered, "I came back, washed my mouth out with some water from a canteen I borrowed from one of the ground crew and climbed into my bird. Once we had everyone on board, Cal came up, patted my shoulder and slipped a white envelope into my hand. He told me to hold it for him until he got back. There wasn't time to talk, so I jammed the envelope into my uniform.

"The wind was just as bad the second time, and the mission was more dangerous because we had to fly through the Guard lines to drop the teams behind them. I was really worried about SCUD missiles and grenade launchers. Summers kept a sharp watch calling out the elevation of the terrain as we flew along only about ten feet above it at any given time."

Craig felt sweat popping out on his brow, and shame swept through him as he lifted his hand to wipe the moisture away. Sabra's lips parted, and her eyes grew sad, but her hand remained strong and stabilizing on his. Taking a ragged breath, he forced himself to go on. "Things got really tense near the drop zone. We'd already had two grenade launchers shoot at us. Luckily Summers saw the flash from the barrels, and I was able to haul the bird up and out of target range. But each time we did that, I knew we were exposing ourselves to enemy radar. It couldn't be helped. I was afraid we'd been spotted, but I had to drop the two teams near an ammo dump they were going to blow up. That action was necessary to create a diversion that would allow a much-larger force to sweep down and catch the Guard off-balance."

More sweat broke out on Craig's upper lip, and he could feel perspiration trickling from his armpits. His voice was shaking now as the adrenaline began to surge through him, like it always did when he relived the event. Sabra reached over and gently wiped the moisture from his brow and upper lip with her fingers. The empathy in her eyes gave him the strength to continue. "We were almost to the drop zone when it happened. The wind jostled us badly and threw us off course. I was wrestling with getting us back below radar range and Summers was calling out the elevation."

Craig shut his eyes tightly, his voice breaking, his breathing becoming erratic. "Neither of us saw it coming. Neither of us... I don't know how many times I've replayed it in my mind. Why didn't we see that third grenade being fired?" He squeezed Sabra's hand more tightly. "I remember Summers screaming out, jabbing his finger toward the right, but it was too late. The grenade hit the main rotor, and the bird flipped up, like a wounded thing. Shrapnel and fire showered through the cabin. The Plexiglas shattered and blew in on us. The fire was over my arms as I wrestled with the bird, trying to stop it from sinking tail first.

"We slowly turned over, the rotor screeching and I heard screams from the rear. Brent was slumped forward, hit by something. Probably shrapnel. All I could do was try to control the helo enough so that we might survive the crash. Everything slowed down, as if I were moving in slow motion. Smoke clogged the cabin, and I lost my sense of direction. No matter what I tried to do to control the bird, it wouldn't respond. I figured out later that the cables to the rudders and tail assembly had been severed by the grenade blast.

"We went down. The bird flipped onto its side and crashed on the slope of a very steep dune that felt like concrete. It hit on Summers's side, and I thought the jolt would snap his neck. I heard the metal tearing, and I remember Cal's voice above everything, ordering his men to not panic. I was amazed at his calm—that he was even conscious, much less thinking clearly. He was such an amazing man...."

Wiping his face savagely, Craig squeezed his eyes shut. Every word became a major effort, and his chest rose and fell as he went on, perspiration covering his entire body now. "When the bird came to rest, I managed to cut myself free of the harness, and I pulled Summers out through the nose. The screams of the Recons were awful. It was so dark, and the fire's dancing light hurt more than it helped. I scrambled around, trying to locate the hatch. Since the bird was on her side, one of the escape routes was blocked. I managed to climb up on top, and I tried— God, I tried to get to that other door. It was jammed from the grenade blast, and I couldn't open it. The fire was getting worse, and I could hear the screams of the men inside. They couldn't escape through the cabin because it was already consumed by fire."

Craig opened his eyes and slowly lifted his hands. "I

tried to open that door. The fire was so bad. I threw myself against it, I lost count of how many times. The screams—those screams for help… I could hear the men pounding against the inside of the helo. I heard Cal crying out." His hands shook and he let them fall into his lap. "There was an explosion. I felt this blast of heat, and I was thrown through the air." His brow furrowed deeply. "It was the last thing I remembered."

Shaken, Sabra slid her arms around his damp neck and held his broken, dark gaze. "Oh, Craig, how awful…."

"For me? No," he said harshly, "I survived. I was the only one to survive. It was a lot tougher for Summers and Cal, and the other Recons." He managed a tortured grimace. "I was the lucky one."

"Were you captured by the enemy?"

"No. Another helo with an Air Force flight surgeon on board was sent in to pick up survivors. I—I don't remember anything until I woke up at a burn unit behind the lines. My hands—" he picked them up and studied them darkly "—suffered third-degree burns. They were suspended away from my body when I regained consciousness. The left side of my face was pretty much totaled, too. I had a real deep gash on my left cheek. But compared to what those men suffered before they died, it was nothing."

Sabra gently touched his set jaw, feeling the tension in it. "You did what you could."

His hands closed slowly into fists. "It wasn't enough," he rasped harshly. "I should have kept working that hatch. It was starting to give way…. I should have—"

"The lock mechanism had melted from the blast," Sabra interrupted quietly. "Or it jammed, Craig. If you couldn't get it open, no one could have."

He shrugged wearily, the silence deepening. "I remember a woman doctor leaning over me, telling me I'd broken my left ankle in two places and cracked four ribs on my left side. My right arm was fractured. When I told her how I'd gotten Summers out and then tried to open that door, she said it was a miracle I was alive. I shouldn't have been able to do any of it with so many broken bones. Adrenaline, I guess…''

''It was,'' Sabra whispered, fighting back her tears. ''How you could walk on a broken ankle, much less try to force open that door covered with fire is beyond me.''

''I'm no hero,'' he said flatly. ''So don't look at me like that. I should have rescued them. I should have gotten to them—''

''No!'' Sabra gripped his hands—now knotted, white-knuckled fists in his lap. His skin felt damp and clammy. ''No,'' she rattled, ''you did as much as you could do, Craig. What you accomplished was beyond ordinary human strength and courage. I know Cal was your friend. I can't even begin to imagine how you felt, hearing him scream.…''

Blindly, Craig reached out, sliding his arms around her, pulling her hard against him. Tears squeezed from beneath his tightly shut eyes. Her arms went around him, strong and steadying. He buried his face in her hair, his heart pounding wildly in his chest.

''Let it go,'' Sabra whispered, holding him as tightly as she could. ''Cry, Craig. Cry for Cal. Cry for Brent. And for Linda and the children.…'' She slid her trembling hand across his hair and her voice cracked. ''I'll hold you, darling. Just let it go, please.…''

The huge fist of pressure, followed by the burning sensation that was always there in the nightmare, came swiftly. Sabra's husky voice and firm touch broke down the last barriers within him. She was holding him, and the whole poisonous nightmare spilled up through him. His throat constricted, a huge lump jamming there, and he gasped for breath, pressing his face against her hair, trying to avoid it. Trying to stop it. But it was impossible. Sabra's soothing voice shattered the hold the nightmare had on him. The past warred with the present, the choking odor of oily smoke and burning metal warring with her sweetly feminine scent. A sound like that of an animal being wounded tore from his contorted lips, and he clung to her, as the first strangled sob ripped out of him.

Sabra caressed Craig's damp cheek, feeling the slow, hot tears begin trickling down his face. She pressed her jaw against his brow, allowing him to bury his face against her. A second sob shook him, making his whole body tremble in the wake of the violent release. Tears scalded Sabra's eyes, her heart breaking with the sounds that began to tear from deep within him. Craig had gone through so much. He needed to cry—to release the horror that had lived in him for the past two years. She kept rubbing his shoulders and down his back. With each stroke of her hand another sob broke loose. Why was it so hard for men to cry? Sabra had long ago lost count of the times she'd cried. It was a wonderful, healing release. Didn't men realize that? What in their stoic natures prevented them from being human?

She knew all too well that the military frowned on men crying on the battlefield, believing it showed weakness. Craig's arms were so tight around her that her rib cage hurt, but she didn't care. He was holding on to her as if she were the last person on earth, afraid to let go for fear that she, too, would reject him.

Gradually, over the next fifteen minutes, his harsh sobs diminished. Sabra was able to settle next to him, her body a fortress for him after the fury of his emotional storm.

She guessed that with his military background, Craig would be ashamed that he'd cried in her arms. Frustrated, she realized she could do little to prevent those feelings. Now that he'd told her the whole story, she knew what she'd already believed. Craig's only real fault was the depth of his guilt at not being able to rescue the men he'd loved as brothers. Sabra could only guess how awful he must feel to have lived through such a horrifying experience, but her heart broke for him.

"Here," she offered tremulously, handing him the edge of the sheet, "you can use this as a handkerchief."

Craig slowly eased away from Sabra, taking the proffered fabric and wiping his face dry of the perspiration and tears. It hurt to look up and meet Sabra's eyes. What would she think of him now? He'd admitted his cowardice. He'd told her of his inability to help his dearest friends in their worst moment. Would he see the accusation in her lovely gray eyes as he had in Linda's? Anguish cut through him in a new way, because he was vulnerable now as he'd never been before. Allowing the sheet to drop aside, he risked everything, and looked up—into Sabra's luminous eyes.

Instead of accusation, Craig saw her pain for him. Her lips were parted, glistening with spent tears. Her tears. As she reached out and touched his cheek, trying to smile, he released a tightly held breath. "How can you look at me like that?"

"How can I not?" She framed his face with her hands and looked deeply into his reddened eyes. "No one in their right mind would accuse, Craig. You did nothing wrong. My God, you almost died trying to help your friends." She picked up his scarred hands. "Look at this. You burned your hands so badly that you'll carry the scars for the rest of your life. You walked on a leg that shouldn't have supported you. You should never have been able to pull at that release handle with your broken ribs and arms.'' Her voice cracked. ''You're a very brave man in my eyes. I don't know that I'd have had the courage you did. Somewhere in the back of your mind, you must have known that your helicopter could blow up, but you disregarded it and went after your friends.'' Tears ran down her cheeks, and Sabra ignored them, holding his wounded gaze. ''You rescued Summers. That has to be enough. With all your wounds and broken bones, you tried. It's enough, Craig.''

Her quiet tear-filled words acted as a balm to Craig's raw emotions. He saw not the least accusation in her eyes. Amazed, he took her hands and held them in his own. Sabra was crying—for him. No one had cried for him, only for those who hadn't made it back. He bowed his head and shut his eyes. ''When I got flown to Germany, the old uniform they'd cut off me came with me. I—I asked a nurse to look in the pockets. She found the small plastic bag with the locks of hair. I kept asking her to find the white envelope, but she couldn't. I remember being frantic, knowing how important that letter was. I didn't know what was in it, but I knew I had to find it. I was nearly out of my mind with pain, but the pain of losing that envelope was worse. They had me on drugs, and I remember floating in and out for days.

''Every time I regained consciousness, I asked that nurse for the envelope. I don't know why she didn't tell me to go to hell, because I bugged her incessantly. About the fourth day I was in Germany, I woke up and saw a dirty white envelope, the edges burned away, lying on my chest. When I realized it was Cal's letter, I started yelling until finally a nurse came running into my room—a different nurse. I begged her to open it and read it to me, because my hands and arms were a mess.''

Craig took a deep breath and looked at Sabra. ''I think Cal knew he wasn't going t make it. I'll never forget what he'd written. He'd asked me to take the letter to Linda, to give it to her.''

''Did you?''

''Yeah, after I got out of the series of hospitals I was in. I didn't make it to Cal's funeral. I couldn't be there for Linda and her daughters the way I wanted. I was going through so many operations, it wasn't funny, and without the use of my arms, I couldn't even call. I had a nurse dial her, and she held the phone to my ear so I could tell her how sorry I was.'' His mouth flattened. ''All Linda could do was cry. I don't remember a whole lot about the call, anyway, because I was on painkillers at the time.''

''You tried, Craig.''

''Yes,'' he admitted softly, ''I tried. But I knew Linda was blaming me. I could hear it in her voice.''

''How long was that after Cal died?''

''Two weeks.''

''Listen,'' Sabra said hoarsely, ''she was in a state of shock, Craig. For that matter, so were you. You were on drugs, and I'm sure it skewed your perception.''

With a shrug, he said, ''Four months later, I finally slipped out of the hospital and went to see her. I was expecting the worst. Linda had moved away from Camp Reed, back home to Seattle. She and the girls were living with her parents. I—it was a mess. Her parents looked at me as if I was some kind of monster. The oldest girl, Sammy, started crying when I came into the house. Claire, their youngest, who Cal had named after my mother, just lay in Linda's arms, staring up at me as if I was a stranger. Before—before we left, Claire had known me. I would go over to their apartment for dinner, and that little girl treated me like an uncle or something. She'd hold her arms out to me the moment she heard my voice.'' He looked away. ''Maybe it was my burns. I had a pretty ugly face at the time. I guess I didn't look much like my old self. The kid was probably just frightened.''

Sabra laid her hand on his arm, hurting deeply for him. ''Did you give Linda the letter?''

''Yeah, I did. Her parents were there behind her, silently accusing me for not saving Cal's life. Sammy was crying and clinging to her mother's skirt, and Claire was just staring up at me with those huge green eyes. I felt like a coward. I felt like apologizing for having lived. I gave Linda the plastic bag back, too. I tried to explain, but her father started cursing at me, and I couldn't handle it. I left. I left without saying goodbye. I did apologize to Linda, though.''

Swallowing hard, Sabra held his watery gaze. ''You shouldn't have apologized for anything, Craig.''

''Maybe... At least I got her the letter. At least Cal got to tell his family that he loved them.''

''Did Linda read the letter right away?''

He shook his head. ''No. She just pressed it to her heart and looked up at me with tears in her eyes.'' He released a breath. ''Hell, Sabra, it was a messy situation all the way around. I found out later that the State Department hadn't told them how Cal died. They said it was top secret and they couldn't divulge the details. About a year after that, Linda contacted me. Over the phone, I told her exactly what had happened. She cried a little and thanked me and hung up.''

''Did she thank you for trying to save Cal?''

''No. She was hurting, Sabra.''

Nodding, she smiled slightly and touched his scarred cheek. "You've been through so much alone, Craig."

Ignoring her compassion, he added, "After I got out of the military hospital, they wanted me to resume flying. I went back to get some flight time." His mouth flattened. "I couldn't do it, Sabra. I went back to Camp Reed and stood on the tarmac, looking at the same type of helicopter I'd flown in Iraq. I got shaky and vomited. I couldn't get in the bird." He wiped his mouth with the back of his hand. "I knew they thought I was a coward—"

"No!" Sabra bit back the rest of her cry. "No," she told him in a low, off-key voice, "you weren't *ever* a coward, Craig. Not ever."

"The instructor was understanding. Each day, we'd meet at a specific time, and each day I'd get a step closer to that bird. Finally, after a week, I forced myself to sit in the pilot's seat. I started sweating like a dog and wanting to cry. I remember vomiting out the window. I'd never felt so ashamed. So—so cowardly. He'd been over there. He'd flown missions just like mine."

"Only," Sabra rasped, "he hadn't suffered through a crash like you had."

"That's true," Craig said tiredly. He forced a bitter smile. "Well, the upshot of it was I couldn't fly. I froze at the controls. The instructor would get the bird going, ready to fly, but I couldn't lift it off. The muscles in my arms and legs would freeze. I couldn't do it."

"Everyone has a personal wall," Sabra said, holding his tortured gaze. "We all hit it if we've been pushed beyond our emotional boundaries. They shouldn't have forced you back into the cockpit so soon. They should have given you more time."

"Time? After that little incident, they sent me to a shrink. He said I was unfit to fly, which was true. I resigned my commission and got out, Sabra. I wasn't going to embarrass myself like than anymore. Then I went home to New Mexico to heal. I stayed home for six months, got some kind of grip on myself and looked into Perseus. Morgan knew I was an ex-marine pilot, but he never questioned me about why I'd left. I think he knew.''

''Morgan is very astute about people,'' Sabra agreed gently. ''He was in a war, too, so he knows.''

''Yeah, I think he did know a lot about me, but he never said anything. It takes one to know one, I guess.'' Craig held up his hands. ''Of course, the scars were pretty obvious. I think he put two and two together.'' With a shake of his head, Craig added, ''For some reason, I didn't care if Morgan knew. I trusted him, and I knew he trusted me. When I told him I didn't want any assignments that involved flying, he just said, 'Fine.' That was the end of it. After that, I began to relax more. I got the jobs done for him, and I began to feel like I could do something right. In a way, I think Morgan was assessing my stability. He gave me missions that would build what was left of my confidence. Over the past six months, I really began to mend.''

''Morgan is wonderful with people,'' she quavered, hurting for both Craig and her boss. ''I'm beginning to understand your initial reaction to this mission now.''

He shot her a wry look. ''Yeah, well, it sort of took the wind out of my sails, believe me. Maybe it wouldn't have been so bad if Jenny hadn't just been killed.''

''You've been reeling from one trauma to another,'' she said, even more aware of the level of stress on him.

Craig met her luminous gaze. ''Well, now you know everything, Sabra.'' Holding up his hands, he said, ''I'm no hero. I've screwed up in ways I never thought possible.

I've lost lives. I'm a coward behind the stick of a helicopter. I'm a loser, big-time.''

Shocked, Sabra stared at him. It was on the tip of her
tongue to refute his allegations. But she realized Craig
saw himself that way because he was still blaming himself
for everything that had happened. What war did to men
was unconscionable in her opinion, making them feel like
cowards when in reality they were terribly brave under
inhuman circumstances.

Gently, she slid her hand up his arm until it came to
rest on his slumped shoulder. She saw the fear in Craig's
eyes and understood it now. ''The man I see in front of
me,'' she said quietly, ''is a hero to me. You did the best
you could, Craig, and that's all anyone can ask of you—
ever. I don't care if Linda or her parents ever forgive you.
I don't care if you can never sit in the cockpit of a helicopter again.'' She tightened her hold on his shoulder.
''What about the man who saved my life last night? You
didn't lose it when they tried to kill us. No, you kept your
wits about you. If anything, Craig, I was the one who was
shaken up. You were thinking all the time. You thought
of digging the trenches for us to hide in.''

''Maybe I just got lucky.''

''I don't think so.'' Sabra leaned upward and placed
her lips against the tight line of his mouth—a mouth that
held back so much force of emotions. Gently, she slid her
lips against his and felt the hard line dissolve beneath her
exploration. Time was not on their side. As much as she
wanted to love Craig again, she knew it was impossible.
She felt him groan, his mouth opening and taking her
deeply. Smiling to herself, she sank against him, allowing
him to absorb her presence. She was the less wounded of
the two of them. Let her kisses help heal him, if only a
little bit. As she slid her arms around his shoulders, Sabra

didn't fool herself. She knew PTSD wasn't something that was easily chased away. The healing took place on an individual's time clock. Some men never got over it. She did realize how far Craig had come in such a small amount of time. That spoke of his courage—a courage he no longer admitted he had.

Easing her mouth from his, she smiled into his stormy eyes. "I wish we had all the time in the world right now, Craig."

He ran his hand along the smooth line of her spine. "So do I, but we don't." Frowning, he eased away from her and reluctantly pushed the covers aside. "We need to shower, get dressed and start thinking about a new plan of attack."

Sabra watched him stand, then slid off the bed and moved into his welcoming arms. "Do you think Jason is there?"

"I don't know, but we're going to find out. First things first. We need another rental car. Then we're going to hide out the rest of the day at another motel. We'll start work tonight. There's less chance of being detected then."

"So, you think Garcia spotted us on the hill?"

"It's hard to say. This could be an inside job. Someone in the police department could have tipped Garcia off."

With a quirk of her lips, Sabra said, "I hope not."

"We can't trust anyone right now," he said, leaning down and placing a kiss against her temple. How Sabra could want him to hold her after what he'd told her was beyond him. He was still reeling from the release of his dammed emotions. Sharing had been less painful than he'd thought, but then, Sabra wasn't an ordinary woman. Craig couldn't trust his good fortune at finding someone who wasn't accusing him of being a coward.

As he stood there with her in his arms, Craig could no

longer convince himself that the unnamed feeling that swelled so powerfully through his chest was anything but love—and he was stunned by the force of it. Looking down into her warm gray eyes, he realized just how much he cared for her. His emotions ragged and confused from the events of the past hours, he said nothing. The situation right now was too dangerous for him to contemplate his feelings with the kind of attention they deserved.

Still, his burgeoning emotions made him hesitate. But how could he let Sabra know? Why would she return his love? He had no right to think he deserved someone as beautiful from the heart outward as she was. Besides, he rationalized, the mission would be jeopardized by further emotional involvement with her. If there was ever a time he needed to force away any romantic notions and count on his realist nature it was now.

Even as he questioned his own motives, Craig decided to set aside his feelings until he and Sabra could have the safety and leisure to explore them properly—if it was meant to be. With his past, Sabra probably wouldn't be interested in him beyond these moments of passion born of the fires of danger.

"Come on," he said gruffly, "let's get going."

Chapter Ten

"We need to get a change of clothes, so we'll blend in like tourists," Sabra said as she slipped on her shoes. Craig had showered, though he hadn't been able to shave, and his darkly shadowed jaw made her pulse race. He stood in the bathroom, the door open, pushing his hair into place the best he could with his fingers. His wrinkled, white cotton shirt outlined his magnificent chest—the chest she'd slept on last night, where she'd heard the thud of his brave heart.

Frustration trickled through Sabra. Craig still thought he was a coward. What would it take for him to see himself as she did? Telling him obviously wasn't enough. As she walked toward him, she smiled softly. But when he turned his head and met her gaze, shock bolted through her. The look in his blue eyes was once again coldly efficient. Sabra's world spun out of control, and her smile dissolved. Craig was suddenly unreachable, and she felt stripped. Hurt flowed through her as he moved briskly past her.

Craig scowled. He saw Sabra's vulnerable features register shock, then confusion. Her lips were still pouty from his kisses, and he longed to pick her up and carry her back to bed. He shook his head, forcing his heated thoughts away. "First, we need to get a rental car. We'll leave the equipment here, for now. Then we'll change motels and get some clothes and toiletry items."

"Good idea." Sabra struggled to get a grip on her rioting feelings. Craig had always been up-front with her. He'd warned her he was bad news to any woman—especially her. Why had she let her heart get involved?

"We'll wear our weapons."

She hesitated. "I can't. I don't have a jacket to hide the holster."

Craig grimaced. "Okay." He slipped into his shoulder-holster assembly, picked up his weapon from the carpet and took the bullet out of the chamber. "We're going to have to be careful. I didn't get a look at who was after us."

"We should take back alleys or side streets."

"Right." He pushed the clip back inside the pistol and holstered it. Sabra handed him his jacket, and he shrugged it on. "If we get attacked, we need to split up."

She sat on the bed, frowning. "I wish we had backup."

"We don't. At least not until Killian gets here with the Learjet. We need to call in and find out his arrival time."

Sabra felt his hand brush the top of her head in a brief caress, the gesture surprising her. She quickly looked up at him, but Craig's face was expressionless. Still, she gloried in his small, meaningful touch. Why had he done it? There was so much she wanted to talk about, but none of it was relevant right now.

"Ready?" he demanded.

"Yes." Sabra rose and gathered what was left of her courage. As they approached the door, she whispered unsteadily, "Craig, I'm not sorry about what happened between us. No matter what goes on out there. Okay?"

He placed his hands on her shoulders. "Do you think I'm sorry?"

Sabra shook her head and drowned in his hooded blue eyes. "I—no, but I just wanted to let you know in case…" She couldn't say it. *In case she was killed. Or he was.*

She chewed on her lower lip, unable to hold his burning gaze. "There's something I need to tell you, Craig, before we leave this room." Even if he didn't love her, she knew he respected her. And that was enough.

Craig's heart pounded with dread, but he nodded. "Okay, what is it?" It was impossible to steel himself emotionally for whatever Sabra might say, but he suspected it wasn't going to be anything good. As desperate as he was, he had no guard against her. He smoothed the fabric of her blouse across her shoulders, where he felt the accumulated tension.

"Once," Sabra whispered, looking away, "I loved a man. His name was Captain Joshua David. He was a pilot in the Israeli Air Force. I—I met him when I was with the Mossad. I met him at a party one night for officials. He came over and told me he'd fallen in love with me with one look. I didn't believe him, of course, and to tell you the truth, Josh was a jokester who played tricks on everyone. I didn't know it at the time. I just thought he was one of the crazy, drunk pilots at the party.

"Over the next year, Josh made a point of seeing me. He was very extroverted—always smiling. I wondered how he could be that way with the job he had to do. His life was on the line every time he rode that plane into the sky. We'd lost many pilots to the enemy, and I couldn't figure out how he could laugh and smile so much.

"Josh kept telling me he loved me, but I wouldn't believe him." She compressed her lips and shut her eyes. "Then I was at the office one day, and I heard that one of our pilots had been shot down. We didn't know who it was, if he was dead or captured. My father came to my office and told me it was Josh."

She forced herself to look up at Craig. "I cried like a baby when he told me. Then we had to wait two weeks before we found out that Josh had died."

He saw the tears in her eyes. "What did you learn out of that?" he asked her gently, framing her face with his hands, holding her agonized gaze.

"I never believed him," she said in a strained voice. "I always thought he was joking. I guess—I guess, somewhere along the way, I did fall in love with him, Craig. He was a nice guy. He was loved by everyone. There wasn't a mean bone in his body, and he was so patriotic. Oh, he'd steal kisses from me every once in a while, but he'd joke about that, too. Sometimes he'd send me flowers, but then he'd turn around and say he'd meant to send them to his mother or aunt instead. I—I just couldn't trust myself to trust him, I guess."

Craig took his thumbs and wiped the tears from her cheeks. "Maybe he was afraid to be serious with you. Maybe he was afraid you'd turn him down."

Sniffing, Sabra said brokenly, "I don't know. I don't know to this day. I just carry this awful pain around in my heart. I feel guilty in a way, Craig. I never took him seriously."

"He didn't take you seriously, did he?"

"Well…no, but Josh was like that with everyone."

"You never knew when he was being real or joking."

"Y-yes, I guess that's the bottom line." Sniffing again, Sabra moved over to the bedstand and got a tissue. She wiped her eyes and blew her nose.

Craig studied her in the silence as she turned toward him, her eyes bright with hurt. "How long ago did this happen?"

"Five years ago."

"And you still carry him in your heart. I think you loved him, don't you?"

She sighed and walked up to Craig. "If I did, it went unfulfilled."

"He was probably scared to death to tell you seriously that he loved you," Craig said. "Maybe joking was the only was he dared say it. Those words are a big step for most men. Especially if they're afraid of responsibility."

"The responsibility of loving me?"

"Could have been. I've known some men who were so afraid of fearing their feelings weren't returned, they never said said anything at all to the woman they wanted most."

"I see." Miserably, Sabra sighed. "I just felt gutted by it, Craig. I must have cried half a year away after that."

"Then you loved him." He shook his head. "He was never intimate with you?"

She shook her head. "No…just a stolen kiss every now and then, that was all."

His throat tightened. "I'm sorry." And he was. He could see the pain in her ravaged eyes. "My mom always said it was better to love and lose than never love at all. I guess, in a way, you know that better than most of us."

"Over the years, I came to the conclusion that if Josh did love me, he was afraid to get serious. For a while, I was so angry at him. Looking back on it now, though, I can see that I wasn't so stellar in our on-again, off-again relationship, either. One day I thought he loved me, the next, I knew he didn't. I didn't have the guts to confront *him* on it, either, Craig.''

Craig walked over to her and dropped a light kiss on her cheek. ''How has what happened with Josh affected your relationships since then?'' It was an important question to ask. Did Sabra think he didn't have the guts the guts to level with her? *Was* he afraid to tell her how he felt? Hell, he wasn't sure what he felt. Maybe he was like Josh. Still, what was most important now was their safety. The mission came first.

Sabra glanced up at Craig's darkened features, then back down at the floor. ''I question every man's intent toward me,'' she admitted. ''I shouldn't think they're Josh David in disguise. The first two years, I was afraid of getting involved with a man again, for fear of reading him the wrong way. When I did have a relationship, I misread it anyway.'' She waved her hand helplessly. ''I was never any good at it, I guess.''

''I found out the hard way about talking, Sabra.'' He saw her lift her chin, saw the wounded look in her eyes. ''Not that I have all the answers. I don't.'' He opened his hands. ''Over the years, I've had relationships. The woman I wanted to marry, I screwed up on. At that time I was pretty typical of most guys. I didn't know how to communicate. How to talk. Michelle eventually left me because I couldn't get to my feelings, or share them.'' He smiled sourly. ''That was before the crash.''

''And since then?''

Craig shrugged and said, ''I've stayed away from women for the most part, because I knew what it would mean to open up. That scared the hell out of me. I was worried I'd punch a woman in the face if she slept with me, or hurt her in a million other ways. I didn't dare talk to anyone about what had happened. I was too ashamed, too raw from it, I guess.''

She gave him a look of awe. ''But you were able to—''

''You're different,'' he rasped. ''For whatever that's worth, Sabra, you're different.'' The need to tell her about the chaos of feelings she aroused in him was nearly overwhelming. Though he wasn't a joker like Josh, Craig could see the lasting damage she'd suffered from the pilot's way of handling the situation.

Craig noticed immediately the hope spring into Sabra's eyes. Her lips parted softly, and all he wanted to do was sweep her into his arms and love the hell out of her— love the questions out of her eyes. He wanted to convince her that he wasn't pulling a trick on her as Josh had. But was he? Craig was sure the Israeli pilot had loved Sabra. The man had no doubt also been afraid of commitment, or he'd have met Sabra as an equal and told her the truth of his feelings.

''Let's get this show on the road,'' Craig said abruptly. ''We've got a lot to do in preparation for tonight. We're a good team. We know how to work with each other.'' He saw Sabra's face reflect the hurt of his sudden brusqueness. ''Let's use what we have to keep us alive and try to find that little boy,'' he reminded her a little more gently.

Sabra felt a cramp beginning in her right lower leg, so she slowly moved from her position near Craig. It was around 2:00 a.m., and they lay undetected on the steep hillside near Garcia's estate, surrounded by thick vegetation. Wearing the night goggles they'd luckily carried in the camera bag, she could see the comings and goings of the guards near the empty helicopter pad. She and Craig

had been timing the guards' movements and watching for
Jason since nightfall.

Haleakala loomed far above them. Everything appeared
yellow-green through the goggles. Sabra moved slowly,
not making a sound. She saw Craig glance at her, a question in his eyes. Holding up her hand in a sign that she
was all right, she moved to a kneeling position. To her
left, Sabra saw fog forming higher on the slopes of the
inactive volcano. Slowly, the white mist thickened and
began to move silently down toward Kula.

They were surrounded by the darkened shapes of eucalyptus trees. Earlier, they'd rented another car, found an
out-of-the-way motel and changed. The stretchy black nylon was perfect cover in the darkness, but it wasn't very
warm, and the early morning chill made her teeth chatter.

Luckily, they had been able to contact Perseus in the
late afternoon, report in and find out that the Learjet was
grounded for repairs in Los Angeles. One of the engines
had sucked up a flying bird as it came in for a landing at
the Orange County Airport, and Killian was stuck with
the plane on the mainland for at least another twenty-four
hours.

Sabra knew she couldn't talk to Craig. Garcia might
have sensitive equipment placed along the fence to detect
human voices as much as a mile away. They were within
half a mile of his estate, having come around the mountainous side this time, under cover of darkness. Thus far,
no one seemed aware of their presence, but that didn't
mean much.

She stretched her right leg out and, with her fingers,
deeply massaged the cramping calf. Out of the darkness,
she heard the *whap, whap, whap* of a helicopter's blades.
Turning slowly, she looked up into the night sky. Where?
Yes, she saw a darkened shape coming from offshore, its

red and green running lights highly visible through the night goggles.

Sabra felt Craig's hand come to rest on her shoulder and squeeze, to let her know he heard the aircraft, too. Garcia's helicopter wasn't on the landing pad at his estate. Could this be his aircraft coming in? Rising slowly to her knees, she watched, her heart picking up in beat.

The whapping of the blades grew stronger and louder upon approach, and Sabra realized it *was* Garcia's aircraft as it swung widely above the estate before hovering and then slowly descending to the concrete landing pad below. She hunkered down, watching. Lights suddenly flooded the landing area. Jerking off the night goggles, she grabbed for the binoculars and pressed them to her eyes. In the wash of bright light, Sabra saw the passenger side as the aircraft landed. Her pulse bounded. It was Garcia! As the helicopter stopped, the blades whirling lazily, a guard ran around to open his door.

Garcia climbed out. She held her breath. Someone else was there. Sabra nearly stood up. Her hands bit into the binoculars as she saw Garcia hold out his hand to a smaller person. Jason? As the boy grasped the man's hand, she saw Jason's face for the first time. Her heart thudded hard in her chest, and she became aware of Craig's heavier breathing next to her. He saw him, too.

Sabra's mouth went dry as she watched Jason climb unsteadily out of the helicopter. Garcia picked him up, laughing, and turned and walked into the estate, a guard following them. The door shut.

Sabra lowered the binoculars. Her eyes met Craig's. She saw fear in them, and anxiety. His skin glistened with sweat. It was only then that she realized the sound of the helicopter had triggered his nightmarish memories.

Reaching out, she gripped his hand hard in her own.

Sabra could say nothing, so she slid her arm around his shoulders and pressed him against her for a moment, to let him know she cared. There was very little else she could do. She felt his hand tighten around hers, and as she eased back, she read the anguish and turmoil in his eyes. What was the cost to him to sit this close to the helicopter? It was a great sacrifice, Sabra realized belatedly, some of her joy at discovering Jason diminishing.

She saw Craig wrestle with his inner demons. He rubbed the sweat off his face with the back of his gloved hand, his profile hard and resigned. Hurting for him, Sabra stowed the binoculars back in the canvas bag hidden beneath the leaves in front of them. She looked up to see the fog moving swiftly now, covering the lower slopes of the volcano, like a cottony white blanket.

Soon the fog had drifted down to hide them, too. It was damp and wet, and Sabra shivered. The leaves of the surrounding vegetation became purled with moisture. Soon the eucalyptus leaves above them began a steady *drip, drip, drip* as water ran off their surfaces.

Craig made a sign for her to follow him as soon as the outdoor lights around the helicopter had been switched off. The pilot had gone inside, and the landing area was deserted. It was nearly three in the morning. Easing to his feet, crouching behind the foliage, he began to move stealthily toward the estate.

His heart was pounding with fear, and he wrestled wildly with the nightmare of emotions that the aircraft had triggered. But he had to know if Garcia had any kind of detectors—lasers or otherwise—around the fence. The only way to know was to test the defenses. It was risky, and his heart was thudding like a sledgehammer in his chest. Worse, he worried for Sabra's safety. If Garcia had invisible lasers or sound detectors on the fence, they could set of a silent alarm inside the huge estate. In moments, armed guards could arrive, firing in their direction.

His mouth grew dry as he moved soundlessly through the greenery. The fog was an excellent cover and, better yet, might well disclose the light from any laser alarms. At least it was warm moving around. The fog became so dense that he could barely see five feet ahead of him, and he constantly had to refer to the compass strapped to his left wrist, heading toward the no-longer-visible estate.

Craig knelt and gestured for Sabra to come up. Sensing her approach, he glanced over at her. Night goggles were useless in fog, and his hung around his neck, as hers did. He saw the sheen of perspiration on her brow, saw the intensity in her narrowed eyes as she settled close to him. He held up his hand, showing five fingers. They were within five feet of the fence. She nodded, her lips compressing with tension.

Slowly, he got to his feet. He could detect no laser activity as he finally got close enough to see an outline of the wrought-iron fence. With excruciating care, he began to run his gloved hand slowly up the expanse of the first iron rod. It was slippery with moisture, cold to his touch. He made a painstaking search for any wires or other equipment that might be attached to the fence. Finding nothing on the first rod, he gestured to Sabra to test the next one. If they so much as stepped on a branch and it cracked, they could be found out. Despite the chill, sweat trickled down the sides of his face, soaking into the black fabric.

Each wrought-iron rod had to be checked. The fog thickened, eerily muffling all sounds. The minutes dragged by as they continued around the fence and helicopter-landing area. There was a gate at one end of the concrete landing pad, and Craig carefully searched it for wires, but discovered none. Could it be that Garcia had no perimeter defenses? He found that hard to believe. Perhaps the drug dealer felt smugly safe here on the island, Craig thought as he continued to slowly run his fingers up each wrought-iron rod.

Finally, they came to the edge of the fenced-in area. The estate sat on the edge of a cliff, and the fence stopped at the four-thousand-foot drop. Craig turned around and faced Sabra. The darkness was so complete in the thick fog that they could no longer see each other: they were limited to communicating with brief touches of their bodies as they moved back the way they had come.

Gripping Sabra's hand, Craig tugged at it once to let her know she was to follow him. He placed her hand on the back of his belt, silently asking her to hold on, so she wouldn't get disoriented in the fog. As he crouched down and carefully made his way back up the slope toward where their canvas bag was hidden, he prayed they hadn't been detected. Using the compass they were finally able to make their way back to their original spot.

It was 4:00 a.m. The fog was thicker, if that was possible. And they had at least another hour's walk ahead of them. Craig placed his night goggles back in the bag and hefted it quietly across his shoulder. Sabra maintained her hold on his belt as he began the trek down the slope. As they moved farther away from the estate and possible detection, she began to relax a little.

By the time they reached their car, hidden down a dirt road and shielded from the highway leading to Kula, Sabra was rubbing her arms in an effort to get warm. They changed clothes there, and goose bumps sprang up on her skin as she shed the damp nylon in favor of a dark blue sweatshirt and sweat pants. Neither of them spoke as they hurriedly changed, tossed their gear into the trunk and climbed into the car.

They were at least five miles away from Kula before they spoke. Sabra was holding her hands up to the heater, trying to warm them. Craig drove, his mouth set.

"Are you okay?" she asked.

"Yes and no."

"Jason is with them. I'm so glad we found him." She glanced at him. "I could tell the helicopter brought back bad memories for you."

His mouth tightened. "Yeah, it did. But more important, Jason looked okay, and for that, I'm grateful."

Sabra released a long breath. "Me, too." She studied him. "Terry used to hit the deck every time a car backfired, no matter where he was. He said it was an automatic reflex action."

Craig nodded. His stomach was still twisted in painful knots. Nothing was as frightening as the sound of a helicopter, having it land so close to him. The rush of images from the crash had nearly overwhelmed him. "I thought I was going to scream in terror back there," he admitted roughly. "I was so damned scared my knees were shaking."

Sabra gave him a compassionate look. "You have so much courage, Craig. My heart goes out to you. I wish I could help you—"

"You do." His eyes cut to her quickly, then back to the road. The fog was thinning, and he could see fifteen or twenty feet ahead on the highway. Sabra was a friend— someone he could trust with his life. Having her nearby gave him something to hold on to.

Heartened, Sabra smiled unsteadily. What she felt for Craig was good and strong. If only he felt the same way! But he'd been without a woman for a long time—that was what he saw in her. She couldn't dare hope for anything more.

"Sometimes people can be good for each other." Craig shook his head. "Damned if I know what I give you in trade, Sabra. I'm a jumpy, thirty-year-old ex-marine who has insomnia and will hit anyone who touches him when he's asleep."

Sabra heard the derision in his voice and ached for him. "You've always been honest with me, with no apologies," she whispered, a catch in her voice. "You don't joke, you don't make light of serious things. I'd rather share your honesty than have you hide from me."

His heart filled with pain. "Yeah, well, there's no getting around my problems. They're all pretty obvious."

Sabra said nothing. She knew they would go to another public phone, and she'd make the call to Perseus. Her heart swelled with joy at being able to share the good news that they'd located Jason. The feeling was quickly dampened by reality. How could they rescue him? Could they? As soon as they made the call, got something to eat and showered, they would have to get back out to the estate and watch.

She knew Laura would be ecstatic over the news about Jason. Sabra hoped Jake and Wolf could make her friend understand that just finding her son didn't mean all that much. The worst part was ahead of them. They couldn't trust the police. They could trust no one but themselves. A ragged breath eased from Sabra's lips, and she reached out and squeezed Craig's hand. It was a strong, steady hand, covered with scars that would always remind him of his past.

Covertly, Sabra stole a look at him as he drove cautiously through the fog. Dawn was just touching the horizon somewhere to the east of the island, the fog like a gloomy blanket.

"Craig?"

"What?"

"Do you have any dreams?"

He gave her a wry look. "Plenty of nightmares."

Sabra glanced back apologetically. "No, I mean dreams of the future—of what you want your life to be like."

"Me? I live hour to hour. Day to day. I'm afraid to look at the future because of the past that sits on my shoulders in the present." He saw her eyebrows dip. "What are you getting at?"

"Oh, I just wondered."

"Do you have dreams?" he countered.

"Yes." Tentatively, Sabra nodded. "Well, I used to."

"Until Josh died?" he asked out of sudden intuition.

"Yes," she admitted.

"What did you hope for before then?"

"I'd always dreamed of marrying a man who would love me for the way I was, not for what he wanted me to be. I'm afraid I'm not much of a cook or housekeeper. My mother went crazy with me in the kitchen. I burned more stuff than I care to think about. I ended up wrecking several of her pots and pans in the process. I hated to dust. I hated to do dishes."

"What would you rather do?" He studied her shadowed face, now set with unhappiness.

"I loved to play soccer. I liked being outdoors. At night I always had my window open, even in the dead of winter, because I loved the fresh air. I guess that's why I like Perseus so much—most of my assignments are outdoors."

Craig tried to tell himself that as her friend, he wanted to share other, private parts of himself with Sabra. Or *was* it friendship? Damn this mission. There was no time to sort through his feelings. What the hell, he wanted to share with her. "You sound a little like a mustang my brother Joe got from one of his Navajo friends for his fifteenth birthday," he ventured.

"Oh?"

"His friend Tom Yellow Horse gave him a mustang no one could tame—a pinto mare, I think. She'd been on the rodeo circuit and she'd bucked off everyone. She hated saddles and hated being snubbed to a post. She'd lash out with her legs if Joe tried to get near her."

Sabra studied his grim features. "What happened to her?"

"Joe eventually realized that the mare wanted her freedom. She didn't like humans. So he let her go."

"He did?"

Craig nodded. "He got me and Dan up early one morning, kicked us out of bed and made us help him. That mare would charge you if you got in the corral with her, so he wanted our help. I remember opening the gate for Joe and watching his face when she galloped off to her freedom. He cried."

"Your brother sounds like a guy with a heart."

"He is," Craig murmured. He glanced at her then frowned. "You're like that mustang, because you don't want to be saddled with house chores or indoor duties."

"One of my stellar eccentricities…" she whispered, her voice trailing off. How she ached to see that tenderness return to his eyes, but it was gone—forever. All Craig had needed was her body, she reminded herself—her ability to love him that one, beautiful time. Sabra wanted to cry, but choked the tears down deep inside herself.

Chapter Eleven

Sabra waited, gritting her teeth as she knelt on the ground beneath the thick foliage. They were less than fifty yards from Garcia's estate. For the fourth night in a row, they had crept close to the wrought-iron fence near the helo-landing pad. For the past three nights, at exactly 0300, Garcia had arrived by helicopter with Jason in tow. He always left again shortly after 1800.

Sabra had no idea why, since they couldn't contact the police or any federal agency to help them track the helicopter's route. One thing was evident, however: Jason was never out of Garcia's sight or far from his side. Tonight, she and Craig had decided to rush forward shortly after the helicopter landed and take Jason away from Garcia.

Not liking the plan, but having no other, Sabra crouched on the ground, fear eating at her. She hated operations like this one, for there was nothing clean or simple about it. What if, instead of one guard meeting the helicopter this morning, three or four appeared, armed with submachine guns? As it stood, even if only one guard came out, they had to render him, the pilot and Garcia unconscious.

Instead of bullets, they carried pistols loaded with a powerful tranquilizing agent that Killian had provided them with. Almost as soon as it pierced the skin, a victim fell unconscious. Sabra agreed with the decision. They didn't want an all-out war with Ramirez or Garcia—they only wanted the boy back. Sending the message that they weren't going to kill unless absolutely necessary might help Ramirez decide to spare Morgan's life—if he was alive.

Still their choice left them uncomfortably in the line of fire. Sabra had no doubt that the guard had real bullets in his submachine gun, and she was sure the pilot and Garcia, were also armed—and more than willing to shoot to kill. Adjusting the bulky armored vest she wore beneath her nylon suit, Sabra knew it was the only thing standing between her and sudden death. She was glad Craig was wearing one, too. He knew as well as she did that Garcia didn't hire slouches who couldn't shoot straight.

Her mouth grew dry as she glanced down at her watch, a dark piece of cloth shielding the luminous dials. It was 0255. Her heart pulsed strongly in reaction. They would sneak close, wait until just after the helo landed, then leap up on the edge of the concrete pad, open the wrought-iron gate and fire. If Jason was accidentally hit, he would survive the dart tranquilizer—another reason to use them rather than bullets.

She raised her eyelashes and squarely met Craig's dark, narrowed gaze. Anxiety was clearly registered in his eyes. Tension hung around them, and Sabra's thoughts turned to their recent time together. What they shared was like this mission—surprising and unstable. Precious moments of intense friendship, communication and awareness were broken by awkward silences, sudden coldness and confusion. The snatches of sleep they'd gotten over the past few days were always in each other's arms, but they were too tired to make love, sleeping only two or three hours at a time. Each day they'd moved to another motel to avoid detection, and each day they'd hidden in another area to keep tabs on Garcia's movements. The situation was too crazy for anything to be properly resolved. Sabra had been forced to put their relationship on the back burner until the mission was completed.

The only real hope she felt over their situation was the fact that the Perseus jet was finally on the Maui airport tarmac, and Killian was shadowing them from a safe distance. He'd landed two days ago, and they'd met near dusk in a remote motel on the south side of the mountainous island, cross-checking all their information. He'd provided them with tranquilizing darts and other gear for the mission. Perseus had put out feelers, trying to discover if there was a leak in the local police department, but it had to be done carefully. In the meantime, Killian had contacted the FBI for help.

Again Sabra ran the plan through her mind as they lay quietly beneath Garcia's silent estate. They would snatch Jason and make a run for it down the slope to where their camouflaged car waited on a dirt road off the highway, four miles away. Then they would speed down the highway to the airport, another twenty miles away, near the center of the island. They would meet Killian and the FBI at the Learjet, which would be ready to take off, with Dr. Ann Parsons, an emergency-trauma-trained physician, as well as a psychologist, standing by. Sabra prayed that Dr.

Parsons's help wouldn't be needed. Of the utmost importance in every action was Jason's safety.

Trying to moisten her dry lips, Sabra closed her eyes, continuing to review the plan. They each wore headsets, with microphones close to their lips, should they need to talk. Killian had brought a special radio, set at a frequency that wouldn't likely be detected by anyone on the island. And the FBI agents involved were from D.C., not local island agents.

So far, no one knew where the leak was, and everyone was suspect until it could be found. But the two agents with Killian had worked with him a number of times before he retired from active duty with Perseus. Sabra knew Killian's reputation for caution and trusted his choices with her life.

She tried to relax, but it was impossible. Her emotions swung wildly between worry over Craig and worry for Jason. She knew the guard would open fire. He had to be taken out first—and that was her job. Craig would take care of Garcia and the pilot. She had to disable the guard and watch to make sure no others came out the rear door at the end of the building nearest the pad. But what if Craig was wounded? What if she was? If either of them was hurt, they were to be left behind. Get the boy and run. Saving Jason was paramount.

A fierce tidal wave of fear threatened to suffocate Sabra as she ran various scenarios through her overactive imagination. If Craig was shot, she knew in her heart she couldn't leave him behind. But if she didn't run with Jason in tow, all of them would be captured. So much depended upon their swift initial assault—and on luck. She glanced over at Craig's set profile as he watched the estate. How unlike Josh he was. Craig made no apologies for his problems. Miraculously, during the times they had slept in each other's arms, the nightmare had not stalked him. Craig was amazed and grateful, but had warned her it wasn't gone.

Sabra knew it, but she also knew that Craig trusted her as he had no one else since that ugly crash. In trust, there was friendship, and she accepted that. Not that he'd ever said a word to suggest anything more. No, he was very careful about how he phrased things to her, even in their brief moments of passion. Sometimes the look in his eyes belied the distance he'd been treating her with. Nor could Craig stop that endearing half smile, filled with vulnerability, that inevitably pulled at his mouth when she made him laugh. As wounded as he was, there was so much to love about him. Sabra knew he was ashamed of his fears and reactions. And she wondered if he could possibly love her.

Every night when he heard Garcia's helicopter, Craig broke out in a heavy sweat and his hands shook. He couldn't control either action. Sabra hurt for him, but there was no way she could help him. All she could do was hold him for those precious few hours afterward, and let him know through her actions that she loved him with a fierceness that defied description.

Moving carefully, Sabra turned to study the night sky. The fog was beginning to form in earnest between four and six thousand feet on the volcano, as it had every night. If she didn't know better, she'd think Garcia had ordered it, using the fog as a cover for his early morning returns to his estate—to hide from the prying eyes of the law, perhaps. The fog was coming in sooner than usual tonight, and she could see fingers of it reaching the estate, muting black shadows to gray. Would the helicopter come soon? Would it still land, with the fog already approaching?

Worriedly, Sabra glanced at Craig. His face had been

blackened, a black knit cap drawn tightly over his skull, with the headset beneath it, the mike almost touching the hard line of his mouth. Sabra's flak vest chafed beneath her suit. Shivering as the fog stole across them, she began to chew nervously on her lip. If it settled too soon, the pilot might divert the flight to the airport. That would mean putting off the operation to another night, waiting for another chance.

The *whap, whap, whap* of helicopter blades sent a shiver down Craig's back. He felt every hair on the back of his neck rise in response. Cutting a glance to Sabra, he saw that she, too, was aware of the incoming flight. It was 3:05 a.m.; the aircraft was five minutes behind schedule. Earlier this evening, they'd seen Jason board with Garcia. Would he be there now? Gripping the night goggles, Craig settled them over his eyes. Normally, the helo made a low pass directly over them on its way to the landing pad, where it would stop at about one hundred feet, hover, then slowly descend to the waiting concrete. His chance to verify if Jason was on board would be on the pass.

Anxiously, he studied the thickening fog. It was coming in too soon, and a light haze covered the area. Would the pilot assess the situation and leave without landing? The conditions were iffy for a helicopter. As a pilot, Craig had hated fog. Helicopters weren't properly equipped for such weather. Military ones were now, but civilian or commercial helicopters ones such as this didn't have the advanced instrumentation to fly safely through thick fog. Looking up, he saw the lights twinkling beneath the belly of the approaching craft. Soon. Very soon.

He was sweating heavily, exacerbating his concern over Sabra. She could be killed in the coming firefight. They had no lethal weapons on their side, and Garcia would be sure to use some against them. Craig's only consolation was the armored vests they wore over their vital organs. Still, a shot to the head would kill them instantly.

Was Jason on board the aircraft? Craig's hands felt clammy and damp with tortured anxiety. Positioning himself, he held the night goggles steady against his eyes. The whapping of the blades grew more powerful—and more emotionally shattering.

His stomach knotted so painfully he felt like groaning as he swung his gaze skyward. The helicopter was coming in for a landing despite the worsening weather! Good. The fog could work for them, if they were lucky. Right now it was drifting in—thin here, thick there, offering more cover than they'd anticipated. But could they take out the three men before a bullet was fired? One shot could alert the entire armed compound. Craig's heart was pounding hard in his chest. Particles of the nightmare crash blipped before his eyes. Sweat ran down his face. Cursing to himself, he forced the images aside. The belly of the helicopter roared overhead, the vibration pulverizing him. Yes! He'd gotten a brief glimpse of Jason. The child was on board!

Dropping the goggles, he leapt to his feet and made one, sharp gesture to Sabra, confirming Jason's presence. The *whapping* sound thickened as the blades hit the dense fog at the estate. The lights were switched on at the helipad, as always. Craig drew his tranquilizer pistol and crouched, snapping a look to his right. Sabra had her gun drawn, too. Her face was taut, her eyes slitted in intense concentration. He couldn't see the bird, could only hear it laboring in the thick moisture. Helicopters didn't do well in heavy moisture or high humidity. As Craig moved swiftly through the foliage toward the iron gate, he knew the pilot had his hands full right now. *Let it make him less alert,* he prayed silently.

Plant fronds slapped at his body as he lunged up the slippery, damp slope. The fog was thicker, but the vibration of the helicopter shattered through him, shaking his confidence. Blips of the crash again blinded him momentarily. Angrily, Craig forced through the scene. Sabra passed him and moved swiftly toward the gate. It was her job to get the guard who would appear shortly at the door. Craig would leap up on the fence, fire at Garcia and then at the pilot. They would be rapid shots. He'd have to be accurate when Garcia opened the door to climb out. Timing was everything. One missed shot and they could be killed. One mistake and Jason could die, too.

But, as he'd hoped, the fog had become their friend. It was so thick that the lights around the landing pad took on a hazy appearance. He marveled at the pilot's skill. Craig could hear the aircraft descending slowly, carefully. The mist whipped and swirled violently around them, foliage dancing as the whirling blades of the helo disturbed the area. Wind buffeted him as he crouched beneath the fence, waiting.

Sabra disappeared into the fog as she headed for the gate, and his throat constricted with fear. He couldn't see her at all! Would she be able to spot the guard in time? Looking around, Craig could see the fog moving in bands, torn by the helicopter's blades. Straining his eyes, he could make out the white underbelly of the aircraft. Twenty more feet and it would make contact with the pad. His mouth went dry and his heart rate tripled. His fingers nearly cramped around the pistol as he held it ready.

Where was Sabra? They had communications, but they didn't dare break the silence. One of Garcia's sensitive pieces of equipment might pick up their voices, and their cover would be blown. His heart ached in his chest. Why in hell hadn't he told her earlier that he loved her? What if he died? What if she was hurt? Captured? The bitterness in his mouth swept through him. What a fool he'd been. He'd never loved a woman as much as he loved Sabra. Now it was too late.

In the dim, scattered light, Craig saw Garcia sitting grimly on the passenger side of the helo. Right now the guard should be coming out to open the door for him. No one came. Had Sabra gotten to him? Craig gripped the bottom of the wrought-iron fence, ready to aim the pistol. He saw Garcia's strained features, saw the perspiration on his thick, mustached upper lip. The helicopter landed. Anger was in Garcia's eyes as he twisted around, waiting for the door to be opened. The pilot looked harried, stressed by the danger of the landing.

Come on. Open the door! Craig compressed his lips as Garcia jerked the latch and swung the door—wide open. Craig raised his pistol and fired once. The dart sank deeply into the druglord's neck. He slumped, tumbling heavily out of the helicopter.

Craig saw the pilot's eyes widen. The man leaned down. Damn! He had a gun! Craig saw Jason, his eyes puffy with sleep, looking around in confusion. Leaping upward, his muscles straining, Craig took aim as the door swung one way and then another. There! The dart slammed into the pilot's chest. The man let out a little cry, then slumped forward in his harness, the gun dropping from his hands to the deck of the aircraft.

As Craig scaled the fence, he heard a sharp retort of a high-powered handgun. It sounded like a .350 Magnum. Damn! *Sabra?* He reached into the helicopter for Jason. The child gave a cry and threw up his hands to protect himself. The blades of the helicopter were still turning at full speed; the pilot hadn't shut the engine down! It took everything Craig had to climb into the aircraft, wrap his hand around Jason's arm and haul him out of it.

Two more shots were fired. He whirled around, the boy under his arm. Jason gave a shriek and started fighting him. Out of the fog, Craig saw Sabra running toward him.

"I've got him!" he rasped. Just as he turned to go over the fence, he heard a series of shots ring out. In horrifying seconds, he saw Sabra fly forward. Her body crumpled. The pistol flew out of her hand. He held back a scream as he watched her strike the ground. Part of the nylon uniform on her back had ripped away. Had the armor protected her? He turned, dragging Jason with him, heading toward her.

More shots flew through the air. Craig was halfway to Sabra when he saw her rise to her hands and knees. Voices carried above the sound of the whirling blades. Sabra motioned violently for Craig to go back. The fog thinned just enough for him to see three men running from around the front of the estate. To his left, on the slope, he saw two more guards coming toward them. They were trapped!

Jason shrilled and hit at him. Craig tightened his grip around the boy and gestured violently to Sabra, who was now on her feet, running toward them. There was no choice. None at all. Glaring at the helicopter, he ran toward it. The only way out of this situation was to fly the bird out of the estate. More bullets whined around them. One bit into the concrete, shards flying upward, stinging his lower legs.

"Get to the chopper!" he gasped to Sabra.

"Go!" she cried. "Go!"

He tossed Jason into the helicopter. "Don't move," he roared at the frightened boy. He unsnapped the harness on the unconscious pilot. There! Craig jerked the man out of the cockpit and leapt into the seat. Slamming the door shut, he quickly assessed the controls. His hands shook badly. He felt like crying. Anxiously, he looked around. Sabra jerked the passenger door open, her mouth contorted with pain. He saw no blood on her. The armor vest had protected her. He grappled with the control surfaces, his fingers curving around them. He twisted the cyclic, and the blades whirled faster. The machine shook around them. Bullets began pinging against the helicopter. The fog was their only defense. The aircraft shuddered. They had to lift off now or become sitting targets for the guards rushing in to capture them. *Now! Now or never!*

Craig's mouth flattened as he pulled back on the control. He hadn't flown in nearly two years, yet, it seemed like yesterday. The helicopter strained to break the hold of gravity, the blades shaking and pounding above them. Bullets struck the Plexiglas. He heard Jason cry out and saw Sabra lunge to cover him with her body. The Plexiglas of the nose shattered, the material exploding inward, and Craig jerked his head to one side, feeling the hot sting of fragments striking him. The bird was lifting off, but the bullets were striking it with deadly accuracy.

In moments, the fog closed in below them. Craig used the rudders beneath his feet and pulled the aircraft in a steep bank. How close were they to the trees? He had no idea. Gasping, he tried to ride it out by feel alone. There was absolutely no terrain radar on board the helicopter. It was dark all around them. Which way was up? Down? His eyes strained on the gyroscope and flicked back and forth between it and the altimeter.

"It's all right, all right," Sabra gasped, easing away from Jason. "It's Auntie S, Jason. Look. Look, it's me, honey." She tried to wipe away some of the frightening greasepaint that must make her seem like a monster to

Jason. She saw the child's face go from terror to relief. Instantly, he lunged toward her.

"Auntie S!" he shrieked.

Sabra gulped unsteadily and pulled Jason into her arms. They were safe. Safe! She glanced over at Craig. His face was frozen. The wind whipped into the helicopter, buffeting and icy cold. Blood trickled down the side of his face. She felt a huge, bruised area pounding unremittingly in the middle of her back where she'd taken the the hit from the well-aimed bullet. The armored vest had saved her life.

She felt the aircraft moving unsteadily. Anxiously, she looked at Craig again. He was wrestling with the controls. Could he fly it? Was he panicking? What was going on? Afraid for them all, she held Jason to her tightly.

"We're in trouble!" Craig rasped, working the controls. "The oil pressure is going down!"

Sabra could smell something hot and oily invading the cabin. She began to hear a high-pitched screech above them. They were still in the fog. Where the hell were they? How far from the estate? "What can I do?"

"Strap in!" he roared, wrestling with the sluggish controls. "We aren't going to go far. I'll try for altitude. If the engine quits, we'll have to make a crash landing. Get on the radio. Call the airport for help."

Sabra quickly hauled the harness over herself, keeping Jason in her arms. Fumbling because her hands were shaking so badly, she got the radio from her uniform belt and began making a Mayday call to the Maui airport. Where the hell were they? The fog was thinning now. The helicopter was bucking and groaning, the shriek becoming louder. Sabra kept shouting into the radio, using the Perseus call sign for help. She knew Killian and the FBI would be monitoring them. If only they could get to the airport or somewhere near it!

The fog thinned even more. The aircraft lunged and lagged, the whine of the rotor above them coming and going. The smell of hot oil stung her nostrils. She flung a glance at Craig.

"Where are we?"

"About ten miles west of the airport. Tell them I'm following the highway in."

It was a good choice, Sabra thought, as she shouted the information over the racket in the cabin. The fog was completely gone now, and she realized they were roughly a thousand feet above the island, limping along. Jason burrowed his head into her chest, and she held him tightly against her. Her throat ached with tension as she divided her attention between him and Craig. Craig was managing the aircraft. Each time the helicopter dropped a little, she watched him struggle with the controls. The physical effort it took was tremendous, and she saw how pale and taut he'd become.

"Can we make it?" she shouted.

His gaze shot to the oil pressure. They were only five miles from the airport. If only they could get there! If only he could set the bird down before the engine quit. The smell of burning metal struck his flared nostrils. His hands tightened on the controls. "We aren't gonna make it. Prepare to crash!"

The order roared through Sabra. She bit back a scream as she smelled the hot odor of melting metal. Without the precious oil as a lubricant, the shriek and grinding of engine parts continued. The helicopter was ceasing its forward motion. She heard Craig curse.

"It's no good! I've got to shut the engine down or it's gonna explode!"

She saw him reach for the control that would switch the engine down. Cold, icy wind whipped into the cabin. She was frightened as never before. The moment the engine was shut down, the helicopter plummeted downward. Jason screamed in terror, his small arms wrapped around her. Sabra shut her eyes, buried her head against the boy and held him as tightly as she could. She heard Craig gasp.

To his left, Craig could see the lights of the airport. They were less than three miles away! Everywhere else it was dark. Murderously dark. The helicopter was dropping like a rock beneath him. All of his training came back to him in a rush. He pushed the nose down, aiming it toward the island. He heard Sabra give a cry, but ignored it. He had to aim the nose down in order to pick up enough speed to haul the aircraft up at the last minute, to flare it so the swinging blades would catch the last pocket of air. If he didn't do that, they would crash and burn. There was almost three-quarters of a tank of fuel still on board and no time to dump it. If he couldn't bring the wildly swinging, bucking aircraft in for a crash landing, they would all die in the resulting explosion or burn to death afterward.

Below, he saw the highway and a few stabbing lights of cars. Wrestling with the aircraft, he shoved hard right on the rudder and tried to get the bird to move to the west of the highway. He couldn't see any lights of homes. Maybe it was a sugar cane or pineapple field. Craig prayed that wherever he was heading, there were no people below.

He had no way of judging anything except through instinct honed by years of experience. The helicopter was picking up speed, the blades still turning sluggishly. It was a matter of intuition to know when to lift the nose, hopefully at the last possible moment. Because he'd shut down the engine, Craig had no instruments to tell him how close he was to the ground. All he had now was his ability to judge where the night sky met the darkened horizon. The smell of hot metal was still strong and stung his nostrils. The engine could burst into flames at any moment.

Something told him to haul back on the nose. He heeded the voice inside his head. Gripping the controls hard, he pulled back, pitting sheer, brute strength against the gravity-driven force of the aircraft plummeting out of the sky. As he reared back hard against the seat, every muscle in his body screamed in sudden protest. Hot pain raced up his arms as he held the controls in place. *Come on, come on! Come up! Dammit, come up!* His lips pulled away from his clenched teeth. His eyes widened.

At the last moment, he saw the ground racing up at them. It was a sugar-cane field! Had he pulled up too late? Were they going to nose into the earth? Die in the explosion as the fuel sprayed around them like a fiery rain? Horrible thoughts paralyzed him as he called on every last ounce of his strength. It couldn't happen again! Blips of the fire after the crash in the Iraqui desert struck him. Savagely, he shook his head, his eyes on the ground coming up fast below them.

He heard Jason crying. He heard Sabra gasp. The nose came up. The flailing blades caught the last of the air. Bracing himself, Craig held the controls steady. The helicopter groaned and shrieked. The blades whooshed thickly overhead. The plummet subsided. The bird steadied about fifty feet from the ground. At the last possible moment, Craig guided the bird downward, playing the rudders with his booted feet. He felt the tail strike the field first, the jolt vibrating through the cabin. Because he wasn't strapped in, he was thrown forward. The aircraft bobbled. He jerked back on the controls, hearing the tail drag more deeply into the ground.

The aircraft groaned and slammed onto a left skid. Craig felt himself being torn out of the seat, and he threw up his arm to protect his head. The aircraft plowed into the field, metal tearing and scraping. He heard the blades striking, breaking. A person could be cut in half by one of those blades. The aircraft rolled over and over. Craig found himself lying against the instrument panel. Sobbing for breath, he realized they'd stopped tumbling.

"Sabra!" His voice was scratchy with terror. He blinked the sweat out of his eyes. She was hanging upside down, he saw, trapped in the harness. Jason was still in her arms, alive and unhurt.

"Get me out of this," she gasped.

Craig scrambled toward her, feeling like he was moving in slow motion. He experienced pain in his left arm, but ignored it as he pushed himself upward on unsteady feet. In one motion, he took the knife strapped to his left leg and began to saw through the harnesses to free her.

"We've got to get out of here," he rasped. "I smell fuel leaking. This bird could go at any moment."

"I know, I know," Sabra sobbed, allowing Jason to crawl out of the broken window. The last strap was sawn through, and she fell unceremoniously to the floor of the aircraft.

"Get out. Get out!"

Sabra felt Craig's hand biting into her arm, shoving her through the broken nose of the helicopter. She could smell the nauseating odor of fuel around them, as well as the hot metal of the rotor assembly. Craig was right: the aircraft could explode at any moment.

She fell out onto the damp soil, on her hands and knees.

Jason sat there, his eyes wide with terror, looking up at the broken helicopter.

"Craig?" She stumbled to her feet and twisted around. Where was he?

"Get Jason. Get the hell out of here!" Craig shouted. His foot was trapped in some wreckage. *Damn!* He leaned down and jerked on a piece of metal that had been twisted in the crash. He was breathing in sobbing gasps. Yanking at the metal that held him, he cursed. Glancing up, he could see Sabra pick up Jason and start flailing through the eight-foot-tall sugar cane.

"Son of a bitch!" He used all his strength on the metal. There! He was free! In one motion, Craig dived out of the broken nose. He hit the ground hard, rolling to reduce the impact.

Suddenly, he heard a *whoosh*. He was less than six feet from the aircraft when he got to his feet. His eyes widened. Fire had started on the rotor assembly. Damn! Scrambling, he dug the toes of his boots into the damp soil. He had to get away. Any second now the bird would explode.

Craig had made it barely twenty feet from the helicopter when the explosion occurred. A powerful shock wave hit him first, scorching his exposed skin. The next thing he knew, he was flying though the air, knocked at least twenty feet more by the blast. The whistling and shrieking of metal torn loose in the explosion screamed about him. He slammed to the ground, throwing his arms over his head, rolling end over end.

Hot, burning sensation struck him in the legs and arm. Shrapnel. He knew the stinging bite well. Dazedly, Craig rolled over and sat up. The flaring fire from the burning aircraft made it seem like daylight for several hundred feet in every direction. The thick stalks of sugar cane, with their sharp, cutting edges, had been laid out horizontally, flattened like so many toothpicks in the wake of a hurricane.

Above the roar of the fire, he heard a child scream. Jason! Shaken, Craig shoved himself to his feet. He wobbled unsteadily, suddenly dizzied. Where were they? Anxiously, he searched the hellish landscape of dancing firelight and shadows. Stumbling around the end of the wreck, he saw Jason standing about seventy-five feet from the aircraft. His eyes narrowed. Sabra! He opened his mouth to scream, but nothing came out. She lay unmoving at the boy's feet.

Oh, God, no! He dug his feet into the slippery cane stalks, running brokenly, as fast as he could. Jason's small face was dirtied, streaked with tears as he stood helplessly beside Sabra's body. As Craig approached, the boy covered his face.

Craig fell to his knees near Sabra's head. She lay on her belly, her face buried in the flattened sugar cane. One arm was outstretched, the other tucked beneath her body. Gasping for breath, he called her name.

"Sabra? Sabra...." His hands trembled as he rapidly skimmed her body, searching for wounds. Had the blast knocked her unconscious? Slowly, he turned her over on her back, her head and shoulders resting against his knees. A cold, violent fear gripped him. In the dancing firelight, he could see a dark trail down the side of her neck.

Reaching down, Craig's fingertips touched the black surface. It was warm. Sabra's blood. Wildly, he searched her hair and the back of her skull. A piece of shrapnel lay buried in the rear of her neck. Leaning down, sobbing, Craig could see by the glow of the fire that the metal had partially severed an artery. *Oh, God, no! No!* Sabra was bleeding to death beneath his hands! She couldn't die! His mind whirled with options—and near-paralyzing terror.

Jason had come up to him, sobbing wildly, calling Sabra's name. Jerking a look up, Craig realized dazedly that the lights of cars were coming their way, bouncing over the piles of cane stalks. Were they friend or foe? It could be Garcia's men having followed the noisy, limping helicopter. Sobbing for breath, applying pressure to Sabra's neck, Craig knelt in the field, feeling her lifeblood leaking through his aching fingers. Sabra's face was startlingly pale in the flickering light. Her lips were parted, as if in a scream she'd never released. Her body was limp and slack against his. Tears stung his eyes as he continued to place pressure on the wound.

The headlights halted, trained squarely on them. Was it Garcia? Oh, God, he'd kill them all right now. There would be no mercy. With his free arm, Craig dragged the boy behind him, trying to shield him with his body. They had no weapons. No way to defend themselves. Tears splattered down his drawn face. Sabra was dying. With each thud of her heart, he could feel the pulse beneath his fingers weakening—from a beat, to a feeble flutter.

Craig's heart clenched in grief, and he watched helplessly as four men appeared from the two cars. The headlights were blinding him. He couldn't see. Jason stopped crying and clung to him, hiding behind him.

Then, in the harsh glare of the lights, Craig recognized Killian's taut features. He let out a cry for help. Instantly, Killian came on the run, followed by the others. To Craig's relief, he saw Dr. Parsons awkwardly flailing toward them, her physician's bag in hand. As Killian ran up to him, Craig's voice cracked with alarm.

"Sabra's dying! She's bleeding to death. Oh, God, help her! Help her!"

Chapter Twelve

Craig sat numbly in a plastic chair on the surgery floor of the Maui Hospital. The ache in his heart wouldn't stop, the pain encompassing more and more of his chest. He rubbed his smarting eyes tiredly, with dirty, bloodstained hands.

"Talbot?"

He heard Killian's gruff, low voice. Gradually, he became aware of the other man's presence and the fact that he was holding a paper cup of coffee toward him. Woodenly, he reached for the cup, his hand shaking badly.

"You need to go down to emergency and get looked at," Killian said, slowly easing into a crouched position in front of him. "There's nothing you can do up here to help Sabra. Dr. Parsons is working with the best surgeon this hospital has. If Sabra has a chance, it's here and now."

Sliding both hands around the small cup, Craig felt the

warmth of it begin to permeate the iciness inside him. How long had it been since they'd arrived at the hospital? Shutting his eyes, he bowed his head, feeling the last of the adrenaline giving way to utter exhaustion. Tears leaked out of his eyes, small beads clinging to his lashes. Working his mouth against a sob, he stiffly rose to his feet. Unable to meet Killian's gaze, Craig opened his eyes only after he'd turned away. Walking on sore feet and aching legs, he forced himself over to the window. He carefully set the cup down on the windowsill before his shaking hands splashed the burning contents all over him. Not that it mattered. The only thing that mattered was Sabra.

He felt Killian approach and glanced at him out of the corner of his eyes. The merc stood next to him, his mouth thinned, a scowl on his brow.

"She could die...." Craig forced out the statement in a low, shaken voice.

"Yes."

Killian wouldn't lie about anything, especially not something this serious. This heartbreaking. Craig tried to shore up his roiling emotions. "How's the kid?"

"Jason?"

"Yeah."

"They took him to the children's wing. The doctor on duty said he was fine. No wounds. At least, not physical ones."

Craig heard the derision in Killian's tone. "Yeah, he was pretty shaken up."

"It's none of my business, but I think you ought to get looked at and then go visit Jason. He's asking for you."

Turning, Craig said, "Me?"

"Yeah. Why?"

"He doesn't know me from Adam. He knew Sabra."

"Maybe so, but the kid knows you helped save his life. I think he's reaching out." Killian looked at the bank of phones on the wall. "Laura's on her way. I just got off the phone with her and Jake. She's taking the first commercial flight available out of D.C. Shah Randolph, Jake's wife, is escorting her." Killian looked at his watch. "It's 0500 now. She'll to arrive in Maui at 1500 this afternoon. I'll go pick them up and bring them down here, but until then Jason's alone."

Craig stood tiredly and tried to swallow his unshed tears. "Sabra's still in surgery—"

"Dr. Parsons knows you'll be in the hospital somewhere, if she gets done sooner than you think." Killian placed his hand on Craig's slumped shoulder. "Get medical treatment, get a shower and then go see Jason. The kid needs you. He needs to be held."

Brokenly, Craig nodded. Even now, he couldn't be selfish. The boy had gone through a hell few people would ever encounter in their lives. To have endured it at such a young age had probably traumatized Jason forever. Rubbing his brow, he nodded. "Okay, I'll go down. Will you—"

Killian nodded darkly. "I'll stay up here. When Dr. Parsons comes out of surgery, I'll tell her where you've gone."

The lump in Craig's throat refused to go away, no matter how many times he swallowed. Belatedly, he looked down at his hands. They were cut all over from the flying Plexiglas. Dimly, he was aware that he'd probably have to have shrapnel taken out of his legs, too. The pain of a doctor digging the metal out of his body would be easy to take in comparison to the mere thought of losing Sabra. She couldn't die. She just couldn't. He loved her. And God forgive him, he'd never told her that.

As he wearily turned toward the elevators, Craig replayed the awful trip by ambulance to the hospital. If Dr. Parsons hadn't been there, Sabra undoubtedly would have died en route. And all Craig had been able to do was sit there, watching dumbly as Parsons worked to stabilize Sabra's life. Bits and pieces of the crash in the desert had overlaid Sabra's ghostly features as tears leaked uncontrollably from Craig's eyes. He had wished over and over that it had been him hit by that unlucky metal fragment. If anyone deserved to live, it was Sabra. He was worthless in comparison, a man controlled by a haunting past he couldn't overcome, while she was so strong and beautiful and confident. Life hadn't tortured her as it had him. She had hopes and dreams. Craig wished with every bone in his body that he could trade places with Sabra on that gurney.

All that time, Jason had been in his arms, clinging to him, his head buried against Craig's chest. Craig divided his attention between them, keeping his hand on the boy's dirty hair to protect him from seeing the blood, from seeing someone he loved like that. No child deserved such trauma. Craig had rocked Jason back and forth, numbly whispering that it would be all right, that Sabra was going to be all right. The boy had sobbed wildly, almost hysterical in the aftermath. They were lies, Craig thought bitterly as he repeated the soothing words. But he felt helpless and didn't want Jason to be any more upset than he already was. It had been the longest forty minutes of Craig's life.

Now in the elevator, he tried to pull himself together. Only then did he become aware of how badly he stunk, as the odor of fear and the metallic scent of blood registered in his sensitive nostrils. As he left the elevator and headed for the emergency room, Craig saw nurses and patients staring at him as if he were some kind of avenging ghost come to haunt them. He was covered with mud from the field, bloodied by glass and shrapnel. He must look like hell. Or the walking dead.

One of the nurses in ER gave him another cup of hot, black coffee to drink. He sat on a gurney, stripped down to his shorts while a doctor examined him. Later, he lay on the gurney, fighting waves of pain as the doctor pulled more than thirty pieces of glass from his face, neck and shoulder, and two pieces of twisted metal from his lower legs. But the pain of the extraction remained small in comparison to his worry for Sabra. He lay there afterward as his wounds were being swabbed and dressed, wondering how she was doing. How much blood had she lost? Had he put enough pressure on that torn artery to save her life? Had he not?

The agony of waiting shredded Craig. Finally, a nurse showed him to a shower and brought in a surgeon's smock and pants for him to wear in lieu of his filthy, bloody clothes. Craig stood under the warming flow of water, hoping it would ease the pain in his chest. All his injuries were minor, and a shower was permissible. Awkwardly he ran the bar of soap through his hair, then stood beneath the spray again, tears streaming freely down his cheek. Sabra couldn't be torn from him! She just couldn't. He gasped for breath, the water stinging his eyes as he leaned weakly against the stall, his fists clenched against the wall at that terrible possibility.

She had loved someone who hadn't had the guts to tell her he loved her—whatever his reasons. Craig had thought it too soon to tell her. But why hadn't he? Oh, God, why hadn't he? If Sabra had known, it might have helped her fight harder to live. He bowed his head, water running in rivulets across his frozen features as his chest shook with a great sob. In here, no one would hear him cry. It was the only safe place to weep for a loss he was sure was coming. Even with tightly shut eyes, he could see Sabra's warm gray eyes dancing with love for him, and suddenly Craig knew, deep in his injured soul, that she did love him. Sabra wasn't the kind of woman to rush into anything; that's why she'd withheld her real feelings from him.

Why did everything have to happen so suddenly? He'd become so jaded, so hardened against life since the crash. The idea of falling in love with someone as beautiful and warm as Sabra had never entered his sordid reality. Not until she'd crashed into his life, tearing that sense of hopelessness away from him, breathing new life into him, making him reach out and hope once more—and realize the depth of the personal, lonely hell he'd fallen into. Bitterly, Craig opened his eyes and slowly eased away from the wall. Would he ever be able to tell Sabra how much she'd given him? She'd literally handed him back his life. When he'd slept in her arms, he'd felt peace for the first time in years. Her presence strengthened him and allowed him to amass his own strength for healing himself.

Such was the miracle of Sabra, he realized, turning off the faucets and standing, dripping, in the stall. Life hadn't exactly been kind to her, either, yet she'd moved ahead despite it. Craig opened the door and reached for the thick terry-cloth towel. Damn his practical realism. He'd been so good at being logical, he'd almost missed the most important person in his life—Sabra. He rubbed the towel against his face, uncaring if some of the small cuts started to bleed again. Water dripped off his hair, and he went through the motions of drying it, feeling overwhelming numbness coupled with exhaustion.

Jason. He had to see Jason. After donning the green

cotton clothes, Craig went in search of a nurse who could
direct him to the boy. With every step he took it felt like
twenty extra pounds of weight were bearing down on his
legs and feet. He couldn't recall ever feeling this low. But
then, he'd never before had the woman he loved lying on
a surgery table, her life in jeopardy.

Nurse Bonnie Blaire, a pert, young, red-haired woman,
led him to Jason's private room.

"The doctor has given him a mild sedative because he
was hysterical, Mr. Talbot." She smiled sadly as she
halted at the door. "If you want the truth, I think the little
boy just needs to be held...."

Craig nodded wearily. "Okay, I'll see what I can do."
Who didn't need to be held right now? Hell, he ached to
have Sabra's arms slide around him. He'd crush her so
tightly against him that the air would rush from her lungs.
Well, that wasn't possible, but maybe he could help the
boy.

The nurse quietly closed the door behind him, and
Craig tiptoed forward. Jason looked awfully small in the
large bed. Someone had given him a toy—a well-loved
teddy bear. Absently, Craig remembered that Jason's favorite blanket and toy were still in their car at Kula.

He lay on his side, his face pressed into the stuffed
bear. The numbness left Craig's heart as he walked closer.
Jason's eyes were shut, and the tracks of tears he'd cried
had dried across his flushed cheek. Craig reached over
and gently mussed his hair.

The boy gave a small whimper. Craig kept stroking his
head and watched the effect it had on him. The small
hands, once clasping the teddy bear in tight fists, gradually
began to loosen. The blanket that covered him was thin,
and Craig felt him trembling.

Easing down the guardrail, Craig sat on the edge of the

bed, facing Jason. A long time ago his mother had rubbed his shoulders and back when he was sick, so he did it now for the boy. Craig knew he couldn't take the place of Sabra, Laura or Morgan, but at least he could try to give Jason some solace. Little by little, he felt him begin to relax. The child looked so innocent lying there, and he himself felt so beat-up and battered by life. Jason had his whole life in front of him. Sabra might have hers taken from her. And Craig would be left alone.

Pain shattered his heart, and without thinking, he eased himself up on the bed and gently bundled the small boy into his arms, teddy bear and all. Maybe he couldn't hold Sabra, and he knew no one was going to hold him, but he could make Jason feel safe—and loved. Jason moaned a little and buried his head on his chest, his small hand stretching outward, then relaxed completely against him.

Craig's mouth curved slightly as he felt the child entrust himself to him. The feeling was warming. Almost euphoric. He slid his arm across Jason's small back, his own eye-lids closing. Craig could feel Jason's tiny heartbeat against him. The shallow rise and fall of the boy's chest told him he was now asleep. A ragged sigh escaped Craig's lips as he felt his muscles, one by one, begin to release the tension they'd held so long. Then he fell into an exhausted sleep, holding a little boy and praying for Sabra's life.

"Craig?"

He felt fingers squeezing his shoulder tentatively. Sleep pulled at him, and he fought to come awake. The voice was unfamiliar. *Who?* He forced his eyes open and realized groggily that Jason was curled tightly in his arms, still asleep. Blinking to clear his vision, he looked up toward the voice.

Dr. Parsons smiled wearily. "Killian told me to be careful how I woke you."

Instantly, Craig came awake. He eased Jason onto the bed, still keeping one hand on the boy's shoulder. "Sabra?" His voice was hoarse with sleep. His heart pounded hard in his chest, fear gutting through him.

Ann tightened her grip on his shoulder. "I think she's going to make it. Right now, she's critical, but she's in recovery."

Relief avalanched through Craig. He was dizzied by the news. Dr. Parsons still wore her green surgery gown, the cap over her hair, the mask hanging around her neck. Searching her smiling eyes, he rasped, "She's alive?"

"Very much so. We had to give her a blood transfusion. Nearly two pints." Ann lost her smile. "She went into cardiac arrest on the table due to blood loss, but we brought her back, thank God." She patted his shoulder. "She's doing much better."

Cardiac arrest. Stunned, Craig felt tears flood into his eyes. He'd nearly lost Sabra. Somehow, he had known that; such was the invisible line of communication he had with her. Wiping his mouth with the back of his hand, he fought against the tears. "When can I see her?"

"Now, if you want. She won't know you're there, though. It will be an hour or two for the anesthesia to wear off. You can't stay more than five minutes an hour until we upgrade her from from intensive care."

Carefully, Craig divested himself of the sleeping boy. Easing himself off the bed, he made sure that the teddy bear took his place as much as possible. Tucking the blanket over Jason's shoulders, he said, "Will someone be with Jason? He's really shook up over all this."

"I'll make sure a nurse comes in and sits with him," Ann said gently.

"What time is it?"

"It's 7:00 a.m."

He'd slept two hours. It wasn't much, but it was enough. Craig's heart soared with joy as he turned to the physician. "Thank you for saving her," he rasped, and he reached out, gripping her long, lean hand. If Craig didn't know better, he'd have guessed Ann Parsons was a painter, not a surgeon. But he supposed both were artists in their own way. One painted beautiful things, the other used the artistry of her hands to save a life. In this case, Sabra's life.

"I'll be over shortly, Craig."

He nodded and quickly left the room, heading down the hall toward the bank of elevators. Feelings raged unchecked through him as he waited impatiently for the elevator to take him to the recovery floor. The depressing numbness that had sunk its claws into him had miraculously disappeared. The weight that inhabited his legs was gone, too. What was left of his exhaustion was torn from him as he hurried down the hall to the ICU nurse's station.

Sabra was going to live! The thought kept playing through him like a wonderful chord of music. Craig barely felt the tile floor beneath his feet, was scarcely aware of anything beyond an inner joy that made him feel as if he were walking on air. A nurse spotted him coming and must have known who he was, because she met him and walked him to the recovery room.

"She's not conscious yet, Mr. Talbot, but Dr. Parsons said for you to stay with her, talk to her and hold her hand. She won't respond, but that doesn't matter. I'll come for you in five minutes."

Craig stepped inside the room. Sabra was the only patient there, IVs in both arms, the white sheet emphasizing her pale, slack features. Swallowing hard, he moved to

the side of her gurney. Her thick, black hair had been
gathered up in a white towel, and he saw the dressing that
now hid the ugly, gaping wound the shrapnel had made
in her neck. Her lips were colorless, her lashes lying softly
against her taut skin.

Gently, ever so gently, Craig leaned over the bed and
placed his mouth against her slack lips. He didn't care
that she didn't know he was there. He wanted to kiss her,
to welcome her back to life—to him—if she would have
him when this was all over. Life had never seemed so
tentative as now, as he felt the coolness of her lips beneath
his own. Her breathing was so shallow that at first he was
alarmed, thinking she wasn't breathing at all. He eased
his mouth from hers and watched her chest for a long,
fearful moment. Only when he saw the minute rise and
fall of the white sheet draped across her did he release a
ragged breath of his own.

Lightly, he grazed her smooth, flawless brow with a
fingertip, lost in the soft texture of her skin. Even now,
Sabra was beautiful—untouched. Yet the woman had the
heart of a lion, there was no doubt. She had faced death
with him—and won. Slipping his fingers over hers, he felt
how chilled she was and grew worried again. Was she
warm enough? How badly Craig wanted to take her in his
arms, hold her and warm her as he had Jason.

"Five minutes," the nurse murmured from the entrance, giving him an apologetic smile.

Craig nodded. He leaned down, his lips close to Sabra's
ear. "Sweetheart, this is Craig. I want you to know I love
you. I should have said it earlier." He closed his eyes,
choking back a wealth of feelings. "Listen, I just want
you to get well, okay? Dr. Parsons says you're going to
make it. You've lost a lot of blood, but you're going to
be fine. I love you, Sabra. Don't ever forget that. No mat-

ter what happens, no matter what life throws at us, just know I'll always love you...."

Sabra heard voices, heard a little boy's high-pitched, excited tone. Then she felt the touch of a small hand on her arm—a warm little hand. Another voice. A woman's, soft and strained. She fought to come awake, but her lashes felt like weights against her cheeks. And then she heard a very familiar voice, along with a touch that could never be mistaken. It was Craig. She felt his strong fingers wrap around her left hand. On her right hand, she felt the boy's touch. The voices melded together in confusion. She stopped struggling, feeling so very weak. The voices ebbed away, and she felt as if she were floating once again within a warm cloud of light.

The touch of Craig's hand brought her back to consciousness, drew her out of that floating cloud of light. She felt his fingers stroking her arm gently, with reverence. This time she recognized the other voices—Jason's and Laura's. Fragments of scenes blipped in front of her closed eyes—of being hit with a bullet and flying five feet forward. Dully, Sabra felt the bruising pain in her back where the vest had stopped the bullet from penetrating her body. She should be dead, she thought.

Then she remembered the helicopter crashing, remembered jerking Jason into her arms and running as hard and fast as she could through the cane field, away from the smoking aircraft. The explosion... Sabra's brows knit at the memory. She recalled the heat rolling across her, recalled pressing Jason hard against her chest to protect him from flying debris. And then a white-hot sensation had slammed into her neck, making her drop him. It was the last thing Sabra recalled: falling in slow motion to the muddy, wet ground and hearing Jason screaming her name.

"I think she's coming awake."

Sabra heard Laura's tremulous voice and felt her hand on her shoulder. Her whole focus swung to Craig's touch, which never left her hand.

"I think so, too," he murmured.

Craig's voice was low and off-key. Sabra felt the warmth of his mouth press briefly against her brow. She absorbed his unexpected kiss, feeling a joy and lightness flow through her. How she loved him!

Where was she? Was he all right? And Jason? Those anxious questions forced her to barely open her eyes. The first person she saw was Craig, looking down at her, worry in his dark, exhausted gaze. She was alarmed at the bloody scabs on the right side of his face, the redness in his eyes, as if he'd been crying, and the tortured line of his mouth. Opening her lips, she tried to speak, but only a whisper of sound came forth.

"Ssh," Craig said, squeezing her hand gently, "don't try to talk, sweetheart. We're all safe. You're going to make it." He tried to smile and failed, drowning in her shadowy gray eyes.

"Thank God," Laura whispered, leaning over and touching her shoulder, "you're going to be fine."

Sabra divided her limited attention between them, as they stood on either side of her bed. Laura looked gray with fatigue, her eyes red rimmed, filled with tears. Only Jason's bubbly smile encouraged her. The boy leaned over and placed a very wet kiss on her cheek.

"Get well, Auntie S! Mommy says you get to come home with us. We get to fly in Daddy's airplane!"

Sabra's mouth pulled into a slight smile, and she held Jason's sparkling, shiny gaze. Of all of them, he looked the least damaged by what had happened. She found it hard to believe that he could spring back so quickly from the kidnapping. Perhaps that was a testament to his youth—his small, innocent view of the world. Craig's fingers interlaced with her own, and she slowly moved her head to meet his blue gaze. The warmth in his eyes, the unabashed welcome for her alone, made her try to smile again. Weakness spread through her, and though she wanted to speak, it was impossible.

"Honey," Laura said to her son, "I think Auntie S wants to sleep now...."

"Ahh, Mommy, I want to tell her what happened!"

"Not now, honey. Come on, let's leave Craig to stay with Auntie S. Come on...."

Craig watched Laura pick up her son and leave the room. He brought a chair over to Sabra's bedside and sat down. Stillness fell over the room, and only her soft, shallow breathing could be heard. At least the beeps and sighs of the multitude of ICU instruments and monitors were gone. In twenty-four hours, Sabra had gone from critical to serious. No one had breathed a greater sigh of relief than Craig. Gently, he slid her hand between his again and held it. Her flesh was still cool to the touch.

When Sabra's lashes moved, he realized she hadn't fallen back asleep. Clearing his throat, he rasped, "Can you hear me, Sabra?"

She squeezed his hand weakly. Did Craig realize how wonderful it was to be touched by him? To hear his roughened voice once again? Did he know how much she'd feared for his life? Tears stung her eyes, and she felt them bead and slip down the sides of her face. She felt Craig release her hand. Then his trembling fingers eased the tears from her cheeks.

"It's okay," he said unsteadily. "Everyone is okay,

Sabra. You're the one we were worried about.'' He hesitated. ''Worry wasn't even close, sweetheart. God, I thought you were going to die out there in the cane field. I was so scared. So damned scared, Sabra.''

What little strength she had she used to open her eyes again. She saw the tortured look in Craig's gaze, felt the terrible pain in his voice and in his hand as he barely touched her arm once more. She wanted to ask questions, but the weakness claimed her, and all she could do was surrender to that white cloud of light. As she drifted away, she could hear Craig speaking to her, but the words became garbled and distant. Right now, she needed to sleep.

Craig sat for a long time just watching Sabra sleep. Had she heard him? He'd quietly told her he loved her, but he wasn't sure if she'd understood. Dr. Parsons had warned him that the first twenty-four hours, Sabra would sleep a great deal, mostly due to the shock and trauma of the surgery, as well as getting rid of the anesthesia in her system.

He studied her fingers in the silence, looking at the wedding ring on her left hand. It was a fake one, of course, for the mission. She'd never taken it off even though their cover had been blown after the first day. Was that a fluke? Had she worn it for other reasons? His wistful side, which was working overtime lately, said that she wore it because she loved him, wanted him for her husband someday.

With a soft snort, Craig eased out of the chair and placed Sabra's limp hand across her blanketed form. The day was coming to a close, the sunlight streaming through the venetian blinds, creating bars on the opposite wall. The door opened and he looked up. Dr. Parsons gestured for him to come into the hall.

Outside, Craig noted that she was back in her blouse

and slacks. He wondered briefly why Ann, who was certainly attractive, had never married. He knew little of her, knew little of the reasons why she'd gone to work for Perseus. Maybe Morgan had known her before he'd formed the company.

"I just got a call from Jake," Ann said, walking with him down the long hall, "and he wants all of us to come back as soon as possible. I told him Sabra needed another twenty-four hours before she could be moved."

"I don't think it's safe to stay here," he agreed, his gaze constantly roving up and down the hall. When Killian wasn't keeping guard on Sabra's room, he was. They took turns every twelve hours to ensure that Garcia wouldn't get to her and finish the job. Nowhere was safe.

"Jake is worried about that, too," Ann continued in a low voice. She clasped her hands behind her back as she walked. "The FBI has apparently found a leak in the Maui police department." She traded a frown with him. "Sam Chung is a mole for Garcia."

Groaning, Craig halted and thrust his hands onto his hips. "We stepped right into the middle of it, didn't we?"

"Yes, you did. Jake said to tell you that you did a good job. He's as relieved as we are that Sabra's going to recover. Right now, the Honolulu police are investigating Chung. They placed a wire tap on his phone and monitored several calls to Garcia's estate. It's a good thing you never went back to the Westin. Jake thinks they were waiting for you."

Grimacing, Craig nodded. "We just kept moving around, Ann. A different room every night, under different names. It worked, thank God."

She smiled absently and halted in the middle of the hall. "Listen, I know you've got a lot on your shoulders right now...."

"What do you mean?"

With an embarrassed smile, Ann said, "With Sabra, I mean. You do care for her, don't you? At the crash site I saw the look on your face, heard the tone of your voice...."

"Yes," Craig rasped heavily, "there's something there, Ann. But I don't want it all over the place. I haven't even had time to talk to Sabra. I don't need gossip floating around."

Touching his arm, she said, "If Killian suspects anything, he's keeping it to himself. It's just that I saw the look in your eyes..."

Crossing his arms, he leaned against the wall and studied her. "What are you leading up to?"

"Sabra is going to need some care when we get her back to the mainland. I thought...well, since you do care for her, that perhaps she could stay at your apartment for a couple of weeks. That artery in her neck was partly severed. We've sewn it back together, and all should go well, but she has to really take it easy. If she should fall, or make some kind of quick, jerking motion, she could rip it open again and—"

"I understand," he rasped. What would Sabra say to such a plan? he wondered. "What if she doesn't want me to play nursemaid?"

"Then she'll have to stay in the hospital for the next week, and have a full-time nurse for the week after that."

"I see. Well, let me ask her, okay? I don't take anything for granted anymore."

She nodded thoughtfully. "Just let me know. I'll have to call an ambulance once we land back in Washington. Listen, I've got to go check on Laura now. She's got me worried."

Laura was looking extremely thin and nervous, Craig agreed silently. "She looks like she's ready to break."

"I know," Ann whispered, frowning. "I hate to prescribe more tranquilizers for her, but I don't know how long she can go on this way. She's lost ten pounds so far, and she's eating next to nothing. She doesn't sleep, and when she does nap, she gets nightmares about the rape."

He placed a hand on her shoulder. "Take it from someone who knows about nightmares. Just let her talk. It helps a lot."

Gratefully, Ann reached out and touched his arm. "Thanks, Craig. I hope Sabra knows what she has."

Stymied by that last comment, Craig watched the physician hurry down the hall toward the elevators. With a sigh, he turned and went back to Sabra's room. It was his turn to watch her. Not that he minded. He really didn't want to be anywhere else, anyway. He hoped Sabra felt similarly. A part of him waited in anxious frustration for when she'd be completely conscious so that they could talk. Would Sabra want to stay at his apartment and allow him to help her through her next two weeks of recovery? *He'd* never wanted anything more. But what did Sabra want?

Chapter Thirteen

"You look a hundred percent better this morning," Craig exclaimed, greeting Sabra with a smile. He'd just gotten up after sleeping deeply for six hours, and Killian had given up his post outside her hospital door in exchange for a hot cup of coffee.

Sabra gazed up at Craig as he approached her hospital bed. It was 8:00 a.m., and the nurse had awakened her to give her some medication. He had recently showered and shaved and was dressed in a bright purple-and-white Hawaiian print shirt, stuffed haphazardly into a pair of tan chinos. She hungrily absorbed the sight. "I like your new fashion," she teased weakly, her voice rough from disuse.

Craig stopped and looked down at his shirt. "Oh, this—yeah," he murmured, touching it with his hand, "I was in a hurry to get some clean clothes, so I bought the first thing this Hawaiian lady thought I'd look good in, at a shop just outside the hospital.'' He grinned, a little embarrassed. ''Think purple's my color?''

''It looks good on you.'' She wanted to say he looked good in everything—and nothing.

When Craig saw the corners of her mouth lift slightly, his heart took a powerful leap in his chest. Halting at the edge of the bed, he placed his cup of coffee on the nightstand.

''That looks good, too,'' she noted hopefully.

''What? The coffee?''

''Yes.''

He grinned a little, drowning in her clear, gray eyes, in the warmth spinning in their depths. This morning Sabra wasn't so pale. She was completely conscious, and inwardly, he heaved a huge sigh of relief. Resting his hands on the bar along the bed, he said, ''So you're getting hungry?''

''Starved,'' Sabra admitted wryly.

''When did you wake up?''

''The nurse got me up to take some medication about half an hour ago.''

Craig couldn't help himself. Reaching out, he gently stroked her hair, which needed to be combed. He watched as her lips parted softly at his touch. To hell with it. Leaning over, he captured her mouth with his own. Never had she felt so good to him, her lips pliant beneath his, giving as well as taking—a far cry from two days ago, when she'd lain cool and nearly lifeless. Gently, he moved his lips against hers, tasting her, giving back to her, breathing into her his urgent desire for her not only to live, but to gather strength from him. They were wet and warm beneath his, and he felt her weakly lift her hand to place it on his shoulder. Though he longed to deepen the exploration, Craig cautioned himself. A fire of aching need grew in his lower body. The urgency to wrap Sabra around him and love her slowly and thoroughly, nearly caused him to lose control.

As Craig eased his mouth from hers, he opened his eyes and stared down into her lustrous gray ones. The words *I love you*, were almost torn from him, but he bit them back for now. Giving her a slight smile, he rasped, "Welcome back, sweetheart. I was so scared I was going to lose you...."

Shaken, Sabra felt Craig wrap his hand around hers. "The nurse told me I almost died," she quavered, absorbing his nearness and warmth. The burning look in his eyes was unmistakable, and Sabra knew the feeling she had flowing through her was love. Real love. Swallowing against a dry throat, she added, "I don't remember much, Craig...."

With a grimace, he straightened up and continued to hold her cool hand in his. "Maybe it's just as well. I'm sure it will all come back to you soon enough."

"Jason?"

"He's fine. Laura's here, too. They visited you yesterday, but you were still coming in and out of consciousness."

"I remember voices." She smiled weakly. "I remember your voice and your touch, though."

"That's a good sign," Craig said, heartened. Gathering what was left of his courage, he said, "Today Dr. Parsons wants to fly all of us home, including you. She says you can travel. There's only one slight problem."

"What?" Sabra saw the darkening in his eyes and heard reservation in his voice.

"She says you need two weeks of rest and close watching. With that artery mending, you can't be doing the normal things you'd do at home by yourself."

Wrinkling her nose, Sabra muttered, "I won't stay in a hospital, Craig."

Giving her a hopeful look, he placed his hand on top of hers. "Would you settle for my place? For me helping you out when you need help?"

Stunned, Sabra stared up at him. She saw the hope in his eyes and saw him trying to steel himself for her rejection. The idea shocked her only from the standpoint that she'd never in her wildest dreams have expected such an offer. "Well," she stammered, "can—can you stand me underfoot for two weeks?"

Heartened, Craig rasped, "Sweetheart, I want you around for a lot longer than two weeks. I don't want to push you into what I want, though. This is your call."

If only they weren't here, in a busy hospital. Sabra's smile was tremulous with emotion. "If you'll have me, I'll come home with you...."

On the way home in the jet, Sabra dozed. The gurney was in the rear of the plane, in a special area where it could be locked into the bulkhead, much like a seat. Dr. Parsons had come back to check the IV drip, had arranged her blankets to make sure she was comfortable, then had gone forward to be with Laura, Jason, Killian and Craig. Somewhere below was the Pacific Ocean, but Sabra couldn't see much from her makeshift bed. The vibration of the jet surrounded her, and this time it was a lulling sensation.

She watched through half-closed eyes as Jason huddled in Laura's arms. He seemed the least affected by the trauma they'd survived, but Sabra worried for the child, who seldom left his mother's side. More than once she'd heard Jason ask where his daddy was and seen Laura wrestle with an appropriate answer that gave some of the truth, but not enough to shake the boy up.

One of the two pilots came back, making his way through the narrow cabin. Sabra liked him. He was a hard-looking ex-Air Force fighter pilot by the name of Sloan MacKinley. The coffeepot was near her bed, and he nodded in her direction as he stopped and poured two cups of coffee.

"You want any, Sabra?"

She smiled a little. "No, thanks...."

He turned and studied her, both cups of coffee in hand. "You look a little lonely back here. Maybe I ought to get someone to keep you company?"

"That's okay...." Sabra was amazed that MacKinley, who had a rough-hewn face, possessed such sensitivity. But why should it surprise her that some men had this sort of intuitive knowing? Craig possessed it, though at the moment, he was exhausted and sleeping in his seat. She didn't blame him for not realizing how lonely she felt. Looking up into MacKinley's narrowed green eyes, she saw care radiating from them. He was a relatively new employee with Perseus, and she knew little about the man. But then, Sabra realized that those who joined Morgan's organization usually had a lot to hide, one way or another.

"We'll be landing in San Francisco in a couple of hours," MacKinley said, sipping his coffee. "Then we'll refuel and head for D.C. I imagine you'll be glad to get home."

"More than you'll ever know."

"Yeah, hospitals suck, as far as I'm concerned." He managed to lift one corner of his thin mouth. "Gotta get back up to the cockpit. Richmond doesn't do well without his IV of coffee every hour."

It hurt to laugh, but Sabra did anyway. MacKinley's

wry sense of humor was typical of military pilots. He was a lean man, reminding her of a hungry wolf on the prowl. She saw a lot of Josh in him, with his teasing, and the same basic build. On the way up the aisle, balancing the cups of coffee, the pilot slowed his pace and look intently at Dr. Parsons. He hesitated, evidently thought better of stopping, then moved on by her. Sabra wondered if Ann was even aware of the pilot's interest in her. She was quietly working some needlepoint in her lap, apparently oblivious.

Sabra's attention was diverted when she saw Craig get up and walk back toward her. He'd slept soundly since the plane had taken off, and she was glad to see him. Instantly, her heart started pounding slowly with joy. Did he know how happy he made her feel? Sabra ached for the time and place to share that with him. She saw the light in his eyes, shadows no longer plaguing them. Holding out her hand, she felt her fingers touch and clasp his. A sizzling heat tingled upward through her arm.

"Mac giving you a hard time back here?" he asked, leaning against the side of the gurney, studying her in the gloom.

"Yes and no. He's like all the pilots I know."

"Mmm." Craig pressed a small kiss to the back of her hand. "You had an odd look on your face. Does he remind you of Josh?"

Sabra's lips parted. "Are you a mind reader?"

"I wish," he said. "Just something in your eyes, was all. Maybe a look of loss."

With a sigh, Sabra nodded. "When I woke up in the hospital, I started to realize a lot of things, Craig."

He ran his fingers lightly across the back of her hand. "Like what, sweetheart?"

She held his worried gaze. Craig had had so much taken

from him over the years, yet he was able to reach out and make her feel better. Every time he called her sweetheart, she wanted to cry. She tightened her grip on his hand, her voice low with feeling. "That a certain man in my life has taught me I can let the past go once and for all."

Craig stared down at her, shaken. He saw tears gathering in her eyes. She was so beautiful lying there her hair dark against the pristine white of the pillowcase. Despite her injury, Craig felt as though Sabra hadn't been wounded emotionally as he had been in the Iraqui crash, that her inner resiliency had somehow seen her through. He couldn't explain why; it was just something he sensed. And for her, he was glad of that. "Josh loved you," he said in a low voice, "but from what you've told me, he didn't have the courage to act on it."

"But I didn't know that," Sabra said wearily. "I realize now that I had fallen in love with him. I wanted to give myself to him, but that wasn't enough."

"Listen," Craig growled, "any man worth his salt would go to his grave knowing he had everything if you offered yourself to him." His mouth turned downward. "Josh was a guy who lived on the edge, Sabra. His way of life didn't include marriage."

She nodded, absorbing the intensity of his words. The burning anger in his eyes told her how much he was upset for her, for what she'd lost. In reality, she'd never had it to lose. "I guess I'm more of an idealist than I gave myself credit for," she murmured reflectively. "Josh crashed into my life and made me look at other possibilities."

"Such as what?"

"Such as marriage. Having children. I was so busy trying to be the son my father never had that I think I lost sight of a lot of other things that were important to me. They got pushed aside, Craig."

"Josh made you aware of your femininity."

"Yes."

He ran his fingers along her smooth, high cheekbone, her skin soft and warm beneath his touch. "After the crash in Desert Storm, I got real clear on a lot of things," he told her grimly. "I guess all the adventure of what I was doing for a living burned up in that crash. Living in a hospital for nearly a year afterward, going through the hell of one operation after another, I had a lot of time to think. It's funny in a way, Sabra, but before the crash, I had a certain detachment from everything. When you fly, it's easy to drop a load of bombs, or pull a trigger that will send a missile a couple of miles away to blow an aircraft out of the sky." He shrugged. "The enemy shows up as a colored blip on your radar screen, not as a human being who has a wife, children and parents. It's almost like a video game."

"That's pretty removed," Sabra admitted quietly, seeing the torture return to his eyes.

"Yeah, well, the crash took care of that." He managed a twisted smile and studied her. "What has this last mission taken away from you?" he asked solemnly.

The depth of his insight forever surprised her. Sabra realized again how Josh's joking about everything had badly skewed her reality about men in general. Craig was not only thoughtful, but perceptive. She licked her cracked lower lip and whispered, "I'm afraid now."

Tightening his hand around hers, he nodded. "I know what you mean. Life isn't some promise hanging out there in front of you anymore, is it?"

She shook her head, feeling the fear within her. "You were right, Craig."

"About what?"

"Remember you told me that because I'd never had a close call with death, I didn't know real fear?"

He nodded and held her troubled gaze. "Reality is a son of a bitch, isn't it?" He saw the same look in her eyes that he saw in his own every morning when he shaved in front of the bathroom mirror. It hurt Craig to realize that fact, and he wanted, somehow, to give Sabra back her previous belief that life would always be good, always be there. Sadly, he knew that once that veneer had been ripped away, it could never be put back in place.

"Isn't it?" Sabra agreed. She settled his hand against her stomach, her hands over his. "I was so intent on protecting Jason," she whispered unsteadily. "I don't even remember being afraid for myself as I was running away from that helicopter. I was only afraid that I wouldn't be able to protect him. This crazy thought was screaming in my head as I ran. I didn't want someone telling Laura her son had died because I couldn't do my job. The poor kid," she murmured. "I crushed him so tightly against me he's lucky he didn't have cracked ribs."

Craig moved a strand of hair away from her wrinkled brow. "You didn't think of yourself. That's normal, Sabra."

Blinking away the tears, she held his sad gaze. "You're the real hero in all of this, Craig. I know how much courage it took for you to get into that helicopter in the first place."

His mouth contorted. "Wasn't much choice, was there?"

"There are always choices," Sabra said brokenly, "and you took the bravest. That helicopter was our only escape. If you hadn't flown us out, Perseus would have an even bigger mess on their hands right now."

He shrugged and nervously rubbed the top of her hand

with his fingers. "I didn't like the alternatives. I guess I traded one fear for another," he said, trying to joke about it. "I wasn't even aware I could have a greater fear than flying a helicopter, but when the chips were down, I didn't want anything to happen to you or Jason."

"I couldn't believe your skill with that aircraft," she said softly, holding his shy gaze. "I know enough about flying to realize that every aircraft is different, and if you don't have experience flying it, it's twice as hard."

"Don't give me more credit than I deserve, Sabra. Helicopters are basically the same. Maybe the control panel is set up a little different, maybe a toggle switch here or there is changed, but they all have a cyclic and a collective."

Sabra refused to be detoured by his deadpan explanation. "You deserve a medal for your heroism, Craig. I know you'll never get one. I know that no one, except maybe me, knows the true extent of your courage." Her voice grew soft with tears. "I never realized what real courage was until I met you, until you showed me. In my eyes, you're the most courageous human being I'll ever meet."

Craig felt heat move into his face, and he avoided her sparkling eyes, which told him he honestly felt he was a hero. The knowledge was at the same time euphoric and frightening. He hoped Sabra didn't put him on a pedestal, because sure as hell, he'd fall off it sooner or later and end up disappointing her. He didn't want that to happen, but he didn't know how to give voice to his concern.

"Well," he said gruffly, "I'll just be glad when we get stateside. I don't know about you, but home sounds pretty good right now." Good and safe and filled with promise.

"You give my place a new look," Craig said, making sure Sabra was comfortable on the sofa. They'd arrived over an hour ago, with Killian helping to bring over some of Sabra's clothes and toiletries from her condominium in Fairfax, Virginia, not too far away.

Sabra smiled tiredly. "I feel safe here," she murmured. The side of her neck was aching, but she didn't want to take a pain pill. They made her groggy, and her mouth always got dry. She had already taken a long, relaxing bath and was dressed in her white silk nightgown and white chenille robe. Craig stood, hands in his pockets, looking a little nervous. Well, so was she, she had to admit. It was early evening, the light of dusk filtering through the front drapes of his west-facing apartment. Snow was falling lightly outside, covering the lawn and bare trees with white. It was a far cry from Hawaii.

Craig moved to the sofa. *Safe* wasn't a word he'd use in regards to Sabra. She wasn't safe from him, but he didn't think she realized that, and it was just as well. Her face was ashen again, and he attributed it to the long, draining flight. "What you need right now is a nap," he told her.

"I think I do." Sabra moved carefully, placing her stocking feet up on the couch and stretching out. The apartment was warm, and she closed her eyes. "Wake me in a hour or so?"

Craig crouched next to her and rested his hand on her shoulder. "You sleep all you want, sweetheart. You're still healing." He remained at her side until she fell into a deep sleep. Getting up on creaky knees, his body now feeling the full brunt of the crash, he went into the kitchen to fix himself a cup of coffee. Luckily for him, he had some frozen dinners. He was hungry, though his stomach was jumpy. Rubbing that region, he hunted through the freezer, found a turkey dinner and pulled it out.

Sabra's words never left his heart; he was a hero in her eyes. With a snort, he opened the package and tossed the cardboard container into the trash. Eleven men had died with him at the controls, leaving their wives widows and their children fatherless. They hadn't called him a hero. Resting the palms of his hands against the kitchen counter, he dropped his head and stood a moment, feeling the emotions twisting within him. How could Sabra see him as a hero? And was she seeing him through honest, realistic eyes, or some kind of warped idealism?

The apartment was quiet. Too quiet. He left the frozen dinner on the counter and went back to the living room to check on Sabra. She appeared to be sleeping soundly on the couch. He felt restless. He wanted to pace. He wanted to laugh and cry at the same time. Where the hell were all these crazy emotions coming from? He'd never felt like this before. Sabra touched him like an ethereal rainbow with her luminous eyes, her soft mouth and her low voice laced with such vibrant feelings.

Forcing himself to leave the living room, Craig told himself he was just overreacting to the past few days. Funny thing, though; the virulence of his nightmares had ebbed considerably. Was it because he'd climbed back into the cockpit? Or been through another crash and survived this time, with his passengers alive? Shaking his head, Craig shoved the frozen dinner into the microwave and decided that life was crazy at its worst and at its finest. All he needed was Sabra. Did she need him as much?

Snow was falling thickly outside Craig's large picture window. Sabra watched the flakes twirling lazily downward from the gray sky, which embraced the Virginia landscape. Absently, she heard Craig in the kitchen, putting things away after lunch. She felt tension in her shoul-

ders and moved them slowly first one way, then the other.
The strain between her and Craig was evident. She called
herself a coward because she wanted to speak of her love
for him, but was unsure how he'd receive such news. So
she bit back the words.

Hearing him enter the living room, Sabra slowly turned
toward him. How handsome he looked in a dark blue,
long-sleeved chamois shirt and well-worn jeans. She saw
the worry in his gaze and the tightness at the corners of
his mouth. He'd been so nervous since she'd come to his
apartment. Why?

"Do you have a few minutes?" she asked, gesturing
toward the overstuffed sofa next to her.

"Sure...." Craig wiped his damp hands on his jeans
and tried not to stare at Sabra. She looked beautiful and
exquisitely fragile in a pale pink angora sweater with a
cowl collar. The dark pink skirt she wore brushed the tops
of her feet, which were covered incongruously with fluffy
white slippers. The pink emphasized how wan she still
looked, though she was bouncing back surprisingly
strongly from her brush with death.

He eased himself down next to her. Craig had only
allowed himself brief touches—an arm around her shoulder from time to time, a grazing touch of his hand on
hers—in the three days she'd been at his house. What he
really wanted was to take her to his bed and hold her
forever after making hot, melting love with her as they
had in Hawaii. Had that all been a pipe dream? Something
that had arisen out of the strain of the mission? His throat
constricted at the thought. Easing his hand along the back
of the couch behind her, he turned and devoted his full
attention to her.

"I'm afraid," Sabra said with a slight laugh, "that I'm
scared to death, Craig." She rubbed her hands slowly to-

gether in her lap. Stealing a glance at his dark, frowning features, she saw his eyes lighten with surprise. "Well... maybe I'm being dramatic. I don't know..."

"We're both experts on fear," Craig agreed slowly, allowing his hand to slide forward and caress her back. Her hair was shining and lustrous, curling around her shoulders and framing her face. "If you want the truth," he said, clearing his throat, "I've been wanting to sit down and talk to you like this, too."

Sabra saw amusement in his eyes. "You have?"

"Yeah." He touched her hair briefly and forced himself to meet her unsure gaze. "I've got all these crazy thoughts and feelings running around in me. I'm not sure if I should talk to you about them or not. Sometimes I think it's me. Sometimes—hell, I don't know. Being around you, I feel like I'm walking on air, sweetheart. But then I get scared. So scared, my stomach knots up. Stupid, huh?"

She shook her head slowly. "Your stomach—my heart."

"Oh?"

"Every time you look at me, Craig, my heart pounds. I..." Sabra raised her hands in exasperation. "It's never done that to me before. Ever."

"You don't give me knots in the stomach," he offered lamely. "It's fear doing it." He took a deep breath and held her clear, intelligent eyes. "Fear of losing something I don't have a right to have, I guess."

Sabra sat very still, gauging the pain in his voice along with the hope burning in the depths of his eyes. "What are you afraid of losing?"

He looked around the apartment. He was such a coward. Finally, he looked at her. "You," he said, his voice rough with emotion. There. It was out. Fear moved raggedly through him as he saw the look on Sabra's face.

Her lips parted, and he groaned inwardly. How badly Craig wanted to kiss her. "I had this crazy notion," he muttered nervously, "about us. I never believed anyone could fall in love with someone with just one look. It's crazy. Dumb." He pulled away and rested his elbows on his thighs, clasping his hands between them. "I guess life is pretty crazy. I ought to know." He laughed sharply, talking more to himself than her. "I saw you, and I felt my world crumble around my feet, Sabra. I was angry at being pulled for the mission, angry that you were going to be the leader and just angry at the world in general, I guess. But it wasn't you I was angry at. It was me." He hung his head and released a sigh.

Raising his head, Craig looked over at her. "I kept fighting how I felt toward you. I didn't think I deserved someone as fine and good as you. I thought once I told you how much of a coward I'd been, how many lives I'd lost, you'd drop me." His mouth flattened. "You didn't, though."

"Why would I?" she asked softly.

"Because," he said harshly, "I'm not whole, Sabra. Part of me is run by that damn PTSD. I'm still afraid of flying. Every time I think that I climbed back in a helo, I break out in a sweat and get the same fear in my gut all over again." Craig shook his head. "Nothing's changed, not really." He rubbed his hand together, feeling the dampness between them. "I have these moments of hope. Can you believe it? Hope. Me, of all people, feeling that emotion after everything that's happened. You gave it back to me, you know."

Leaning forward, Sabra reached out and settled her fingers against his arm. She felt the tension in his muscles and saw it clearly in his stormy, ravaged-looking eyes. "Craig, I love you." Her voice trembled dangerously as she said the words. Fear shot through her. What would he say? Would he tell her she was crazy? Swallowing hard, Sabra tightened her fingers on his arm. "I woke up in that hospital realizing I'd loved you from the first moment I laid eyes on you." She managed a soft, embarrassed laugh. "Just like my parents, I suppose. Just one look." Taking a deep breath, she watched as he slowly straightened and turned toward her. His face mirrored shock. His lips had parted, as if to deny her halting words. Would he laugh at her? Think she was a world-class fool?.

"You—love me?"

She nodded and smiled a little. "How could I not?"

Craig sat very still, absorbing her words, her tear-filled eyes. Was he hearing things? He searched her face intently. "I'm no prize," he rasped. "I'm a loser—"

"No!" Sabra gripped his hand. "You've never been a loser, Craig. Yes, you've been hurt badly—more than most—but you're not a loser. If you think that, how do you explain climbing back in the same aircraft that nearly killed you before? Surely you knew the risks you took when we climbed on board with you. If you were such a loser, how did you manage to get that helicopter down in one piece, and us with it?" Her voice broke with feeling. "Do you think I love you because I only see your heart, your courage? I see what the war's done to you, Craig. I accept that, too. I accept all of you, scars and all." Her voice faltered. "I—I just hope you can accept me, the way I am. Josh once called me a piece of work, and I don't know to this day whether he meant it as a compliment or an insult. He—he was just that way. You never knew where you stood with him."

Whispering her name, Craig gently slid his arm around Sabra's shoulders and brought her to him. Releasing a ragged sigh as she surrendered to him, settled her head against him, he pressed a kiss into her hair. How brave she was to admit her love. He soared on an inner euphoria at knowing she loved him despite all his problems.

"I love you," he told her gruffly. "I've loved you from the beginning. I was just too thickheaded to realize it at first. I may be slow," he said, his mouth curving ruefully, "but what I feel for you is real. It's not a game, Sabra. I want you to know that." He saw the tears gleaming in her eyes as she lifted her face just enough to meet his gaze. "I'm no prize. But you are." He squeezed her shoulders, wondering how to make her realize just how precious she was to him. "Josh couldn't have found a pearl in front of his nose, in my opinion. He was afraid of you, maybe because of your career in the Mossad. I don't know. It doesn't matter anymore."

"No," she whispered tremulously, "it doesn't." Reaching up, she slid her fingers along his cheek. "I'm so glad to know you love me, too."

He caught her hand and pressed a long, slow kiss to her palm. "Didn't you hear me tell you in the hospital? You woke up, looked at Laura and Jason and then over at me. They left shortly afterward, sweetheart, and as you were closing your eyes, I leaned over and told you I loved you." He shrugged. "I wasn't sure if you heard me."

"No...I didn't hear you say it." She smiled bravely and blinked back her tears. "It all happened so fast, Craig. I wasn't expecting to fall in love. I returned to Perseus so shaken up over Terry's heart attack. I was a mess emotionally."

"We both were," he said, feeling the fear in his gut dissolving for good.

"We have the time," Sabra whispered. "I never thought we would. We could have died in that mission. It was one of the worst I've ever experienced."

He rubbed her shoulder gently, soothing her. "It was rough," he agreed, resting his brow against her hair. Sighing, he felt Sabra's arm stretch across his chest. "This is all I want," he said huskily against her ear. "I want you. I want to build on what we have, Sabra. We got lucky. We survived. I thought we were going to die, too. I don't know how many times I almost turned to you during that mission and told you I loved you. But I was afraid if I did, you'd laugh or turn me down."

"I'm afraid—" she laughed softly "—we're very much alike. Do you know how many times I wanted to admit my love to you? I was afraid, too."

"Fear has a hell of a hold on us, doesn't it?"

Sabra closed her eyes. "We had the courage to walk with our fear, Craig. We didn't let it stop us from telling each other in the end. That," she said, rubbing her palm against his well-sprung chest, "is what counts."

Joy flowed through Craig. "I never thought," he rasped hoarsely, "that I'd ever find someone who'd love me. I really didn't. After that crash, I just gave up living. I had no hope left. I had nightmares for my companions—until you walked into my life." He kissed her brow. "I want to spend the rest of my life telling you how many ways you've helped me, how much hope I have because of you."

Sabra snuggled closer, a contentment like none she'd ever experienced stealing through her. Craig's arms were strong and supportive around her. As much as she wanted to love him, it was impossible right now because of her neck injury. In another week, she promised him silently, she would love him until he realized how very special a man he was—despite the horror of his past.

"I've watched my parents in their marriage," she told

him in a hushed voice, absorbing the strength of his chest beneath her hand. "I'm sure we'll fight—"

"Constructive discussions," he amended. "My parents have a long marriage like yours do, and the one thing I never forgot was that they never fought personally—they stuck to the topic that needed discussing."

She smiled up at him. "Don't you think we have a chance, considering all we've weathered so far? We didn't exactly meet under good circumstances."

Tunneling his fingers through her hair, feeling the silky thickness of it, Craig said, "We have the time, Sabra. And we won't waste a moment of it."

She closed her eyes, feeling his fingers gently massaging her scalp. Her skin prickled pleasantly. Did Craig realize how unique he was among men? He was a toucher, a holder, and that's what she needed most—someone who valued such things as she did.

"I worry about my nightmares," Craig admitted after a few moments of silence. He eased his hand from her hair and touched her flushed cheek. "I haven't slept with a woman since the crash for fear of hurting her."

"You've slept with me four nights in a row under some pretty dangerous circumstances," she told him, holding his uncertain gaze, "and never once did you have a nightmare."

"I think that was a fluke," he admitted, frowning. "The last thing I want is to hurt you, Sabra. The last thing..." He couldn't stand the idea of lashing out and striking her lovely face, possibly breaking her nose or jaw. The thought sent a wave of nausea through him.

Closing her eyes, she sighed and rested against his strong body. "Let's take our lives one day at a time, darling...."

He nodded and said nothing. Just holding Sabra made

some of his fear go away. Right now, he knew that Perseus was working hard to locate Morgan. He might be dead. The thought made him wince internally. What he should be doing was helping Jake, Wolf and Killian. They needed all the help they could muster to keep the company going while widening the search for Morgan.

Having Sabra in his arms, he thought about Laura and the awful pain she was carrying twenty-four hours a day. She had no one to hold her. Especially at night, in bed, when the darkness brought out the fears. In another week, he would go back and help Perseus in any way he could. Would Sabra go back to her apartment then? Or would she stay with him? A part of him wanted to hurry the process and keep her with him. That was the part that feared losing her, he admitted to himself. Loving a woman meant allowing her her freedom, too.

His mind ranged back over the past, to his parents. Although his father had been a rancher most of his life, then bought the trading post on the reservation after fracturing his back, he'd never made a servant out of his wife. If anything, his parents had been a hardworking team who pulled together. Craig wanted that same thing for him and Sabra. She was free to choose whether she continued to work for Perseus, just as he was.

Craig had so many questions for her, but he squelched them as he felt her falling asleep in his arms. She was still exhausted from the mission and the surgery. He smiled faintly as he eased his hand slowly up and down her limp arm sprawled across his chest. Right now all he wanted to do was love her, give in to the sweet, haunting, unfilled need that flowed through him. But that had to wait. Love was more than sex, much more. Making love with Sabra was another way to show her how he felt about her, and he ached to bring them together even more since they'd admitted their love for each other.

Chapter Fourteen

"I've got good news and bad news," Craig told Sabra as he entered the apartment. The cold wind rushed in the open door and a number of snowflakes swirled in with him. Shutting it, he turned around. Sabra was on the couch, reading the newspaper. It was only 1:00 p.m.; and he saw the surprise on her features. Pulling off his dark blue knit muffler, he dropped it on the desk next to the door.

"What do you mean?" She set the paper aside and rose. Her heart tripled in beat as she realized Craig was not only home early, but unannounced. A week ago, at her urging, he'd begun going to work with Killian at the Pentagon to try to help track down Morgan's whereabouts. Usually, he got home late in the evening after spending a good twelve hours on duty. She had persuaded him she was well enough to make her own meals. Besides, he wasn't happy cooped up in a small apartment with little to do.

Shrugging out of his coat, Craig hung it on the peg above the desk. He made sure the dead bolt was slid into place on the door, then turned to meet Sabra. She wore a cream colored sweater that emphasized her olive complexion and dark, ebony hair. He could still see little telltale signs of her recent trauma, but only a small dressing covered the spot where her stitches had recently been taken out by Dr. Parsons. Yes, she looked healthy again.

Opening his arms, Craig groaned as Sabra walked into them and pressed herself against him. It was something he looked forward to each night, hungrily absorbing wherever her body touched his, molding against him. This time she reached up and placed an eager hungry kiss on his mouth. Stunned by her unexpected response, he monitored his returning pressure.

"Craig, I'm well now," she whispered fiercely against his lips.

He pulled away just enough to look down into her dark gray eyes, which smouldered with desire. How many times had he seen that look in her eyes? Every night. It had been hell sleeping apart—him on the couch, she in his bed. Craig didn't want to risk hurting her in the night, and he'd coaxed her into agreeing to sleep separately until Dr. Parsons said she was her old self again. That had happened yesterday afternoon. Hotly aware of her breasts and hips pressing against him, provocatively this time, he gripped her shoulders and gently eased her away from him.

"It's a good thing," he said gruffly. "Listen, we've got to get out of here."

Sabra's mouth fell open. "What?"

"We picked up a dispatch between Garcia and Ramirez

less than an hour ago," he explained swiftly. "That's why I'm home early. The good news is we've located Morgan we think—in Peru, at Ramirez's jungle estate." His hands tightened briefly on her shoulders. "The bad news is Ramirez has ordered hits on every Perseus employee they can find."

Gasping, Sabra pulled out of his grip. "You're joking."

"I wish I were," he said tiredly. Gazing around the apartment, he said, "I want you to pack a bag with just necessities. We're going undercover until this thing blows over."

"What about Laura and her children?"

"Jake already has them in hiding. Killian is making sure Susannah is with them. Shah, Jake's new wife, will be with her, too. Right now, Laura isn't too stable. She knows we've found Morgan."

"And he's alive?"

Craig shrugged and walked back to the bedroom with her, his hand pressed against the small of her back. "We're not sure. From what Killian said, and Wolf double-checked it, Ramirez is the kind of bastard to keep Morgan alive as long as possible. We're sure he's been tortured extensively, but to what end, we don't know. Wolf was in his prison for almost a month, and Ramirez tortured him daily. If he lost consciousness, the bastard had a doctor there to bring him back with drugs so he could torture him some more. He's a real pro at that kind of sick stuff."

Hurriedly, Sabra took her small suitcase from the closet and placed it on the bed. She shivered just thinking about Wolf—and Morgan—being injured by Ramirez. "Are any of the teams back from a mission yet?"

Craig threw a canvas bag on the bed, went to the dresser and pulled open a drawer. Right now, haste was essential. "We have one possibility," he said, throwing underwear into the bag. "Culver Lachlan, who always works solo, just came in from an undercover assignment in Ireland."

"You can't send him into that rat's nest alone," Sabra protested, quickly putting some lingerie and sweaters into the suitcase. She glanced up at Craig's set features. He was tense and worried. So was she. Ramirez always made good on his orders, though this would be the first time he'd made such an open attack against an American company.

"Jake's working on another angle. There's a Peruvian agent by the name of Pilar Martinez who he's trying to contact. A long time ago, Pilar and Culver worked together on a Peruvian undercover assignment, but something happened, and they split up. At the time, Culver was a CIA agent and she was an undercover government agent in Lima. They worked on a huge cocaine bust for three months. But that was eight years ago. Jake knows Pilar pretty well. She was partly responsible for getting Wolf and Killian away from Ramirez. She's worked on a lot of cocaine busts over the years, and she knows the jungles like the back of her hand. Her family is Indian, and they live near where Ramirez hides out. She's the perfect choice for the assignment—if he can find her in time, and if she'll work with Culver again." He frowned. "There are a lot of ifs to this."

"Frankly," Sabra murmured, shutting the suitcase, "I don't think two people on their own could rescue Morgan. Ramirez has five or six estates throughout South America, I know. The one in Peru is deep in the jungle and mountains. Jake can't be thinking of sending them in alone."

"No," Craig said, zipping the canvas bag closed and hoisting it over his left shoulder. "I think he's trying to get the Peruvian government to work with us. But that's iffy, too. Come on, let's get out of here.''

Hurriedly, Sabra picked up her suitcase, but Craig caught her hand and shook his head.

''I'm well. Remember?'' she protested.

''I don't care. You're only one day well, sweetheart. I'll carry the bag.''

''Craig, stop treating me like I'm some fragile, breakable doll.''

He grinned tightly and followed her out of the bedroom. ''Am I?''

''Yes!'' Sabra retorted with pretend exasperation, throwing a look over her shoulder at him. ''And it's driving me crazy!''

''I'm crazy for you.'' Now was not the time to discuss much of anything, except leaving the residence. ''Get my jacket? Let's go down the basement stairs. I've got the car parked inside the garage, and the door is shut and locked.'' He didn't want to take any chances. He'd nearly lost Sabra two weeks ago, and he was damned if she was going to be placed in jeopardy again so soon.

Sabra gave a helpless laugh, shook her head and shared an amused look with him. She opened the door that led down the stairs to the garage below. ''You're hopeless, Talbot.''

''Hopelessly in love with you, Ms. Jacobs.''

She colored prettily beneath his warming gaze as he approached. ''Where are we going?''

''The DV at Andrews Air Force Base.''

''DV?''

''Yeah, it stands for distinguished visitor's housing.'' He halted and smiled. ''The best accommodations on the base for us. Usually only generals and congressional people stay there. It will have everything—a stocked bar, video, television, all kinds of choice food. You'll want for nothing.''

"Nothing," Sabra muttered, following him down the steps. All she wanted was him.

"It's a good place to hide. The Air Police are aware of the threat and have been alerted at the gates to Andrews.'' Craig put the suitcases in the trunk and shut the lid. ''Get in,'' he told her. How fast could Ramirez put hit men onto them? The orders were exactly one hour old. Craig worried because he lived the farthest away from Perseus. Time was precious.

Backing out into the icy street, made more slippery from the foot of snow a recent storm had dumped on the Eastern Seaboard, Craig narrowed his attention to driving without sliding on the unsalted pavement and watching for any cars that might be tailing them. The early afternoon sky was leaden, and not many vehicles had ventured out on the slick streets lined with bare-branched maple and walnut trees.

Sabra swiveled her attention between Craig and their surroundings. She, too, watched for cars that might be carrying a hit man or group of thugs. The snow made everything look white and clean. Trying to relax, she realized that for nearly two weeks she'd been in a safe cocoon in Craig's home. Now their lives were threatened again.

"I don't know how Laura can take all this danger and intrigue," she murmured, watching the traffic. "I think I'd have had a nervous breakdown by now."

"She's a lot stronger than she looks," Craig said, guiding the car onto the interstate that would take them to Andrews Air Force Base. He breathed a little easier, because this roadway had recently been plowed and salted.

"Besides, she's got Shah and Susannah looking after the kids, which takes some pressure off her."

"I'd like to help her...."

Craig shot her a quick glance. "You're supposed to focus on getting well."

"I *am* well."

Craig grimaced. "Let's discuss this when we get to Andrews."

"You've got a deal."

It was nearly midnight when Sabra took a bath, then pulled on a pale green, silk nightgown that brushed her ankles. The DV house was everything Craig had promised and more. Tension had been strong since they'd arrived, however. Sabra didn't put as much faith in the Air Police as Craig apparently did. Three different times, Wolf had called them. First to report that they had intercepted a cryptic message at CIA headquarters and found out Morgan was indeed alive. Sabra had burst into tears over that news. She loved Morgan more like a brother than a boss, and she cried for Laura, too, who had to be feeling at least some relief.

Wolf's second call was sinister. The Customs Department had already intercepted three known Columbian hit men at Miami International Airport. The men had been carrying photos of Perseus employees—among them, Sabra's.

The third call had come less than half an hour ago. It had been Killian, phoning to tell them he would need their help to coordinate the huge plan to rescue Morgan. Sabra had been overjoyed at the idea of getting back into the type of work she was best at. Craig hadn't looked too happy, because he was to go to the Pentagon with Wolf, while she would be working with CIA officials monitoring satcoms from South America, trying to pick up more information on Morgan.

Opening the door, she moved soundlessly down the hall toward the other bedrooms. The house, impressive looking inside and out, was single story with a basement. The furniture throughout was Queen Anne, and Sabra loved the warm cherry wood that adorned the place. It was only a house, though, she admitted—without Craig's presence, it would have seemed hollow and empty.

She heard a noise on her left and hesitated at the half-open door that led to the master bedroom. Pushing it wider, she saw that Craig had showered in the adjoining bathroom. He wore nothing but blue-and-white-striped pajama bottoms, which hung dangerously low around his narrow hips. A soft smile touched her mouth as she watched him unpack his clothes and put them into the drawers. His hair was dark and shining—still wet. The play of muscles on his back was beautiful, and Sabra leaned against the door, appreciating him in silence.

As if sensing her presence, Craig turned.

"What do you think you're doing?" she asked, walking toward him. Sabra had deliberately left her robe behind. The V-cut gown barely hid the swell of her breasts, and she wanted him to take notice of her. Judging from the narrowing of his eyes as he straightened and faced her, her plan was working.

"I was unpacking," Craig said, distracted. The silk gown shimmered in the room's low lighting, and Sabra moved like a graceful ballerina, each sway of her body flowing into the next movement. Her thick hair had been brushed until it shone, draping around her proud shoulders. The look in her eyes was unmistakable—a smoldering glow for him alone. Groaning inwardly, Craig tried to put a check on his desire. It was impossible.

"Why are you unpacking your stuff in here?" she asked, reaching out, sliding her arms around his shoulders.

"This is the bedroom I chose," he said. Sabra's touch was electrifying. He slipped his arms around her waist and drew her against him, seeing her lips part provocatively. She tilted her chin upward just enough so that he could kiss her if he wanted to. He wanted that and more.

"I thought," Sabra murmured, leaning forward and moving her lips against the line of his mouth, "we agreed to sleep together from tonight on?"

It was hell trying to think coherently beneath her gentle assault. He felt the soft, sliding movement of the silk between them, the warmth of her loving body pressing against him, of her lips teasing his. Gripping her shoulders, he eased her away.

"I think we said we'd discuss it," he rasped. An ache filled him and a hot, burning sensation flowed through his lower body. He inhaled her fragrance, wondering if she'd used gardenia soap on her peach-soft flesh.

The corners of her mouth lifted slightly. "Craig, there's no discussion on this. We're sleeping together. That's what I want. It's what you want."

Worriedly, he rasped, "I'm afraid for you—"

"I'm not," Sabra whispered, nibbling at his lower lip, feeling him harden against her belly. She tightened her arms around his neck, closed her eyes and moved her lips across his.

Groaning, Craig gripped her to him. The roundness of her breasts pressed against his chest; the slickness of her lips molded to his and, with the heat of her supple body, conspired against him.

"Love me..." Sabra whispered against his questing mouth. "Love me, please...." She felt him tense for a split second, then, to her delight and surprise, he lifted her off her feet and into his arms. His stormy blue eyes were hungry—for her. She sighed and rested her head against his. "Take me to *our* room."

Hesitantly, Craig glanced around the master bedroom and then down at her sultry, half-closed eyes. "So much for our discussion," he rasped thickly, a hint of a smile on his mouth.

"I love you," Sabra said, running her fingers through his recently washed hair. *"I need you...."*

The words fell across him like fire. He walked down the hall to their bedroom, a smaller room with a queen-size bed in it. As he entered, Craig saw that Sabra had lit some candles on the dresser, their light reflecting in the mirror behind them. With his foot, he gently shut the door.

"You're a woman with a purpose," he teased as he laid her on the pink silk coverlet of the bed, where the soft light glimmered on her features.

"And you don't mind?"

Craig stretched out next to her, reveling in the feminine strength of her body. "No...not really. I guess I'm not used to it, that's all." He smiled a little. "But I'll get used to it."

She sighed and reached up, framing his face between her hands. "With you," she murmured, "I had to use my sharpest tactics and strategy skills to get you to realize I'm well."

Running his hand up her long thigh, the silk warm and sleek beneath his fingertips, he shrugged. "I guess my mind knows it...."

"Your heart doesn't."

"No." He leaned over, sliding his arm beneath her neck and gently cradling her against him. "I feel like a man who got his only wish in the world. Now that I have it, I'm afraid of losing it."

"I understand," Sabra whispered, stretching up and claiming his set mouth. "Let's make tonight a new start for both of us, darling." She felt Craig's hands tightening around her, felt his hand move upward to cup her breast beneath the silk. Heat purled through her, and her voice dropped to a husky whisper. "We love each other. That's all that matters. I don't want to spend one more night without your arms around me, Craig. Please...."

Her plea tore at him as nothing else could. In that moment, with Sabra in his arms, her lips resting teasingly against his mouth, he realized the depth of her commitment to him. "It won't be easy," he warned gruffly, easing her onto her back.

"What won't be easy?" She trailed her hand downward across his flat, hard belly, tracing the line of his pajama bottoms across his hips. She saw his eyes go thundercloud dark, felt his hand stop caressing the side of her breast.

Craig couldn't think any longer, nor could he talk. Sabra's body was like a branding iron, moving ceaselessly against him like the rhythm of an ocean tide. Her fingers eased the fabric away from his hips, and he stiffened as she slid her fingers downward to caress him. Gripping her shoulder, he groaned. Whatever worry, whatever concerns about her injury he'd had, melted beneath her exquisite exploration. All he could do was tense beside her, lost in a storm of electric sensation, drowning in the desire to make her his.

Candlelight suffused the room, flowing across her shoulders and face, revealing her inner and outer beauty. He eased his hand beneath the silk nightgown, drawing it upward, pulling it off her so that she lay naked before him. How vulnerable she looked—with such trust in her eyes as she met and fearlessly held his gaze. Her flesh was hot and demanding. Her lips parted, silently begging him to continue his exploration. At the same time, he felt the cloth he wore being pulled away, and he pushed the pajamas aside. Gazing at her intensely, as if she were his quarry, Craig entangled her legs with his own. Sliding his hand beneath her hip, he eased her on top of him. He saw surprise and then pleasure in her shadowed eyes, which now burned with longing. Trembling with need, he tried to hold himself in check as he positioned her above him. This way, he wouldn't accidentally put too much pressure on her recently healed neck wound. This way he could watch her every fleeting expression, like a greedy man too long without sustenance, too long without love.

As she settled over him, he groaned. The moistness met his hardness, and he gripped her hips, pulling her down upon him even more. He heard a soft gasp escape her, felt her hands grip his arms in instant reaction. Her thighs tightened against him, and he smiled to himself, savoring the melting fire of making her one with him. There was such power in claiming her, in easing into her depths and feeling her heat as she moved with abandoned pleasure.

Like the ceaseless ocean tide, he felt her rocking against him, in perfect rhythm. Whatever worry he'd had was burned away in the molten flames of their joining. The slickness of her body met and matched his and he thrust more deeply into her, hearing her soft cry of joy. Moments glided into one another, like hot wax pooling at the base of a candle flame. Closing his eyes, his teeth clenched with the effort of holding back, Craig brought Sabra into a fast, frantic union with him. Each sliding movement, each explosion heat from the friction between them heightened the pleasure.

He felt her fingers tense and release rapidly against his arms, and he gripped her hips more firmly, thrusting hard and deep into her. The intense explosion within her translated to him, and he felt her stiffen and throw back her head, her hair flying out across her shoulders and back. In those fiery moments, with Sabra a part of him, Craig had never felt stronger as a man, or more in control of his destiny. He moved again, prolonging the pleasure of her climax, and watched as a rosy flush swept up her glistening body. Only then did he release the hold on his own desires. Only then did he give her the gift of himself.

Sabra moaned softly as she collapsed against Craig, her head next to his on the pillow. His breath intermingled with her own, and she closed her eyes and slid her arm across his damp chest. "I love you so much," she said tremulously.

Craig slipped his hand across her back, slick and warm from their lovemaking. "Sweetheart, I'm the luckiest bastard on this planet." He kissed her cheek and saw her lashes flutter open. His smile was male. "I've got you. That's all I'll ever need...ever want." He slid his fingers across her flushed cheek and held her drowsy gaze. "Come on," he rasped, "let's go to sleep. I want to hold you in my arms all night and wake up tomorrow morning to find you beside me."

Sabra smiled weakly as he readjusted her at his side. The sensation of fire still burned brightly within her, and she felt deliciously consumed by it. How wonderful a lover Craig was. Did he know that? Had any woman ever shared that knowledge with him? As she eased beneath the covers, then snuggled against him, she promised to tell him that tomorrow morning, over breakfast.

The candles would burn out on their own, and Craig was content to have the low light dancing in soft, muted shadows on their bedroom walls. Sabra was damp against him, and he pulled the covers up to her shoulders, his arm around her to keep her close. As he shut his eyes and settled down with her at his side, his mind refused to work any longer. Exhaustion pulled at him. Before he plunged into a deep, healing sleep with the woman he loved at his side, Craig realized that no matter what lay ahead of them, they could triumph together. Sabra gave him hope—for himself, for a future he once had thought would never be his. Her love for him was as strong and unerring as she was. Silently, Craig promised her that no matter how dark it got for him in the future, no matter how he had to wrestle with his past to heal, he would do so—not only for himself, but for her. She'd had the courage to reach out and tell him of her love. He could do no less for her.

As he felt her soft breath against his chest, Craig sighed, feeling the last of the tension flowing out of him. Somehow, he knew that tonight there would be no nightmares. They were as safe as possible under the circumstances.

In the weeks ahead, Craig knew, there would be continued danger and tension, until they were able to rescue Morgan. If it could be done, and if he could be brought home safely, then Ramirez would probably cease his hunt for them. For now, their future was clouded with danger, and each day was going to be a miracle. No matter what happened, Craig knew life was worth living again as long as they had each other. He would love Sabra forever.

*   *   *   *   *